About the Author

Kerry Jamieson was born in Durban, South Africa and educated in the United States, where she lived in Miami, Los Angeles and New York. She has a degree in English Literature from the University of Miami and a postgraduate qualification in screenwriting from UCLA. She began her career writing short stories and has won *QWF*'s Phillip Good Memorial Prize and South Africa's FNB Vita Award for Short Fiction. She divides her time between South Africa, Ireland, the United Kingdom and the United States. This is her first novel.

Kerry Jamieson

The Golden Door

FLAME
Hodder & Stoughton

Copyright © 2004 by Kerry Jamieson

First published in Great Britain in 2004 by Hodder and Stoughton
A division of Hodder Headline

A Flame Paperback

The right of Kerry Jamieson to be identified as the Author of the Work has been asserted
by her in accordance with the Copyright, Designs and Patents Act 1988.

1 3 5 7 9 10 8 6 4 2

A CIP catalogue for this title is available from the British Library

ISBN 0 340 83098 0

Typeset in Sabon by
Phoenix Typesetting, Auldgirth, Dumfriesshire

Printed and bound by
Mackays of Chatham Ltd, Chatham, Kent

Hodder Headline's policy is to use papers that are natural, renewable
and recyclable products and made from wood grown in sustainable
forests. The logging and manufacturing processes are expected to
conform to the environmental regulations of the country of origin.

Hodder and Stoughton
A division of Hodder Headline
338 Euston Road
London NW1 3BH

To my parents, Pam and Ed Jamieson, whose
respect for books first inclined me towards writing
and whose love never wavers.

ACKNOWLEDGEMENTS

Thanks are due to my brother and sister-in-law, Rory and Karen, for their support and encouragement and to my wonderful friends – Michelle, Carryn, Amy and Carlie – who were nice enough not to appear at all surprised when they heard I was being published!

Much appreciation, always, to Jackson, Frank, Peter and Hamish, who have shown me kindness, faith and care.

I owe a great deal of gratitude to my wonderful agent at Curtis Brown, Hannah Griffiths, and Hodder & Stoughton's star editor, Mari Evans, for their warmth and efforts above and beyond the call of duty.

And last, but never least, thanks to Sue Rae Fox for her mentorship, friendship and enthusiasm.

'On September 10th 1990, the Ellis Island Immigrant Museum opened its doors to the public. It is the fourth largest museum in the City of New York but, to date, only Island One of the complex has been renovated. Island Two and Island Three (on which the hospitals and contagious diseases wards were housed) remain as they were when Ellis Island was abandoned by the immigration authorities in 1954.

Though the history of these deserted halls is undoubtedly intriguing, nine successive American administrations have refused to reveal their hidden secrets. The reason – or the excuse – remains the same: it would be too costly an undertaking . . .'

Francis O'Malley
'Enigmatic Isle'
Editorial: *The New York Record*
14 January 2001: A8

'One hundred and fifty-eight thousand immigrants entered the United States through Ellis Island in 1929. By 1933, their number had fallen to less than twelve thousand. This dramatic decrease can be partially explained by the global economic depression resulting from the Wall Street Crash and restrictive, new immigration policies. However, these reasons alone do not suffice as justification for the radical reduction in influx. The immigration slump of the early thirties is a baffling anomaly and endures as one of America's most puzzling historical mysteries.'

Arthur S. Humphries, Ph.D. History
Revisiting America's Past
New York: Haven Press, 2000

Foreword

It was all jazz and mint-juleps in America. Every man in New York owned a yellow car and the ladies' shoes had real diamond buckles. Each shop window displayed a sign that pleaded NEED HELP and a strong, young man could have his pick of work . . . Those were the stories that circulated around the lower decks of the transport liners, passed from traveller to traveller like shared cigarettes.

The passengers sat outdoors, huddled together in groups because the mid-Atlantic was a frozen sea and the icy air sliced through their coats as easily as sleet tears through leaves. The steerage cabins had no portholes; they stank of urine and rats' nests, so many travellers preferred the cold decks to their stifling quarters. They told their embroidered stories to re-assure themselves, and the stories became holy entreaties that mixed with the chill fog from their lips. In the purple, glassy dusk, the smoky prayers entwined themselves around the wings of the gulls and twisted up to heaven.

Will Carthy sat apart from the rest and practised his answers to the immigration inquiries. He didn't want to make a mistake. There would be thirty-two questions (and a cursory medical examination) before he could enter America. Will watched the wake surge up behind the *Celtic*'s propellers and experienced an inner turbulence of his own. For every hour of the eight-day voyage, Will anticipated the inspections and worried.

As long as the sun was up, most of the passengers occupied

3

themselves with seasickness but at night there was music and dancing with girls who didn't speak English or who didn't understand Will's accent. Fiddles and flutes were dragged from Hessian sacks and hurriedly tuned to the cadence of the waves. Will would dance till his knees ached – he had always been a bit of a lad in the dancehalls – then he would discover, suddenly, that he was drunk and uncharacteristically carefree. He would pass out beneath the curved belly of a life raft and the cigarettes flicked from the upper decks would mark his face and hands with fine, black ash. With each new day, the anxiety returned, however – as a palpable twitching behind Will's heart and constant indigestion in his stomach.

The *Celtic* steamed into New York on a Sunday. It was too late to go ashore by the time the ship dropped anchor and the harbour master held them a mile out, expectant. The septic-green water disgusted the Italians. They pointed at it and tut-tutted. Already, they longed for the aching blue of the Mediterranean which had the white columns of temples hidden beneath its surface. On the far side of the river, the Manhattan skyline stood like a monument in miniature; the children half closed their eyes and tried to pinch the buildings between their fingers.

The night settled down and the lights of the city came up all at once, as if New York was being switched on for business. It was more brilliant than fireworks.

Will had never seen so many lights before. Some were small and gold and sophisticated, some flashed brazenly on and off with ruby audacity. One shouted out across the water: DRINK COCA-COLA – IT'S REFRESHING!

The cavity of Will's chest was too tight to contain his swollen heart. America was a fragile bowl with so much hope to bear, a transparent vessel made entirely of glass and light and floating on water. Will began to wonder if it would be able to bear the weight of him and the burden of his emerging dreams.

At dawn the next morning, a boat pulled alongside the *Celtic* and the crew threw a rope up over the railings. At the end of it was a basket full of long, yellow fruit that smelled as sweet and syrupy as the black molasses Will had added to the horse-feed in winter.

'Twenty cents a hand!' the man called up to them.

The passengers crowded round and pulled the fruit apart. The basket went down lined with coins and Will tasted the exotic, round creaminess of his first banana.

Tenders took the immigrants ashore in groups of thirty and Will attached himself to a bedraggled throng of people, hoping he was moving in the right direction. The sun pressed down on the back of Will's head and the sweat ran through his only suit as he waited in a line that staggered back and forward between the barriers like soggy string.

There were fountains on the forecourt but hardly anybody sipped from them. Rumours had filtered back to the old countries about those who drank the water on Ellis Island: they forgot their homes and their families altogether and were lost. Will didn't buy that sort of talk but still he convinced himself he wasn't thirsty.

Every now and then, there was a damp thump and a fluster of activity as one of the ladies fainted. Will examined the mother standing in front of him, assessing her potential as a woman in distress. She was as stout and upright as a coal stove. She didn't so much as sway on her feet and Will felt somewhat disappointed. He approved of women who could swoon just right, so that they were easy to catch. Back home, there had always been some girl or other falling gracefully in Will's direction.

The line edged forward towards the Great Hall. As he progressed, Will lost sight of his bag – it was his stepfather's duffel bag from the War and it had been snagged on barbed wire and trudged through a dozen muddy trenches but it was all he had. He caught a last glimpse of it, lying tagged among samovars and bagpipes and golden triptychs on the burning lawn.

Will experienced a moment of heated surliness as a prodding baton urged him along but he didn't argue with the officials who kept the masses in line with their bluff, American yells. Their nerves were frazzled by the ignorant arrivals' babbling queries, by the vomit on the steps which somebody had sprinkled with sand from a fire bucket and by the dirty pieces of luggage which pulsed with maggots in the sun.

The Kerryman standing behind Will kept asking him how tough he thought the reading test would be.

'I can't read good but I only want a job as a busboy at the Excelsior Restaurant in Yankee Stadium. Babe Ruth takes his coffee there. You don't need to read good to serve Babe Ruth his coffee, do you?'

Will glared at him. As if reading could ever be reduced to something a man could take or leave, as if it wasn't the most important thing next to family.

The Great Hall was a vast, bare vestibule. At last, there was shade. Will rested his palms against the cool, white wall-tiles. Rows of benches filled the middle of the room and there was the powerful smell of disinfectant poured out neat. The inspectors separated the immigrants as they entered, filing men to one side and women to the other.

After another hour of waiting, Will reached the head of the line and someone thrust a Bible into his hand. It lay open at the Twenty-third Psalm. Will recited the passage by heart; any

Catholic could have done it but the literacy inspector looked astounded.

'What do you weigh?' he asked Will.

Nobody had warned Will about this question; he was unprepared for it. For a second, apprehension hiccoughed through him. Was there some kind of weight limitation? Was he over the mark? Then he looked at the man's ingenuously raised eyebrows and understood that he was only casually interested.

'Two hundred and twenty pounds,' Will said.

The literacy inspector let out a slow, sinking whistle.

'Six foot five?' he asked Will.

'Six four,' Will said.

The man nodded, impressed, and pointed Will over to the doctor's station.

'Show the doc your tackle next,' he said.

Taking out his privates for examination was the worst part of the ordeal. Will knew he had nothing to be modest about but he felt awkward and ashamed; the women and children were waiting only a few feet across the room. Will had pushed into a few accommodating girls in the alley behind the aptly named Fiddler's Feast in Gort. There never seemed to be a lack of wet, willing places on offer where Will Carthy was concerned but even those hurried couplings had been more discreet than this. When the doctor lifted and poked him, Will's instinct was to punch out at the man. He didn't, though; he was so very nearly through.

'You look OK,' said the doctor and he motioned Will over to the next station.

It was a conveyor belt of humiliations that day. The next inspector wielded a type of crochet hook – a slim, steel rod with a nasty twist at the end – and said, 'Hold still!' as he used it to lift Will's eyelids up, so he could peer beneath them. Will's eyes watered and the hook looked like a knife that was out to blind him. He tried not to blink until, mercifully, the man shoved him along.

The sound of crying children was everywhere – that staccato, discordant wailing of babies being ineffectively jiggled by desperate mothers. Will hadn't eaten anything since his breakfast banana. He had heard they served bread and tea in the immigrants' canteen if you were lucky enough to be processed during a mealtime but it was already late in the afternoon and Will hadn't seen any sign of food.

The thirty-two questions were next. It had all happened so quickly after hours of waiting that Will felt horribly disorientated. The early questions covered the statistics of simple, human existence. Then came the answers you had to learn. It was best to be bland, to lie about passions and pleasures. It was important, Will had been told, to look at your shoes when in doubt and to be meek. Will looked down at the tiled floor and saw that it sloped towards a row of drains in the centre of the room – just the way they said the tiles had in the secret execution chambers of Dublin's British jails.

Name? Will Michael Patrick Carthy
Age? Twenty-five
Colour of hair? Black
Colour of eyes? Brown
What is your height? Six feet, four inches
Complexion? Fair
Marital status? Single
Calling or occupation? I'm a horse handler and a groom
Are you able to read? Yes
What languages? English and Gaelic

Can you write? Yes
Country of birth? Ireland
Town of birth? Kinvara
Last permanent residence or country? Ireland
City or town? Kinvara
Your race or people? The Irish
Nearest relative or friend in country from whence you came?
   My half-sister, Isobel
Final destination? New York City
By whom was your passage paid? A charity of the Catholic
   Church
How much money is in your possession? Twenty-five dollars
Have you ever been in the United States before? No
Will you ever return to the country from whence you came? No
Length of stay in the United States? I hope to stay permanently
Do you intend to become a US citizen? Yes
Have you ever been in a prison, an almshouse or an insane
   asylum? No
Are you a polygamist? No
Are you an anarchist? No
Do you advocate the overthrow by force of the American
   government? No, I do not
Have you come here because of solicitation of work or employ-
   ment offer? No
Were you previously deported this year? No
What is your condition of health, mental and physical? I'm in
   excellent shape
Are you deformed or crippled? No

Will finished up the rote answers and the official thumped a
stamp down onto one of the pages of his passport. Will read
the impression it left twice to make sure he believed the words.

The ink was still damp and he was careful not to blur it with his fingers. *MAY 1924: AUTHORIZED TO ENTER*, it said. Will noticed that his once-crisp passport had been soiled somehow; there was a mysterious, dark ring across the bottom of its red, cardboard cover. He was in, though. America lay ahead.

A final official marshalled Will to the left and ahead he saw the separation stairs – that dreaded flight with its two steel handrails which divided the masses into three streams. Those who had passed the inspections went through to the trans-portation hall. Those in the middle were herded into offices to face further inquiries or hearings. Those on the right were never going to be Americans. They were moved on into holding cells where they would be housed until they could be returned to their country of origin. The stairs divided men from their wives and children from their parents. It happened quickly and always there was that untenable decision which would change the course of lives and generations – to stay with the weakest of your kin and sacrifice your dream or to push forward alone and at any price. It was a test of heart and mettle: the American crucible.

Finally, Will reached the bottom of the stairs and was free to make his way to the greeting gate. Off to one side, he saw a man holding up a sign that read *CATHOLIC AID SOCIETY: WE WELCOME OUR IRISH FRIENDS*. Before Will could reach the man, however, a brassy woman in the official, blue blazer of the traveller's assistants took hold of him by the coat sleeve.

'The American Express Company has a booth in the corner,' she said. 'They offer fair rates of exchange. We don't suggest you change your currency on the street. Directly ahead of you is the railway ticket office. Beside that, you'll find the ferry company's window and . . .' her voice trailed off as she looked at Will properly for the first time.

'Oh, my!' said the traveller's assistant. She smiled a big smile that was covered in lipstick. 'You're one of those who's off to Hollywood, I expect,' she said.

'No,' said Will. 'I'm heading to Orchard Street. To the boarding house of a Mr Tulliver from Limerick.'

I

___

It was that indeterminate time of day when the tarnished, sulphur light made it difficult to distinguish dawn from impending darkness. Down along the river, the mournful horns of the Gateway liners wallowed in across the water like whale dirge and the low sun sent a long, crooked shadow from the short, upright man Will Carthy was following.

The man was walking fifty feet ahead of Will and, by coincidence, he also seemed to be making his way down to the piers. Will could only see the stranger's back as they both hurried along. The man was compact and he walked in a curious way with his head slightly cocked as though he listened to voices that were just a little too distant to discern. When he reached the waterline, the stranger stopped and the soot from the chimneys of the island factories settled on the shoulders of his coat – delicate as ashes.

Will caught up with the man and they stood awkwardly beside one another, looking out over the water with mutual expectation.

Will had run all the way from the Whitehall Street subway station to Battery Park, beating at the doors of the train as soon as it stopped and pushing his way out ahead of the last commuters. It was already a quarter past seven. He hoped he was not so late that Isobel would be worried. Most of the claimants would have come at five. Some would have rushed straight from their sacred jobs. Others – the majority, it now seemed – were idle these days and so indulged in punctuality or that dreadful, uncomfortable earliness which marks the unemployed.

Castle Clinton – the woefully flat, brown stone fort at the tip of Manhattan – was almost deserted. There had been a time when cannons had pushed out from its walls like the muzzles of sniper rifles – trained nervously at the harbour, waiting for the masts of Confederate ships. The enemies were different these days and there was not much point in trying to prevent their entry; they were already ashore. Now the building housed an aquarium that was all but abandoned. Inside, the fish swam round and round in their circular tanks and longed for the nearby river and, ultimately, the sea.

Will watched three bankers settling down for the night in the dark green shade of the Park Service oak trees – a small knot of figures, organizing themselves in the growing gloom. They wore suits which had once sported pinstripes as straight as accountancy columns down their length but which were now the uniform grey of New York dust. The bankers were laying their bedrolls back-to-back, so they could guard each other against the gangs of cut-throat boys that roamed the parks by night, or worse, the Hooverville police.

Will lit a cigarette and examined the man he had followed to the water. The man was still trying to hear those far-off voices. In his mind, Will christened the man 'the listener' – his lopsided ear was that pronounced.

The listener's frame was stiff except for his tilted head and he wore spectacles that cut severely into the sides of his face – the defining trait, Will thought, of people who enjoyed self-flagellation. Something about the listener's polished shoes suggested a newly arrived foreigner. He appeared prosperous. Unlike the bankers who were sleeping rough, Will and the listener were in work; their work characterized them. But, while the natural posture of Will's spine made him unintentionally superior, the listener's carriage was plainly smug.

Together, apart from the riff-raff, Will and the listener waited for the second-to-last ferry from Ellis Island to reach Manhattan.

Aware of Will's examination, the listener silently acknowledged his presence with a clipped bob of his chin. He doubtless represented a society or an organization, like the man from the Catholic Aid who had been sent to meet Will all those years ago. These association men were the least eager of those taking the ferry. It was only duty to their old countries that brought them down here with their list of names and their authority to release.

Will put his right hand into his coat pocket and felt the bills crunch there. Their rustle reassured him that he had made the right decision when he had agreed to the overtime. The two extra hours on the job had made him late but he had the money in cash.

Will watched the ferry moving in towards them across the greasy water. It thumped against the quayside bollards and rolled on the waves of its own tide. The wash of the engines set off a glinting from the water and, for a few seconds, Will was almost blinded by a golden dazzle before the ripples settled and the bile-green face of the river reappeared.

An immigration officer, wearing a navy suit with wilted epaulettes, squeezed past Will and made his way down the gangway to open the iron gates. The ferry passengers tumbled ashore like a load of damp laundry dumped from a bucket. Their cardboard suitcases bumped the backs of their neighbours' knees but there was no common language with which to apologize. They bumbled up the gangway towards Will and when they came within ten feet of him, he smelled their stench – the rancid sting of sweat mixed in with the dull, copper odour of women on their monthlies. Will turned his face down into the collar of his shirt and felt utter disdain for the immigrants and then a rush of guilt.

The listener took a handkerchief from his pocket and covered his nose as though he feared a plague.

This was the place where steerage finally cleared. First and Second Class travellers had been off-loaded by tender boat while the *Aurora* was still at anchor in the deep channels but passengers from the lower decks were shuttled over to the immigration blocks and it might take hours or days for them to be allowed ashore.

Will wished he could have afforded a decent berth for Isobel. Instead, he now had a welcoming gift for her – some spare cash for a new dress from Macy's. They would make a day of it and head uptown for some shopping and an ice-cream, maybe even a picture show if his bonus ran to it.

There was a destination board propped against the cabin window of the ferryboat. The officer wiped it clean with a wet handkerchief and lettered ELLIS onto it in yellow chalk.

Will boarded and headed to the stern, securing a solitary post at the handrail. He flicked his cigarette into the river and watched it swirl hypnotically before going under. It was Will's first time on water in years. Not since he had taken this very ferry in the summer of 1924 had his feet felt the sway of decking. In Will's childhood, there had been boats and buoys and fish slipping like quicksilver into the hold when the nets opened, but that was in another country and another time.

The listener stood opposite Will and arranged his limbs and aspect in a way that suggested he was expecting photography.

The reversing engine sucked the ferry clear of its moorings. Off to the left stood the vague, verdigris monolith of the Statue of Liberty, holding her torch against the pumice sky, and it was suddenly very clear that night was descending. Will looked back over the city as they pulled away. He strained to see the construction site where he worked. It wouldn't be hard to locate – it was about the only one still in funds, surrounded by derricks and bright blue cranes – but it was simply too far uptown to be visible from here.

As the skyline shrunk, Battery Park showed its curved edges and Will became more aware than ever that it was an island on which he lived and an even smaller island to which he was going, and it struck him that an island off an island must be as isolated as any place could be.

Will checked to see if the railing would take his weight and leaned his tired back against it. He began to imagine how he would go about locating his sister. He always played this game in his mind, trying to select the fewest possible number of words he would have to use to get his message across. Just her name should do it. 'Isobel Phelan, please,' he would say. The trick was never to let the men in authority catch an accent, though Isobel's name itself – like a Gaelic bell – would give them both away as Irish this time. Perhaps he should just say, '*Aurora* steerage,' and be pointed in the right direction. He could pick Isobel out beyond the barriers with her flaming hair and her one ever-so-slightly lazy eye which gave the impression that she was always just about to wink.

Nobody else looked quite like Isobel. Will never caught a glimpse of a girl from across a street and thought, for a second, that it might be her. He did that with other people sometimes, people from home, and when the person he called out to turned and revealed themselves to be a stranger, Will was swept with a sadness that took a long while to pass.

The deeper water brought white horses with it. The bumping of the ferry was taking its toll on the listener's rigid posture. The man started to lean nonchalantly back on the rail, just as Will had done, but the top chain of his section had not been secured.

Will had developed a predilection for falls. The force of gravity had become something of an obsession with him since his father's death. Pat Carthy had been a Galway fisherman with a fondness for the shape of pint glasses. When Will was seven years old, his father had lost his footing outside a riverside pub one night and fallen into the Shannon. He was so drunk that only the bubbles of Guinness in his blood had known which way was up. They had floated him to the surface three days later and a boatman with a gaffe hook had fished him aboard. Since then, Will had trained himself to anticipate the moments when gravity would swoop in and suck down; it was a valuable intuition in his line of work.

Will's legs were already carrying him across the deck as the listener began to topple. The man's arms went up and made mad wheels in the air like a paper windmill on a sea cliff. All decorum was lost. Will reached out and grabbed the listener by the shoulder of his coat as he began his tumble towards the water, and pulled him clear.

'Thank you,' the listener said, a patina of oily sweat on his forehead.

He was foreign, from the Netherlands or Germany – somewhere in Europe, at least. Just those two words had marked him out.

'I do not swim,' the listener added.

The surge of fear had passed and the man pulled himself free of Will's grasp. He managed another awkward 'thank you' before he strutted away into the enclosed cabin.

After a few moments, Will glanced through the window to see if the man had composed himself. He saw the listener take a handkerchief from his pocket and wipe his hands. Then the man wiped at the shoulder of his coat. Perhaps he had just spotted the factory ash that had melted there like black snowflakes or perhaps it was because Will's hand had touched him in precisely that spot.

Will's stomach went small and spiteful. He would tell Isobel about the listener as soon as he saw her but the man's fastidiousness wouldn't make Isobel angry; it would probably make her laugh. The thought of the reality of Isobel's laughter made something tender at the back of Will's throat leap in anticipation. He felt an excitement beneath his skin, a buzzing of electricity in the wiring of his veins.

Up ahead, the red brick buildings of the Immigration and Naturalization Service came into view. They were built on a shallow, nondescript atoll in the Hudson. The Indians had called the place *Kioshk* – Gull Island – a reference to the flocks of birds drawn to the rich oyster beds along its shoreline. In the 1600s, it had been known as Gibbet Island because pirates had swung from a gallows tree there as a warning to other errant sailors – the opposite of a welcome to those venturing into the Dutch colony of New Amsterdam. The island had been used as an ammunitions dump for powder kegs and dynamite during the Revolution, the Civil War and the Spanish–American dispute. Finally, it had been renamed after Samuel Ellis who had owned it in the 1780s, and in 1880 it had been chosen as a replacement venue for the outmoded and undersized immigration station at Castle Clinton.

Over the years, the original mound of land had been connected to two other manmade islands created by using the landfill excavated from the New York City subway in 1904. These three parallel landmasses were eventually linked on their port side by a spinal causeway, so that together the islands formed the letter 'E' to God. The buildings looked grand but the white limestone lacing and gingerbread woodwork that candied their eaves and doorways was deceptive; the buildings themselves were fierce. They loomed over the ferry port and Will felt a nervous anxiety in their shade.

Six years had passed since he had shuffled his way along the immigration lines but still he felt a queer disquiet. The structures hadn't changed at all in those intervening years. Trees had been planted on the grass forecourt to offer some shade and scaffolding had been erected on either side of the concrete paths to form the framework for canvas awnings but these were seldom used.

As a deckhand twisted their mooring line around a cleat, a man in the uniform of a senior immigration officer loped over to their bow to meet the listener and help him ashore. The listener flapped like a self-important pigeon at the officer's greeting. He refused to take the hand that was offered to him, preferring to let his chest lead the way. The listener's status was obvious. Judging by his reception, he was probably an inspector from the Public Health Department. No wonder then that he kept washing his hands with invisible soap.

Will walked against the human traffic. A horde of newcomers was pushing its way down to board the last ferry but the mob parted to make space for him as crowds tended to do when Will Carthy was in a hurry.

Will made his way into the building and up the stairs to the receiving room. It wasn't busy; nothing like when he had arrived and the hall had held thousands. He approached the commissioner who sat behind the main counter. Authority made Will edgy and the immigration men who could say 'yes' or 'no' to America were feared in Ireland more than the *gardai*. The commissioner looked up and gave the small start men always gave when they saw Will standing unexpectedly over them. The man's name was stitched into his breast pocket in a gold thread that was turning into a metal of a less precious sort – brass perhaps – with age. It read: OFFICER S. W. OAK.

'Help you?' Officer Oak asked Will.

'Isobel Phelan,' Will said.

It came out all right. Flat and long and bland like real American.

'You sponsoring her?'

Will nodded.

'You're late,' said Oak.

'I know,' said Will. 'It couldn't be helped.'

'You kin?' Oak asked him.

'I'm her brother,' Will said. 'Will Carthy's the name.'

'But she's Phelan?'

'Different fathers,' said Will.

Oak's eyes bounced up to heaven and then back down again in a knowing manner.

'My mother was widowed,' explained Will. 'She remarried after seven years of grieving.'

Then he stopped, damned if he was going to explain to this man that Donald Phelan had been a soft-spoken, gentle man – utterly unlike Will's own father – and that he had given Will's mother some tenderness and the daughter she had always wanted when Will himself was already fifteen.

Oak pulled his languid body out of his chair and strolled over to the end of his counter.

He called out to another guard, 'This Mick's here for his sister.' Oak looked back at Will. 'What ship you say she's on?'

'The *Aurora*,' Will said.

'Off that Gateway ship that came in last night,' Oak added to his subordinate clerk.

The clerk sorted through a series of files and found the one he needed.

'You go with my junior there,' said Oak. 'He'll connect you up with her.'

By bizarre whimsy, the junior clerk's name was Junior; it was also stitched onto his uniform in front of an un-pronounceable last name that was probably Polish.

Junior encouraged Will along with a flick of his hand. Will followed him up a set of stairs and onto a viewing balcony.

'Shout out when you spot her,' Junior said and yawned without covering his mouth.

Isobel wasn't there. There were only a few dozen passengers left and Will could see right away that Isobel wasn't among them. He looked for her hair first but no red showed itself. He scanned each face. These were the dregs. The children with bulbous knees bisecting skinny legs, the women with arms dragged long and thin by the weight of babies. Will felt guilty that he had allowed Isobel to be left among them. She, unlike this lot, was wanted.

Junior looked up at Will.

'No?' he said, sounding only half surprised. 'I'll have to look her up then.'

Junior led Will down the stairs and back to the front desk. He managed to check his watch twice during the short journey.

'Not there,' Junior said to Oak.

'You sure you got the right ship?' Oak asked Will.

Will took the telegram from his inside coat pocket. It was still in its envelope, perfectly preserved and cared for since the hour of its arrival. Will showed it to Oak and, once the commissioner had read it, he nodded at Junior.

'The man's right,' Oak said. 'It says she's on the *Aurora*.'

'God damn it,' said Junior and he opened the file he had been carrying all along.

'Spell the name,' he said to Will as he pored through the pages, using his finger to trace the endless lists.

'I-S-O-B-E-L.'

'I meant the last or family name,' Junior said.

There was a slimy, snickering eel in his voice.

'P-H-E-L-A-N,' said Will, carefully.

'Fallon?' Junior asked.

'Phelan,' said Will, giving the 'e' its proper length.

The man shook his head, as if Will were crazy.

'Fallon,' he said again. 'Nope. Not on the *Aurora*. Not today.'

Will held the telegram out to Junior, so that he could read it for himself.

'I know that says July 10th and all, but it ain't right. She didn't come in,' said Junior.

Will was starting to experience real anger but he quashed the feeling.

'Maybe you've got it spelled wrong,' Will suggested.

'It's still an "F", right? I mean no matter how crazy you say it, it's obvious to me that it starts with an "F".'

'It starts with a "P",' said Will, spelling it again. 'P-H-E-L-A-N.'

The man swished to the 'Ps' on his list and read with his finger once more.

'I've gone through every "P" and every "F" in steerage and she ain't listed.'

'Second Class?' said Will, hopefully.

'She maybe came through Second?' Junior asked.

It was clear he was hoping this was the solution.

'Maybe,' said Will. 'There's a chance, I suppose.'

Junior made a study of his watch again.

'OK, I'll check,' he said.

Junior went into an office. Will waited. Through the glass of the main doors he could see that the last ferry had almost finished boarding; it would leave in ten minutes. Will waited another few moments then went over to the greeting gate. It suddenly seemed logical that Isobel had been in the ladies' restroom when Will had looked for her before, so he had missed seeing her. Once again, Will checked the faces of the families and the single men, even the tots who hugged their mothers' skirts. The small formations had not changed and Isobel couldn't still be freshening herself up.

Junior tapped Will's shoulder and showed him the list from Second Class. There were twelve names registered under 'P': Pappadopolous, Pargeter, Parnel, Patrick, Paulson, Payton, Pendleton, Philips (Mr Andrew and sons – two), Philips (Mr Walter and wife), Postlethwaite, Priel and Purkiss.

Something frightening and insectile was starting to twitch its membranous wings in Will's gut.

'You're not saying she travelled First Class, are you?' Will looked down into Junior's eyes without blinking and the man added a shaky, 'Are you, Sir?'

Will shook his head.

'No, I don't think that's likely.'

'She has your address, Sir?'

Will nodded.

'I suspect she's somehow made her way there then, Sir. Women travelling on their own are required to be detained until a male relative or sponsor calls for them. They aren't really allowed to leave of their own accord but sometimes they manage to slip past us with other families or claimants and we don't catch it. I'm not supposed to tell you that but it does happen.'

'She's not on your arrival list, though,' Will said.

'Oh, that's right,' said Junior, crestfallen that his explanation made no sense after all. 'She didn't ever get here then. She's still at home in Paddyville, safe and sound. She's decided against making the trip, Sir.'

Will shook his head. If that were true, he would have heard about it by now. Another telegram would have arrived from Mr Kelly at the Merryman Hotel, informing him of Isobel's delay and the reason for it. Mr Kelly knew how keen Will was to have Isobel with him; he wouldn't have left Will to worry like this.

'Every person who leaves a ship in New York City, travelling steerage, comes through this very hall, Sir,' said Junior with finality. 'She's not on the list. She never came through.'

2

Will had lived in the same room for five years – an uncompromising square with sour-milk walls and a sagging ceiling. It was situated on the top floor of a boarding house on Orchard Street. One hundred years ago, the roots of peach trees had plumbed the soil where concrete foundations now drove in and scarred. The groves had been dense with life and the rich brown smell of earth. Bees had drizzled softly down on the heavy boughs; breezes had moved quietly through them. Plump fruit had dangled in sweet, pink flashes against the bottle-green leaves.

Now there was black tar on the roads that went tacky in the worst of the heat and rows of block tenements, their shining fire escapes like the spinnings of giant, iron spiders. The heat was ferocious from May through September and the children would open the fire hydrants and flood the sidewalks with steaming puddles. Produce rotted quickly in these streets, beer went warm between mug and lip and weeds sprouted like sawblades in the cracked, concrete courtyards ringed by the tenements. Though not a solitary tree grew through the asphalt, and the only fruit was the wasp-stung dregs in the hawkers' crates, Orchard Street's name had endured.

A name was an important thing here. That was why the literate immigrants fought so tenaciously with the Ellis Island clerks when they tried to turn a 'Ribinowitz' into a 'Robbins'. A man's name was what reminded him who he was when the breadlines made each man the same desperate, hungry animal. The name of the place where a man lived reminded him of the place where he had lived, even when it bore no physical resemblance, so the boarding houses off Mulberry Street had names like the *Belli Cipressi* and the *Fiesole* and the *Ponte Vecchio*. Down near Germantown there was the *Tirolhaus* and the *Rhein Ansicht* but they were all alike really: tiers of inexpensive rooms that looked over the glum roofs of next-door buildings.

The names of the boarding houses in Will's neighbourhood all harped back – as so many hearts there did – to Irish beauties. On Canal Street there was the Kerryvale Resthouse and a tenement called Dunlaorie Waves where the windowsills were painted the blue of dissolving clouds. Heat cost extra in winter and, since the windows had no screens, in summer the bluebottles dozed in and bruised themselves for hours against the grimy panes.

Once, there had been an Irish bakery called Our Daily Bread on the corner of Houston Street. The early morning doughboys used to carry crates of soda bread out to their delivery truck, showering the sidewalk with the fine flour they sprinkled on every loaf. Will remembered how his boots had made black prints in the white dust and that the street had smelled of hot rolls and melting raisins right up till noon.

The bakery was abandoned now. The butcher had also gone out of business. The grocer was closed, too. The newspaper stand had moved to Union Square Park in search of customers but still mysterious broadsheets blew through the neighbourhood like rags discarded from a passing paper angel.

Across from the blank storefronts was the Four Green Fields, a local bar established in 1899. It had become a coffee house after the Eighteenth Amendment of 1919 ordered prohibition and had prospered for a while as the place where the Irish contingent of 'New York's finest' preferred to take their Canadian whiskey in mismatched teacups. Business had boomed during the last six months of junkbond heaven but since Black Monday, the owner dealt mostly in poteen and cigarettes – a purveyor of cheap, transient happiness to the hopeless unemployed.

Whenever Will passed the alley that ran down the side of the Four Green Fields, he listened intently. Almost sure that one day he would catch again the last few notes of '*In the Mood*'.

Over all, it was a sad neighbourhood that dead-ended on East Broadway – which was where things should have been getting started. Beyond that, there was only the river and the hunchbacked silhouettes of the black island factories.

Will came out of the Essex Street subway station into the gloom of nearly nine o'clock. He hadn't eaten since lunch and he was tired in the way that only unrelenting heat and punishing manual labour can make a man tired. Will almost heard the ghost of jazz from the alley beside the Four Green Fields as he passed. Outside the echoing, clapboard box that had once been Our Daily Bread, he looked down at the sidewalk to be sure there was no white flour in which to press his footprints. The sidewalk was unbroken black; the fact of Will's passing no longer showed.

Fifty yards further on, Will climbed the few crumbling, concrete steps which led up to Tully's. The front door had been painted the colour of snakeskin during a weekend of drunken patriotism the previous St Patrick's Day. Tully himself had adorned it with the interlocking gold curlicues of a Celtic border. It was so eye-catching that every now and then a wedding party would knock on the door and ask if their uncle, who owned a Brownie camera, might take their photograph standing in front of it. Invariably, Tully said 'no' and he would fling open the door unexpectedly every few minutes after the request in the hope of pushing the bride and groom down the steps if they had dared to disobey him.

The accommodation at Tully's was far superior to that offered in the other coldwater flats on the Lower East Side. In the station apartments that clung like rancid cocoons to the sides of the elevated train tracks, the families lived seven to a room. The boys and girls shared a bed. The babies slept wrapped in blankets in the precarious washstand bowls. The mothers took in sewing while the fathers smoked for a living and played *bocce* in the public parks. Tully's was better; it had been well built and it was always clean because of Rose Marie, the proprietor's only daughter.

Rose Marie and Aidan were at the kitchen table when Will came in – just the two of them, no Isobel. Perhaps she was having a wash upstairs in Rose Marie's tub. Aidan was one of the newer residents at Tully's – a skinny, edgy boy Will had never taken to. He was one of those people who presume intimacy too early and who always seem to be asking for unlikely favours. Will nodded a reserved greeting at Aidan and noticed that Rose Marie was wearing a fresh dress; its sleeves were rolled down which was unusual for dinnertime. A small daisy grew in Rose Marie's hair behind one ear. She brushed her skirt straight and looked expectant. Will realized that she was waiting for Isobel to come out from behind him. She was expecting Isobel to be with Will and all the while Will had been hoping that Isobel had made her way into Rose Marie's care.

'We knew you must have stopped on the way,' Rose Marie said. 'You're ever so late.'

Her voice was excited, like bubbles over smooth, blue pebbles.

'She never came, Rose Marie,' said Will and he realized, hearing himself give voice to it in his own way – accent and all – how much the situation baffled him. 'She didn't make it here then, I suppose?' Will asked futilely.

'No. There's been no sign of her. She never showed up at immigration?'

Will shook his head. 'There wasn't a telegram either then, was there?' he asked.

'No, I've been in most of the day,' said Rose Marie.

Rose Marie went out into the hall and across to the front room where her father was playing '*Ain't We Got Fun?*' on his phonograph. Tully Tulliver was a hundred and twenty pounds of sinewy skin topped with a bald and knobbly skull. He grew the nail of his baby finger as long as a Chinaman's, so that he could click it against the stack of coins that formed on his hall table every rent day. Tully hated the Jews and the English and he misquoted scripture loudly because he was hard of hearing.

'Was there no mail today?' Rose Marie asked her father.

'There's only ever bills,' he shouted. 'And get those worthless boys out of my kitchen. They're coveting my dinner.'

Rose Marie came back in. 'No telegrams and no letters. You didn't miss her there?'

'No chance of it. I stayed long after the last ferry. They must have checked every scrap of paper for the last week looking for her. No sign of her name even.'

Will had really pressed the officers of the immigration service. Oak had stayed late in an attempt to see the problem through and then offered Will a free trip home on the staff boat or else he would have had to spend the night in the detention cells.

'It's a mistake only,' said Rose Marie and she dragged the

flower from her hair and threw it into a paper bag in the corner with the fish bones. Her lower lip was petulant.

'I'm worrying now that Isobel's tried to make her way here and she's got lost,' said Will.

'You couldn't miss us,' said Rose Marie. 'Not with our front door. Anyone would tell her the way if she asked. She's not lost. Only delayed.'

Will began to feel better for the first time in hours.

'Not true,' interjected Aidan who had only been waiting, it seemed, for the opportunity to contradict before speaking. 'The crooks are all just waiting one road back from the wharf to fleece the new ones.'

Rose Marie glared at him.

'Weren't you meeting your one for a drink?' she asked.

Aidan leapt up and shrugged into his coat. Five men lived at Tully's and at least four of them met a girl named Connie every month for a drink. It had rather shocked Will when Rose Marie had made it clear that she knew what these drinks involved. She was often surprising him like that lately. Maybe Will was old-fashioned but he had preferred it when she had needed detailed directions whenever she started out anywhere and when she had constantly asked his advice about the subway.

Rose Marie had arrived from Limerick in November of 1929 when the newspaper headlines were all still shouting CRASH!. She had proceeded to declare every depressing corner of the city remarkable. Rose Marie had lifted Will's spirits with her sturdy, country arms – always elbow-deep in washing water – and her resilience.

Rose Marie was a girl toughened by six older brothers. She had nut-coloured hair and freckles on her ordinary nose. Will had once thought she was nice and had defended her whenever one of the drunks called her 'the plain one' in the Four Green Fields. Rose Marie had reminded him of Isobel in the beginning. Not in any physical sense or by any trait of personality but simply because she was a young girl who had seemed, at first, to need him. Now, he found he was constantly trying to extricate himself from a relationship she had inferred but which Will was certain he had never encouraged.

When the news had arrived, telling Will that Isobel was finally going to join him, Rose Marie was the first person he had told. Will had sought her out in the kitchen and read the telegram to her, expressing his first, tentative worries about where Isobel might stay.

'She'll stay with us, of course. I know just where her bed will fit,' said Rose Marie. 'It'll be as if I had a sister.'

'I think she's hoping for work as a maid or a nanny,' Will had told Rose Marie. Actually, Isobel had used the word 'governess' in her letters but she was young and had grand notions. 'She would live in with her employers then,' he added.

'Until she does, she's a sister to me,' said Rose Marie with finality and Will had felt a pull towards her because her words were kind and kindness was a rare commodity in the city.

'I'm telling you,' said Aidan as he opened the front door to go out, 'she's got herself involved in something unsavoury.'

The statement was vague and ominous. It unsettled Will worse than all the reams of paper he had searched that day without finding Isobel's name on a single sheet.

With Aidan finally out of their way, Will softened a little towards Rose Marie.

'It was a bath wasted anyway,' he smiled at her, trying to be light.

'I keep trying to tell you lads,' said Rose Marie, and she leaned in quite close over him, 'a bath is never wasted.'

The stairs were steeper after work than in the mornings. Will trudged up them. He had a small gas cooker in his room and he boiled a kettle of water and spooned some tea into a strainer. The heat – like a musty, wet towel – clung to his body. It was packed, as if in boxes, around the doorway and along the base of each wall. Will couldn't escape it and it made everything stink. Even his freshly ironed shirts, hanging over the wire he had strung across the corner, seemed to exude a muggy fetidness. Some nights, Will would lie awake for hours just to hear the fresh crackle of the ice truck delivering its blocks to every doorstep on the street. He would imagine running his hands along the ice's sleek surface and he envied the dog who sat in the back as cool as a collie bobbing in a seaside rock pool.

After Rose Marie had fed her father and washed the dishes, Will heard her pass his door and sit down heavily on the top-most step. That was his signal. He went and sat on the floor with his aching back against the frame of his door and Rose Marie sat similarly in her doorframe above him. The way the stairs curved right near the top prevented Will from seeing her but they didn't have to speak loudly to hear one another.

This evening ritual had evolved by accident during Rose Marie's first week in the house when she had been lonely and Will had talked quietly with her, long-distance, until she had fallen asleep. It was an arrangement her father could grudg-ingly approve of. As long as Tully could hear their muffled voices calling to one another over that stretch of step, he was assured they were not in a room together and was satisfied. Often, Will and Rose Marie thought they had the house to themselves and then, in the middle of a conversation, some uninvited comment would drift up from one of the lads on the floors below and remind them that privacy was rare in the tenements.

'What will you do?' Rose Marie asked.

'I'll put in a call to home tomorrow. Ask for word of her.'

'Was she never on board the ship or was she never on the island?' asked Rose Marie.

'That's the question,' said Will.

'They must have a ship's manifest you can look at. That way you'll know if she ever got going.'

'The telephone call should tell me that, too,' Will said. 'I hope she's not here, is all. I hope she's not lost.'

'Stop coveting my daughter!' Tully yelled up the stairs.

Rose Marie giggled and went into her room. Will closed his door and lay down on the planks and modest mattress he called a bed. His window was covered with a purple velvet curtain. It was third hand and had probably enjoyed life as a sofa cover and a dress before ending up here. The fabric was dark and Will had to leave it pulled open at night for fear of oversleeping in the morning, so sometimes, if he lay with his head just right, there would be an hour or so when he could see the moon. Sounds drifted in from the back tenement that shared their courtyard. There was a new baby in one of the cheap flats and its constant bawling had made Will irritable over the preceding week. Tonight, it was quiet.

A few minutes later, Will heard Rose Marie's socks moving quietly across the floorboards above his head and, to comfort himself before he fell asleep, he imagined her coming down the ever-so-few steps that separated his top-floor space from her attic bedroom.

In the dream, she was a different girl, really. She certainly didn't look like Rose Marie. She was somehow more confident, more American, and she had the blonde hair Will had always favoured on a woman. In fact, the only similarity she bore to Rose Marie was that, in the dream, this girl came down the stairs from Rose Marie's room.

She would appear at his door in some soft, sweet-smelling garment that would slip from her shoulders as she slid naked into bed beside Will and warmed the expanse of his back with her hardy, round body. It got so he ached for this vague girl in a way he had never had to ache for a woman before coming to America.

3

'Your sister come?' asked Frenchie.

He was standing in the site's transport lobby, smoking a foul, French cigarette. It was the cigarettes that had given him his nickname; he was actually from somewhere poor in Georgia. Frenchie had caused a stir by showing up to work on their first day in short trousers that fell just above his knees, and that particular daring-do had made him seem a little Gallic, too. Frenchie was a man who spoke without thinking, worked without thought for sweat or muscle strain and never gave a subject too much thought, particularly when he held strong opinions on it.

'No,' said Will and Frenchie nodded, satisfied with that.

Frank had also showed up early and he stood behind Frenchie with his empty paint can under his arm. Will searched through the issuing pile for a hammer with a smooth grip.

Once, he had chosen one with secret splinters and after the day's work his hands had swelled up like boxing gloves. Rose Marie had pricked each blister with a needle until it leaked its stinging, transparent pus and Will had slept with his fingers in a bowl of salt water for a week, trying to encourage calluses to form.

The three men boarded the Otis to take them up to where Lem would already be waiting. There was an unwritten law of hierarchy on the site which said that nobody went up until their riveter arrived, except for the heater who had to get his bolts fired.

On the twentieth floor, the sun was shining and the girders were already warm to the touch. Lem was stoking the coals in his portable forge. His face was as red as a blacksmith's. Black soot emphasized his wrinkles and made his eyes and teeth appear startlingly white.

'Weather looks good,' said Lem, by way of greeting.

Weather was their biggest worry. Rain that made the going slick and wind that gusted them off balance and creaked the steel. Ice was the enemy; the way it beaded invisibly on the frost-blue girders and waited for the worn tread of an incautious boot. Until he stepped out of the elevator and onto the staging platform, Will never knew what to expect. It might be as calm as deep sleep on the street but up where they were going, the wind would be blowing the seagulls about like white kites. Or it might be peaceful all the way to the top. Once, when they had still been working down on five or six, it had been so calm that a balloon had drifted up from a careless child's hand and Will had reached out and grabbed the string as it passed him. The child, who was watching from below, had clapped delightedly and Will had made sure he took the balloon away from view before he popped it and got back to work.

'You see your sister?' Lem asked Will, and Will shook his head for the second time.

Nobody asked any more questions. They had always taken Will's silences for a sign of profound intelligence. Will was their riveter. They took their tone from him. When Will began his morning ritual, they all followed on. He tightened the buckles on his dungarees. He checked that no shirt tail was loose and that no flap of clothing was free for the wind to snatch or the burning rivets to set alight. He pulled his cap on tight. He tugged at his bootlaces and double-checked their knots.

When he felt ready, Will walked out onto the highest beam that had nothing below it but the naked street. It was still. He imagined his soles sucked at the steel as he walked out; imagined that their suction made it impossible for him to fall. He acquainted himself with the sun. It was drifting across the sky above his left shoulder. Disorientation caused accidents as much as panic or carelessness or exhaustion. Will took in the teams below him and the teams beside him. He breathed in.

The shift whistle blew and the derricks came to life like elephants waking. They swung the steel girders towards the building's frame. The skyboys took hold of them and nudged them in the right direction, walking backwards along the beams as casually as a man might walk from his bed to relieve himself in the night.

The girders came from steelworks in New Jersey. A relay of sixty trucks bore them under the Hudson and through the midtown traffic six times a day. The base derrick secured them and passed them up to the relay derricks in bundles of twenty. With shuddering stealth, the girders made their tortuous way from the street to the sky. When they reached the riveters, the bottom-most girders were still warm – not from the sun, the teams had realized after a while, but from the furnaces in which they had been smelted only hours before. It was moving that fast and the teams had to keep up.

The waterboys brought them water – on Fridays it was sometimes clandestine beer. The hosemen flattened the dust for them with sprinklings of water. The welders cleaved and buckled the joints but the riveters made the building go up.

There were forty gangs of riveters at work on this site. Each gang had four members and each of the four had a distinct job. On Will's team, Lem was the heater. He took ten rivets at a time from a barrel and heated them in a forge of burning coke until they were as red as firecracker wrappings. The rivets looked like bolts with bulbous heads and Lem would choose one from the fire with his three-foot tongs and flick it to the catcher.

Sixty feet away or above was Frank. He caught the rivet as it flew through the air with his empty paint can. Some catchers had the newfangled, steel catching cone but Frank's paint can was the first can he'd used to paint the first house he'd bought for the first and favourite of his succession of wives, and it was lucky. Frank took the rivet from his lucky can with pincers and tapped it against the girder to loosen any stray cinders. He positioned the rivet into a hole on the girder and Frenchie, the bucker-up, supported it in place with a hand-held clamp. That was when Will took his riveting hammer and drove it home, spitting heat and raining sparks down through the daytime sky.

They performed this ritual seven hundred times a shift – more than a rivet a minute in a seven-and-a-half-hour day. The money was good: steelmen earned fifteen dollars and forty cents on weekdays, and double time on Saturdays if they could face to work the six-day week. If one member of a gang didn't show for work, the other three were laid off for the day with no pay. All four men signed their names on the same wage card, their earnings and their futures inextricably linked in the company's books. It was a good, hard job that had come Will's way by accident; it had literally fallen at his feet.

Will had been collecting wood for Rose Marie in the lot on West Thirtieth Street. The contractors had announced that truckloads of timber from the demolition of the old Waldorf Astoria would be dumped there for public use during that first

Depression winter. It had been December then and, above Will's head, the wreckers had been clearing the site, prying loose the masonry and lumber of the old hotel with their pinchbars. They were not a gregarious lot. They worked with intense concentration. They seldom made mistakes, so when the man fell, he fell silently – as if he had acknowledged in the second his foot slipped that the error was irreconcilable.

Below, Will sensed the fall more than he saw it. He dropped the pile of wood he was carrying and stretched up his arms in the futile gesture of a man who was willing to catch, but it was impossible. The body hit with a plump thump. The sidewalk absorbed the impact and the man's blood sprayed out of his eyes in two quickly dying fountains. A few spots landed on Will's shirt and on his right cheek. They burned quite hotly there for just a second until the chill wind froze the droplets to red ice.

Will stood with the same blank amazement as the rest of the gawkers for a few seconds then his feet started to run. He raced past the line of men whose faces were all looking back over their shoulders and up the steps of a temporary structure that was serving as the site office. Will didn't even knock before he entered.

'I need a job,' said Will and the typist stopped typing and glared at him over her thick cat's-eye spectacles. The only man in the room didn't even look up. The nameplate on his desk read PATRICK FEENEY – FOREMAN.

'There are a hundred men in line before you. A thousand even. We're fully staffed.'

'You're not,' said Will. 'Right now, you're one short.'

Patrick Feeney looked at him then.

'He just fell,' said Will. 'He's dead there on the sidewalk of Thirtieth Street.'

'Jesus Christ!' shouted the foreman and he shoved past Will at a run.

Will waited for two hours, alternating between sickness and anticipation. He followed the story with his ears. Amid the clicking of the secretary's typewriter keys, he heard a policeman's whistle get shriller and shriller as the crowd pressed in to look. He heard the ambulance siren mourn its way from the hospital and warble through the onlookers to the body. He heard the halted traffic's hooting. Then it grew quiet again and Will caught the hiss of the acetylene torches being re-lit above his head and the resurgent whining of the structural saws.

Foreman Feeney came back in with a pile of papers in those pastel colours that suggest officialdom – police reports, accident forms, compensation claims. Feeney threw them down on his desk where they fanned out like a deck of cards.

'You still here?' Feeney said to Will.

'I need the job something terrible, Sir.'

'He was nineteen,' said the foreman. 'The man who fell. His father welded the *Titanic* when she was in the Harland and Wolff dockyards in Belfast. I remember taking him on because he made me laugh so when he told me that. I said to him it was the grandest reference I'd ever heard of. I hired him on the spot for making me laugh so.'

Will was silent. He needed the job very badly.

'Can you rivet?' Feeney asked.

'Best riveter in New York,' said Will.

Feeney smiled faintly.

'Show up on Monday. We have some gangs starting. You need to fit in with three others. And don't tell me later you can't get along. All four's got to get along.'

'I'll get along,' said Will and started out.

'You one of Foxy Nolan's men?' asked Feeney, suddenly suspicious.

'Never heard of him,' said Will.

That was a lie. Will had heard of Foxy Nolan but he would never work for someone like that; the kind of agitator every foreman in the city feared most. Once Foxy Nolan had burrowed his way onto a site, the management might as well give it up for lost. He was the termite that could bring any enterprise crashing down from the inside before the brass ever got wind that it was being eaten away.

'You sure?' said Feeney.

It was a feeble question. If Will were one of Foxy's secret spies, he was unlikely to admit it.

'I'm my own man,' said Will. 'I'm not with no Foxy Nolan,' then he added hurriedly, 'whoever he might be.'

Foxy Nolan was a name Will knew from Ireland – a man who had been born without the sense of touch. Foxy Nolan, so the tales went, had almost no discernible reaction to pain. He received and inflicted it with equanimity. Foxy was a character composed of equal parts myth and madness. They said he had come to New York at eighteen – which meant he couldn't be more than twenty-eight now – and he ran a gang, or rather a gang ran after him. He had failed as an actor out in Hollywood for some reason – despite his extraordinary good looks – and had started out with cockerels. He raised them and fought them; nobody ever knew how he instilled such hatred or valour in their hearts. Foxy made his fortune off the fights he organized and he was the palest complexion welcomed in Harlem on a Saturday night because of the money he attracted to such illegal events.

Foxy had moved on to dogfights next but he never smelled of dogs. No scars ratcheted his body; no odour of blood or sweat trailed in vapours behind his person. Eventually, Foxy had decided there was money to be made in unions – running them, and organizing when the men would work and when they wouldn't. It had been enormously lucrative right up until the traders had started to use their bearer bonds for cigarette papers. Now everyone scrambled for work, nobody complained, and to organize a strike was futile with five hundred men clambering at the gate to offer themselves as scabs. Foxy Nolan was a dangerous man to know and a lethal man to cross. Will hoped he never ran into him.

'You never heard of him even?' said Feeney with a disbelieving tone.

'No,' said Will. 'Should I have?'

Apparently, Feeney realized he would have to take Will at his word.

'What's your name then?' said Feeney.

'Will Carthy,' said Will.

'Good Irish name,' said Patrick Feeney as Will walked out.

Pooled on the sidewalk was a circle of ice where the boy's blood had been.

When the whistle blew for lunch, Will went for the elevators and travelled down into the humble-bumble boredom of the street.

The Columbia Hotel had a public telephone that was secreted away in a mahogany booth beneath the staircase. Will was relieved to see that the booth was unoccupied. He felt ill at ease walking past the front desk in his boots and his roughneck shirt.

He placed a call with the operator and stayed inside the booth, holding down the receiver for fifteen minutes, until the phone rang.

'The Merryman Commercial Hotel,' said the voice of Mr Kelly.

Isobel had made beds and served beer to the horse market crowd at the Merryman for nearly three years to afford her half of the voyage. Mr Kelly had hired her and given her a room when their mother (and her father) had died of the influenza in 1928.

The way Mr Kelly's voice drifted in and out of earshot like storm-surge made Will think that there must be an undersea gale blowing in the Atlantic. He imagined the telephone cables being battered about in the deep, cold water. In Will's mind, the intercontinental wires of the AT&T Company ran through the deserted, drowned city of Atlantis – all up and down the fish-flooded streets just like regular telephone lines in a real, breathing city.

'Mr Kelly, it's Will Carthy calling you from New York in America,' said Will. 'Can you tell me if Isobel made her passage on the *Aurora*?'

Mr Kelly's voice crackled back at him, 'So Isobel's there with you, safe and sound by now, is she?'

Will's question and that answer he had dreaded passed each other beneath the blackest-bluest part of the ocean, between the white façade of the Atlantis City Hall and the entrance to the Atlantis Palladium Theatre.

'Hello? Hello?' said Mr Kelly.

Will waited a few seconds to accommodate the dreadful delay and then said, 'She's not arrived here, Mr Kelly. She wasn't on that ship you said.'

'That's grand,' said Mr Kelly. 'My nephew was going down to Cork. That's the nephew who's a dentist now, not the nephew whose leg got broke on the bicycle . . .'

Will thought of the minutes ticking away on the operator's stopwatch.

'. . . anyhow, I mustn't ramble if you're paying the exchange. My nephew who's a dentist was going down to Cork and he was only too pleased to travel with Isobel and see that she made it aboard.'

Will knew the nephew in question. He was a sharp-tongued, straight-laced man without a sliver of imagination or malice.

Mr Kelly droned on, 'He said there was another nice girl there from Offaly somewhere and Isobel took her right under her wing. They were going to share a berth and my nephew who's a dentist stayed to wave them off . . .'

'But she's not arrived on that ship,' said Will. 'Is he sure she got on?'

Mr Kelly's story wasn't finished, '. . . he even waved her away from the quayside. They had streamers, some of them. Isobel had a right proper send-off, and I'm glad she's made it there to you in one piece anyway.'

Will decided on resignation where Mr Kelly was concerned.

He said, 'I'm sure she has, Mr Kelly. And my appreciation to your nephew.'

'Not a bother,' said Mr Kelly. 'You still building those big buildings?' he asked and Will cut him off, leaving him to blame the operator.

He placed a second call to Rose Marie, hoping Tully would let her answer the telephone for once. He was relieved to hear her voice but afraid of her answer to his question.

'Isobel's not arrived, has she?' Will asked her.

'Oh, Will!' she exclaimed. 'No, I'm afraid it's bad news.'

'She's not shown herself then?' he asked.

'No, and no word from anyone either.'

'Ah well,' said Will. 'There's an explanation, no doubt. I'll be in later.'

With that, he hung up and he went out of the telephone booth and back up into the sky.

It had been less than a day – less than half a day really – Will told himself. But Isobel was so achingly beautiful. They had always been so close despite their age difference, so if Isobel were in the city, wouldn't Will be able to look down from here – about as high as any man could be – and see her hair? The trouble was that Will didn't feel her. Isobel didn't seem close like she had when Will had held her as a baby and her warm kitten breath had tickled his fifteen-year-old chest. Isobel was a big soul; her small body took up space. Will knew he ought to be able to sense her nearby, but he didn't.

Will decided that when he got back to Tully's, Isobel would be there. Rose Marie would have moved her into the attic, the two of them giggling at their battle to get Isobel's trunk up the stairs. Will would hear both their voices that evening: Rose Marie's and then Isobel's would call 'goodnight' to him from the top-most step. He could almost imagine it.

'No overtime today, lads,' said Will.

For once, nobody complained. It was Friday and they were all aching in different parts. Will made them check their laces before he let them head back to the staging platform. When a man was tired, he was more likely to slip up.

Will flung his hammer down onto the pile and signed off for the day. As he passed the foreman's office, Feeney himself came out and pulled him aside.

'After extra cash?' he whispered.

'Why even ask?' said Will.

'I've got a job for you,' Feeney said. He was holding a cylindrical cardboard tube, the kind the architects were always walking around with. 'Scarper these papers over to this bigwig's house on the park. There's five dollars in it for you.'

'My sister's waiting for me,' said Will, determined to believe it. Isobel would be there; he would see her when he walked through the front door of Tully's.

'Oh,' said Feeney. 'I heard she never made it through.'

Word travelled this fast through the site: passed along in the canteen, mentioned over smokes and water during the breaks.

'You heard wrong,' said Will. 'I'm expecting her today when I get home.'

'I wouldn't expect too much if I was you,' said Feeney.

Will suddenly felt a prickling dread that Feeney was right. He didn't want to go home, now. More than anything, he didn't want to not find Isobel waiting there.

'Anyhow, if she *is* there she'll be there in an hour after this is done.'

Will took the cardboard tube Feeney held out to him. It felt oddly substantial. There was an address typed on a sticking label. Will knew the street though he had never been there himself. It was the street name used in conversations when working-class storytellers were trying to imply a neighbourhood of great wealth.

'Can you find the place?' asked Feeney.

'I know it,' said Will.

'You do, do you?' said Feeney in a scathing tone.

'I know of it,' Will corrected himself and Feeney nodded at that.

'We all know of it, boyo,' said Feeney. 'My telephone rings two minutes ago and the bosses say they need these plans returned to the bigwig today. They've got to be sent now, they tell me. This bigwig's a specialist in something for buildings but he's no architect, he's no surveyor and he's no construction man, so you figure it out. You'd think with our schedule they'd be focused on this job but no, these papers

are about some other building altogether. I've had a peek and
they don't make any sense to me, so don't even bother yourself snooping. I can't get my head around what this fellow's
actually supposed to be doing but he's a bigwig, like I said, so
go in round the back like you're supposed to.'

4

The house was situated at the end of a road of trees, one of those ways off the park that led nowhere except to the heart of its own opulence. The three-storey mansions had been built from tan granite in the late 1800s, built by Scottish railroad magnates, Russian coalfield barons and German steel tycoons. The houses had Georgian roofs of grey slate and windows the size of museum mirrors. There were no numbers on the front doors, only discreet digits on the area gates that led to the tradesmen's entrances.

Will opened the gate of Number Seventeen and followed a row of stepping-stones that ran along the side of the house. It was leafy and lush here, one of the soothing sanctuaries the rich had made for themselves inside this city. A tortoiseshell cat licked its paw on the sun-baked wall and stretched. A small bell around its neck tinkled and a startled wren shivered from a magnolia bush. There was little traffic noise. Will could hear the sound of a piano being played somewhere and the high notes of water from a neighbour's fountain.

The path opened out into a large back garden protected by a high wall on which a green creeper crept, spangled with star-shaped flowers, and from each corner bed came the tall, silver ringing of birches. By the back steps, a tap dripped into a stone drain.

Will went up to the door. It was open and led into a green and white kitchen. He was about to knock when he was greeted by the soles of a woman's feet, propped up on a

49

kitchen chair. The woman was sitting at a central table and her feet were in the splash of sunlight coming in through the door. Her lap cradled a dozen broken bits of china and she was attempting to piece the object back together. She saw Will standing there but she didn't jump. She remained utterly unmoved by the shadow he threw into the room.

'Come in,' she said. 'I can't get up or it'll be even worse than it is now.'

Her accent was slightly Southern, Will was sure, but it had been varnished over with learned Yankee vowels.

Will went in. He held the cardboard tube he was meant to deliver in front of him, as if to show her that he was there on legitimate business, but she didn't ask him about it. He watched her choose one broken piece of china and try to fit it into the puzzle. So far, she had a base – like a small bowl – that was still intact and nothing else. The woman clicked her tongue and picked all the pieces up and put them on the table in two neat, parallel rows.

She had the light colouring Will had always been attracted to in a woman. This woman's hair was streaked with three distinct shades of yellow – lemon, gold and honey. She hadn't succumbed to the waved bob like Rose Marie had done the very week she had arrived. This woman had left her hair long and slightly tousled, an unkempt look that was popular with bohemians, Will imagined, or the wives of communists. The woman was unaware that the sleeve of her blouse had come down off one wood-brown shoulder; she was more tanned than was fashionable with the rich, so she must be a maid. But if she was a maid, she was daring . . . no shoes in the kitchen and her hair loose.

Will turned his attention to the cylinder he was carrying.

'It's for . . .' he nearly said 'the bigwig' but then he looked down at the tube to read the recipient's name which was typed on the label above the address. Unfortunately, it was a complicated name and Will wasn't sure how to pronounce it.

'Mr Trichardt?' the woman interrupted. 'Trickheart' was how she said it.

Will nodded, gratefully. The woman got up and went over to the porcelain sink to wash her hands. She was in no hurry and Will understood, by her incautious ease, that the house belonged to her or she belonged to the house. Her hands suggested proprietorship over everything they touched. They moved over the bar of soap . . . the faucet handle.

She looked over at Will again and he saw that her eyes were very dark blue, almost purple, and she was slim and languid like the cat on the wall. She turned off the tap and shook her hands to dry them. A spot of water landed on Will's face – precisely where the blood of the demolition boy who had fallen from the old Waldorf Astoria had landed. The spot of water warmed itself on Will's skin; he didn't wipe it away. He felt as if he could watch this woman in her kitchen all day, without words.

She took an apple from a bowl on the draining board and hopped up to sit on the counter. She bit into the fruit. It was small and so green it must have been as tart as lemonade but her face didn't show the bitterness.

'What's in it?' she asked, pointing at the tube Will held.

'I don't know,' said Will. 'It's private.'

'Let's look,' the woman said, trying to make a co-conspirator of him.

She reached out and took hold of the free end of the tube. She tugged at it a few times but she didn't snatch; the tugs were gentle and playful. Will felt very uncomfortable.

'Is the man himself here?' he asked.

Will wasn't good at conversation and he wasn't good at being rude to women. A man he might have told to, 'Push

Off!' but this girl was refined. Despite her casual manners, there was no doubt about that somehow. She was not a kitchen maid but she was not easy to categorize either.

Will held onto his end of the tube until the woman smiled and laughed and then he let it go. She laughed just like Isobel with her mouth open and no apologies. Will suddenly knew that this was a sign. He should have gone to the shipping company offices after work instead of coming here for the extra money. He should have gone straight to Isobel yesterday instead of working those two hours of overtime. Meeting this woman today – a woman just as beautiful as Isobel – was a warning to him about procrastination. It was each trivial delay and all those small, inane regrets which culminated in tragedy.

The woman popped the end off the tube and shook it. There was a single plan in the container. She spread it out on the counter beside her.

'It's just a schematic,' she said, slightly disappointed.

'A blueprint,' said Will and she looked up at him, surprised. 'My father was a builder,' Will added and he had no idea why he said it except that, in Ireland, a builder came above a fisherman.

In truth, Will only knew a blueprint from a schematic because of Lem. Lem had owned his own construction company upstate before the Depression and he was trying to encourage Will to learn the details of the job.

'You ought to be more than a pair of hands, Will,' Lem always said.

Will pointed at the small ruler printed on the sheet.

'See, it's got a scale and everything.'

The plan was a small-scale representation of a building – not a house but rather a facility of some sort. The rooms were large and there was extensive service and utility access in the walls. At the bottom, where the builder's name usually went, was a logo – a drawing of a door that had opened just a quarter of the way, as if enticing.

'Buildings,' she said, 'aren't interesting like people.'

'A woman would say that,' Will blurted out.

Then he worried that she would take offence. Since he had no idea who he might be offending, he looked down at his shoes. Then he thought how tired he was of looking at his shoes and he looked instead into the startling circles of her eyes. They were very dark blue now and Will saw they were a disconcertingly accurate gauge of her mood.

'Only I work on a building and it's very interesting,' Will added.

The woman smiled again, rolled the plan up and put it back into the cylinder.

'You should give it to him,' she said. 'To Mr Trichardt, I mean. If it's official.'

'A schematic's a rough technical sketch, a blueprint includes services like plumbing and electrics,' Will said suddenly.

'Is that the difference?' the woman said, sounding genuinely interested. 'I always wondered. I'll remember that and I'll remember that it was you who told me. Who are you, so I can remember?'

'Will Carthy,' he said.

'Will Carthy,' she said. 'Not William?'

Will shook his head.

'Christened Will,' he said.

He would learn later that she preferred the proper name to the contraction but she seemed to accept that he was just an ordinary Will. He didn't ask her name. It seemed brazen in this gleaming kitchen – as rude as the lewdly polished copper saucepans in the rack.

There was lavender in a vase on the windowsill and an enormous flush of herbs growing in a silver bowl in the centre of the table. Will didn't know the names for them, only the smells. Each one carried with it something distinct and unique – a certain aromatic dish or a happy moment remembered.

The woman slid off the counter and tapped her fingers on the table beside the broken pieces of china.

'I broke that jug on Monday,' the woman said, 'and I have given myself a week to mend it. I was just about to find two pieces that matched when you interrupted me.'

'I'm sorry,' said Will, not meaning it but thinking she had wanted him to say it.

'It was a welcome interruption,' she said.

There was suddenly a blue jay on the windowsill, peering at its reflection in the glass – fascinated by what it saw and unaware that it was only seeing itself. From somewhere inside the house, something squeaked and moved across the carpet. The blue jay flew off, disturbed, and Will looked towards the door from behind which the sound had come. The woman pulled her sleeve back up onto her shoulder. Will had thought she was oblivious to the fact that it had fallen loose but apparently she had known.

'You should give it to him now,' she said. 'I'll take you through.'

The kitchen opened into a hall. They went down it, through a reception room and into a larger living space. The house was heavy with thick oil paintings and clocks and the dense, stifling aroma of too many freshly cut flowers and too much cut glass. Will checked to make sure he wasn't leaving dirty footprints and when the woman stopped to knock at a door, he shone the nose of his boots against the back of his calves.

The woman didn't wait for a response but entered boldly.

Will wasn't sure if he should hover in the doorway or follow her. He decided to go in.

A man, who was probably her father, was sitting behind a desk as large as a California Redwood. He had both hands resting on it, palms down, and the surface was almost entirely clear of objects.

'Something came for you,' said the woman.

The man looked disapprovingly at his daughter's bare feet. She rested one foot on top of the other as if her feet ashamed her now. This strange posture gave her back a delicious curve.

'Come in,' said the man. 'I'm Jonas Trichardt.'

He had deep-set, yellow eyes and a widow's peak from which his hair was slicked back in black and silver streams. His breathing was odd, Will noticed. Oxygen was not there for the taking. Each inhalation was a conscious seeking out of breath. Jonas had a hard mouth and deep lines ran down the sides of his lips because once he had been used to laughing. He wore a suit and a striped, silk waistcoat buttoned all the way up. The chunky gold chain of a fob led from his braces to his breast pocket.

'Are you with Starrett Brothers & Eken?' Jonas asked.

'Yes, Sir,' said Will. 'At least, they're the master builder. I'm with a team that's been subcontracted in.'

'Manual labour by the look of you,' said Jonas.

'Yes, Sir,' said Will, and he tried not to sound as proud as he was. 'Riveting.'

'How tall are you?' smiled Jonas.

To a man like Jonas Trichardt, constructed with an economical use of anatomical parts, Will's bulk was a carnival oddity.

'Six feet, four inches,' said Will.

'Isn't that ungainly?' Jonas said. 'I mean, for the work you do?'

'No slip-ups yet, Sir.'

'Well, there only has to be the one in your job.'

There seemed no disputing that and Jonas gestured out with one of his perfect, creamy hands. Will rested the cardboard cylinder into his palm.

Once again, it was opened and the plan was shaken from it.

'Do you read plans, Mr . . . ?'

'Will Carthy.'

'Do you read plans, Mr Carthy?'

Will took a second's glance at the woman but she was purposefully looking away, inspecting books on a shelf behind her father. He saw her movements pause for an instant. She was waiting to see what his answer would be. Will had told her in the kitchen that he knew something of construction maps. Could he trust her with a little lie at this point?

'No, Sir,' he said.

Will saw the woman's lips tweak up a little and he felt happy. They had a secret, something private between them, which excluded her father.

Jonas rolled the plan open on his desk.

'I am a populace engineer,' he said. 'Do you imagine you know what that is?'

'No, Sir,' said Will.

'It's a scientist,' said Jonas. 'A man of science whose field of expertise is people and their movements. Not individually, in a physiological sense, but as a group. Have you heard the term "humanism"?'

'No, Sir,' said Will.

'"Anthropology"?' said Jonas.

'No, Sir.'

'"Ergonomics"?' said Jonas.

'No, Sir,' said Will.

'Well, you wouldn't have heard of that last one,' said Jonas. 'It's a concept I'm interested in developing. Even the word is mine. In the most basic of layman's terms, I am an expert not in predicting human behaviour – which is the job of the psychologist, the pseudo-scientist – but rather in moving them from place to place and organizing that movement efficiently.'

Will wondered if the man was having him on. It didn't sound like an actual job.

'In a skyscraper, let us say, the flow of humanity is in and out but also up and down, three-dimensional. It's a challenge to think of human movement in that way. How do we facilitate the flow in the most expedient manner possible?'

Will could see that the woman's face was starting to curl down, as though she felt Will was being humiliated. Was he?

'Do you know how we do it?' Jonas pressed.

'No, Sir,' said Will. He wouldn't give the man another 'No, Sir'. Not one. Not ever again.

'Well, I do. That's why I have the job I have and you have the job you have, Mr Carthy. It's Darwinian really. Have you read Mr Stoddard's most excellent book *The Rising Tide of The Coloured Peoples*?'

'It's on my list,' said Will. The woman's lips turned up at their corners. 'At the moment I'm wading through *Principles of Federal Democracy* by Alexander Lawson.'

Will only knew about the book because it was the one everyone dreaded having to read out loud to demonstrate their literacy on Ellis Island. Mostly, the Catholics got handed the Bible or *Lives of the Saints* and the Jews got the Torah, but the African darkies always seemed to end up with *Principles of Federal Democracy* which everyone knew was a college man's book.

Jonas's expression went sullen.

'A populace engineer copes with large numbers of people

who often behave as a flock . . . You are Irish, by the sound of you – a man who must know something of sheep,' he said.

'I know something of people,' said Will, 'and that it's hard to move them when they decide not to go.'

'I agree,' said Jonas, and he smiled. He looked genuinely delighted, as if they had some common interest after all.

'Lily,' he said. 'Did you offer Mr Carthy some water?'

'No,' said the woman, but Jonas Trichardt had given her a name at last. She was Lily to Will now. A flower. 'Would you like a drink, Mr Carthy? We have a secret stock of gin,' she said disingenuously.

'No, thank you,' said Will. 'They give us water at the site.'

'I'll need papers delivered regularly,' said Jonas. 'If your bosses decide to put in a tender for this job of mine. You could augment your wages by twenty dollars a week, if you want to be my errand boy.'

'I'll run your errands for you,' said Will. 'Not a bother.'

'Jonas can't get about like he used to,' said Lily.

She had called him 'Jonas', not 'my father' or 'Daddy'.

'My wife thinks me an invalid,' said Jonas and, in an attempt to prove her wrong, he stood up with pronounced force and walked around his desk.

His wife?

The man looked fifty and the woman was in her mid-twenties. Will had an unnerving sensation; a house of cards he was building in a faraway place had suddenly been blown down by a stray gust.

Jonas Trichardt walked smoothly with a properly straight spine. His suit hung at the shoulders as if, at his tailor's, he had imagined himself to be a bigger man. Behind him, Jonas pulled a small, steel cart on which was strapped a cylinder attached by tubes to a rubber mask with an elastic face strap. The wheels of the cart squeaked as they revolved across the carpet behind him. It was the noise that had alerted Lily to his presence when they were in the kitchen.

'It's oxygen,' Jonas said. 'I was unlucky enough to be gassed in the Somme. Mustard gas. It does the lungs in.'

'I know,' said Will. 'My father was in the War. My step-father, really.'

'Gassed, was he?' said Jonas, daring Will to imply he knew what being gassed was like.

'No,' said Will, and he left it there.

'I was twenty-five when I went,' said Jonas.

The man must be only thirty-five or forty then, Will figured. But Lily?

'There will be more papers on Monday. I'll let you know,' he told Will.

It was a dismissal and Will turned to go but then Lily called out, 'Before you leave, could you do something for me, Mr Carthy?' It was a very awkward request to make in front of her husband. 'Jonas can't manage it,' she added.

'Of course,' said Will.

'Could you check a light in the kitchen?'

Jonas didn't come along to oversee this mundane, domestic task. It was starting to get grey outside as Lily pulled a chair beneath the chandelier and put a dishcloth over it to protect the upholstery from Will's boots. Will hopped up onto it.

'I don't know what's gone wrong with it,' Lily said.

'Switch it on,' said Will.

Lily flicked the switch but the chandelier remained dark. Will carefully reached round and felt the connection of each flame-shaped bulb. The fourth one was loose and he tightened it up. The fixture popped into light.

'Loose bulb is all,' said Will.

'Is that what it was?' said Lily. 'I thought a filament had blown. And the bulbs come from Bergdorf Goodman's.'

'No, nothing like that,' said Will.

'Well, thank you,' she said. 'I expect you need to get home now. Normally, we have an odd-job man – I suppose that's what he is, I'm not sure really. He drives Jonas around and he's sometimes here to help me with things but he's off today. I wouldn't have had to ask for your help otherwise,' she said. 'But thank you.'

Just then, an enormous woman shuffled in through the back kitchen door. She carried with her half a dozen brown paper bags from the market.

'I did my best but there wasn't much going, Mrs Trichardt,' she said.

'That's alright, Mrs Harrigan,' said Lily. 'We all have to take what we can get.'

Will went past Lily and past the housekeeper and out into the garden where pale moths were anticipating the moon.

On the corner of the park, near Columbus Circle, there was a flower stall. Its bright buckets held a selection of blooms and Will asked the seller, on a whim, if he had any lilies.

'How many do you want?' asked the seller, coming round from behind his table to search through his produce.

'Just one,' said Will. 'To see what they're like.'

'Funeral, is it?' asked the seller.

'No,' said Will, appalled.

'Lily of the valley,' said the seller and handed Will a stem. 'Five cents.'

So that was what it looked like – white as goose wings, a temporary sculpture.

Will looked at the flower for a few moments then placed it into the loosest pocket of his jacket. He touched it all the way home as he sat in the subway; he felt its remarkable shape on his fingertips.

At the front door of Tully's, Will stood for a few minutes before going in. He strained his ears, hoping to hear Isobel's voice from within. If she was upstairs, though, he wouldn't be able to hear her from here. He would take the lily in to her but perhaps that would be tempting fate.

Will saw Rose Marie's shadow through the kitchen curtains but he knew that he didn't want to give the flower to her. He brought Rose Marie's face to mind and couldn't imagine how he had ever thought she was anything but plain. Rose Marie pulled the curtains back just then and looked forlornly down at Will. Slowly, she shook her head at him.

Will put the lily down at the base of the cold, stone steps – the way his grandmother had left knotted string on the threshold as a talisman against the entry of evil.

5

The next day was a Saturday, the second Saturday in July, and Will put on his best suit and his only hat and headed down to the Harbour Master's office which was situated on a bleak quarter-mile of cement near the South Street piers. The compound was comprised of several flat, grey buildings that squatted next to the river. Seagull droppings drizzled down their windows, cripple-legged pelicans perched on rusty pylons, and oil dripped from quayside davits and spiralled on the mossy water between the coastguard cutters.

In the Department of Public Enquiries, Will was hurriedly handed a request form to fill out but it was almost noon before a secretary took him in to see a Mr Vole. The man's office was like the interior of a wasp's nest – paper from floor to ceiling and no two sheets stapled or pointing in the same direction. Mr Vole, ensconced behind his desk, was similarly dishevelled. His frazzled hair refused to lie down flat and his middle finger sported a large bump where his pen rested and a permanent tattoo of ink.

'You have a passenger query,' the man said to Will.

It was a statement, not a question.

'Yes,' said Will. 'It's about my sister.'

Together, they went through the whole process again. Will provided Isobel's personal details and the circumstances of her non-arrival.

'What day was this?' Vole asked.

'Just this past Thursday,' said Will. 'Thursday last.'

'Give me the exact date,' snapped Vole, as if he couldn't work it out for himself.

'Thursday, July 10th 1930,' said Will.

The man stood up and peered at the numerous shelves that ran, buckled by weighty tomes, along the wall.

'Vessel?'

'The *Aurora*.'

The man muttered to himself, 'That's a Gateway ship.'

He ran a hand along the shelf.

'Gateway, Gateway, Gateway,' Vole intoned until his finger settled on the correct ledger. He brought the enormous leather-bound book back to his desk and thumped it down, crushing the layers of paperwork beneath it. He fumbled through the pages, looking for a passenger manifest.

'Apparently, the boarding inspection was carried out the night before they actually came ashore,' said Vole. 'That happens when a ship gets in near dark; the shipping companies prefer to delay the tenders till the next morning. Here it is: Wednesday 9th in the evening . . . and the girl's name?'

'Isobel Phelan.'

'No middle name?'

'Isobel Fay,' said Will.

'Yup, here she is,' Vole said, and Will's heart elated then sank.

His head hadn't yet decided what would be good news but this must surely be positive: some acknowledgement of Isobel's existence at least. Will stood up and pulled the book around, so that it was facing him the right way up. As he did so, Vole retreated nervously back into his chair.

There was Isobel's name in the ledger, written in the boarding inspector's hand or in the hand of his assistant who had obviously been hired for his rapid and legible penmanship.

PHELAN, ISOBEL FAY (MISS) – EI.

The shape of her name was graceful on the page.

'What does that mean?' asked Will, pointing at the two capitalized letters at the end.

'Ellis Island,' said the clerk. 'She would have had her jacket tagged with a yellow card that said EI. That way those who don't speak English usually end up being dumped in the right place.'

'She does speak English,' said Will, defensively.

'Either way, she cleared through Ellis,' said Vole.

'So she did travel as a steerage-class passenger?'

'Yes, Mr Carthy. She would have been processed on Ellis by the late afternoon or early evening of the 10th at the latest.'

'She wasn't there,' said Will.

'You didn't meet her?' asked Vole.

'I was a little late,' said Will.

Vole looked scandalized by this innocuous confession.

'I did eventually go to meet her but she wasn't there,' explained Will. 'Where else should she be recorded?'

'The next list she would make would be the commissioner's report on Ellis.'

'She's not on that. I've checked through it with Commissioner Oak.'

'Not possible,' said Vole.

He closed the book with a bang and walked round to put it back on the shelf, as if Will would allow that to be the end of it, the end of Isobel.

'But that list you have was written here in the harbour once the ship arrived?'

Vole sighed exasperatedly. 'Once First and Second Classes have cleared, the boarding inspector makes a list of those still left on the vessel who then have to clear through immigration on Ellis. Your sister was one of the travellers who gave her name as one of those remaining steerage-class travellers.'

'She made it this far then.' Will made the statement to reassure himself.

'Unless someone else used her name,' Vole added, casually.

'How could that happen?' said Will. The thought made him shudder.

'Well, the inspector would have checked all their passports and papers. He would have tried to, at least, but if someone looked a little like her, had her documents and gave her name . . .'

Will remembered something Mr Kelly had said on the phone the day before, '*There was another nice girl there from Offaly somewhere and Isobel took her right under her wing. They were going to share a berth . . .*'

'Who wrote her name there in your book?' Will demanded. 'Whose writing is that?'

'We have over two dozen vessel inspectors here, Mr Carthy, and they all take an available clerk with them to do the writing when they go out . . .'

Will pulled the logbook out from the shelf again and slammed it onto the table, opening it back up to July 10th. Vole let out a high, effeminate shriek at the thump the ledger made.

'Whose writing is that? It's very good writing. You must recognize it.'

'Yes,' Vole stammered.

'Who writes like that?' demanded Will.

'It's a boy named Samuel Fisk. Sammy Fisk, we call him.'

'Where is he now?'

'I can't tell you that, Mr Carthy. He's probably aboard one of our cutters if he's doing inspections.'

'Find out!' said Will, and he picked the book up and thumped it down onto the table again to make his demand emphatic.

Vole picked up his telephone and dialled the switchboard. After a few minutes of queries, he said shakily, 'Fisk has been out this morning but he's coming in with Inspector Dryer now. They'll dock at Quay Five.'

'Thank you,' said Will and added, 'She's seventeen years old, you know,' by way of atonement.

He was trying to explain how desperate the situation was making him, but Vole just kept nodding hurriedly and Will could see that the bureaucrat only wanted to be left alone.

Will took the time to have one last glance at the way Isobel's name looked on the page – squashed in among the hundred unrecognizable names of lesser immigrants – and then he left Vole in whatever peace he might manage to attain amid his chaos.

The cutter tethered up and Will waited for the crew to disembark. He could see the liner they'd been out to. The logo of Gateway Shipping was large above her water line – a blue angel with bird's wings soaring above a series of rolling waves – but this wasn't Isobel's ship, the *Aurora*. That vessel had already departed on her way back to Ireland.

Inspector Dryer was an old naval man. He had maintained an impressive moustache and he rolled from side to side as he walked, the same way Will's father had done on land. Behind Dryer was a well-built, young man with a tousle of dark curls pushing out from beneath the peak of his uniform cap. They made him appear somewhat girlish and he had a sweet face that must have made him a target for bullies in the schoolyard.

'Mr Fisk?' said Will. 'Could I have a word?'

It was a question Will hardly ever asked anybody. If he could, Will went out of his way to avoid speaking with people. He didn't like strangers to hear that he was Irish unless he was in an Irish pub or at an Irish parade. It was all very uncomfortable – exposing his naked foreignness like this – but it was for Isobel.

'About what?' said Inspector Dryer, trying to shelter his clerk from unnecessary bother.

'It's about my sister,' said Will.

'Oh, God! Here we go again, Sammy, I've warned you about the girls.'

'I think you may be able to help me,' said Will.

'Does your sister look anything like you then?' roared Dryer. His walrus moustache quivered at the snipe. 'She must be a bracing girl!'

'No, we had different fathers,' said Will.

'Irish, are you?' guffawed Dryer.

'I'll be in directly, Mr Dryer,' said Fisk. 'Go ahead if you like.'

Dryer walked off towards the grey buildings, still chuckling to himself.

'My name's Will Carthy but my sister's name is Isobel Phelan and it was written in the ledger in your hand.'

'What ledger?' said Fisk.

He had started to walk off, too. Already following his boss back to the relative cool of the offices. Will kept pace with the man as he walked.

'The manifest ledger for the *Aurora*. Isobel arrived as a steerage passenger two days ago. Wednesday it was. Maybe you saw her?'

Fisk stopped walking. He sighed and smiled a little.

'I write a thousand names a day, Mr Carthy,' said Fisk, as if that answered Will's question.

'Maybe you remember Isobel, though? I think you would.'

'I don't look at them. I don't see them. My hand's scribbling away faster than a typewriter. It's all just work, and have you

67

smelled them? Seen the sight of them? You stand as far away as you can just to avoid looking at them.'

Fisk started towards the buildings again.

'I can't find her,' said Will.

'Probably doesn't want to be found,' said Fisk. 'That's my experience of missing women anyway.'

Sam Fisk walked through a side door which had EMPLOYEES ONLY painted on it.

'She's seventeen!' Will shouted through the door.

He checked the knob to see if he could follow Fisk in, but the door was locked.

It was almost three o'clock by then and Will was trying to work out what he should do next. He saw a group of long-shoremen leaving an annex to the Port Authority building through a side door. Some of them carried mugs of coffee. It must be the dockers' cafeteria. In the late afternoon, when lunch was finishing up, workers' canteens often didn't bother to ask for a wage slip as proof of employment. If you looked the part, you could sometimes pretend to be an employee and get a company-subsidized meal for a few cents. Will thought he would try his luck; he went in.

It was hot inside. It smelled of damp wool and oxidized metal. Will went up to the counter and asked if there was anything like a meal still going. The sweaty serving woman looked at his suit for a few seconds then said, 'Mashed potatoes, sprouts and some pan fat from the chicken . . . Oh, and terrible coffee.'

'Lovely,' said Will.

The server slopped the dregs onto a tin plate.

Will went into a corner to eat; he kept his back to the wall. The canteen tables were wood and they smelled as if they had once been used for scaling fish. Will picked unconsciously at the surface of the table with his finger. There was the tip of something sharp and cartilaginous sticking out from a crack in the wood. Will twanged it with his fingernail to try and work it free as he ate.

A few men were watching Will from where they played dice on the lid of an Indian tea crate. Out of the corner of his eye, Will saw a few more men form a group at the door. The air in the canteen dimmed as their figures blocked the sunlight coming in from outside. They all looked Will over and he stayed hunched over his plate, growing more edgy. Will wasn't sure if they were union men looking to protect their jobs from an outsider or if they were company men thinking he was a unionist trying to stir up trouble. Perhaps they imagined he was one of Foxy Nolan's professional snoopers. Whatever they thought, it wasn't good for Will.

Then Will saw Sam Fisk standing in line for the terrible coffee. The boy's refined, pale face was a smooth mask among the stubble, scar tissue and razor burn of the longshoremen. Will looked back down at the table and saw that it was a fishbone he had been fiddling with – small and ruthlessly curved with tiny teeth all along its edge.

Fisk paid for his mug of coffee and started to head back to his office. He spoke to the gang of watchers at the door and, after a few minutes of unnerving delay, they reluctantly hulked off.

'Hey!' Fisk's voice carried across the canteen.

Will looked up. Fisk had been about to go out, too, when he had turned back. He stood half in and half out of the door-frame.

'Your sister's not a redhead, is she?'

The fishbone came free in Will's fingers like an axe pulled from a stump. His heart boomed deep and round like cannon fire.

'She is,' Will said.

Fisk came over to him.

'You seemed so sure I'd remember her that I got to thinking about the ones I did remember from Wednesday night. And there was only one. A redhead. Pretty.'

'Yes, that's her. That's Isobel.'

Will was elated. He smiled and shook Fisk's hand in both of his own. Some of Fisk's terrible coffee spilled onto the floor.

'It's OK,' Fisk said, 'I can't tell you any more than that, though. That's it. There was a line and I was sitting behind the trestle table we always set up. This girl came forward when it was her turn and handed me her passport. Dryer wrote her tag and tied it to her coat button. I checked her name and wrote it in the register. That's all.'

'She didn't say anything to you?'

Fisk frowned and considered.

'I'm not sure,' he said. 'She smiled. She looked well, happy. She had a perfect face except for one eyelid lower than the other. At first, I thought that maybe she'd been crying – her eyes were a little red – but then I realized she was just tired because she had a terrific smile the whole time.'

'That's Isobel, no doubt,' said Will. 'She fell out of a tree when she was six. The fall didn't hurt her much but she looked up to see how far she'd dropped and a branch came free and bumped her face. The bits of bark got into her eye. I remember trying to flush them out with warm milk half the night. She was really brave but that eye was just a touch lazy after that. The right eye, it was.'

Fisk smiled. Will's enthusiasm for his sister was contagious.

'She's OK then,' Will told himself, flooding with relief.

'She looked well on Wednesday and that's only three days ago. I'd say she's still fine. You'll find her.'

'She didn't say anything else, though?' Will asked, hoping for more.

'I might have tried to talk with her more but there was a line behind her and we shuttle them through as fast as we can. I think she might have said, "Bless you." No, she said, "Blessings on you." That was it.'

'Isobel always says that,' said Will. 'Every night before bed, ever since she was little.'

'Mystery solved,' said Fisk. 'She made it to New York City and she's misplaced herself for a day or two.'

'She's not on the commissioner's list on Ellis Island, though,' said Will.

Fisk's face frowned deeply and went dark.

'She isn't?'

'No, where else should her name be?'

'That would be the only place, really,' said Fisk.

He got up abruptly to go.

'Thank you anyway,' said Will. 'At least nobody else got hold of her papers. The girl you describe – that's definitely Isobel. I thought maybe another girl was travelling with . . . Anyway, it sounds fine now.'

'The doctor's list,' said Fisk, suddenly. 'If she felt unwell once she got ashore, she'd be put in the infirmary on Island Two. She could be there, I suppose. Then she might never have made it onto the Ellis Island commissioner's list because the medical inspection comes first. That's where she'll be, Mr Carthy.'

'Call me Will, please.'

'Sammy,' said Samuel Fisk.

It was all so obvious that Will wanted to whoop out loud. Isobel had been under the weather and she'd been taken into the hospital; they'd been slow in contacting him. He wanted to crack the skull of whoever had forgotten to let him know. If Isobel was in a fever, though, she might not be well enough to communicate. That worried him a little – Isobel being sick like that – but it was better than Isobel alone in the city.

'Thank you, Sammy,' Will said again. 'I'm grateful to you.'

'Don't be,' said Fisk, and he took his cold, terrible coffee and left.

Will tried to reach Commissioner Oak by telephone to see if the man would help him. He thought Oak might connect him to the hospital wing or go and see if Isobel was there, but the official worked weekdays only, it seemed.

Will got a public telephone number for the Ellis Island infirmary from the operator but when he dialled it, the line simply rang. He told the operator he was desperate but she said curtly, 'I can make it ring but I cannot make them answer it, Sir!'

Will had been standing in the dank phone booth on the docks for thirty minutes and it was almost evening when somebody finally picked up the receiver on the other end. It was a nursing sister with a voice as sharp as surgical scissors.

'It's not our policy to answer private calls on the weekends,' she said at once, 'but your constant ringing is bothering my patients.'

'I need to know if my sister has been admitted,' begged Will.

'We don't give out information over the telephone,' said Sister Scissors.

'I'm worried that she's sick, I'm her only family. Please!'

'You'll have to visit and be identified by the patient before we can give you any information.'

'Can you tell me if she's there, though?'

'No,' said Sister Scissors and then she thawed slightly and added, 'I can tell you that I have no critical charges at the moment. So if your sister is here, she's certainly not calling at death's door.'

'Thank you for that,' said Will. 'I'll come tomorrow on the first ferry to see her.'

'No ferry tomorrow,' said the sister, 'and no visitors. It's Sunday.'

Will's stomach sank but he had been told there were no chronically ill patients. Isobel had something minor. She had probably been seasick and unable to eat anything. That would have made her weak. Maybe she had passed out and they were simply nursing her back to strength.

'Monday then,' said Will.

'Don't ring again. You're probably keeping her from her rest.'

'I won't. I'll see her soon,' said Will.

He thought he'd try to get a message to Isobel, though he was sure Sister Scissors wouldn't help.

'Her name is Isobel. Please tell her that her brother, Will, is coming to get her. I'll be in to see her on Monday . . . if she's there.'

That night, Will explained to Rose Marie what had happened. He sat in his doorway; she sat on her step. He knew she was there because the wood creaked when she swayed her weight from time to time – a humble, rhythmic sound like a house settling down on its old bones late at night.

'That's exactly what's happened,' Rose Marie said after she had heard Will's story. 'Why didn't any of us think of it?'

'Too busy imagining a disaster,' said Will. 'Like at work – they all talk about the accidents, never the progress.'

'Aidan has a black eye,' Rose Marie said. 'He's been brawling.'

'Over work?' said Will.

'There's some rumour about that a few under-the-table jobs are going begging on a building site somewhere. All the labour for it has been brought in from out of the city so far. The unionists can't figure it out and they're hopping mad about it. Foxy Nolan's on the case, they say. The contractor's housing his workers in a dormitory in the Village but nobody can get in to talk to them. Apparently, it's new boys every week. There's security outside so local lads can't even pick up a tip on who to speak to for the work. Aidan went down and tried to get in through a back window but they dragged him clear and beat him. He's a fast runner else he'd be in worse shape.'

'Jesus, Mary and Joseph,' said Will.

'He'll be fine but they're guarding the work something fierce now. I'm glad you're safe where you are.'

'I can't take so much as a day off, though, Rose Marie. The foreman's just looking to give your job to the next man who's fresh and eager. They line up at the site every morning even though they know the place hasn't taken a new man on since May.'

'What are you doing tomorrow?' said Rose Marie, changing the subject.

'Worrying about Isobel all day,' said Will.

'I'm going to the park for the July Fair. You should come, Will. It'll be grand and you could get something for Isobel when you see her.'

'I want to be well rested,' said Will, wondering if he would end up looking like Rose Marie's escort for the day. If she kept clinging to him as she had done for the past few months, none of the younger lads would feel right asking her to walk out. Will felt he ought to mention it to her. He fancied Aidan might try his luck with Rose Marie if the boy knew Will was amenable.

'Hospital visiting ends at six on weekdays,' Will told Rose Marie. 'I have to make the early ferry after work on Monday or I'll be sodding late again.'

'You'll make it. We'll have Isobel with us before the end of the week,' said Rose Marie with her usual, jutting optimism.

Will wanted to hug her just then. There was a lot to be said for her humanity. Then he thought of Lily and the bare soles of her tanned feet and something in him shivered.

'I'll join you for a bit tomorrow,' he said.

'It'll be a great day for certain,' said Rose Marie.

'Goodnight then,' said Will.

'Sweet dreams, Will,' said Rose Marie, as if she was having a sweet dream herself at that very moment, and then she sighed.

6

Lily Trichardt was at the fair in a silk dress the colour of banana ice-cream. At first, Will thought it was impossible luck, seeing her again so soon, but her presence made sense. Her house was only a block from the entrance to the level, grassy field that stretched along Central Park West where various sponsors had decided to hold their 'Jump Into July' fair. It was the first really scorching day of summer and Lily wore a straw hat with real daisies around its brim. Will caught sight of her at once between the sunlight and the lime-green trees. She had a sash of little girls around her and she was admiring the frills at the tops of their socks.

Rose Marie had led Will around all morning but now he gently loosened his hand from the knot of her fingers. The figure surrounded by children was undeniably Lily. Though Will had only seen her that one time, there was no doubting her. Lily was like Isobel in that way. There were few physical similarities between his sister and this woman but rather a shared shine on the skin that came from some soft, internal illumination.

Will wanted to go up to Lily and touch her bare shoulder. More than anything, he desired some tiny measure of physicality between them. It would easily pass as an appropriate means of catching her attention in public. Will would touch her and say, simply, 'Hello again!' but it was not hello again. They had not first greeted with a 'hello', Will remembered. They had started right in on a conversation, as though his conscious body had come late to a ghostly communication his spirit had already begun with her at an earlier time.

Then Will saw that Jonas Trichardt was at the fair, too. The man sat behind a fence of patriotic bunting on a platform erected for specially invited guests. He wore a cream suit and he had his legs casually crossed to show that the soles of his shoes were almost new. He looked like a dandy from the movie posters at the Lyric, except that his oxygen cylinder was beside him and his fingers were perpetually curled around the cart's red rubber handle in the same way an unstable man keeps his cane close at hand. The plastic oxygen mask hung loosely around Jonas's neck. He must be using it today – perhaps the outdoor air exacerbated his lungs. If Jonas was a scientist, as he had said, he was probably accustomed to a more rarefied atmosphere, Will thought. It was likely laboratory air, screened through pipes and conditioned to be cooler and more dispassionate than that breathed by the man on the street.

These ideas came cruelly to Will. He started to seek out instances of his superiority over Jonas Trichardt. Some were deliciously obvious: he was taller, healthier and immensely stronger but still he felt uneasy. It was the way the other man spoke. Though Will had managed to follow everything Jonas had said to him the previous Friday, Jonas's speech suggested reserves of intellect Will felt he couldn't match. Wiles were a different thing to wisdom and Will didn't know which of the two would come out on top in a verbal punch-up.

Will and Rose Marie found a shady spot and sat down in the grass with outstretched legs. Rose Marie noticed Will spying on Jonas immediately.

'Do you know him?' asked Rose Marie.

She had that female astuteness which allowed her to hit on

the truth through pure intuition every now and then, without ever being particularly clever.

'He's a scientist. The company I work for is bidding on a tender he's offering out,' said Will.

'Lah-di-dah,' said Rose Marie. 'I bet he has a white car.'

White cars were the epitome of sophistication in Rose Marie's mind – being both impractical and garish. She lost interest in Jonas and flipped through the pamphlets they had accumulated throughout the morning.

'There's a strong man contest,' said Rose Marie, reading from a programme. 'You ought to enter that.'

'I'm not parading about,' said Will. 'They love a parade leader in this country but it's not how I was brought up.'

If a man wanted praise in Ireland, he had to do something. When Will had scored the winning goal in the all-Ireland inter-county hurling finals, the lads had hauled him up onto their shoulders. He had roared and brandished his hurley about for a bit but, afterwards, he had been chided into buying a round for the whole team, for being so foolish.

'You'd win,' needled Rose Marie.

'Buy us a Coca-Cola,' said Will, changing the subject, and gave her the money.

Rose Marie got up from where she had been sitting on his jacket and went off into the crowd, leaving Will free to watch Lily. Between the legs of the passing human circus, Will could see glimpses of her. Lily hadn't seen him and it was like watching her on stage. In his mind, for the past thirty-six hours, Lily had moved according to his will. Here, the way she brushed her hair from her face and made tiny, fluttering gestures with her hands was unpredictable and thrilling.

It was mostly green in the park. The grass had been freshly mowed for the event and the trees had their new leaves on, but around Lily there was a concentration of colour. There were puffs of cotton candy and little girls with bows the colour of cotton candy in their hair. There were stalls with red, striped awnings, selling scented drawer sachets for the ladies and paperweights for the men. A chestnut pony with an orange plume on his harness was plodding the children round a paddock for five cents a circle. The tin calliope warbled out its incessant cheerfulness and the balloon man still held a whole rainbow of plastic souls by their strings.

Everybody was in their Sunday finest but there were two distinct types of people present – those who had walked here from their homes near the park and those who had come by subway and bus. Some of the children were playing the games and munching their peanut brittle but on the outskirts of every privileged group was a child who clutched an apple and waited to be told when he could eat it.

The mother of this boy invariably wore a heavy coat despite the heat because the coat was newer than the tawdry dress beneath it. As Will glanced about him, he saw more and more unfortunates. Mostly, they were women but the odd out-of-sorts father was there, too.

The Margaret Sanger Society was handing out discreet newsprint brochures and the women in their winter coats took them guiltily and stuffed them low in their pockets.

A breeze, on its way up from the lake, ruffled through the crowd and, on the platform, Lily rubbed the tops of both her arms. Mrs Harrigan, the Trichardt's housekeeper who had a bosom as big as a bowsprit mermaid's, swooped in and draped a gold shawl over Lily's shoulders. All the other ladies on the platform were older – very old – and they had their grey hair pinned up and their gloves tightly buttoned. Lily's gloves were made of yellow lace and in the French style, so that her scarlet-painted nails peeped out.

Rose Marie came back and handed Will his bottle of

Coca-Cola. She followed his gaze and, like all the ladies there, her eyes stole a lingering glance at the yellow dress.

'That would look fine on me,' said Rose Marie.

'It would,' said Will, kindly.

'Yellow's my colour. Not many can wear it,' declared Rose Marie. 'Even this month's *Woman's World* says it. It's a difficult colour.'

'A difficult colour!' laughed Will. 'I thought green was the only difficult colour. Green with envy.'

Rose Marie gave him a playful shove.

'You must buy me a yellow dress one day, Will. All wrapped up in tissue paper and in a proper box from the Saks Department Store.'

'When I make my first American million, I'll buy you and your husband a trip on a Pan American airplane to Miami Beach,' he said. 'No expense spared.'

Rose Marie went quiet.

Thankfully, the Salvation Army band started up with an explosion of cymbals at that moment and they listened for a while. Will watched Lily swing back and forward against the platform railing, as if an invisible rope tethered her there. After a few brass band classics, the group started in on '*The Star-Spangled Banner*' and several veterans, those who could, tottered to their feet from their wheelchairs and saluted. Jonas Trichardt was the first man up, Will noticed.

There was a 'Healthy Boys and Girls' parade at noon. The children marched about in their white vests and gym shorts and did sit-ups and stretches and lunges in unison, all with perfectly pointed plimsolls. The American Eugenics Society was awarding medals for it. Will took a pamphlet entitled *The Menace of the Feebleminded* from one of their representatives and lay down to read it under the trees while Rose Marie went off to dance the Charleston on a plywood dance floor sponsored by the YWCA.

The gist of the American Eugenics Society's message seemed to be that inferior races would soon take over the world with their indiscriminate breeding. However, if the Nordic races took a superior male specimen and a superior female specimen, the resulting offspring would likely be superior. There was little arguing with that. What they considered superior was less clearly stated. The brochure mentioned height, optimum weight, fairness of complexion and mental acumen. There seemed to be a preponderance of concern over eyes.

There was a quote from Stoddard, from the book Jonas had mentioned to Will during his visit to the Trichardts' house, '*It is tantamount to a eugenic crime to turn the possible parents of defective children loose on society*.' Government-supervised sterilization was the answer, it seemed. The science looked all right. There were pages of graphs and a few experiments to show the inadequacies of the dull-witted brain. The tract ended by saying that the American Eugenics Society, supported by the likes of past presidents and famous jurists, had over eight million members nationally and countless sympathetic friends among distant allies.

'Find any spelling errors, Mr Carthy?'

The voice was Lily's. She was standing over Will, using the tree as a pole from which to swing back and forward. Lily's body was restless in this way. It was always moving but it kept an inclusive arc. Will wondered if she knew that she was using her energy to trace and retrace the same limited extremity of space.

'No,' said Will.

'That's good. Jonas is their secretary and he'd spit if you caught a mistake.'

'I didn't know you were here,' said Will.

It was a stupid, clumsy thing to say.

Lily laughed. 'You didn't follow me then?' she said. 'I rather hoped you had.'

Lily took the bottle of Coca-Cola from Will's hand and put it to her mouth. She didn't wipe it; she put it straight between her parted lips and swigged.

'You don't have germs, do you?' she said, seeing Will's slightly shocked expression.

'No, just an inferior make-up apparently.'

'How do you mean?' she asked.

Will flapped the pamphlet at her. 'Dark eyes are a result of interbreeding between the races.'

'I like dark eyes,' said Lily, adamantly.

'That'll be the downfall of the whole movement, I expect,' said Will. He tried to wipe the grass stains from his trousers. 'People who just like dark eyes and won't be swayed from their thoughtless course of action.'

Lily looked carefully at him then. The bottle was caught between her mouth and the sun. Light glinted off its edge.

'People can be so reckless in that way,' she said.

Will laughed. She had a clever turn of phrase.

'You're here with your wife,' said Lily. 'I thought you must be. A man wouldn't come on his own unless he had a girl to show off for, or a cause.'

'I'm here for the pony,' said Will. 'I like horses. And she's my landlord's daughter.'

'Ah,' said Lily. 'Useful for rent stabilization.'

Her wit charmed him. Rose Marie never said things like that; most women never said things like that.

'She asked me to come with her. I couldn't say no,' explained Will.

'She dragged you along? All one hundred pounds of her?'

'My sister's in hospital,' said Will, suddenly. He wanted Lily to have the truth from him. 'I can't visit her today, so this passes the time until tomorrow.'

Lily flopped down next to him. Will looked to see if Jonas had caught the casual fall.

'I'm an expert at passing the time until tomorrow,' Lily said. 'You should ask my advice on it. I could sign you up for decoupage or flower arranging,' and then, because she knew she was being facetious, she added, 'but I'm sorry for your sister. Is she very sick?'

'I don't know. I'll talk to the doctor tomorrow evening.'

'If you want our doctor to see her, I'll get him to do it,' said Lily, and she said it in such a way that Will knew, unequivocally, that Lily would follow through on her offer and pay the bill for it, too, if he only dared to ask her.

'Thank you. It's not necessary, though. She's only not well from the travelling.'

'She's new in town?' said Lily, and she sounded pleased.

She didn't get a bad smell under her nose the way some begrudgers did when Will mentioned that a new person was soon to make their home in New York. As if to be glad of Isobel's arrival meant that someone precious to the established residents had to depart to make way for her.

'I'd want to help if I could,' said Lily. 'Not this kind of stupid help for stupid people. . .' she indicated the whole fair and Will's pile of pamphlets '. . . but real help. I was only sixteen when it started but if I'd been old enough, I'd have gone off to the War with Jonas. To nurse at the front.'

Will looked carefully at Lily; she seemed very young to him in that moment.

'And I know that only people who never went ever say that,' she added, redeeming herself.

'You'd have made an awful nurse,' said Will.

That seemed to take Lily aback and her mouth let out a little huff of air as though she had been punched lightly in the stomach.

'I've seen you trying to put that jug back together, remember?' he explained.

Lily laughed loudly at that, so loudly that Will saw Jonas's head come up in the distance and look around for his wife, but his eyes never alighted on them under the trees. After a moment, Jonas relaxed and resumed his conversation with the man beside him.

'Glad it wasn't your shattered leg I was working on in the trenches?' Lily said after the giggles had subsided.

'I was never at risk from you,' said Will. 'I didn't go to Europe. There were exemptions for necessary workers and I was employed on a farm.'

'What sort of farm?'

'A seaweed farm in Galway,' said Will.

'You're having me on!' said Lily.

'I am not,' said Will. 'We harvested seaweed from the ocean. A few of us men would wade out, up to our necks sometimes in cold, rough surf and we'd attach steel hooks to these enormous sheets of orange weed. The hooks were tied to ropes and harnesses and several lads on the beach would urge these great old carthorses to drag the stuff ashore.'

'What did you use it for?'

'To make iodine for the soldiers. The War Office in London was putting huge demands on the industry; desperate for the iodine on the front they were, so I was excused from the fighting.'

Will didn't tell Lily about the fields as red as old blood where they laid the seaweed knee-deep to dry. He didn't tell her about the face of the boy he had come across buried under that weed, the crabs eating his eyes. Will had found himself in the wrong place that time. He had looked up, startled and frantic for help, and he had seen two lads he had grown up with – passionate Fenians to the end – calmly glaring over at him from a distance.

'What have you found there, Will?' one of them had called out to him. 'And careful what you say now.'

Will had looked down at the collar of the boy's shirt. It was that distinctive khaki colour which marked him as a Black and Tan. Probably, he had simply wandered away from his barracks on a pass one evening and ended up in the wrong pub. People often went missing like that in Ireland during the early twenties.

'It's nothing at all,' Will had called to the two anxious lads, and he had simply covered over the two black eye-pits in the boy's white face and pretended to go on about his work.

Over the weeks that followed his unimaginable discovery, Will had avoided newspapers and gossip. He had not wanted to know the name of the boy he had abandoned fecklessly in death and he never did come to learn it. Will had decided then not to dig around in the seaweed once it was laid – leave that to the crabs and the gulls and the frilly-lipped sea slugs. But he had known in that moment, despite everyone's constant assurances to the contrary, a terrible truth. The way a man does know the worst of himself when others never guess it. Will knew that he was that most deceitful of physically powerful men: the private coward.

'Does it make you guilty?' Lily asked, and Will froze.

What had he said to give himself away? Then Will realized that she was merely asking about his absence from the War.

'At home, nobody would dare ask you what you did in those days. Afraid you'd say you were in the Irish freedom struggle and ask them for their side in the matter.'

People seldom asked Will about how things made him feel and they never asked him where his sympathies lay. Nobody had ever questioned him about an abstract emotion like guilt or doubt or faith. It seemed intimate, a conversation better suited to stern wallpaper than the kind of open, speckled light that came through the leaves of the tree.

'Then I shouldn't ask either,' said Lily. 'I'll wait for you to say.'

Will looked over to the dance floor. He could see that Rose Marie's cheeks were growing flushed as she flapped her arms and kicked her legs out. The music was reaching a crescendo; soon she would be walking back this way.

'I might see you again tomorrow,' said Will. Lily seemed uncertain about that and rather flustered at being dismissed. 'I'm supposed to be coming over with your husband's plans,' he added. 'But it depends on the state of my sister, I'm afraid.'

'Oh, yes,' Lily said, relieved that he wasn't just bored with her. 'Well, I hope you do . . . If your sister's well enough to be left, I mean. I'll try to have my jug further progressed for you,' she said with flippancy. 'Just to prove I'm not a complete waste.'

Lily walked back to the platform, going out of her way to wend through the crowds, so that, by the time Jonas saw her, it looked as if she had come from the coconut shy.

Will bought Rose Marie a coffee cake before they headed home. It had been made with real butter icing and was Tully's favourite indulgence. Rose Marie looped her arm through Will's as they strolled back to the bus stop. They were far enough away from the fair by then for him not to worry about Lily seeing them together. It felt companionable. It was the way he had intended to walk proudly with Isobel and, if Will didn't look to his side and see Rose Marie's old floral dress there, he could almost believe it was yellow silk he was escorting.

Yellow was a colour that wouldn't quieten down, Will found. It buzzed in his head like a bee refusing to settle. He couldn't sleep that night and he remembered how rock-sure he had felt under the trees with no internal complications, no twisting of the spirit. That calm had fled now. Maybe it was because Lily had reminded him of the boy in the seaweed grave, or perhaps it was because tomorrow he would see Isobel after all their years apart. The terror of not seeing Isobel ever again had drifted away and the fact of touching her in reality, of taking her hand while she slept and waiting for her eyes to open, took the fear's place and finally put him to sleep.

7

'I'm glad you've found her anyway,' said Frenchie when they broke for the day on Monday. 'I didn't like to say it last week when you weren't sure but some dreadful things happen on the ships. I mean to girls travelling on their own.'

'Too right,' said Frank. 'One of my aunts was on a ship where two of the girls made charges of lewd behaviour against an officer. An officer! Not even a steerage man.'

'Lewd behaviour! That's rape they're meaning,' said Frenchie. 'Half of them get here pregnant.'

Frenchie was prone to exaggeration but Will had heard the stories. Girls being robbed, beaten, violated and sometimes jumping overboard before they reached New York harbour out of desperate loneliness or disgrace. Dying of shame like that wasn't something Isobel would do, though; Isobel was more liberal than she ought to be. Will had her letters and he knew her from those. They had arrived every few days over the past five years and he had sensed her growing up in them. Changing from a little girl of twelve into the young woman he had never seen except in photographs.

'But Will's sister's alright,' said Frank, hurriedly.

'Of course she is,' added Frenchie.

'She's a little ill. She's had her first dodgy American hotdog is all,' said Frank and they all laughed.

Will left them in the lobby and popped his head through the foreman's door.

'There's supposed to be a package again today,' Will said to Feeney.

He was about to explain that he wouldn't be able to take it. He wanted to see Lily but Isobel had to come first now.

'Not that I've heard of,' said the foreman. He scratched through the papers on his desk, as if he might come across some pertinent pages unexpectedly. 'Try again tomorrow.'

Despite his relief, Will felt a sudden drop of spirits – like a stone sinking all the way down through deep water and settling on the bottom. There would be no Lily today but that meant he would definitely make the earlier ferry over to see Isobel.

The ferry was busy. Two new liners had surged into port that morning – one with a blue Gateway angel painted on its prow and the other with a Cunard crown and laurels. The families on their way over to Ellis Island were speaking in the usual torrent of tongues. The few children became the victims of the adults' anxiety and impatience. Cheeks were pinched rosy and socks dragged up to cover scabbed knees. Mostly, it was small groups of men going over to meet their brothers or uncles or cousins, though – the women were usually left behind in the old country, the family split until money could be sent back and a place prepared for them.

In the receiving room, Will had to stand in line to meet an unfamiliar commissioner. There was no sign of S. W. Oak with his name fading on his jacket. Will explained his story to the new official. By a piece of luck, Junior was on duty again, though. Junior confirmed that he and Will had been unable to find Isobel the week before. The new commissioner picked up his telephone and placed a call to the hospital wing. He spoke into the handset for a few moments with his back turned to Will and then he swung round on his chair and said, 'Junior will take you over to the forecourt. Speak to a doctor out there by the name of Challis.'

Peter Challis was as thin a man as Will had ever seen. His white coat flapped in the wind off the Hudson and his trousers sucked about his spindly legs. In the sturdy breeze, Will wondered how the doctor could hear the chests of the people he took aside and branded with his icy stethoscope.

'Dr Challis,' said Will. 'I'm Will Carthy, I'm to go with you to the hospital.'

'I'll be done in five minutes,' said Challis.

Will stepped aside as the doctor grabbed a boy by the scruff of his neck, tugged his shirt tails free from his trousers, and placed the stethoscope against the sharp ripples of his ribcage. The boy's breathing rattled. Will could hear it from where he was standing a few feet away. Challis pulled the boy aside and a nurse helped him put his coat on then chalked a large letter 'N' on the back of it. His mother was babbling questions and Challis pulled her out of the line, too, and shoved both of them into the cluster of unfortunates already huddled behind him. They each had a letter on their backs: a 'P' and an 'X' and another 'N'.

After a few more cursory exams, an elderly doctor came down the steps to relieve Challis who threw his stethoscope down onto a table with a kind of angry hopelessness. Challis massaged his temples with his fingertips and motioned for Will to follow him. The doctor moved quickly, as if everything needed to be as expedient as his examinations.

'What are the letters for?' Will asked him.

'"P" for pregnant. "N" for pneumonia. "X" for mentally unsound.'

'You can decide in one exam?' asked Will.

'I'm a doctor,' said Challis. 'I can decide in a second.'

They went through several official doors and left the building through a rear exit.

'We're supposed to have misplaced a patient, I understand?' Challis asked.

'I'm only hoping you're caring for my sister,' said Will.

When they came out of the leeward protection of a wall, the wind punched them. Challis walked out onto a metal causeway that ran across the water for a hundred feet and connected to the parallel landmass that was Island Two. The wind was blasting across the expanse of the river and the high cry of wheeling seagulls sounded like the ricochet of bullets. When the waves crashed against the pylons, seawater splattered Challis's coat and Will tasted salt on his lips.

They couldn't talk until they made Island Two and went in through the front door of the main building to a reception desk. A nurse was seated there, deciphering a doctor's handwriting on a chart. Her spectacles seemed to shadow her eyes rather than promoting them and Will was instantly sure that she was the scissor-voiced sister he had spoken to on the telephone.

'It's your opinion that we've lost your sister,' said Challis. He leaned over the desk and grabbed a clipboard. 'This is the admissions list for the last week,' Challis said.

He handed the pages directly to Will; perhaps he had already perused them for himself and knew all the answers.

'I don't see her name here,' said Will.

The constant, tidal fear that had washed him for the past few days came surging back into Will's stomach.

'Then she was never admitted,' said Challis. 'Our paperwork here is impeccable.'

'I'd like to look.'

'Our patients deserve their privacy,' said Challis.

'I'm going to look,' said Will, rephrasing his request.

'I could have security prevent you.'

'The last guard was back on Island One. We passed him outside the records room and he was lacing up his shoes. Presuming he doesn't pause to finish doing that, and presuming he hears you calling him across the river once I've ripped this phone out of the wall, I'm guessing I'll still have enough time to get through any wards you may have here before he can stop me.'

Challis and the nurse glanced at the phone on which Will had rested his hand.

'I'll not cause trouble if you let me see for myself,' Will added.

'The women's ward is this way,' said Challis and he ushered Will through a set of swing doors, leaving the nurse to cautiously pick up the phone and check that the switchboard was there and ready to take a distress call at any moment.

The room was surprisingly modest in size and unpartitioned. There were ten identical iron beds wrapped in light green sheets with military corners. On the top shelf of the nurse's station was a large fern – an ideal plant for hospitals, Will thought, since it thrived even when very little care was actually proffered. The three staff nurses who sat, looking bored, behind their station stood up when they saw Dr Challis enter. They had starched pinafores like iron breastplates and each displayed the worn caretaker's look of constant disapproval.

There were five women in the ward. Two female patients lay in their beds; they were reading romance novels in two different languages. Another looked very ill, she was sleeping. Two more looked positively chipper. None of them bore the remotest resemblance to Isobel.

Will asked the youngest of the nurses, 'Do you remember a girl with red hair? She would have been here very recently.'

The nurse looked afraid and glanced at Dr Challis for direction.

'Don't look at him!' Will shouted. 'Did you see her or not?'

The nurse shook her head. Not a strand of her hair shifted out of place beneath its crown of pins.

Will pushed past Challis and threw open the doors in the men's ward just across the corridor. There were only two patients in this room. They were playing chess and they looked up at Will with dead, sunken eyes.

The children's ward was next. There were three occupants. Their bodies were small in their beds, their feet plumping up the sheets only a third of the way down their mattresses. Enormous pillows swallowed their heads. One was entirely wrapped in bandages, a small swaddling of white.

'Boiler explosion on a Greek steamer,' explained Challis. 'She won't see again. There will be horrible scarring. She would be better off dead.'

The mummified shape in the bed was too small to be Isobel.

Will pushed past Challis again. Doubting he would ever be allowed back here, he had to be sure. He went down the corridor, slamming open doors. Some flew ajar onto supply closets that housed mops and bottles of blue disinfectant, some opened onto empty offices or dispensaries with shelves of medical supplies. One was a bathroom with rows of cubicles. The last three doors were locked.

'Open them,' Will said.

Challis looked reluctant.

'Please,' said Will, and Challis saw that if he didn't comply, it meant violence.

The first locked door concealed a large, sunny room. There was accommodation for thirty patients in this empty ward.

There were the ferns and the clipboards hooked to the footboard of each iron bed. The second locked room was a mirror of the first, so was the third. Ninety immaculate but unused beds lined along blank walls. Will walked among the vacant stations. He had run out of locked doors.

'Five years ago we might have had every bed full,' said Challis. 'Now that immigration's slowed down, we keep them free in case of a disaster in the harbour. A sinking or a fire onboard a ship.'

At the side of each bed, there was a steel cabinet painted white. On the top of each cabinet, a mesh basket in which a washcloth and a brand new bar of soap nestled. It seemed such a waste of resources in these lean times to leave the rooms perfectly stocked like this but, then again, it was a government installation.

The soaps were smooth and ivory-coloured. What Rose Marie called 'beauty bars'. Will picked one up discreetly and slid it into his coat pocket. He would take it home to Rose Marie. She was always going on about not having money for soap and such.

'We have thirteen patients in total at the moment,' said Challis. 'That's how I'm so certain your sister isn't here. It's not as if she's gone missing in the crowd, is it?'

Will wiped sweat from his forehead.

'This was the last place where she might be safe,' Will told Challis.

'We've had no unidentified bodies this week. There have been no deaths of unknown patients for over a month. Your sister never came here.'

Will nodded and looked up through the barred windows. Across the blowing water, he could see the impressive building blocks of Island Three.

'What's out there?' he asked.

'The contagious diseases ward and then Staten Island,' said Challis.

'I'm going over there,' said Will.

'You can't,' said Challis and his voice was very sharp. 'There are three people out there. All men. One has German measles; the other two have something much worse.'

Will ignored the doctor's protests. He went back to the front desk and out into the howling wind. Challis's coat flapped against his sides as he pursued. Will started out across the iron walkway and Challis kept pace with him for a while.

'I want to see them,' said Will.

'Sometimes what they have is incurable not just contagious,' said Challis.

His voice had taken on a different tone. No longer condescending and cool but genuinely fearful.

'I'll take my chances,' said Will.

Challis, seeing that Will wasn't going to stop, ran back to the start of the steel walkway, lifted a flap on a control panel, and pressed a button. Ahead of Will, the steel walkway buzzed and swung away from its joint, so that Will was faced with nothing but a gap of twenty feet of water and a drawbridge far beyond his reach. Below, the waves looked like ocean-surge with foamy spittle at each choppy crest.

Will stopped and turned back.

'I can swim,' he roared out to Challis and pulled his jacket off. 'Tell me what they have!'

'Rabies,' Challis shouted. 'From a mad dog they tried to corner on a boat from Tunis. They both have it and there's no cure.'

Rabies wasn't something Will knew anything about but the idea of enraged dogs stopped him. He threw his coat down on the metal grid at his feet. Challis waited until he thought Will was calmer then walked out to join him. Unexpectedly,

Challis made a compassionate human gesture: he offered Will a cigarette. It was shop-bought and tailored, the kind of cigarette Will hadn't smoked in a year. The doctor cupped his hand and offered Will's match meagre shelter, enough to get the cigarette lit, and then he lit his own. In that unlikely location, in that howling wind, they stood side by side and smoked.

'Do you know how rabies victims die?' Challis asked.

Will shook his head, miserably.

'They die of spinal fractures most often. The convulsions and the dementia are so extreme that they snap their own backs, usually after hours of writhing and thirst. They become hydrophobic first – terrified of water, unable to swallow it – but before that, they will start to snap at their carers. They will try to bite. Their saliva becomes stringy and thick. If they attack and break the skin, the victim is infected and that's the end of them. We aren't even staffing their room any more, Mr Carthy. There's one nurse out there for the measles patient because there's hope he might pull through but there's nobody else, I promise you.'

Will looked over at Island Three.

'What about the other buildings? There's half a mile of space out there.'

There were quite a few buildings on Island Three. Two were almost as large as the Great Hall on Island One.

'It's our refuse buildings and storage facilities,' explained Challis. 'It's mostly deserted now. Empty except for the trash and the surgical waste and those three tenuous lives.'

'Where are the patients kept?'

'There are a few holding cells in the smallest building. The Immigration Service made use of them when things were busier to hold the criminal element who tried to enter the city from abroad. There's not so much of that these days, though.

We've managed to stem the tide of incoming refuse. Now, we're using one of those cells as the death room. It's locked and we have the two rabies patients chained in there together like dogs. Part of me hopes they might rip each other's throats out, otherwise it could take hours, maybe days.'

Will must have looked stricken.

'That's the limitation of human compassion,' said Challis. 'The dog we darted with an overdose of morphine. It fell asleep and then it died peacefully.'

Will sat down on the wet, steel sheeting and thought of Isobel. Unashamedly – and with a grief that was in part exhaustion – he rested his face in his hands.

'It's for the best,' said Challis, misinterpreting Will's sorrow. 'If you had all the facts you would understand it better.'

He placed his palm on Will's shoulder and patted him gruffly.

There was nothing more to see out on the river. Will left Ellis Island quietly and took the ferry back to Battery Park and then the subway to his neighbourhood. He would have to deal with Rose Marie's interminable questions about Isobel; hopefully, the bar of soap might distract her.

Will made a stop at the Pike Street police station. He went up the steps, his feet bathed blue by the official precinct light. Inside a woman was bleeding into a towel, her face torn by a broken cider bottle. She was howling that the man who lay passed out at her feet owed her money. There were flyers posted on the wall. One of them caught Will's eye because it had a detailed drawing of a small dog on it.

STOLEN! said the headline.

'Olivia Pickford's dog,' said the desk sergeant, noticing Will's interest. 'Taken right from her kitchen where it slept on a velvet cushion.'

'Olivia Pickford the actress?' asked Will, and the desk sergeant nodded.

'It's our number one case at the moment,' the sergeant said and Will tried to ascertain whether or not he was joking, but couldn't.

Will asked to speak to anyone who could file a report for him. The desk sergeant sent him upstairs to speak with two detectives. They were playing cards and they put their hands down carefully on their respective sides of the metal desk, as if they intended to resume the game shortly.

One of the detectives got up to look for a 'Missing Person' form but couldn't find one in the cabinet where they were supposed to be kept. The other rifled through his desk and discovered an old sheet.

'My lucky day,' he said, flapping the crumpled page. 'I done it in pencil last time.'

'You're just a lucky kind of guy,' said his partner.

'The last lady left before we got it finished, so it weren't never official,' the detective assured Will, as he rubbed out the answers with a crusty eraser.

'Everybody's going missing,' said the lucky cop. 'You're my third this week, matter of fact.'

Will gave the man Isobel's name and her age, the details of his search so far. The lucky cop listened; he wrote very little down.

'You're a regular Pinkerton,' he said, as he prepared to ask the required questions. 'Colour of hair?'

'Red,' said Will. 'Auburn, really. Light auburn.'

'I got "*Blonde*", "*Brown*", "*Black*", "*Grey*" or "*Other*" here on the form.'

'Tick "*Other*" then write "*Red*" next to it,' suggested his partner.

The lucky cop obliged him.

'Eyes?'

'Green,' said Will. 'Very green, almost emerald.'

'Good,' said the lucky cop. 'I got "*Green*" here as a choice. Shape of face?'

'She has a strong face,' said Will. 'A strong jaw and strong cheeks, a long forehead.'

The policeman's pencil wavered between his choice of "*Round*", "*Square*" or "*Oval*" on his form.

'That sounds like an oval,' said his partner.

'Height and weight?' he asked Will and then, before Will could answer, he said, 'I'll put down average height and average weight.'

'She's tall for a woman,' said Will.

'Right,' said the cop but he didn't change the checkmark he had made in the "*Average*" box.

'She's not average,' insisted Will.

'I'll have it read out to the beat shift in the morning. Every cop round here will be looking out for her. Any chance she went out West? A lot of people are going to California these days. The way you tell it, your sister's maybe movie star material.'

He smirked when he said 'sister'.

'She's seventeen, you say? She's a little bit young for you, my friend,' said the other detective. 'That's my advice, anyway – just in case she's maybe not your sister like you say.'

Will picked up his hat and put it on. Normally, he would have waited until he was out on the street, out of respect, but under the circumstances he didn't feel the need to bother.

8

Will believed his head was clearest when it was high above the street and blown through with fresh air. Below him were the tops of the other towers, the charcoal smoke from the factories, the pale blue plumes from the Italian pizza ovens on the far side of Delancey Avenue and the white steam from the irons in the laundries down in Chinatown.

The truth was inescapable here: Will's failings were plainest beneath the unforgiving steel of the sky. How could he have waited four days to report Isobel missing? Yes, he had believed she was safe in the Ellis Island hospital but how had he allowed himself to be so sure without hearing her voice?

Will walked out onto the girder they had just fused into place like a man walking out onto the diving board at a public swimming pool. Will could almost imagine that the girder would bend like a diving board beneath his feet and that it would twang with reverberations as his weight left it. He couldn't leave Isobel behind, though, not until every possibility had been exhausted.

The next step would be to try the churches and the community centres around which the Irish congregated. He could even search out the homes for single mothers – Will dreaded that Isobel might have fallen pregnant before the voyage or that some man had taken her, fumble-drunk, on a pile of preservers in one of the lifeboats. If that was what had happened, surely she wouldn't know if there was to be a baby yet. There was no way it could be left like this – halfway between the pavement and the sky. Will would have to save any swan-dive he might contemplate for when he knew Isobel's fate for certain and, as awful as he was feeling now, he hoped that time would be soon. The prospect of months of not knowing – or worse still, never knowing – came in over his heart like low storm clouds.

Frenchie had started in first thing that morning on his stories about the white slave trade to China and the secret brothels the Jews ran in Soho – each tale more ludicrous than the last – until Lem told him to shut up. Lem was a man who had earned Will's respect over the preceding months. Of the four of them, Lem was the solid one – the stoker – who stoked each thought around in the fire of his mind before taking it out and offering it up for discussion. Next to Will, Lem was the only man who could tell the crew how it was going to be without risking contradiction or sour murmurs.

Now Lem walked out to meet Will at the end of the girder. Will retreated from the very edge when he saw Lem coming and sat down. Lem's brow was creased with concern, so Will started to swing his feet over the street to prove his intentions were carefree. Lem sat down beside him.

'There's not a chance she's still aboard the *Aurora*?' asked Lem.

He knew Will's mind was circling this problem the way the crows in deep winter circled above the nearly frozen bodies of the pavement sparrows.

'How do you mean?' said Will, but he looked over into Lem's red-looped eyes with hope already welling up inside him.

'I don't know for sure but it came to me that if your Isobel was sick aboard or at the last minute something prevented her taking the tender boat ashore, might she not still be on the ship and halfway back to Ireland by now? I mean if she fainted or something after giving her name to your Sammy Fisk fellow but before getting on the tender boat, she might have been taken to the ship's infirmary, mightn't she? I'm not sure what the procedure would be then, but it seems to me that you won't be certain she's even missing till that ship makes Cork.'

Will took in a breath of dizzying air. He could smell the hot, dull scent of the burnt rivets. They smelled somehow delicious, spicy and metallic.

'That's true,' he said.

'The list you say her name was on, that was taken on the deck of the *Aurora*. That's where Sam Fisk last saw her but there's no one yet said he's seen her on American soil, is there?'

'I haven't been thinking with my head straight,' said Will.

He felt like a fool but he was gladder to be a fool in front of Lem than in front of Frenchie or Frank. Terror made a man stupid, Will had discovered.

'I'm not saying it's so,' said Lem. 'Just that it's likelier than white slavers.'

Will smiled at that, more to cover his embarrassment that he'd been considering Frenchie's stories than because the stories themselves had been funny.

'They say it'll be the tallest building in the world for a hundred years,' said Lem with satisfaction.

They always reverted back to this when they were feeling small. The building was the greater thing that made each of them feel a little bigger than he really was.

'It's to be the pinnacle of human achievement,' said Lem. 'Someone told me those very words are in *The New York Times* this morning.' Then he added, generously offering Will a piece of his own inadequacy with the question, 'But what's a pinnacle exactly?'

'It's a spike,' said Will. 'Like what they used to impale fellows on.'

'Jesus,' said Lem respectfully. 'It don't sound too good.'

'It can be,' said Will. 'Like when it's a spire on a cathedral or a high day in your life.'

'You know a lot about bloody pinnacles, Will,' said Lem, jesting.

'I'm Catholic,' said Will. 'We're big on sharp things – spears and burning swords and pointy reckonings.'

Lem smiled, knowing that Will's fancy talk meant he felt better. Lem watched Will get up and noted that Will checked his shoelaces before he walked back to the elevators. That was a good sign, too.

It was Tuesday and Feeney had the cardboard cylinder containing the maps and papers for Jonas Trichardt waiting for Will when the elevator doors opened on the ground floor. The foreman placed the tube into Will's hand without stopping the conversation he was having with one of the architects. Will took the tube the way an Olympic runner takes the baton – silently, and knowing in which direction to head.

As he walked, Will pushed his hair back from his face and tried to pat it down but it wouldn't go. At the site tap on Thirty-First Street, he ran his hands under the water and wetted his scalp. He was looking forward to the journey. The start of the civilized street on which Lily lived brought him closer to her. The smooth, oily swing of the gate into the tranquil garden brought him closer still. A sight of the tortoiseshell cat was a good omen, Will decided. To hear the sound of the fountain was even better. The kitchen door was open and that meant Lily was a mere few feet away, just inside, and in three . . . two . . . one second he would catch his first new sight of her.

The kitchen was empty. There was a white tea towel in the middle of the table where the bowl of herbs had stood the last time Will had been there; the bowl itself was in the sink being soaked under a running tap. In the middle of the tea towel were the dozen fragments of the jug. Lily had matched three pieces together and half of one side of the china object was showing the curve it had once sported. Will smiled to himself. Lily had done this for him. There was some element of anticipation in her as there was in him, even if it was only a modest, private joke.

The way the shards were arranged this time made it clear to Will that one crucial piece was missing. It was so obvious. He was good at puzzles and he saw the gap at once.

'It's practically finished,' Will said to the empty room and Lily came out into the kitchen from inside the pantry.

'It's barely started,' she said, 'but it's progressing.'

Her hair was down and brushed this time; it shone. She wore a white skirt that was very short – the kind the most daring of women were starting to wear for sports – and what looked like a man's sweater made from white cotton crochet. She wore ankle socks and no shoes but Will could tell that she was about to go out.

'Jonas's friends have tennis courts,' she said. 'I play with their son on Tuesdays.'

Will didn't like that and the fact that he didn't like it bothered him. What right had he to object to other people's sons playing tennis with her? It was a game he couldn't play himself. He had never seen it played. He didn't understand it, except that there seemed to be no logic to the scoring.

'I'm late already,' Lily said.

'Oh,' said Will, supposing she would run out the door now,

but pleased that she had stayed long enough to say she was going.

'Jonas is already there. I said I'd wait for you . . . for the plans . . . and leave them on his desk.'

Lily took the tube from Will and leaned it against the leg of the table.

'I have something for your sister,' she said.

Lily made a little 'Ta-dah!' of announcement as she came out of the pantry with a small, square picnic basket. She opened the lid and showed him the delightful collection of gifts she had assembled. They showed such a tenderness of feeling for Isobel, the new American, that Will felt a flush of gratitude. Nestled in a beautiful, embroidered shawl was a map of the subway and one of the Manhattan streets, both folded in a neat, leather carrying case. There were four prepaid bus tokens and a hair ribbon and a pair of ladies' binoculars with mother-of-pearl inlay that looked expensive. They still had the manufacturer's tag tied to them but not a price sticker.

'They're so sharp you can see your future with them,' said Lily and she laughed happily. 'When the salesman in the shop told me that, I thought Isobel had to have them since her future here is the newest and the most uncertain.'

Lily meant it kindly, not yet knowing the truth that Isobel's future was fragile indeed. It must have taken a while to assemble the gift, at least a few hours of shopping, which meant Lily had been thinking of Isobel – of Will, really – since they had met on Sunday. What Will loved most was the practicality of the items. They weren't the kind of things he would have suspected Lily would buy. They were thoughtful and – in a light, frivolous way – wise.

'It's just grand,' said Will.

He thought of the few dollars he had been going to give

Isobel in an envelope. He had planned to tell her they would go and choose her a dress at Macy's together. The idea of money as a gift seemed crass now. Lily's present was the kind of thing Will should have thought of buying.

'Will she really like it?' asked Lily.

'She would love it, Lily.'

Will had said her name for the first time – the first time in her presence – and the sound of it, once uttered, made him touch his lips in a gesture like a nervous tic. The name made her real: Will had spoken her.

'Only I don't know where she is,' he confessed.

'What?' said Lily.

They sat down together, a mutual sinking into the kitchen chairs.

'She's just disappeared and that's not something Isobel would ever do to me unless . . . unless she's in some terrible situation I can't even imagine. She can't just be gone, can she, Lily? She can't just be gone forever. I've waited for her for so long – years. And then I was a little late collecting her and she's vanished. She could be dead. Dear God, what if she's dead? I'm terrified of what might have happened to her and it's me to blame for it all.'

Lily listened to the confession and never interrupted. Will told her about his meeting with Dr Challis and his hysterical search of the wards – the tumultuous events of the past week. There were parts Will left out, though. He left meeting Lily herself out of it completely, though she was somehow inextricably woven into the story of Isobel lost.

'I hope she's still on the ship but I think you have to see that last place to know for sure,' said Lily. 'That third island.'

'The contagious wards?'

'You won't need to go in. You won't have to touch anything but you have to go out there and see for yourself.'

Lily made it sound feasible – plausible, even – the way it had started to sound in Will's own head as he had driven the rivets home that day. As the bolts had gone from angry red to black in the wind, Will had thought he would have to risk exploring the contagious wards; something about Challis's story didn't sit well with him. Then there were still the possibilities presented by the *Aurora* docking in Cork. He would ask Mr Kelly to see if his nephew (who was a dentist) wouldn't go down to greet the ship and ask after Isobel.

'It would be illegal,' said Will. 'Trespassing on government property.'

'Go at night,' said Lily. 'Go tonight.'

'I will,' he said. 'I'll not ever stop till I find her.'

There wasn't any more Will could tell her. He touched the raw seam of glue in the jug's reconstruction.

'How did you actually break it?' he asked.

'I dropped it on the table top and it bounced onto the floor,' Lily said. 'Jonas snuck up on me and I got a fright. These past few weeks, he's been working on a project outdoors somewhere and the wheels of his cart have become a little rusty. That's why they're squeaking. They need a good oiling but I haven't asked our man to do it; the noise they make has given me an early warning of his movements for the past few days,' Lily laughed nervously at her need for an alert of her husband's approach. 'Jonas doesn't seem to even notice it.'

The telephone rang in the hall and they both jumped at the noise. Lily went out to answer it. Will got up and went over to where the herbs in their silver pot dripped limply in the sink.

This bowl had probably been on the kitchen table the day Lily had dropped the jug – Will had seen it there on his visit and Lily had said her jug had smashed on the table first and then fallen to the floor. Will pushed back the lush leaves and hunted gently along the soil with his fingers. Sure enough, there was something sharp hidden away in there: a piece of china about the size of a silver dollar. Lily would never finish the jug without it. Will put it in his pocket just as Lily came back in. He had some notion that he would give it back to her later – in a box with a ribbon, as a joke.

Lily looked solemnly at Will and said, 'I've been officially summoned.'

When Rose Marie's socks were finally silent on the floorboards above Will's head and the moon was long past the place where he could see it beyond his curtain, Will got dressed in a black fisherman's sweater and canvas work trousers and creaked his way out of Tully's. The streets got quieter and more feral after dark. Shadows sat plump and pulsating in the doorways and gassy, green genies hissed from subway manholes. Will walked between the illegally posted playbills and the illegally strung electric cables of the dock-side drinking houses and made his way down to the water.

There was only one guard on the dock and he was quaffing from a clay cider urn. His swigs weren't surreptitious either which meant no brass was about. Will slipped down into the smallest boat he could find. He unhooked the rope from its quayside cleat and dragged an oar from beneath the dinghy's wooden bench. Each tug of rope and each splinter in his hand reminded Will of the very best days on the sea with his father. That, in turn, led to thoughts of Donald, his stepfather, who reminded him of Isobel. Isobel had been Donald's gift to Will's mother and when Will had witnessed Donald's tenderness towards his only child – his unexpected delight that the baby was a girl and the profound joy he took in caring for her – Will saw what a man could be and that he himself could be such a man: kind.

Once Will was clear of the dock and out on the inky water, he started the outboard engine and gunned along. The boat was well serviced and it seemed to Will he was back where he ought to be – not among the turrets of a new, silver city but out on dark water and heading in a predetermined direction. There were green lights on the harbour buoys and orange ones. Will kept to the left of the green and to the right of the orange and hoped he was steering true.

The lights of Ellis Island seeped through the gloom. The government kept the building façades on Islands One and Two lit like the faces of the museums along the park. The complex seemed to glow whitely and shimmer like the holy hall of judgement glimpsed from outside the pearly gates.

The causeway between Island One and Island Two was marked with red lights that twinkled on and off in hypnotic rhythm. The second causeway – the one between Island Two and Island Three – was dark. Will powered underneath its shadows and tethered his guideline to the pylon nearest the manmade wall. The boat rocked there. Every now and then its prow crunched up against the wall but that couldn't be helped. Will jumped out into water that was deeper than expected. It soaked his jumper and the wool became a heavy weight against his chest.

For no reason at all, Will thought of the man he had saved on the ferry when he had come to claim Isobel the previous Thursday – the listener who had kept his ear cocked for voices and who had washed his hands without soap or water. If Will hadn't grabbed him, the listener might be at the bottom of the river – ripely rotten – by now.

Will thought of the unnamed boy's body hidden beneath the seaweed in that Galway field. He imagined the boy's crab-eaten hands grabbing at his feet now and pulling him under the river's surface. Will shivered as his thighs pushed against the dense, hungry water. In Will's mind, the boy's face was raked by gulls' claws, his wounds were riddled through with the arms of wet anemones but still the boy's eyeholes looked sightlessly up at him through the dark water with a fearful animation and, when his mouth opened in a grin, his gums were spiked with the teeth of sharks.

Will's body heaved up onto the shale shore. He was panting under the rigours of his imagination. He crouched down in the long grass and swaying sea-oats that formed the border between the manmade beach and the lawn.

When everything looked still, Will ran for the main block and hunched along its wall. It was a single-storey building with evenly spaced, barred windows along its walls. It was quiet. Will hunkered down beneath the sharp light from a window and told himself that, whenever he chose to stand up, authority might be there or it might not. Dr Challis had told him there was only a solitary nurse on duty. Perhaps that was the case. It was complete faith now. Neither stealth nor strategy would help him.

Will popped his head up into the rectangle of pane and saw that the bright room was empty. There was a bowl of soup on the table – red, tomato – and it was sending up curlicues of heat. The sister must have just stepped out. Will slid along the bricks. Now that he was there and actually trespassing, he was less afraid. It seemed partially unreal and, at the same time, quite rational to be investigating in this way. It was clear to him that the authorities had no intention of offering practical assistance.

Will's imagination was on a loose rein tonight. Now, he had a fantasy that the nurse might throw open the window above his head and say, 'Mr Carthy, why are you skulking about out here? Come in and visit.'

Isobel would be sitting propped upright in a bed, eating

tomato soup with her hair freshly curled as if it had just come out of rags.

The windows Will approached next were dark. He estimated that by now he would need almost twenty seconds of running time to get him back to his boat, taking into account the curve of the buildings and the slipperiness of the shale on the beach. He held his breath again, wondering if his luck would hold, too.

There were limpets growing on the walls here because this was the cold side of Island Three; it was where moss would grow on a tree in Ireland. The barnacles' shells were as sharp as tern beaks and they snagged on Will's sweater as he pressed his chest against them. From Island Two there came the baleful wail of dogs and Will's blood stopped pumping entirely and listened in every vein. No baying answered from his vicinity. Will assembled his courage and looked into the next window.

At first, there was just the dull, black glass and nothing beyond it. Then, as his eyes grew accustomed to the dimness, Will saw that he was looking into another empty room. There were rows of beds made up like all the others he had seen on Island Two, but nothing else. He moved on and discovered that all the rooms he peered into were the same.

As he neared the far end of the island, he slipped down into a thin walkway that ran between the two largest buildings. It was so narrow that Will wondered what purpose it would serve. Stranger still was a single, round window like a porthole in the middle of the solid wall, halfway along its length. Why put a window here? It looked out over two feet of sand and then the exterior wall of the next-door building.

When Will's eyes focused on this odd window, he saw something scratched into the glass. Will hadn't brought a flashlight with him but he could see that several letters had been crudely etched into the pane using a sharp object – the diamond in a wedding ring or the edge of a tin can lid. The letters were odd to him, not the regular alphabet nor the Gaelic one. He tried to memorize them so that he could ask one of the lads at work if they knew what the shapes meant. There was a Russian boy working on the elevator shafts who might be able to read this: the shapes could be from some Eastern European alphabet – they were that foreign.

Will shuffled along and came out at the far end of the alley. He turned to his right, crept to the neighbouring structure and peeped through yet another dark window. He kept the top of his head just below the sill and he heard something move inside, just a brick's width from his ears. A single course separated Will from dreadful, human suffering. Not Isobel, Will begged – it was an incantation to God. The keening he could make out was a soft up-and-down wail in a throat, almost inaudible, like the grizzling of an exhausted baby. Will put his face to the glass and tried to look down but the floor space directly below the window wasn't visible from this angle. He heard the noise again and risked a whisper, 'Hello?'

Something smashed against the pane and, for a second, Will was absolutely certain it had smashed through the glass and was about to take him by the throat. He leapt back and saw a face at the window with fangs in its blue mouth. The creature's canines squealed as they slid along the pane. Eyes with green veins in them bulged out at Will. A trail of saliva, thick and yellow as month-old custard, smeared the window. The thing's tongue salivated against the glass and its hot breath smudged Will's view and then cleared and then smudged it again in hot blasts.

Will saw that the thing was human. It had once been a man. The man tore at the metal brace that was locked around his neck with bloody fingers. Now that the initial terror had diminished, Will saw that the man's teeth did seem elongated but that was probably just the tilting shadows from the moon. The man's cheek slid through his own viscous deposits of fluid on the glass and then his body dropped to the floor below the window again with a snarl.

That's the rabies, thought Will, and he felt the adrenalin that had dumped into his bloodstream stinging in his feet and behind his eyeballs. His nerves were shattered. He hadn't found any access point to either of the two enormous buildings on the far side of the island except that tiny, defaced window and he would never fit through that. He ought to investigate inside but he didn't have the heart to push on.

Will could hear a distant hissing and pumping in the air and when he looked up there was a trail of black in the night sky that was darker than the sky itself. A tunnel of smoke was rising from the heating stacks. The last building on Island Three must house the hospital boilers and the other equipment, like lawnmowers and maintenance machinery that was necessary to run the enormous facility – just as Challis had said.

Will crept back to his boat, forcing himself to check the last two windows near the nurse's station as he went. The remaining rooms were square with no hidden corners and Isobel wasn't in any of them. Will accepted what his own eyes had told him. His sister wasn't anywhere in the Ellis Island compound. She hadn't been held or secreted away and she wasn't keeping herself from him by choice. Where it mattered, in the sinew, Will knew that Isobel would not do that to him.

He would ask about the scratchings in the round window, though.

As he pointed the borrowed boat back to shore, Will shuffled through the stories he had heard on the site that day, selecting the least painful one to consider.

'Once I heard of a girl who was sleeping up on deck on account of the smell below,' Frank had said. 'She turned over in the night and slipped right beneath the ship's railings into the sea. She must've been drunk or something 'cause she never made a sound. They found the blanket she had rolled out of the next morning but no sign of her and not a soul onboard had heard any calls for help. She just fell asleep and the water never woke her up.'

Perhaps Isobel had fallen asleep underwater. She had drifted off on deck that last Wednesday night when the *Aurora* had been waiting in New York Harbour and she had simply turned over in her sleep and fallen overboard. The water had caught her and cradled her down into its green depths. Between the rabies and the rapes, it seemed the kindest story he could give himself.

Will tried not to think too much as he steered towards the Port Authority and tied the borrowed boat back at its mooring.

Will refined his fairy tale all the way home, until it was as if the waves had crept up the hull of the ship and lapped onto the deck to carry Isobel away with them. Will left the fall from the ship out of it entirely. Isobel was simply lifted by water and deposited, as if by an angel, on the silt-soft bed of the sea.

9

People didn't seem to understand that Isobel's loss could not be forgotten or that Will's guilt went so deep that no words could comfort him. They didn't know how, when Isobel had fallen as a child, she had always come running to Will. That, to her, Will was better than a best friend and unquestionably heroic.

Other people didn't know about Isobel's letters to Will. That she had written, in the most ladylike terms, to tell him of her first sex with a local jockey. She had taken three pages to confess it, breaking it slowly to Will in case he was desperately disappointed in her but trusting him to love her still. Will had wanted to hold his sister deep beneath his shoulder then. He had wanted to tell her not to make a habit of giving herself away. He had tried to say all these things in his next letter but he was not a good writer. The jockey had been Isobel's first lover and her last (as far as Will knew) and Will found himself hoping now that the boy, whose name he couldn't remember, had been tender with her.

Often, Isobel's letters to Will had been about the sea. She had known he would be missing it. Isobel always told him how the waves looked from her window in the Merryman Hotel as she was writing. She didn't seem to guess that he was missing her more than the sea. More, even, than the graceful forms of horses.

Will had asked Lem for advice and the older man had restated his suggestion that Will wait for the *Aurora* to reach

Ireland. Will had checked on the liner's return passage and it was taking a convoluted route home – it had stopped in Charleston and Miami before heading out again across the Atlantic.

Will felt he had to do something to make himself seem useful. Lem recommended that Will try the Catholic Aid and the Holy Roman Union, too, and Will sought out their buildings all over the city. He wore the soles of his workboots out with all the walking he did. He was tired all the time and sleep didn't ease his tiredness. After the first week of fruitless searching, Will had begun to appreciate that there were places in the city where a man could post his grief. He had never noticed the corkboards before or the shop windows that looked like newspaper classifieds, curtained with collages of paper. Will had soon discerned that he needed to carry cards around with him – short, begging notes that he could leave behind – and he had done this right away.

Will had sat down one evening shortly after his night investigation on Island Three and inscribed a pile of cardboard squares with a bold message. After consultation with Rose Marie, Will had decided on:

> *MISSING PERSON*
> *DESPERATELY MISSED*
> *Isobel Phelan, half-sister of Will Carthy*
> *Contact Tully's Boarding House*
> *20 Orchard Street, New York City*
> *Isobel, please call . . . your new home is waiting for you*

The direct appeal to Isobel at the end had been Rose Marie's idea. It was a sop, Will believed, to try and tell him that she still believed in Isobel's survival as much as he did. Will doubted this. Rose Marie was a hardy and practical girl; she had mapped out Isobel's fate in her mind a few short days after the girl's non-appearance. Pretending to keep Isobel alive was only Rose Marie's way of keeping Will close. Will was certain that Rose Marie had already given Isobel up for dead.

Will had added his sad card explaining Isobel's disappearance to the rows and rows of tattered cards on the peeling notice boards of halls and societies. Most times, to get a pin, he had to take someone else's card down. He chose the oldest one, the least hopeful, and put it in his pocket – he didn't like to throw them away – and then he put his card up in the middle of the board, covering the others. Will knew that in a matter of days his card would be moved aside by newer, fresher losses and Isobel's name would be pushed to the back.

Will even spent a few lunchtimes accosting people in the street. The strangers he asked didn't know Isobel and the people who took the time to scour the notice boards did it more out of boredom than any intention to help. Eventually, Lem had noticed Will's behaviour and had gently led him into a pub for a secret pint before the afternoon shift.

Will had started going back to church, too. Not to pray but because a church still seemed the place to go when a man was desperate; Will's upbringing made him cleave to altars and gesticulation and the humdrum comforts of rosaries.

On the last Sunday in July, Will found himself in St Terence's, a modest church in the low hundreds on the border of Harlem. He had made an alphabetical list of all the Catholic institutions in the city and he was nearing the bottom of it. There was little hope after this. Will had been to those churches that were close to the building site during his lunch hour and those further afield in the evenings. They were all the same inside, having soaked up the sentiment of the Depression early on. The Crash had actually helped the Church's cause. The numbers willing to kneel and take direction grew every day. The congregation looked as if it was comprised of perpetual mourners – grey in colour and countenance. The organ's requiems seemed fitting.

Will stood in the vestry and waited for a choirboy to summon the priest for him. The smoke from the votive candles was sweet and strong. When Will parted his lips, he could appreciate its smell on his tongue; it tasted brown and stringy like Chinese noodles. Will admitted to himself that death didn't seem so enormous or such a terrible thing here. Maybe the peace of churches stemmed from their tall noise-lessness, a contrast to the flat and vocal streets. They were cool, too, and the relief of that was breathtaking. Will could feel the chill dripping off the stone walls and refreshing his lungs. Outside, the world was as hot as a steaming stew; the heat clogged every pore.

The priest looked the same as all middle-aged, Irish priests – not like the young zealots whose religious fervour burned as brightly as burgeoning sexuality nor like the elderly fathers who carried disappointment with them like blankets round their shoulders. The intermediate priests looked only tired, not as if their faith had deserted them. This man introduced himself as Father Farrell and asked Will if he cared to sit. They took places beside each other in the last pew. Will told Father Farrell about Isobel and the man sighed out his practiced measure of empathy.

'There are plenty like you,' Father Farrell said. 'It reminds me of the War – dispossessed souls on every corner.'

'Would you mention her, though?' asked Will.

'Are you a member of this congregation?' asked the priest, pointedly.

'No,' said Will. 'But I'm first and always a Catholic.'

It was a lie. Will hadn't really thought of himself as a Catholic above all else since coming to America. Rather, he valued himself as a success or a failure depending on what wages he had earned for the week and what his prospects for promotion seemed to be on any given day.

'I could mention your Miss Isobel Phelan of Kinvara, Galway during the announcements after Mass,' said Father Farrell. He wrote the information down in a small notebook as he said this; Will could see dozens of other names denoted on its pages in Father Farrell's blunt pencil.

'Thank you,' said Will.

Will rested in the pew, unwilling to leave quite yet; he took some comfort from the way the stained glass mottled the floors and the people's faces with jewelled light.

'Perhaps you'd like to be here to hear me mention your Isobel, my son?' said the priest.

'No, thank you, Father,' said Will, deliberately missing the point. 'I trust you with it.'

On his way out, Will passed the church notice board near the front door and he stopped to pin up one of Isobel's cards. The board was mildewed despite the heat and Will saw that there was a leak in the roof and that some fractured water pipe was drizzling green fluid down the wall. Half the notices were crinkled and washed out. He saw one sign that intrigued him. It was only half legible but Will took it down and examined it.

He had focused on it because of the heading LOST! and the missing person's name: Felicity Bell. Will didn't know her; he had never even heard of her. She was just some stranger who had somehow managed to get herself lost like Isobel. But Felicity Bell was young, her card gave her age as eighteen, and that struck a chord with Will. Both the girls' names were like chimes and hard to forget. It seemed impossible that two such girls could go missing at the same time. Felicity Bell (her card said) had not been seen since July 4th – only a few days before

Isobel had disappeared. It had been Independence Day and she should have had fireworks in her eyes and not a worry in her head. Will wished Felicity Bell's card stated where she had last been seen. He couldn't contact its writer because the address was illegible.

A picture of Felicity Bell came into Will's head. He imagined her with pretty, dark hair and the soft, chocolate eyes of a hart. Will wondered if the missing had a place where they went and encountered one another. If so, he hoped Felicity had found Isobel – that each was a comfort to the other.

Will tore the card across, so that he was left with just the piece of paper that had Felicity Bell's name on it. He kept this scrap in his shirt pocket. It meant that Isobel was not alone.

Since Tuesday the 15th, there had been no deliveries to Jonas Trichardt, so Will hadn't even had the sight of Lily to comfort him for almost two weeks. But near the end of July, Feeney handed Will the map cylinder and he took the subway full of staring, solemn faces to the park. He walked down the quiet pathway of Number Seventeen.

There was a moment when his heart actually quickened with the mystery of whether Lily would be there to show him the jug's progress or not. He knew she could not have finished it; he had kept that piece of china to give to her later. Where had he put it now? He couldn't remember. His mind had been full of Isobel.

Will trotted up the back stairs into the kitchen and found Jonas Trichardt sitting at the table. It was a Tuesday again, Will realized – Lily's tennis day.

'Will Carthy!' Jonas said, looking up over his newspaper. 'Do come in.'

Will shuffled forward a little awkwardly; he was already in

the middle of the room. Will was surprised that the man had remembered his name. He had been to the house twice but he had only met the man for a few minutes weeks before. A man like Jonas Trichardt must have minions doing his bidding all day. Did he greet them all personally like this? Will would have to watch Jonas; he caught things Will didn't think he was noticing.

Jonas walked away then and Will followed him. They went through the house with Will's boots ringing on the terrazzo floors to announce them. Jonas's shoes had leather soles and he moved silently, only the wheels of his cart squeak, squeak, squeaked as they rolled along. Jonas led Will into a living room and sat himself down in a red, leather chair. Will's shirt was sweaty; it stuck to the small of his back and he felt dusty and at a disadvantage.

'Do sit,' said Jonas. 'That's why we have help, to clean up after any mess.'

Will sat down on the seat beside Jonas and accepted the crystal tumbler of what turned out to be very fine whiskey. Will knew what was fine because of his stepfather who had encouraged him to taste as a boy; he had developed a remarkably mature palate for someone so young.

'You would prefer beer,' stated Jonas, suddenly, as if regretful at a faux pas he had made at his guest's expense.

'No,' said Will. 'The single malt is fine by me.'

Jonas actually laughed at that. He had a good laugh, though rusty.

'You do intrigue me, Mr Carthy. You're often quite . . . un-expected.'

Will wondered if Jonas meant the timing of Will's last visit to the house. That it had coincided with Lily being late for her game of tennis.

'You sit in my chair with your muscles and your menace

and you admire my refined whiskey. It's altogether remarkable,' said Jonas.

'There's no menace,' said Will.

'The appearance of menace,' said Jonas. 'And a valuable thing it is. Yet, despite your physicality, you seem quite eloquent.'

'I read,' said Will, explaining it all with that finite sentence. 'As well as working,' which explained the rest.

'A literate, working man. I see men like you as this country's future, you know. A land populated with well-read, physical men to make it great and beautiful, illiterate women to decorate it. Don't tell Lily I said that, though. We've had her accent softened by elocution classes but she remains a Southern firebrand. She's from aristocratic stock of French descent, of course.'

Will didn't know what to say to that.

'European races are mentally superior,' said Jonas. 'But for every one of us – strong, able men – the hordes spawn a feeble, morally inept, diseased, wayward waster. The strong can't keep up. We're being swamped. Some think it's inevitable but I don't believe that.'

It surprised Will that Jonas classified himself among the strong and able.

'The world's big enough for all kinds,' said Will.

'But what kind of world will it be? Beauty will become our rarest commodity,' said Jonas.

He sipped from his golden whiskey and looked Will in the eye.

'Take Lilian . . .' Jonas said, and Will's organs stiffened inside him '. . . for example,' he continued. 'She is earthly perfection but it took me twenty-five years to find her. She was living in a backwater town near New Orleans. Her family were fifth generation Americans – descendants of Lafayette, no less – and she was living in a room above a bawdy house on a dusty side-street of town. That's what great American families have sunk to and do you know why? Because the blacks will farm cheaper, the liberals will buy from them and, if we let the Chinese in, they'd do it all cheaper still. Thank God for the Immigration Acts,' and Jonas smiled to make light of what he had just said with loathing.

Will knew the Acts to which Jonas was referring. They had been implemented in 1924; Will had arrived just before those very Acts had virtually slammed the door to America shut. The Acts assigned quotas to immigrants from specific countries and made it nearly impossible for unfavoured nationals to enter.

'I had something of a say in those Acts, you know. I'm well connected politically. My friends and I see things in the same way.'

'When did you meet?' asked Will, casually. He was never eager to talk politics.

'I met Lilian at a dance, 1918 it was,' Jonas said. 'And I decided then and there that I would have her. I was just an architect back then but already I was interested in greater things than buildings. At the time, I was in the South pursuing my hobby. I was a collector. I used to collect all manner of things, antique rifles and so on – my father had money and that sort of requisitioning trip was how we both filled our time. After the War, I became more serious about things, though. I came back to marry Lilian and I brought her here to the family home. A good wife is an asset above coral.'

That was a misquote from *Proverbs*. Will had heard Tully do it often enough to discern when syntax from the Bible was bent.

'A good wife has value above coral,' Will corrected and

Jonas put his glass down heavily on the table beside his leg.

'Do you have my plans?' Jonas asked.

Will handed over the tube he had been clutching all this time.

'You're a part of something greater than yourself simply by the work you do,' said Jonas. 'I envy you your ability to do it.'

To underscore this statement, Jonas lifted the plastic mask to his face and leaned over to turn a wheel on his cylinder. The oxygenated gas escaped with a hiss and Jonas took a long, deep inhalation. His eyes half closed like a man on the wings of an opium pipe and then Jonas put the mask down and lifted his whiskey glass again.

Will scrabbled for neutral ground and thought that news from the site might be best.

'Once it's done, they say it will be unparalleled in history,' he said.

'It is brave,' said Jonas. 'It is that.'

'A building unrivalled in the history of human enterprise.' Will found that he often quoted the bravura of the news-papers when it came to the construction site.

'Ah,' said Jonas, 'you meant the building.' As if he had been speaking of something else.

Just then, Lily came in wearing her tennis skirt and a yellow blouse. She kissed Jonas on the forehead and then she did a startling thing: she went over and kissed Will lightly on the forehead, too. The peck was bestowed with childish ebullience but it was a moment of such excruciating dis-comfort that Will downed his entire glass of whiskey and stood up, wishing Lily would go over and stand beside her husband, proving her alliance to Jonas, rather than hovering beside Will's own chair.

If Will had been the Trichardt's lawyer or one of Jonas's

business associates or even their chauffeur on his birthday, a kiss might have seemed right, polite, but Will was no more than the man who ran Jonas's errands and the kiss was an error. Will would lose the five extra dollars he was earning every time he came to this house; he would lose the chance to talk to Lily in her kitchen.

Then something caught in Will's mind as his eyes met Lily's. If he didn't work for Jonas, could he still see her? Not here in this house but somewhere else? A restaurant or the park – somewhere pretty that was worthy of her. Not at Tully's or the Four Green Fields. Not anyplace Will spent his spare time. Somewhere better. Somewhere loftier. Might Lily not, when her ailing husband finally died, consider him?

The carriage clock rang out a quarter hour and that ended any speculation. Will looked at the clock and saw its fineness. He realized it would probably cost him more than a year's salary to own it second-hand. Some of the Trichardt's class of people had been equalized with the working man because of the losses they had sustained in the Crash but Jonas Trichardt hadn't so much as flinched at the fall. Where had his money been? Had the political allies he had mentioned whispered to him about what was coming before it came?

'Come and see our project,' Lily said to Will.

That was a mistake, too. It implied connections Will preferred Jonas not to suspect. This girl was very indiscreet. Her voice was full of promises; surely her husband heard them.

'I won't get up,' said Jonas. 'If you can put up with her nonsense, you're a better man than I am. In fact, you are. You are a better man than I am all round, Will,' but he said it so flippantly that it was obvious to Will that Jonas meant the very opposite.

How could Will tell Lily to respect her husband? It wasn't

his place. What was more, Will didn't want to tell her. He watched Lily's lithe hips sway beneath the skirt that was designed to show the swing of hips. As they walked down the hall, there were two close walls and both of them encouraged Will to throw Lily up against them and plunge down on her. It was hot in the house and Will could see that Lily's hair was clinging to her neck. Tiny beads of sweat shone above her lips and Will closed his eyes for a second to stop them looking and to steady himself.

Lily took the jug from the pantry shelf and showed it to Will. It was more than half finished. The glue showed badly. It looked patchy and rather pathetic and he loved it. Will imagined them taking tea somewhere on a white veranda near the sea. Lily would pour the milk into Will's cup from this very jug and they would smile about it.

The piece of china Will had found in the herb bowl and taken away with him created an obvious hole in the jug; it was the reason Lily hadn't progressed any further. Again, Will worried about it. Where had he left the remnant? Was it still in his coat pocket? He must remember to look for it, so that he would give it to her one day. Will was starting to think Lily would appreciate that more than any pricey dress, or was he wrong? It was getting difficult to discern how much of his fantasy was really Lily herself and how much was what he needed her to be.

'It's almost finished,' Will said, putting his finger through the hole in the reassembled jug.

'I've suffered a small setback, though,' Lily said. 'I've started to realize there's something missing. One piece at least.'

'Well, I get the feeling that you'll finish it on the day I bring the last drawings to your husband. The day they finalize the quotes for this building and break ground, you'll have your jug fixed.'

She looked at him curiously.

'They've already broken ground on it, haven't they?' Lily asked. 'I was under the impression the project's finished and it's only teething problems they're tendering out for.'

Will hadn't realized that. For some reason, he imagined the project for which he was ferrying papers was still in the planning stage.

'They started it months ago but it's top secret, so I never hear much about it.'

'Where is the building, though?' asked Will. 'I might go to see the unveiling and perhaps you will be there, too, as the wife of an important man.'

Will always tried to make light when there was something significant to be said. He was trying to tell Lily that he would seek her out, even after the days of delivering plans were over. He wanted a response from her that said the same thing.

'Once I've finished overseeing your jug construction here, there'll be no need for me,' he joked.

'Then when it's finished,' Lily said, holding up the jug, 'I will just have to break something else.'

Will laughed a little. It was out of joy, not humour.

'I have whole cabinets of china,' Lily said, happily. 'I could break something different every week for a hundred years.'

She turned and smiled at Will and, for a fleeting second, Will saw Isobel when she had turned to him at some dance they had attended together right before he had left Ireland. Isobel had looked back over her shoulder and she had smiled: a flash of such beauty across a room that Will had almost been driven mad with tenderness by the sight of it. His face must have registered his sudden pallor of devastation. Where was Isobel? Why had she been taken from him like this?

Lily leaned forward then. Will didn't move. She took his hand and held it. They stood that way for a long time. Not looking at one another but rather out the door into the milky twilight that was slowly dripping into the garden. Their fingers fitted. Beside him, Will heard Lily swallow in the way a person swallows to keep down tears. He didn't dare look over at her. He just let his large hand hold hers. He touched the mysterious, soft plumpness at the base of Lily's thumb, the warm creases along her palm, the enticing, fleshy clefts between her fingers.

They stood like that, contented and watching, until the creeper turned from a green and glowing thing into a dark tangle of snakes.

It was impossible for them to know that from the outside, if the gardener had been passing across the lawn at that moment, they would have looked to him like two lost travellers on a railway platform, hopeless and close to parting.

By the time Will got home, Rose Marie was already in bed. There was no talk with her on their secret stairs; there hadn't been for over a fortnight. Will knew somehow that there wouldn't be again. He would not miss their conversations as much as he once might have. Rose Marie had become more irritable over the preceding weeks. She slammed doors; she stamped up the stairs; she tugged often on Will's coat sleeve.

There was Lily now. Will had to care for her. He wanted her to be his to care for. And there was Isobel, too, no less of a worry. When Will thought of Isobel, though, he felt flushed out with cold water, a stone bowl or a grinding stone where his heart should be.

10

It was the day of the last resort. Will came in from work and hung his coat on a peg in the entry hall of Tully's. Rose Marie was waiting for him in her kitchen. It looked shabbier to Will now. The runners of the drawers slid on greasy residue and Will could see that the constant washing of the floor was eating away at the wooden legs of the sink stand. Rose Marie was sitting at the table in a melodramatic pose and that meant bad news. She must pick these vignettes up from stills in her movie magazines.

'A man called from home today,' Rose Marie told Will. 'He asked me to tell you he's the nephew of a Mr Kelly and a dentist and he left the name of his exchange in Cork and his number.'

Will didn't ask if Mr Kelly's nephew had left any further message. If he had and the message was happy, Rose Marie would have been out on the street waiting for Will's shape to turn the corner.

Will went into Tully's front room where the old man was listening to '*The Mountains of Mourne*' on his gramophone and walked over to the telephone that sat on a doily like a statue of Mary on a shrine.

'You're not to use that instrument!' said Tully from his chair.

He wrenched the record from beneath its needle, as if to underline that his attention was now entirely upon Will.

'You're coveting a better man's possession, which is a sin in the holy book.'

'Shut up, Tully!' said Will and placed his call.

Mr Kelly's nephew was curt and to the point, the opposite of his affable uncle.

'Mr Carthy? Your sister is not on the *Aurora*. It's been all over the Americas and the British Isles before reaching home but it finally made Cork last night. I went down personally the minute she docked and spoke with the Purser and the Second Officer. They remember Isobel and she was offloaded by tender.'

Will glanced at Tully whose face was looking more and more like a beetroot that was baking in its own juices.

'Did they seem odd to you, the crew?' Will asked into the phone.

'They seemed nice and well educated,' said Mr Kelly's nephew, meaning it as a slur against Will.

'Did you have the chance to look about?' asked Will.

'Did I scour the decks for her, do you mean? No, I didn't. Isobel was no longer aboard. The Second Officer caught sight of her in the tender boat as it pulled away from the ship. She's in New York City, Mr Carthy, and if she's lost it's through nobody's fault but your own.'

Hearing another voice say it – instead of the one inside his head – jarred Will.

'I'll find her,' said Will.

'She worked for my uncle for almost three years with never so much as a nick from a kitchen knife,' said Mr Kelly's nephew, self-righteously.

'She's fine,' said Will. 'I'll find her.'

Will hung up and his fairy tale of Isobel's demise distorted horribly in his mind. Isobel's eyes opened in her underwater bed. She realized she was drowning and flailed at the water, choking. Then her bare feet found the sand and she pushed off from the bottom, breaking for the skin of the surface, gasping for air and taking in only salt water.

Will leaned against the wall. He wanted to slither down it like a fainting woman and huddle on the floor until he could think of an answer. Think of a new approach . . .

Aidan came into the room. He was wearing his heavy jacket – the one he used for skulking – and he said to Will, 'Could you do me a favour tonight, Will-o?'

'A favour will kill you faster than a bullet,' said Tully, sagely.

Will didn't want to spend the evening in his stifling room. The call to Mr Kelly's nephew had been his last hope except for word from the churches or hospitals, and that would never hold good news. He wasn't keen to get involved with one of Aidan's schemes either but it served as a distraction.

'I only ask because I've heard you're good at keeping things hid,' said Aidan and he raised an eyebrow in a suggestive way – like he knew a secret. 'I used to live in Ballyvaughan, you know.'

Ballyvaughan was the town a few miles away from Will's home in Kinvara. Both places were deep in the West where communities were small and gossip was a county sport.

'What's that supposed to mean?' Will asked and he thumped Aidan twice in the shoulder – as hard as he could without flooring the boy.

Aidan let out a sharp sound. He winced and massaged the bruised spot. 'I only mean you're great at the hurling, is all,' he said, petulantly.

But that wasn't what he meant and Will knew it. Aidan was just the kind of boy who followed the rebels around like a dog. Always looking for a leader to pat his head. He might have been in with the Fenian boys or, if not in, then on the fringes of their gang. He might have picked up a story about the boy in the seaweed.

'I'm only asking a favour. I can keep my mouth shut, too. Do me the favour, Will-o.'

'What is the favour?'

Concentrating on Aidan's inane whining in the here and now seemed preferable to mulling for the time being.

'Don't do it,' said Tully. 'This boy's trouble. I've always said so.'

'I'm asking Will,' said Aidan, in a wheedling tone that reminded Will that the boy was no older than twenty. 'It's not a big thing. It's something that has to be done tonight, though.'

Will didn't want to talk to Rose Marie about his telephone conversation with Mr Kelly's nephew. He didn't want to consider Isobel. Aidan was, no doubt, into something dangerous but Will felt that tonight of all nights he might be willing to go along with that.

'I can probably help you,' said Will. 'What do you need?'

The Four Green Fields was smoggy. The fumes from the stale pipes stretched themselves into tall, thin shapes in the muggy corners, so that the smoke started to resemble the ghosts of dead drunks. The eyes of the men who called the speakeasy home watched Aidan and Will unblinkingly as they bought their cider and went out into the back alley to talk. Two other men joined them surreptitiously. Will didn't know their names and he didn't want to.

Water ran along a shallow gully in the middle of the narrow lane, though it hadn't rained in days; suds from dirty washing scummed its surface. City mushrooms, rank and vile orange, grew up the drainpipe beside the outhouse door.

Privies had been ostensibly banned in New York City in the

1920s but many places, including Tully's, had installed indoor sewage exclusively for the landlord's use and still required tenants to suffer the putrid outhouses. When inspectors called – which was seldom – they were shown the modern plumbing and, if they happened to glance down at the privy from an upstairs window, were informed that it had been filled in and converted into a toolshed.

'We're going down to that workers' hostel again,' said Aidan. 'There's the four of us going and we're looking to find whoever can say yes to hiring us.'

'I thought they already cracked your skull for you,' said Will, remembering how Rose Marie had told him the story from her step a few weeks before.

The two other men nodded at Will. Their mouths were pointed and vicious in the light from their cigarettes.

'What they don't know is that I found a way in last time,' said Aidan. 'I let them catch me because I knew when I went back I could go in quiet-like.'

'I have a job,' said Will. 'It pays me good and if I take a beating, I'll be laid off and lose it. That'll blow it for me and three others.'

'You're not going to take a beating,' said Aidan. 'Look at yourself.'

The other men nodded in agreement, following Aidan's direction. If Aidan was their leader, they were a sorry crew indeed, Will thought. They were just boys, really, but desperate for the cash and Will knew that feeling.

'You might just give someone a beating,' said Aidan, gleefully.

Will wondered why Aidan thought that the possibility of pummelling another man might appeal to Will so much that he would be swayed in his resolve. Will wasn't a violent man. He always kept his rage in check. But Aidan had hinted that he knew about the boy in the seaweed, knew how Will had abandoned the body to rot away, so that the boy's family would never know where and how his life had ended. Oh God, was Isobel some kind of divine retribution for that boy? Had Will's penalty for that cowardice swung around at last?

'Tell me what you know, Aidan, and be bloody straight,' said Will.

'There's work somewhere in the city building a factory . . .'

'What sort of a factory?' interrupted Will.

'Nobody knows, but they're bringing in strangers to build it. The word is they're Canadians from over the border. Now why are they railing in Canadians when we want the work? The unions say it isn't right.'

'The unions are dead,' said Will. 'Is that who you're spying for?'

The men skittered nervously at Will's suggestion. Aidan dragged his boot along the lip of the sidewalk.

'I'll come with you and have a look for myself,' said Will. 'I'll try and get you in, but I want to know who you're doing it for, Aidan.'

'For nobody but myself,' said Aidan.

'Because if Foxy Nolan or some other union rouser is sponsoring this little outing, I want nothing to do with it. My name gets tied up with any union and my job's taken from me quick as lightning.'

'It's just us,' said Aidan.

'OK,' said Will. 'Tell me about the place.'

The building was tall and wide with railway tracks denting the rough cobbling in its immense front yard. The tracks led under the wooden doors of the high-ceilinged warehouse and there was the distinct – but not unpleasant – smell of chilled beef hanging.

'It's only meat packing,' Will whispered to Aidan.

'They're rooming them above,' said Aidan.

Will and Aidan were perched on the fire escape of the building opposite the warehouse. They had been exploring – leaving the other two men to watch their backs – for twenty minutes. It was quiet. Every now and then a cigarette flared red in the shadows where the guards were hidden and there was a low light from somewhere inside the warehouse. It glowed through the enormous skylights in the tin roof.

'They have them in bunks in the loft. They come about thirty at a time but never the same lads from week to week. They bring them in on a train from Montreal, in a private boxcar, and they roll it right in there and offload the lads inside.'

'Sounds more like whores than workmen,' said Will. 'How do you know so much about it?'

Aidan didn't answer.

'How long have you been watching this place?'

Aidan was silent. Too much time to think, too many hours to fritter away, too many days with no work led a man to this.

'If we go up there, we're not going to find builders, Aidan, and we're not going to find a foreman with a book of hiring slips either. It's all just stories,' said Will.

The starving prisoner may well imagine well-laid tables, the thirsty legionnaire might see lush mirages, but the jobless man dreamed of lucrative employment – respectable positions just waiting to be filled.

'We'll go over and have a look and then you can decide,' said Aidan.

'There's lookouts posted,' said Will.

Aidan nodded.

'Last time, they were only on the inside stairs – one at the top, one at the bottom – and three on the fire escape but they might be on the roof now, too.'

Will looked for tall shadows. The shape of a man at this hour was like a dark tear in the night's cloth that seemed to expose an even darker space behind.

'This isn't about a job, is it?' asked Will but Aidan was sidling off, dissolving into the shadows which gathered him up like a drop of sable mercury.

The roof they were on was connected to the roof of the warehouse by a pipeline that had once had a conveyor belt running through the middle of it. In that way, sacks of grain or coal could be unloaded from railcars and directed straight into the warehouse's second storey or into the overflow building across the yard.

Will put his weight on the aerial pipeline to see if it would bear him. The creak it made seemed as loud as a wolf howling in the quiet. There was still some traffic in the streets beyond the warehouse and loud thudding emanated from a shunting yard just beyond the compound fence. Will waited until he heard the heavy roll of steel wheels on the neighbouring tracks and then he started across between the two buildings with Aidan behind him.

When they reached the other end, Will held up his hand and Aidan stopped. He waited for the crash of a shunt and dropped down onto the roof. The clatter his fall made was well disguised. Will hunkered down for two minutes in case a guard had heard them. There was no response. Aidan came down behind him and softly, slowly lifted the edge of a filthy skylight. Will dropped through into the roof and onto the top of a wooden crate – one of dozens that were stacked in the loft.

Aidan followed Will in but he landed on the packing crate beside Will's. His foot went through its plywood lid with a crack that sounded like a branch snapping in a snow-muffled wood.

Will clenched his fists and wanted to cuff Aidan on the head but there was no response to this sound either. In the light from the lower level, Will could see Aidan's face wrenched in pain. His mouth was an open slash of black against his pale skin. Will looked down and saw that Aidan's leg was gashed and bleeding. The wooden lid had splintered into a spike which had driven up through the skin of Aidan's shin, sliding along the bone before embedding itself deeply in the calf muscle.

Aidan couldn't speak. Air was coming out of him in quick, sharp blasts. Will didn't know whether to pull the wooden spike from Aidan's leg or leave it there and carry the man. The going would be treacherous, especially if they took the same route back along the narrow pipeline. Any escapades for the night were over now anyway. Will tried to get his hand in under Aidan's boot to pull it free and caught sight of the name of the company stencilled on the side of the crate: *PHILIPPE LE ROUX COMPANIE DE QUEBEC* and below that *MATÉRIAUX DE CONSTRUCTION*. Building supplies, Will guessed.

Will wrenched Aidan's foot out of its boot and the man almost passed out as he flopped back against another crate. Will left Aidan to pull the shard from his leg and staunch the flow of blood with his sock. Will reached into the box for Aidan's boot and felt cool tubes wrapped in rough paper. Will pulled a handful of these small cylinders free and looked down at them. *AVERTISSEMENT: EXPLOSIFS!* it said along the sides of the yellow wrapping and there was a smudgy skull-and-crossbones straight off a schoolboy treasure map printed along its side.

'Holy Christ, dynamite!' said Aidan, too loudly.

Just then, a door opened on the floor beneath them and a

voice said, 'Check the loft. They came in through the skylight.'

Will's arms went under Aidan's shoulders – fortunately the boy was slight – and he pulled him up, ignoring the crashing their course across the box tops caused. They were over the last obstacle just as the flashlights began to swivel above their heads. Will slammed through a set of doors at the far end of the loft and into a dormitory housing about thirty sleeping men.

The expletives were French when they came and the room was rank with the smell of unwashed bodies and something like the cordite from blasting caps.

'Told you,' said Aidan, as they hobbled through the rows of cots.

'Not now!' said Will furiously.

Fortunately, the unexpected awakening had addled the men's brains. They had barely got to their feet by the time Aidan and Will reached the far end of the room. Will had time to notice that they were sleeping in their clothes; their trousers were patchworked with smoky stains. There was no way out, except for a large hole in the floor through which a steel chute ran. It had been designed to allow bags to be slid down to the chilling room on the lower level.

'Get on it and slide!' shouted Will.

He plopped Aidan down on the chute and gave him a shove. Will jumped on after the injured boy, leaving an excited French cacophony behind him. Together, Will and Aidan slid down to ground level in a dizzying spiral. Will collected Aidan at the bottom and gathered him up under his shoulder again.

The room was a cold storage unit. Blocks of ice the size of Fords ran in lines along the floor, strung up against them were hundreds of carcasses of beef.

Will's hands were suddenly cold and when he went to flex

them, he realized he was still clutching one of the sticks of dynamite.

'Throw it!' said Aidan, desperately.

He tipped out his pockets onto a bloody butcher's block and Will scrabbled to find a box of matches among the contents.

'Light it and throw it!' shouted Aidan. 'Else we're dead.'

'Are you crazy? There are two dozen men upstairs!' argued Will.

'Throw it out there then,' said Aidan.

There was only the pressure of panic in Will's mind. No consequences. There were what seemed like a thousand heavy footfalls above his head. Will struck the match and the fuse sparked to life. Will had never seen a stick of dynamite before, except in the movies, and he didn't know how long the fuse would sizzle. Will threw the dynamite hard. It landed deep among the ice and the raw beef and they waited.

Several men were coming down the chute behind them, clambering along it with their feet slipping out from under them, not sliding on their backs as Will and Aidan had done.

They carried pinchbars and two-by-fours and Will thought he saw the black muzzle of a shotgun.

Jesus, had the fuse gone out?

Did a stick of dynamite require some other kind of detonator?

The blast was immense and, despite his expectation, it took Will by surprise. The warehouse seemed to suddenly swell, blooming open in a white flower of light. Will had a second's perfect recollection of looking into the floodlights at Yankee Stadium and then there was a roar of black wind torn through with hot shards and splinters, and a balloon of heat lifted Will and Aidan up and crashed them into the back wall.

The other group of men blew apart like shattered glass, too, landing among the bloody bits of meat and the fractured icicles.

Will thought: let nobody be dead. God in heaven, let nobody be dead.

He grabbed Aidan and they headed out through a side door, making towards the nearest stronghold – a collection of train engines billeted for the night beneath a signal tower in the distant shunting yard. Will's ears were full of church bells; no other sound punctured their tremendous ringing.

The warehouse was on fire behind them and Will had a deep, hollow ache in his chest where a side of beef had hit him. He felt lucky at that, the hook that was embedded in it had clanked against the wall just beside his face.

Despite the injury to his leg, Aidan – his face black and stricken – was running, too.

Will took the forbidden stretch of stairs in Tully's up to Rose Marie's bedroom. He brushed his knuckles against the frame of her door but he couldn't hear her inside. He opened the door carefully and called out to her in an urgent whisper, 'Rose Marie!'

There was no sense in trying to locate a light switch. Tully pulled the circuit breaker each night before the house went to sleep; it prevented his tenants from squandering his electricity.

Will stepped gingerly into Rose Marie's room and felt for the matches on her dresser. His fingers found the upright form of a candle with a matchbox beside it. For the second time that night, Will struck a match.

Rose Marie turned over in her bed. She saw him and – dreadful this – smiled as if she had anticipated Will's coming for a long time and it had happened at last. Will felt an awkward guilt at the sight of her shining, expectant face.

'It's Aidan,' he said. 'Can you help me?'

Rose Marie went into action at once; she shrugged angrily into a dressing-gown and dragged it closed around her, belting it tightly.

'Don't shout!' said Rose Marie.

Will heard her admonition as a whisper through his damaged eardrums; he determined to speak softer.

'Sorry,' he said quietly and he guessed that his volume now sounded normal to her.

'What's happened to Aidan this time?' she asked and her voice was tight.

Will led her to the stairs and she went down them until she could see Aidan at the bottom in the gloom. His shape was propped up against the banister, half-crouched, like a man about to vomit.

'You'll have to get him up here,' she said. 'I'm not dragging the bloody sod.'

Will went down and hauled the half-conscious man up the three flights.

'It'll have to be cold water,' said Rose Marie. 'I'm not bothering to put the electric on to boil a kettle for him.'

Will plonked Aidan down beside the steel washtub Rose Marie kept hidden behind a curtain in the corner of her room. She poured a stream from her jug down Aidan's leg and pulled at his trousers until they tore all the way up the seam to the knee.

'What happened?' she asked again.

'I fell on a steel pipe,' said Aidan. 'We were drinking.'

Will's face was the colour of cold ashes and his eyes seemed wild. He could still see the burning building behind his eyelids and the tremendous destruction.

'Get me the soap,' said Rose Marie.

Will looked about the room and his gaze alighted on her bedside table. On its surface was her rosary, and a book that wasn't a Bible with its cover facedown. Beside that, on a small embroidered pillow, was the bar of soap Will had stolen for her from the hospital ward on Ellis Island. The small shrine startled Will but he went over to it and took the soap. He turned the book over quietly and saw that it was a cheap romance with a lurid cover. Rose Marie must save up for this sort of rag every week from the pittance her father gave her for food.

Will handed Rose Marie the soap. When she saw it, she wasn't embarrassed, only displeased.

'Not this,' she said to Will, as if he ought to have known. 'You gave me this.'

'I know,' said Will. 'I only stole it for you. It wasn't a gift like.'

'Get the carbolic from the drawer,' Rose Marie said and she pointed at the dresser. 'The second drawer down. Not the top one.'

She was adamant in her directions and she watched Will open it to be sure he had obeyed her.

Rose Marie hoarded; Will could see that. The second drawer down was lined with small piles of objects, categorized by theme. There was a thick stack of six-month-old magazines – *My Lady's Fashion* and *Silver Screen* and *Starlet*. There were handkerchiefs with tatty edges, all neatly pressed and folded, and matchbooks – many of them were from places Will knew and had been. He found the bar of brown soap among slivers of others, preserved in scraps of newspaper. Rose Marie lathered the soap and ran her hands up and down Aidan's shin, picking at the wound with a determined brusqueness that was cruel and efficient at the same time.

Will could imagine Rose Marie as a nurse. Rose Marie was capable and, no matter what light he imagined glowed from Lily, Will wasn't sure how that woman would have coped under the same circumstances. Perhaps he underestimated Lily, though. He tried to imagine Lily in her impoverished childhood home near New Orleans. She must have been a strong girl then; strength like that endured.

'You've been up to no good,' said Rose Marie.

She was really quite furious by now; her cheeks were flushed vermilion. Rose Marie scrubbed at Aidan's leg until he winced. That seemed to satisfy her and she stopped rubbing. She wrapped a towel around Aidan's knee.

'I haven't any bandages. You'll have to sacrifice one of your handkerchiefs, Will.'

Will gave Rose Marie the handkerchief he always carried in his pocket and she wound it round Aidan's leg. Then, because there was no more pain she could inflict on Aidan, she turned and said to Will, 'These exploits won't bring your sister back, you know. You're only distracting yourself with nonsense, so that you don't have to face any of it. She's dead by now!'

Will looked down and saw that his trousers were flecked with tiny holes where the flying debris had torn them and where the small sparks had burned through. His smart, white shirt was quite tattered, too.

Will remembered how the smoke from the factories had settled on the shoulders of the listener's pale coat. He thought of the boy buried in the seaweed – his blanched face drilled with two black eyeholes. Will thought of how his own footprints had looked like black pockmarks in the white flour on the sidewalk outside Our Daily Bread.

Black on white.

Black and white – the way nothing in life was.

11

That night and all the next morning, Will waited for retribution. He expected a hand on his shoulder at every turn, the serious voice of a police officer over a bullhorn. In his mind, they always had English accents. But Orchard Street was silent. Will avoided Rose Marie and looked in on Aidan who was still asleep at seven o'clock, sweating beneath his sheets. Will wished he could have stayed in bed, too. He couldn't afford to lose his job, though. He would be thrown out of Tully's; he would go hungry. Some of the men he encountered on the streets these days were thinner than any American ought to be. Their cheekbones were like the ribcages of junkyard dogs; their eyes starved.

Will took the long way to work – getting off at the subway stop before his usual one, so that he could walk past the morning newsboys and see the headlines.

CITY LAYS OFF 200 POLICE! shouted the headline of *The New York Times*. Will glanced at the smaller stories on the front page but saw none that even suggested an explosion at a meatpacking factory.

There was a story about Olivia Pickford's stolen dog, however. The actress had found its butchered body on her doorstep the previous morning. The police suspected a disgruntled former employee. The story chilled Will more than any of the others he scanned. Somehow, he had believed the dog would be ransomed and returned.

'You buying, Mister?' said the newsboy.

Even this snipe had grown more surly and less forgiving since the previous October.

'Nope,' said Will and kept on walking.

The warehouse fire – they might use the word 'sabotage', Will thought – had missed the early editions. He would have to wait till lunch when the evening papers would be out. How many were dead? None. Please God, let there be no casualties. It all depended on the structural damage Will's stick of dynamite had imposed. He had thrown dynamite! It seemed like another life, happening to another person: an Irish life, not an American one. The hand he could remember throwing that burning fuse belonged to a man who came out at night, bitter and vengeful.

Will made it to the site and went up in the elevator with Frank and Frenchie. He didn't speak to them; they didn't ask about Isobel. Will had put his message about Isobel up on the staff notice board in the staging lobby and he checked it each morning. He noticed that several flyers had been stuck higgledy-piggledy all around it but a respectful border of half an inch haloed his card.

Will saw Lem resting down on one knee when they reached their station. He knelt in the habitual stance of the stoker, as if always proposing. On the subway, Will sometimes saw men with leather patches on only one of the knees of their trousers and he would smile inwardly, knowing they were stokers when the rest of the carriage's travellers must think them odd. The men in the dormitory had had similar sooty marks on their clothes, Will remembered. He felt a pang.

Lem had taken to checking the notice board, too. Each day when he saw Will's card there, he knew Isobel was still lost. On the day Lem saw that it had been removed, he would know that the girl was dead or discovered somehow. Lem was the one who moved the other pinned pages aside, so that

Isobel's name was always in the centre. Once, he had caught a lad about to take Isobel's pin to hang his own sign about a bicycle for sale.

Lem had said, 'Move that notice and I'll kick your head in for you,' and the boy had blithely used another pin without a second thought.

Will had chosen a bad hammer that day. He hadn't selected it carefully and he wouldn't be allowed down to exchange it until the lunch whistle went. It felt insecure, the heavy head had a small amount of play on its shaft and that meant Will was battling to strike the rivets home with the single blow he was used to. His rhythm was off. Will was halfway across the girder before he looked down to check his shoelaces. One of them was loose, dangling down towards the street, teasing gravity like a boy teases a dog through the slats of a fence.

Will knelt down and tied the lace; he felt wobbly and then he thought of Lily and that stabilized him. He grew taller, more secure. If Isobel was lost, then Lily's presence in his life would somehow make things right. Will knew he would always keep looking, that his eyes were destined to roam the faces of redheaded strangers for the rest of his life, but what else was a brother expected to do? In his dreams, Isobel accused him as she never would have in life. She had become malicious in his mind. She chided him about losing her, charged him with not wanting to claim her from wherever it was where the lost people of the world lived.

'We're making bad time,' said Frenchie, only to make conversation.

It didn't matter. They were going up by four floors a week and below them, like worker ants in a colony, the building teemed with hundreds of finishers: glaziers and electricians and plasterers and plumbers and painters and flooring men and tilers and carpenters. In the lobby, the artists were due to move in to carve the cornices and illustrate the murals. The finer things were already being completed beneath Will's feet. Invisible to the street, the inside of the building was beginning to be polished and primped while above, near the shoulders and head of the structure, the creation was still a skeleton – just steel bones sticking out like bad fractures against an X-ray of sky.

There was no shelter up here and Will's body had begun to brown. Most of the teams worked without shirts now, though only Frenchie maintained the ludicrous short pants. Will's wide back was burnt and his face was dotted with freckles which had finally become a dark, even tan. The burnished colour of his skin made his eyes blacker than before.

At lunch, Will walked the beams of three floors, seeking out any man who might have paid Curtis, the waterboy, to bring the newspaper up.

'Can I have the news when you're done?' Will asked a bucker-up on level fifty-two when he found him sitting behind the *Daily News*.

'You can pay me half for it when I'm done,' said the man.

His crony laughed at him and accused, 'Jew!'

'I'm Church of England,' said the man and Will thought to himself, 'I should have known.'

Will gave the man his seven cents for the paper and took it into the shade of the elevator housing. He sat with his back to the wall, so nobody could read over his shoulder, and he looked at each and every article. He found the story he was expecting on the bottom of page six. It read:

FIRE DAMAGES MEAT STORAGE

A fire believed to have been caused by a gas explosion damaged a meat packing and storage facility in the South

Village last night. The lost meat is believed to have been valued in excess of a thousand dollars. The building's owners, Marconi Meats, Inc., are concerned that their insurance company may not cover the costs of the repairs and the replacement of stock since their gas inspection certificate expired last December . . .

There was more about the woeful state of Marconi Meats insurance coverage and then the final sentences:

Though a night watchman was on duty at the time, he was some distance from the blast when it occurred and nobody was injured. The police department arson investigation unit is satisfied that the event was accidental and no claims of negligence are being levelled at the owners of Marconi Meats, Inc. or the City.

Will experienced all-consuming relief followed swiftly by a feeling that the article concerned another property altogether from the one on which he had been trespassing the night before. Then Will thought about Aidan and wondered what the hell the boy had managed to get him into. This story was no story. There wasn't a hint of the men being housed in the attic or the piles and piles of crated equipment and supplies. Jesus, if the fire had reached that crate of dynamite . . . Will felt glad that somebody had wanted the story gagged but he was unnerved at the same time. Who had quashed it? This was more than even the unions could manage. Maybe five years ago, when the Workers Movement had been at its strongest, some powerful man at the top might have put a subtle call in to the senior editor but those days were gone, weren't they? Were the unions beginning to build solidarity again and would they have any sway over journalists, the police and the fire department?

Will thought next of organized crime. The Sicilian families had made their power felt far beyond the red, green and white striped awnings of the sandwich shops in Little Italy. Was this game their doing? Did the families protect these itinerant, Canadian workers?

Will was going to talk to Aidan. He was going to lean all his weight on Aidan's injured leg until the boy sweated out the truth. Will needed to know what he was in on and he was going to have to teach Aidan a serious message about keeping his mouth shut. Aidan was too young to remember the days in Ireland – the Black and Tan years – when parents had taught their children the value of silence. The boy who didn't learn that lesson might run out into an evening field and find his father in the middle of a row of turned soil with a bullet in the side of his head.

Will's future had become linked, in one night, to the lips of someone he considered an irresponsible boy. It made him queasy.

The only good news was that the police weren't looking to pin the fire on two unidentified men. If the papers were to be believed, nobody was helping the authorities with their inquiries. Nobody had got a good look at Will or Aidan. The French Canadian lads had, but they seemed to have been moved on without investigation. It was troubling. Will couldn't worry about Isobel and Lily and Aidan. It was too much.

After he had finished with the news story, there was no time to go down to the issuing department and get a replacement hammer. Will would have to work out the day with the one he had. For the first week since Will's team had started, they were about to be overtaken in the riveting stakes.

Will felt sure the blame for their slow progress fell on his shoulders. Nobody said much about it and they weren't being paid piecemeal but it was a matter of pride and hierarchy that they stayed ahead of the others.

Will picked up the pace and made a practice swing with his hammer. The whistle to resume was still thrumming in the air when Frank fished the first glowing bolt out of his pail with his tongs and Frenchie positioned it. Will swung the hammer back, determined to drive the rivet home in one stroke, when he felt the head of the tool sail free. There was a sudden absence of weight at the end of the shaft and the discrepancy made Will step back, almost toppling Frenchie from his station. Will looked immediately over his shoulder and saw the man on the team to the left of him swerve sideways to dodge the hammer's head and fall.

It happened in less than a second. One minute, the man was standing and the next, the human instinct to duck had sent him plummeting two storeys onto the rope cargo net. The net had been strung to catch falling masonry and prevent it harming pedestrians as they skittered along the sidewalk hundreds of feet below. The net was taut but it was designed to hold rubble and the odd wooden plank. The fallen man bounced across its surface like a rubber ball and flew towards the edge. He reached out his arms towards the building as his body began to slither towards the brink.

Will ran. He didn't check his laces; he didn't think. He threw the hammer shaft to Frenchie and he raced along the beam like a sprinter towards the tape. When the beam ended, Will's body kept going. He flew through the air like a long jumper, pedalling his legs.

For a while, Will maintained altitude then gravity began to pull him down. Below him was the street and the net which would never take his weight. He landed in it and it tore at his skin in various places. He got his arms under the man's chest – in just the same way he had clutched Aidan the night before

– and then he felt one side of the net come loose. It swivelled away from the side of the building and, as it tore completely free, Will intertwined his arms through as much of its rope as possible and hung on to the man. The net held where it had been tied at its other extremity and swung, with two men attached to it, in an arc across the street before ramming back against the side of the building.

Thankfully, the glasswork wasn't in on that level and Will held onto the man with all his strength as they crashed through the temporary barriers that formed the wall. The other workers remained bizarrely silent as the net, trailing debris, landed with an enormous crash on the floor of the forty-fifth level.

The man was writhing in agony and Will rolled onto his side to see if one of the steel pipes had penetrated him anywhere. The man he had rescued was a greenish shade of white and his arm was hooked behind his head at an acute angle. His shoulder had been dislocated when Will had wrenched his arm to take his weight.

It had happened in less than thirty seconds. People on the street below had heard the crash of the two men's landing; there had been several complaints to the site office of dust and wood chips landing on the ladies' hats as they passed below but nobody had seen the men fly through the air attached to the trapeze of a cargo net.

An ambulance arrived to carry the worker to hospital. The medic pored over Will's bruises and suggested he take the rest of the day off but Will refused. He took the elevator back up to his team and was greeted with suspicion and something like fear. Men patted him on the back but the afternoon's work was sluggish and wary. They didn't seem to understand that not a single person more was going to slip off the edge of the world on Will's shift.

The awkwardness lasted for the rest of the day. One of the waterboys had been sent to get Will a new hammer and it arrived still shining in its coat of bright, red paint. The wholesale price tag from Central Supply was still on it. It was brand new, selected from the secret stash of equipment they stored in the basement with the heavy machinery and, Will supposed, the dynamite left over from the blasting of the Waldorf Astoria's foundations.

It was the first day of August and the weather was at its hottest. The evenings came sagging in and there was respite from the concrete heat only after seven o'clock at night. Will felt drunk on the sultry weather and the shock. The bruises were painful, deep inside his skin. He felt tired but pleasantly floating at the same time, as if nothing was real and no action had a consequence. The half euphoria was the result, Will supposed, of an altered sense of perspective, of knowing how close death was – like the man whose breath you could feel on your shoulder when the subway was crowded.

When he went through Lily's kitchen door with his delivery that night, he found her sipping gin from a tall glass.

'Jonas is at a meeting. A very important, unmissable meeting, apparently,' she said and there was a sour sound to her voice – a hint of wormwood. 'He's always leaving me alone these days.'

'Really? I only nearly died today,' Will said, rubbing his palm across the bowl of herbs and smelling the mixture of their scents.

'Oh God,' Lily said. 'Are you OK?'

She kept making rapid, nervous gestures with her hands, plaiting her fingers or knotting them, or brushing the fine down on the backs of them. Will suspected it was only to dissuade herself from touching him.

Will put his head into his torn hands and said, 'I can't find my sister!'

'Jesus, still not?' said Lily and she forgot herself at once.

She went down the hall into Jonas's study and came back with a tumbler half-filled with whiskey. She made Will sit down at the table. Will could smell the sage; it was the strongest herb. It smelled as old as the stones in the Burren, blue with lichen and the hosts of memory.

'I've waited nearly a month,' said Will. 'The ship she took is back in port in Cork and Isobel's not on it. She's not here. She was on the ship, someone remembers her, but now she's gone. She's not in the hospital, not in any of the wards and they have a man with rabies kept chained up out there . . .'

Right then, Lily did an extraordinary thing. She went down on her knees at Will's feet and rested her head on his thigh. Both her hands clutched at him and she said, 'Will, I'm so lonely, too.'

Lily started to cry in great racking sobs that didn't ease up or stop. Will put his hands on her head like a blessing and let her weep there. He thought of the man falling from the building; how close he himself had been to dying. He wondered again if any of the men at the meat factory had been killed in the explosion. The newspaper had either lied or been deceived and maybe they had been wrong about the fact that nobody had been injured, too. Was he a murderer?

'Jonas used to try and dance the Irish jig,' said Lily, calming at last. 'He was dreadful at it.'

She started laughing through her tears.

'I think the War and that gas changed him. It changed his mind. He used to be gentle and tender and we made love in a garage, in the back seat of a brand new Packard, at his father's country club.'

In her mind, Lily could hear the band playing the '*Blue*

Danube' and Jonas's fingertips were on her collarbone, sliding back and forward there as if across a keyboard. The delight of his touch was almost enough to cause her to explode.

'Now there are people he actually hates, really hates. Not just sometimes when he's annoyed but on principle.'

The dark was stealing across the garden like a cat stalking low and close to the ground. Will could hear the leaves of the herbs growing in their pot as he lifted Lily's face, with its lipstick-free mouth, up to him. Will's tongue found hers and he let his lips linger daringly along its cool, moist surface. Lily's skin was salty from her tears and Will kept his eyes open to see her face as her body slid up onto its knees and pressed against him. Her hands pushed on his chest in a culmination of resistance then her muscles went hot and liquid inside her.

It was not going to be stopped and the universe never meant it to be. Jonas did not arrive. The telephone did not ring. No neighbour knocked. God did not say a word.

For fifteen minutes, there was no Isobel. There was just the incredible, brown stretch of Lily's skin and her two pink nipples and her rounded stomach and her hips jutting out and teasing him and the fuzz of blonde hair between her two, straining thighs.

Will breathed her in – a scent like twilight in a damp garden, curried with lime juice and bay leaves. Unselfconsciously, he let the twinges of Lily's skin and her wetness tell him where she wanted to be touched next. He smelled himself, too. Steel and coriander and a pinch of clean sweat. His tongue entered her, quivering, and Lily let out a sigh that came from deep within her lungs, as if she had been holding her breath underwater. He felt her fingers move gently across his bruises and run along the ruby puckering where the ropes had burned him. Lily did it with a kind of fascination, as if seeing that he had pain, too – though physical – was a bizarre comfort to her. She touched her mouth to the wounded places and it did not sting at all then Will pulled his body up to cover hers and he entered her: unhurried, not fearful, and fully.

Afterwards, they lay tangled together on the floor, parts of his body indistinguishable from hers. They stayed like that for half an hour, not speaking, beneath the star-punctured night. As if to move was to end it and start the guilt and the worrying about her husband and his sister, and whether or not a possible baby was, by now, thirty minutes old or thirty-one.

Will left quietly. There was no speech between them. The smell of the sage was lost as soon as Will was in the garden and the less intuitive plants – the roses and the honeysuckle and the night-blooming jasmine – plummeted in and splashed their scent around like coarse women.

12

Will felt like a rag in one of the laundry vats the Chinese men stirred with their wooden paddles on Bowery Street. He contained a strange, interior brew that wouldn't settle. It simmered in him; each minute brought a new churning of uncertainty then new bubbles of soapy, green delight. One minute, he was elated by the thought of Lily – the brazen nudeness of her skin – and then Isobel intruded . . . Isobel who would not be forgotten. Will's mind couldn't seem to choose what was most important at any given minute of the day. Fantasies rolled over and over in the boiling vat of his thoughts and in between their sinkings and surfacings, Will tried to catch his breath.

There was his work and the heat. Those two things remained steadfast. He had to make the early train. He had to take the elevator up. The rivets were constant. The steel was constant. Only his mind was fickle; only his heart swerved and centred like a drunk behind the wheel.

The cards about Isobel's disappearance – which Will still carried in his various pockets – had grown blurry around their edges, tatty, and they seemed older than they were, like relics unearthed from a civilization whose power had passed. Will found himself referring to Isobel's photographs more and more often to reacquaint himself with her appearance. The photographs proved she had actually existed, and smiled, now that she seemed to have been swept from the earth. Will looked at them and tried to convince himself that a girl so full of life could not have been easily extinguished. Once, when he was holding his favourite picture of Isobel, something in Will's mind suddenly realized that the photograph was almost exactly the same shape as the memorial cards they handed out at funerals and he had put it down hurriedly, as if it burned.

At the same time, Lily was growing bolder and brighter. Her lines were defined and shocking – gold trimmed in black. Lily occluded Will's thoughts, so that every attempted progression of logic returned to the image of her face.

One thing Will could do was inflict some fear on Aidan. In the absence of anything more constructive with which to occupy himself, and fuming at his impotency, Will waited until the house seemed quiet that Saturday evening before sneaking down the stairs. He stopped outside Aidan's room. There was no keyhole but the boards of the door had warped so much in the summer heat that it was easy to find a spyhole. Will looked in.

Aidan was lying on his bed with his leg propped up on two pillows from the green, velvet chairs in Tully's front room. Rose Marie had fixed things as she always did, assuming responsibility for the boy as she had assumed authority over the whole house. Aidan was reading one of the dreadful, gore-filled tabloid sheets they sold up and down the busy market streets. Will could see that this particular piece of pulp wasn't even in English but the drawings were provocatively lurid enough to appeal to Aidan's blunt tastes.

The lettering of the headlines reminded Will of the scratch marks he had seen in the strange, round window on Ellis Island. He must remember to ask about those etchings. He had drawn them from memory onto the back of a cigarette packet which he had subsequently lost, but he imagined he could recall the letters well enough.

Will didn't knock or request permission to enter Aidan's room. He pushed the door in hard, so that it cracked against the wall, leaving a mark in the old, grey paint. This was how Will entered when he intended to show that his anger would not be easily allayed. There was no way Aidan could misconstrue his meaning.

'It's not in the papers, our little lark,' Will told Aidan. 'So maybe you can explain that to me.'

'We were lucky, I guess,' said Aidan.

It was an attempt at surliness and Will wasn't having any of it. He pulled the sheet off Aidan's leg and saw that yet another clean handkerchief had been doused in iodine and was covering Aidan's wound. As always, the sight of iodine – so like the blood it was intended to staunch – brought back memories of the boy in his seaweed grave. The handkerchief was one of Rose Marie's best ones from Ireland – linen from home that was now soiled and ruined.

Will took Aidan's leg in his hand before the boy had a chance to move and dug his thumb deep into the healing gash. Aidan cried out and his face scrunched up like a ball of wastepaper. Sweat ran immediately, as if from a faucet, down Aidan's forehead and he looked as if he meant to cry.

'Try again,' said Will.

'I don't know or I'd tell!' cried Aidan. 'Jesus, I'd tell you if I knew, Will.'

'I have a reason to live, even if you don't,' said Will.

When Donald Phelan had said similar words to the Republicans who had travelled the Irish countryside, recruiting for their cause, he had meant that his reason to live was Will's mother. Will realized that when he himself repeated the words now – though they were mere mimicry of his stepfather – he meant Lily.

'You come clean now, Aidan,' said Will, coaxing the boy.

'Foxy Nolan asked me,' said Aidan.

Down inside, Will had known this would be the answer but it frightened him nonetheless. Will thought at once of the cockerel spur Foxy supposedly kept on a ring around his thumb. He used it, so the tales went, to gouge out men's eyes. The mention of Foxy Nolan's name invoked volatile responses; if he was involved, Will knew things couldn't get much worse.

'He wants to take the work those Frenchies are doing and give it to us Irish lads. He asked me to see what was what, in case he could muscle in. That was all.'

'You've already told him about Thursday night then?' asked Will.

'He sent a man this morning,' said Aidan. 'I'm pretty sure it was Foxy's man: a girly-looking, little fellow in a winter coat. I said it was French Canadians we'd found and that they were housing them above Marconi Meats but that I didn't know where they'd been taken or where they're actually working. I told this fellow I buggered the whole plan up by setting the place ablaze and now they've likely moved the Frenchies on to somewhere else.'

'Does Foxy Nolan know my name?' demanded Will.

Aidan shook his head and Will plunged his thumb between the ruby lips of Aidan's wound again. The boy started to cry in earnest.

'Yes! He knows you came along to help me out. Your name's good! It's good with him, I promise.'

'My name's my own,' said Will. 'And don't you go giving it in allegiance to a man I never met.'

Will got up then and started back to the door. He could see Rose Marie's shadow – a soft, blue, listening shape against the pale paint of the kitchen doorframe near the bottom of the stairwell.

'It's not Foxy who's kept it quiet with the papers, is it?' asked Will.

'No,' said Aidan, miserably. 'He's not got sway like that, I don't think. He'll be as dark as the rest of us about the press hush job, I reckon.'

'So it's over as far as I see it, Aidan. Nobody's lost their life, have they?'

Aidan shook his head. 'They've moved them, is all. They're OK.'

'It's over then,' said Will. 'And I'm out of it. You tell your girly-looking, little man in his winter coat to pass that on to Foxy Nolan.'

Aidan nodded solemnly. Will went down the stairs. He would have to say a magnanimous hello to Rose Marie. By the time he reached the kitchen, she was sitting – as innocent as could be – at the table, pretending to peel half-rotten apples for a pie.

'Might you be up for a proper drink, Will?' asked Rose Marie. 'My father's at the church bingo.'

Her voice had that high, plaintiff note Will had come to dread. So unlike Lily, whose voice was low and thick like a wad of fresh money hot from the teller's drawer.

'Where were you thinking of?' asked Will.

'Just a small glass at the Fields.'

Rose Marie had started going to the Four Green Fields on her own whenever her father left the house. Will didn't like it; it made people talk badly of her.

'I'd better take you,' said Will, feigning gallantry. 'That place gets rough.'

He was thinking of the men from the night before, the ones who had dragged their boots along the sidewalk behind him and Aidan. The ones with the starved, feral set to their faces and the carnivorous eyes.

Rose Marie looked delighted. A mild sheen lit her face; it was a pale glow compared to the sun-soaked shine of Lily's whole body but there would be no chance of another glimpse of Lily tonight. Will had seen all he was going to see of Lily for the day. She would be soaking in a bath drawn by her maid at this hour. Her hair would be pinned up, sticking in tendrils against her neck. A silk dress and stockings would be laid out on her bed and a dinner party would be ahead of her.

Will could imagine Jonas at the head of the table with Lily seated opposite him. In Will's head, there were any number of stuffy, waistcoated men between them, punchbowls of pink liquor between them, pink roses like a fountain of pink champagne between them, and the men on either side of Lily would be vying for her smile – each piece of pained conversation she offered them like a fishbone in her throat.

Despite prohibition, the Four Green Fields offered its regulars their choice of liquor. Will ordered Rose Marie a pink gin and himself a glass of whiskey and he pushed his way out past the groups of sweaty men and into the back alley. A few crates had been set up here as makeshift benches and tables because of the scorching evenings. Above their heads, the tenement laundry flapped like the wings of dark crows against the night. A slight wind slipped down between the barriers that had been erected to shield the drinking from any police car cruising by on Broome. There were a few orange boxes and a bicycle with no wheels that balanced precariously like a man on stilts. Between these struts, pieces of cardboard (that were too shabby even to be stolen for Hooverville shanties) had been wedged.

'What's this then?' asked Rose Marie, glancing down at the rosy fizz in her glass.

'It's what the ladies are drinking,' said Will and Rose Marie changed her expression rapidly to one of approval.

'Lah-di-dah,' she said. 'You've got very fancy all at once, Mr Carthy.'

Will just wanted to see the drink in Rose Marie's hand. It helped him to imagine it in Lily's hand at that posh table he had conjured far uptown. Will watched Rose Marie as she primped and pressed her skirt over her knees. She seemed to think she was in a grand restaurant or a Dublin ladies' bar. He sometimes wondered if Rose Marie knew there was a depression on, or did she live in the pages of those movie magazines she hoarded, imagining limelight and the burst of flashbulbs?

'What was the other night all about then?' Rose Marie asked, as if Will would tell her.

Will had never shared intimacies with Rose Marie, not ones that mattered at least, and it surprised him that she imagined he had. Perhaps women always did this: concocted closeness.

'It was a favour for Aidan that went wrong,' Will told Rose Marie.

He ended the sentence with a gulp of whiskey and a deliberate glance away, so that Rose Marie might know that he wasn't going to say any more on the matter.

'And what about Isobel?' Rose Marie asked.

Jesus, could this woman not leave his sister alone? Every day, Will was trying to find Isobel or else lose her – at least for a while. In the ridges and recesses of Lily's body, he had tried to lose her. When Lily's flesh was in his hands, forgetting Isobel had seemed almost possible but always, afterwards, his sister's face came inexorably to the fore – a force as relentless as gravity.

'I don't know what more there is to do. I have written the *gardai* and the New York Chief of Police. There's been no response back. It could take months. There's been no news of her and I've not got a cent, so it's not a kidnapping for ransom.'

'You do have a cent!' snapped Rose Marie, outraged. 'You have enough for a wife and a family, let alone one, sad, little sister.'

'But I don't have my little sister, remember?' Will said.

'Perhaps she's chosen to desert you,' said Rose Marie.

She seemed content with this suggestion, smug even. As if Isobel being away from the scene was more than she could have hoped for.

'She would never have done that,' said Will, thrown by Rose Marie's cruelty.

He frowned a little; he couldn't help it. Was this what happened to a good, Irish girl in New York? This hard edginess, so that Rose Marie's face seemed all sharp angles in the dusk. Her profile had become quite pointy against the growing shadows. Had Isobel been transformed, too, or was this stoniness always there in certain women and poverty – deprivation after the promise of plenty – brought the worst of it out in them?

'I will find Isobel,' Will said. 'I will know what has happened to her.'

'You don't think she's maybe dead?' asked Rose Marie.

Will emptied his trembling tumbler in a few gulps.

'No,' he said softly.

Rose Marie took this as resolve on Will's part. She leaned over to squeeze his fingers and reassure him but he clutched his glass with both hands. Rose Marie lifted her own drink to her lips and sipped it in the way an obstreperous child drinks from a mug, refusing to share.

It was quite dark by the time Will walked Rose Marie home. They were both concentrating on where they put their feet, a little drunk. The tenements were lit by candles at this hour because most landlords turned off their electricity as Tully did. From far-off streets, the rowdy ones, there came the sounds of glass smashing and shouts and feet slapping the sidewalk as victims ran. Orchard Street was quiet, though. There were no cars here. A van belonging to some embattled business was parked silently on the sidewalk – a dog or a boy probably asleep in the back to discourage thieves.

If Will closed his eyes, he could imagine Orchard Street when the place had borne real fruit trees: the peach groves of Mr Delancey – rows and rows of trees, fuzzing with orange fruit. Will dreamed of the hum of bees in summer, the crisp crunch of jade-coloured leaves beneath the pickers' fingers. Will tried to smell the memory of peaches among the gutter dust, and failed.

When they got inside, feeling along the walls to orientate themselves, Rose Marie whispered to Will, 'Would you like another?'

She kept half a bottle of Canadian whiskey in the stove drawer where none of the men in the house would ever think of looking.

'I won't have more,' said Will. 'You go on up to bed now.'

His head was swimming from the sweet liquor. His stomach felt stretched and swollen with nausea.

'Will you look in on Aidan?' whispered Rose Marie.

'I will do,' said Will.

Rose Marie patted in the dark for the banister. Will heard her stumble over something; she let out a mild curse as she climbed over whatever it was and headed up the stairs. Will took a few seconds to find the matches in his pocket but by the time he had managed to light one, he saw that Rose Marie had found her way. In the flare of the strike, he saw the hem of her skirt disappearing up the curve of the staircase.

There was a boot lying on the bottom stair; that was what Rose Marie had tripped over. It was a careless and dangerous place to leave something lying about. It was odd, too – just that one boot. It was Aidan's. A boot belonged to a man, took on his shape and adopted the nature of his work. Will's own footwear was marked with ash from the hot rivets. Aidan, who had worked briefly for the Park Service a few months back, had mud from a municipal flowerbed still caked along the sole of his boot. But there was just the one half of the pair. Maybe Aidan had thrown it down to hit Tully when the landlord had decided to whine about Aidan being a layabout and a malingerer. Tully discouraged anyone from being home during the day, though he only ever ventured out for Mass and church-sanctioned bingo himself. Tully considered bingo to be on a par with the contribution bowl.

On his way up, Will intended to wake Aidan and smack some manners into his dumb head but first he needed the privy. He went out through the screen door at the back of the empty pantry and down the few steps into what would have been a garden anywhere other than the streets of the Five Points.

This garden grew weeds like razor wire. They sprouted in unswerving rows through an uneven dumping of dried cement that was supposed to be a level foundation for half a dozen washing lines. The wind had come up and, above Will's head, the black lines snapped against each other in the dark like live electric cables. Every now and then, a hot, wet shirt – sticky as tar – slapped against Will's face when he didn't expect it. He made his way, stumbling a little between the lines, and set off a bell. It jingled high and ludicrous into the night and set a dog barking in a distant street. The bells were installed to warn the tenement housewives of boys who snuck in to steal their shirts to sell on. Usually the bells were taken down at night and hung above the babies' cradles but this one had been forgotten.

Will reached the privy. Its door was three-quarters closed like the logo on Jonas Trichardt's maps. Just outside it, Will came across Aidan's other boot. It lay at a strange angle and Will bent over to pick it up. The movement almost made him retch. The boot was heavier than the one at the bottom of the stairs because it was still attached to a leg and the leg – with Rose Marie's best, bloody handkerchief still tied around it – was attached to the rest of Aidan's body. Will dropped the boot and swung the outhouse door fully open. The stench of human waste from eight apartments jumped out at him. Perhaps, too, it was the stench of a man who had soiled himself at the moment of death.

Aidan's face was as round and white as the absent moon's. A deep, black fissure that smelled of old pennies and salt ran across his throat and his weasel's face was surprised – jaw slack, eyes open and afraid.

Will's first thought was that the killer might be coming up behind him. He spun around and immediately sensed the emptiness of the abandoned space. The invader had fled, perhaps as long as an hour ago, though Will doubted it. With the garbage people were having to eat these days, the need to use the outhouse facilities several times in the night was not uncommon. This murder was fresh or it would have been discovered sooner.

Strangely, the nausea left Will; he was suddenly sober. He saw that Aidan's other foot, the bootless one, was still in its sock. There was a pathetic hole through which the comical tip of Aidan's toe peeped out. Will placed the boot he had carried from the bottom of the stairs down next to the boy's body and took in a breath to shout.

'Rose Marie!' he yelled, once and loudly.

In the next few seconds, candles spluttered to light in

several surrounding windows. A glass bottle flew past Will's face and smashed to pieces on the concrete. No warning preceded it. The men who worked needed their sleep and those who didn't were always after a fight.

From the top storey of Tully's, right under the derelict eaves, Rose Marie's head and shoulders leaned out through her windowframe.

'What?' she whispered, harshly.

'Call for the police!' Will said. 'Aidan's got himself dead.'

Rose Marie didn't wait for explanations. She was away from her window in a flash but Will knew she wasn't going into the street to get help. She was coming down to look for herself. He went towards the back door and met Rose Marie as she flew out of it. He took the weight of her body against his chest and held her.

'You don't need to be seeing it,' he said.

'How?' she said, her expression stricken.

Will took a step into the garden and spoke loudly. He knew there were ears straining to hear the story through every open window overlooking the wretched space.

'Murdered, it looks like,' Will said.

Every candle was extinguished in a moment. Several casements were slammed down in spite of the blessed breeze the night was using to scour out the boiling rooms. Rose Marie went for the telephone and Will sat on the back step and contemplated the two boots lying out near the privy. The tenants would be using chamber pots tonight, he thought to himself, and then he thought how utterly unlikeable Aidan had been.

Half an hour passed before the policeman's hand Will had been expecting for two days – though for that other, unrelated offence – came down heavily on his shoulder.

★   ★   ★

There were three constables. Will thought that was a generous allotment for a Mick who had managed to get his throat slit in a Lower East Side outhouse. It must be a quiet night at the precinct and a nice one for a walk with the breeze and all. They were not the same men Will had spoken to about Isobel's disappearance.

The youngest of the three seemed most concerned about Rose Marie; he kept touching her shoulder where the nightgown didn't quite cover her skin. Rose Marie took it all in her stride, as usual, and offered the officers tea but she didn't offer them sugar. They came, in her hierarchy, between the priest and the boys who delivered the heating oil – the former was offered biscuits with his sweet tea, the latter boiled water and the leftover leaves from the night before.

After the police had asked their questions and made illegible notations in their leather notebooks, there was a lull in conversation.

'I was in the Pike Street station house just the other week . . .' said Will.

'Oh yeah?' said the senior officer, suddenly interested.

'It was about my sister. She's one of your missing persons at the moment. You should be on the watch for her. Her name's Isobel Phelan?' Will said with a hopeful query in his voice.

'Doesn't ring a bell . . .' said the policeman. 'Turn up dead, did she?'

'No,' said Will. 'You're still supposed to be looking for her.'

'Well, we have a murder tonight in case you didn't notice,' the officer said, pointedly. 'Perhaps you'd rather shed some light on that.'

'He mixed rough,' said Will.

'Like with who?' asked the man.

Will shook his head and shrugged. Foxy Nolan's name wasn't coming out of his mouth.

'I reckon it's a robbery. This Aidan lad of yours likely resisted and your felon had a razor to hand, thought he'd try it out. Your friend's wallet's gone.'

Will didn't point out that Aidan was probably already asleep before he had been dragged down the stairs. In those circumstances, it was unlikely he would have had his wallet on him. No way was Will Carthy going to breathe a word that Foxy Nolan's ally – the girly-looking man in the winter coat whom Aidan had told Will about – had probably had quite sufficient time to meet his boss for a drink while Will himself was having a draught with Rose Marie. The man could have told Foxy what he knew and Foxy would have had plenty of time to send his man back to Tully's to finish Aidan off.

What Will couldn't figure out was why Foxy Nolan felt he needed Aidan dead. Aidan had screwed up his assignment but that happened from time to time. He was a no-hoper and Foxy must have known that. Aidan had no intelligence that Foxy Nolan might find a threat.

Perhaps the killing had been provoked; Aidan could certainly give a short-tempered man reason enough to kill him. That was the explanation then: the girlish man had come back to conclude his talk or bring a message to Aidan from Foxy and Aidan had tried his clumsy hand at some sort of crude blackmail and that had been the end of him.

Policemen always seemed to have shoes larger than those of the average working man, Will thought. As one of them came down the stairs, he managed to knock over the umbrella stand.

'You live right at the top?' this officer asked Will.

'No,' said Will. 'One down. The young lady here's at the top.'

Will indicated Rose Marie with a movement of his teacup.

'You woulda been goners, too,' said the policeman. 'The suspect's gone and kicked both your doors nearly off their hinges. He woulda killed anyone who was home. You're lucky to still be with us.'

Rose Marie started to cry – ugly, elemental tears that had nothing to do with coyness or fashionable flirting.

'It's a thievery gone wrong,' said the sergeant. 'The suspect killed your lad when he startled him in the commission of his robbing. Likely, he thought the house empty. Saw you, Miss, and your beau here heading out. Saw your father leaving earlier in the evening. Maybe he'd been watching the place for hours.'

Rose Marie howled again.

Without knocking, two men came in through the front door carrying a canvas bag that looked second-hand. The sergeant directed them into the courtyard. They went out to roll Aidan's body up in the used shroud.

'You'll hear from us in a few days after the doctor's had a look-see,' said the officer. Will didn't think that would happen. 'Then it's off to Potter's Field, I expect,' he added.

'No,' said Rose Marie. 'The Hibernians will bury him.'

'Good. They can pick him up then, too. City Morgue.'

The two men carried the mummy of Aidan's body through the kitchen. One of them had taken a wooden clothes peg from a washing line and used it to plug his nose. The policeman who had been questioning them roared with laughter at that and slapped the prankster on the shoulder as he passed. They toppled over one of the kitchen chairs as they exited but Rose Marie just continued to sit at the table, leaving it where it lay.

The upturned chair was still lying there half an hour later. Rose Marie had left the front door to swing on its hinges, too; the departing police had left it off the latch. Aside from those two oddities, the house was dark and peaceful again by the time Tully came home from his night at bingo, bitterly begrudging the two dollars he had lost to God.

13

After his first sex with Lily and Aidan's murder, Will began to doubt what was real and what was not. He moved through streets without knowing them. The green door of Tully's looked foreign and not a part of his life at all. Will's day-to-day existence became unfamiliar to him; food was strange. He drove home the rivets. He listened for the music behind the Four Green Fields and he checked for his footprints where the flour-snow had lain outside Our Daily Bread but it was all just passing time, rituals to be observed until he could see Lily again. Will thought about the black-red line across Aidan's throat, and the boy under the seaweed, and Foxy Nolan and Isobel. He wondered when it would be his turn to be sought out and slain. He wondered if Isobel already had been.

On the following Wednesday, Will had to take Jonas's maps into the man's study and hand them over to him. Lily was there, standing behind her husband, but he had no opportunity to speak with her. Will handed Jonas his cardboard cylinder across his desk and, hidden from her husband's view, Lily lifted her skirt from between her legs and slipped her knickers aside. She rocked silently against her fingers, her head thrown back in abandon, her back pressing into the spines of Jonas's books and Will could do nothing but watch without staring.

After a few seconds, Will had to look away. Either that or have her, and something in him suddenly hated Lily because she was three feet away.

*　　*　　*

When Will arrived at work on Thursday, a week into August, tension at the site was running high. Unsubstantiated rumours said that the unions were planning something; there had been an act of vandalism on the site the previous night. The way the men kept using the word 'something' to describe what had happened meant they knew nothing concrete about it. There was a dim unease among the workers and less laughter in the issuing lines as they waited for their equipment. A makeshift fence of orange security tape surrounded the site office and nobody was allowed in or out. Management was nervous. There were more men in suits around the place than was usual. One of the workers claimed he recognized one of the partners from the architect's firm. Whether it was one of the Starrett brothers or Eken, nobody was sure but those prestigious pinstripes had never been down to the site before. Even Lewis Hines – the official photographer who dangled precariously from the derricks to get his shots of the building for posterity – was sent home to spend the day developing in his dark room.

A husky man with a roughly repaired harelip and cauliflower ears was checking the workers' names against a list as they arrived in the equipment room.

'What's all this?' Will asked Frank.

'There's been messing with the site,' Frank answered. 'They even searched the stokers this morning before they went up, looking for weapons. Have you ever heard such shite? Everything we use is a weapon. Give me a brickbat over a knife any day.'

'What do you think is up?' asked Will, though he knew it was pointless to ask Frank for an unbiased opinion on anything.

'I reckon the unions are planning on bringing in some rabble to demand their fair share of our jobs. I reckon it's a Foxy Nolan type of thing. He wants his lads in on this site and he ain't happy about the types they're hiring at the moment.'

'Canadian fellows, is it?' asked Will.

Frank looked at him oddly.

'No,' he said. 'Where did you hear that? It's niggers most likely. Probably Jews as well who don't have no right to be working here in the first place, if you ask me. Next thing they'll soften and we'll have slink-eyed Chinks making us green tea and I happen to know it's only green because they piss in it.'

'Piss is yellow,' said Frenchie, coming up the line to join them.

'Not Chink piss,' argued Frank. 'That's green.'

Will wondered if the disturbance had anything to do with him and Aidan and their amateur investigations of the previous week. He went forward and signed next to his name on the rapidly assembled employees list. WILL CARTHY was at the very top of page thirty. That was bad. It wasn't hidden among the others; it looked bold. There were no spelling mistakes, no typing errors in it. Will wondered if Foxy Nolan had a man looking out for his name on lists like this one all across the city. Foxy knew where Will lived, of course, but to know where a man worked, and to mess with that, was a rougher message.

'Another man has to vouch for you,' said the goon with the harelip.

'I'll vouch for him,' said Frank. 'He's Will Carthy alright. He's the biggest man on our site and he'll knock your teeth in for you, if you push him right.'

The harelip looked up at Frank's fighting words and then his eyes moved over to Will. He gave Will a small, mocking smile – his torn lip and its scraggle of scar slid up over brown teeth. Will didn't return the taunt.

'There'll be no teeth-knocking today, Frank. We're here to work on a building is all,' said Will, mildly.

'A great building,' said Frank.

He stressed the word 'great'; they were back to their usual self-congratulatory bravado on being in work.

Will knew he wasn't going to be able to cope with any more on his own. Back home, in Kinvara, there were few problems that stretched beyond the town limits. Anything could be taken care of with a walk down to Ginty's and a chat with the O'Doyle boys – four brothers, each one born exactly nine months after the one before. You'd explain the complications of your dilemma and together the five of you would decide on the best way to settle the matter. Sometimes, it was a sister treated badly or some misunderstanding to do with land or horses or a bill due, but nothing more than that. Here it was bigger. Will had no brothers, no family. He thought of Isobel, the last of his kin, and her loss stabbed at him. Will was alone and without resources. Not weak exactly but vulnerable to Foxy Nolan who knew his name, thanks to Aidan. Will was vulnerable, too, to the man who had slit Aidan's throat without hesitation – there had been no tentative wound on the boy's neck to indicate the killer had paused for a second to reconsider.

The riveting gangs called for a water break at half past ten and Will's team sat on a girder in a row, like swallows on a wire, dangling their legs over Fifth Avenue.

'I'll wager any man here that Foxy Nolan's behind whatever's been done to the site office,' said Frank.

'That man's nothing but an out-of-work actor,' said Lem, scornfully.

'Have you met him, Lem?' asked Frank, somehow implying that if Lem had, he wouldn't dare make disparaging remarks.

'No,' said Lem. 'Have you, Frank?'

'No,' said Frank. 'But I know his story . . .'

Will could tell that Frank was gearing up to tell one of his tales; he was a good storyteller, though. They each put a cigarette to their lips and a match was passed along the line.

'Foxy Nolan came to America on a contract from MGM out in Hollywood,' Frank began. 'Meyer Bennett himself oversaw his screen test and wanted him to play this clean-cut cowboy fellow. Foxy's just that type – he's as smooth as silk, like he never used a razor in his life. Before they ever start shooting the picture, though, Meyer Bennett decides to treat the crew to a weekend in Mexico on the beach. So, they're staying in a swank hotel and they all think Foxy's a nice enough fellow. The girls in Mexico love him and one particular young piece of skirt takes his fancy. So, Foxy leaves the dinner table one night and heads off to his hotel room with her. She's all bare shoulders and long, black hair like they have in Mexico and Foxy's wearing this new white suit he's gone and paid too much for to celebrate his new good fortune.

'Meyer Bennett and all the suits are up half the night drinking and snickering about what Foxy must be up to with this bit of Mexican tail. Next morning, Foxy's late for breakfast and Meyer and two of the suits decide they're gonna knock on his door and kinda embarrass him like.

'The way I heard it told, Meyer and the suits thought the hotel must be doing some kind of roasted pig on the spit for lunch – like they do out at those fancy California parties – only it ain't a pig that's been cooking, it's this little Mexican girl. She's been so beat up and burned with Foxy's Ronson that the suits can smell her while they're walking up to the room. She ain't dead but she's nearly dead; her face is all kinda melted together and there's a towel shoved down in her mouth.

'They find Foxy Nolan – still in his white suit – sitting on the beach, sipping one of them cocktails with a pineapple twirl and a blue umbrella in it. There's a whiskey stain all down the front of him and Foxy keeps saying the stain ain't never gonna come out. That's all he has to say: the stain ain't never coming out.

'MGM cancel Foxy's contract and they pay off the girl's family. I reckon their journey back to Hollywood was an awkward and silent affair but – and here's the kicker – when they get back Stateside, since there's no proof of no crime, Foxy Nolan takes them to court and sues for damages. There ain't no reason, he says, why his contract ought to have been cancelled, see? Nobody even wants to tell the story on account of the smell of the girl and all, and Foxy walks away with ten thousand dollars US.'

They had all stopped swinging their legs by then. Will's cigarette was a fragile rod of ash where he had forgotten to finish smoking it. Will had heard a version of the story before, though the details had been masked in euphemisms. After that incident (Will had been told) Foxy Nolan had moved to New York – another rich hunting ground for natural predators. He was no longer welcome in Hollywood where he had become, in the history of the movie studios, a breathtakingly handsome screen test on a single reel in their storage basement. The executives kept looking for another man like him only without the malice – not understanding that the malice was the very thing that made him beautiful.

'It's a bunch of hooey,' said Lem, speaking at last.

'I also heard about the suit thing,' piped up Frenchie. 'Only it was Jack Dempsey not no Mexican girl. The way I heard it, Jack Dempsey had just won a fight in two rounds and the champ and a dozen adoring fans all pile into this bar where Foxy Nolan's having a quiet drink. In all the pushing and shoving, Jack Dempsey bumps into Foxy and he spills the whiskey he's drinking down the front of this favourite white suit of his. Foxy turns around and he lands a punch right in the champ's kisser and floors him like he's got a glass jaw. Jack Dempsey's out cold in the middle of the bar and the crowd's gone dead silent.

'Then, as casual as can be, Foxy Nolan takes off the stained jacket and drops it down on the champ's chest and says out loud, so everyone in the joint can hear, "Make sure he gets that laundered properly and returned to me," and he drops a calling card down on top of the jacket, letting Dempsey know exactly who it is punched his lights out for him and exactly where he lives. That's how much brass Foxy Nolan has.'

'Even worse hooey,' said Lem but he was smiling. It was a good story.

'That ain't the best part,' said Frenchie, puffing up with anticipation of a great punchline. 'My cousin works as a bellhop at the hotel where Foxy was staying at the time and he tells me that white jacket got returned the very next day . . . No note or nothing but it was cleaned like brand new and there were two tickets in the pocket for Dempsey's next fight. Front row seats.'

They all chuckled. Even Will felt a smile on his lips; it felt uncomfortable and strained from underuse.

'I bet I can spot the girl with the best legs from up here,' said Frenchie, changing the subject now that he was no longer the centre of attention.

They were fifty stories high, so they all laughed at him again.

'They're just like ants below,' Lem said.

Then, walking down the street in their yarmulkes and dark

coats, came a group of Hassidics. The Jews carried weighty bags and they stuck close together so that, from where the riveting gangs sat, they looked like a knot of dark hair cut by a barber that had blown out onto the street and floated along the pale sidewalk. Will wondered how it must feel to be that obviously foreign in this hostile city. Will often worried about his accent getting him into trouble but that was nothing. His mere appearance didn't mark him as an outsider the way the Jews' dress did.

The mood on the beam went immediately sombre. Frank spat and the riveters watched the pus-coloured glob fall until it was out of sight. The Hassidics crossed Thirtieth Street and made their way below the safety netting. Will hoped that they had made it into the building before Frank's spittle hit the sidewalk.

'Maybe they're the problem everyone's on about?' Will asked.

He was trying to get a handle on the source of the tension.

'No,' Lem said and he shook his head. 'They ain't it. We've known they were coming for weeks. This trouble's new.'

Will was glad that the information was coming from Lem's mouth. The others were fools or boys; Lem usually knew better.

'Those fellows are doing some woodwork in the entrance,' continued Lem, as they unwrapped their mid-morning snacks from twists of paper. 'The "grand foyer" is what they're calling it. They're carving some wall panels. The plasterers are about done down there, so it's time for the Jews to move in. They're master carvers. You should see the beautiful things they can turn from wood.'

Frenchie and Frank stopped eating their soda bread sandwiches and their eyes called Lem a traitor.

'You know,' added Lem, uncomfortably, 'for Jews like.'

The riveters nodded approvingly, as if they understood Lem perfectly now that he had qualified his praise.

'Murdering kikes,' said Frank under his breath and he kissed the crucifix that hung round his neck.

'Want the latest?' said a young voice.

It was the waterboy named Curtis – the one who could be persuaded to bring beer up on a Friday. He had leaned down beside Lem in a conspiratorial stance. He always brought the gossip; it cost a dollar. Will divvied up fifty cents and Frank and Frenchie dug in their overalls for the remaining coins.

'They found a beehive in the site office this morning,' said Curtis.

'A what?' asked Frank.

'A beehive was hanging inside the door and there were maybe ten thousand bees all going crazy inside. Mr Feeney went in without knowing and he's got stung something wicked. He's got a reaction to bee poison and it's put him in the hospital. It's supposed to be a sign about workers, they reckon. Like workers and worker bees, you know. The unions reckon the management here ain't being square.'

'Every guy I met on this site is square,' said Frank. 'Here we're all New Yorkers and white men.'

Nobody seemed willing to bring up the fact that eighty percent of them were foreigners who had been in America for less than a decade.

'Except for the new Jews,' added Frank.

'It must be a warning about another site the company's running then,' said Curtis.

Will thought of the rows and rows of beds in the makeshift dormitory above the meatpacking warehouse. The extensive equipment stored in the attic. The secret building site nobody seemed to know about. The dynamite.

'This company ain't working on no other projects,' said

Lem. 'This building's it, except for a few tenders they're bidding for.'

'Unions must have a whiff of something off,' said Curtis. 'Somebody involved in this site ain't being square.'

'The unions ain't nothing no more,' said Lem. 'There are too many scabs like us willing to take the work; that's what broke the unions' backs in the first place. You can't blame us either; we've got kids to feed.'

'Anyway,' said Curtis, interrupting Lem – he was a good few years away from worrying about kids to feed. 'The Animal Control had to be called in and they gassed the bees with smoke. They just put the whole swarm to sleep by pumping it through the window and now there's a million bee bodies to get yourself stung on if you go walking in the office.'

'You're shitting,' said Frank. 'It's all blarney.' He grabbed Curtis by his collar. 'I want my thirty cents back.'

'My thirty cents,' said Frenchie.

'You only put in two nickels.'

While they argued, Will took Curtis's shirtsleeve in his fist and pulled the boy close to him.

'You hear things, right?' Will said into the boy's ear.

Curtis nodded.

'You hear anything about girls gone missing, you let me know.'

Curtis seemed a little bewildered by that.

'Cats?' he asked.

'Not cats,' said Will. 'Nice girls who've vanished or places working decent girls for profit. Not cats, though.'

'I ain't heard of anything like that. Do you mean those stories about the Chinamen who dope them and turn them into slaves?'

'Like that story, only true,' said Will. 'You'll know it when you hear it. Then you come straight to me and tell all. There's two dollars in it for you, if it's true.'

Curtis pulled his shirt free and slipped away to the next group of steelmen. He could sell his scandal three more times before the whistle went to get them back to the job.

14

Lily was in the garden when Will got there. He hadn't seen her for a day; hadn't spoken with her since they had made love. She was wearing a skirt that wrapped around her waist and clung to her body. It was the colour of white roses, so pallid and crisp it was almost blue or green. A big sunhat was on her head and she was weeding between the stones, though there was little to find that didn't belong there: the Trichardt property was tended by a team of gardeners.

'Will!' she said.

It was almost an exclamation. Will was beginning to believe that she looked forward to him as much as he looked forward to her. The gooseflesh that suddenly freckled Lily's shoulders hadn't much to do with the cool shade thrown by the house. She put her gardening fork down – threw it, so that it spiked into the ground. It was these tiny gestures that reminded Will that Lily hadn't always had money. He had seen some of the Southern boys throwing horseshoes in the park and Lily made just that gesture – quick and flicking and final.

Lily left her basket and her thick gloves on the path and took the cardboard tube from Will's hand. She ran ahead of him, disappearing through the kitchen door.

'Cook's day off,' she shouted back to him. 'Come in and try our shower.'

Will went through the house but Lily was nowhere to be seen. He was suddenly unsure if Jonas was home or not. He didn't want to shout Lily's name in case she was being reckless. Instead, he said formally, 'Mrs Trichardt?'

There was no answer.

Lily was no longer downstairs. Will looked into Jonas's study. There were papers strewn everywhere. Maps were draped across the back of the chaise longue. Blueprints were propped on an architect's reading stand. It seemed as if Jonas had departed suddenly. Will walked past all this disarray and made his way over to Jonas's desk; he explored its surface.

As before, the desk was virtually bare. It gleamed, as if it served more as a platform of intimidation than a resting place for office supplies. There was a gilded lighter on its surface and a box of Tampa cigars with a Red Indian on the cover – that was about it. Will opened the lid of the box and took out one of the cigars. It left a definite hole among the others but Will felt daring. Let Jonas try and figure it out.

Part of Will wanted Jonas to know that he was enjoying his wife. Will slipped the cigar into his shirt pocket. The only other object on the desk was a folder. It had the same logo all the plans had at the bottom – a quarter-open door. The logo on the file cover was in gold leaf and the afternoon sun glinted off it for a second. Will was used to this small image by now, though he had grown tired of opening the tube on his way over to the Trichardt house and trying to pore through the plans. They didn't make that much sense to him and they didn't seem that interesting. There were no street names on them, no identifying locations as on most maps. Will was starting to imagine that Jonas was using these plans as theoreticals – that they weren't plans to be implemented at all – but then Jonas didn't seem like the kind of man to have a grand undertaking and keep it locked inside his head.

'Are you coming up?' yelled Lily.

Her voice was as loud as a smashed plate in the house. Will left the study and put his hand on the smoothly varnished banister of the central staircase. He had never been upstairs in the Trichardts' house. It would be hard to slip out once he was up there.

'Is the man of the house not in?' he called out.

Lily leaned over the top of the banister; her naked, brown skin was an extension of the polish.

'What man?' she said quite nastily and then she smiled sadly.

Water was splashing. The bathroom was the size of Will's room at Tully's and he hadn't ever seen a shower like this plumbed indoors. As a boy, Will's mother had stood him in a steel tub and poured jugs of soapy water over his head – freezing him in winter. As a young man, Will had even showered outdoors when it rained but to be dripping wet inside was strange.

Will let the soap roll in his hand, creaming his fingers with silky bubbles and then, without preamble on neck or breast, he pushed his hand between Lily's legs and slid it along her slit. She gasped and threw her hair back; it stuck in a wet, shining mass against the blue tiles. Will turned her to the slick wall, pressed her into it with his hard body, and felt the way the icy tiles and the rivers of steaming water turned her nipples into hard pegs. Water had never run off him hot like this. Their eyes were blinded by it, their feet were covered in it and still it showered down, inundating their intercourse with stinging heat.

Afterwards, Will took Lily again, slower this time and with more grace. He laid her gently on the satin cover of her bed. One day, they would lie together between sheets, unrushed and indulgent, but not today. An unexpected voice might call from downstairs at any moment; they might hear a footfall or the squeak of wheels on the hall carpet.

'It's my room,' Lily said. 'Jonas sleeps next door. I want you to know that.'

Will had heard that this was the modern fashion among rich, married couples but he found it profoundly strange. Will's own mother and his stepfather, Donald, had slept side by side every night. There had been few secrets in their cottage – there had been no room for them. It was not like this house which had space enough to accommodate complex conspiracies.

'He decided on that,' said Lily. 'Ever since . . . Well, since quite a while ago.' She was almost pleading with Will to understand. 'I wouldn't have let you otherwise because I do still love him in a way.'

It was not something Will especially wanted to hear but it was Lily's way of alleviating her own guilt at the pleasure to which she was submitting.

'It's between us,' said Will, taking Lily's face in his hands. 'It's not to do with anyone else, husband or otherwise. What happened couldn't have been stopped. I couldn't have stopped it anyway.'

'I couldn't have stopped it either,' Lily said; she seemed to relax once that had been acknowledged.

'Might as well order back the sea,' said Will.

'But where to from here?' Lily asked.

'I don't know,' said Will.

It seemed the answer he gave to almost every question these days.

Lily got dressed again. As she mopped the shower floor and hung up their towels, Will looked around her room. It was plainly decorated, flooded by green-glazed light diffused through the ivy that grew outside. The walls displayed simple pictures; the furniture was light and there were cushions and silk throws. The worn spines of the books on the shelves showed that they had been read and re-read. It wasn't the room of an immensely rich, young woman. It was a room that ought to be upstairs in a well-to-do farmhouse somewhere sunny and Southern. It didn't belong to the rest of the house, just as Lily herself didn't.

Will kissed Lily softly on the lips, always mindful that it might be his last taste of her for a while or forever.

He said, 'You stay up here and read something. I have to go.'

Lily ran her hands along his dusty work shirt and felt the cigar in his pocket. She pushed it free with her fingertips.

'Jonas will notice,' she said. 'He does notice things like that. He counts. He's a great old bean-counter, is Jonas.'

It seemed profoundly sad to Will that a man who didn't care to comprehend that his wife was sleeping with another man, would dare to mention that he suspected someone of pilfering cigars from his office.

'I'll put it back,' said Will. 'It was an urge, is all. I'm bad with taking little things like this. I collect bits of garbage from all over town sometimes.'

He thought about the bar of soap he had stolen for Rose Marie; Felicity Bell's card.

'No,' said Lily. 'You should smoke it and enjoy it. God knows Jonas doesn't enjoy anything anymore.'

'Lily,' Will said, just to say it – it was not a query, merely a statement of her name.

'Will,' she said, in the same way.

Will felt unexpectedly at ease in the ludicrously opulent house. His mother would have laughed and said, 'What on earth do they need all this space for?' and Will tended to agree with her but Lily didn't really need it. Lily only needed a way out. She lived within that one room that was hers alone the way Will had lived within the walls of his own self-sufficiency for so long that he had begun to imagine he was impermeable.

Back in Jonas's study, Will opened the cigar box and placed the pilfered smoke back inside. He smiled to himself, as if he had borrowed something and then returned it before the owner had a chance to notice that it was missing. Will closed the lid of the box. The sun was setting and, at this angle, it glinted continuously off the image of the quarter-open door on the cover of Jonas's file. That was the purpose of gold leaf, Will supposed, to draw attention to itself. Casually – he didn't think about it, he really didn't – Will opened the cover of the file and looked down at its contents. The pages inside were printed with lists of names. The names were simply typed, set out in three rows across each page. There were about twenty pages in all, covered with names in alphabetical order.

Will turned to the 'Cs' to try and find his own last name. He did it without prospect; it was a game a child might play. Will just wasn't yet ready to leave Lily's house. He could hear that she had put on a record upstairs and he could make out her feet moving on the floorboards, the way he could sometimes hear Rose Marie's feet at night. It sounded as if Lily was dancing up there and Will smiled to himself.

There was no CARTHY, WILL MICHAEL PATRICK on the list.

Will closed the file's cover and then opened it again. The chorus to the song was coming and it was a catchy one. Will thought he would wait to hear it drift down the stairs and then he would go. Inside the folder, each sheet of paper had the quarter-open door logo at its head and just below that, in lower case letters – as if it was the name of some mighty corporation – were the words 'golden door'.

Will went to the 'P' page; he was tapping his feet in time to the tune. It was just about his favourite part of the song, the part where he would swing Lily around if they were dancing together, when he saw his sister's name.

PHELAN, ISOBEL FAY

It took Will longer than he would have imagined for his brain to take it in. For weeks, Will had scoured notice boards and lamppost flyers and graffiti musings and phone books and rosters and sign-in sheets for Isobel's name and, suddenly, here it was. It was listed among a hundred other names – not especially longer or shorter than any of the others. Will touched the ink to make sure Isobel's name was set and that he couldn't wipe it away like sleep from his eyes.

Isobel's name remained. His sister's name was on a list in Jonas Trichardt's office. There was no mistaking her; there could never be two. Will had always known that Isobel was unique. She was alive. Her name confirmed that. She was listed among others who had done something or gone somewhere as a group. Will flipped to the front of the file, trying to find a heading or some clue as to the subject of the list. There was nothing – just the names. He wanted to laugh out loud. Isobel must be somewhere nearby; everything was going to be explained. She had made it to America; that was the most important thing. Will swallowed the elation and tried to ascertain what it all might mean.

'Lilian, you've left your gardening tools on the path again!'

It was Jonas's voice and it sounded so close by that Will imagined the man was already in the room, that his snooping had been discovered. Actually, Jonas was only just coming in through the back door. Will heard the man's cart squeak on the tiles of the kitchen floor then he heard the swishing of its wheels on the hall carpet.

Will closed the file. In the split second before Jonas entered his study, Will had time to do two things: he grabbed hold of the cardboard tube Lily had thrown casually on the chair and he convinced himself that what he had seen was real. He would never let himself doubt or question it. Even if he never found the file again, he would trust himself to know this fact for certain: Isobel Phelan was on Jonas Trichardt's list.

Will decided to find his voice then, 'Nobody's home, Mr Trichardt,' he said.

The words came out as smooth as steel; they didn't quaver.

'Will,' said Jonas, coming in and seeing Will standing innocuously beside his desk.

'I thought my wife was home.'

'No,' said Will. 'The back door was open, so I was just going to leave your maps here.'

He indicated the tube and put it down on Jonas's desk. He laid it across the closed cover of the file, not even giving it a glance.

'That will do fine. Thank you,' said Jonas.

'I am home!' Lily shouted suddenly from upstairs. 'I had my music on. Who's here, Jonas?'

'Your friend Will was just leaving,' Jonas said.

'Oh,' Lily said and she lied like a lawyer, 'Say goodbye for me.'

Jonas looked Will right in the eye.

'Goodbye,' he said. 'From my wife.'

Will started towards the door. The coolness of the shower that had glittered on his skin minutes before was turning hot and rancid; he sweated through it.

'Do you smoke, Will?' Jonas asked before Will could make his escape.

'Sometimes,' said Will.

Jonas picked up the cigar box from the table.

'Take one with you,' Jonas said.

He flipped open the lid and, by chance or uncanny ability, he took the exact cigar Will had replaced only minutes before and handed it over to him.

'Enjoy it,' said Jonas. 'Who knows when you'll have something as fine again?'

15

When he received his last budget cheque from the City, the director of the Manhattan Public Library System had made the most rational resolution under the circumstances: he had auctioned off the few dozen leather chairs that had once been dotted in clusters throughout the ten stories of the Fifth Avenue building and ordered several hundred benches that might look just right outside a school principal's office. It turned out to be the most practical decision he had made during his time in office and a legacy that would save countless lives in the lean winters that were to come.

Once, men on their luncheons and ladies with children and earnest, bearded scholars had each selected a plush chair and settled in for a few hours. Now, the lobby of the library had rows upon rows of spartan pews where men sat scrunched up against one another with barely enough room between their elbows to spread their newspapers. In the heat, the smell of their bodies was bad and many took to sitting in their shirt-sleeves with their jackets thrown over their knees to minimize perspiration.

The library assistants looked harassed and spent their time wondering if their municipal paycheques would clear that week. Will approached the youngest librarian he could find and asked her for help. The badge pinned to her chest said simply ASSISTANT. There was no name stencilled on it for fear that the men, who had nothing better to do with their days, might get familiar if they felt they knew the smallest personal detail about her.

Will didn't bother to whisper when he spoke to the assistant. Once, even the click of a heel would have rung through the tall rooms, but now there were so many feet scuffling and throats being cleared and papers being turned that the library sounded as loud as a subway station.

'I need information on something called "Golden Door",' said Will.

'What is it?' asked the librarian's assistant.

Will had hoped she might know. He had hoped that the phrase might be common knowledge but the girl's face remained blank and impassive.

Though he loved books, Will hadn't often been in a lending library. He read whatever he could lay his hands on; gardening books discarded by the houses near the park after the first blush of summer was past, novels left in piles outside the better schools, the rain making soggy mush of the cardboard boxes in which they had been abandoned. Will carried them all home. He tried to reach the meaning in every sentence, often reading phrases several times until he felt sure he had the point. Will didn't like to use a dictionary; he found that painstaking, having come to the alphabet later in life than most boys.

He tried to explain Golden Door to the library assistant.

'It's likely to be some sort of company, maybe a construction company.'

'Have you tried the Department of Commerce?' she asked.

'No,' said Will. 'I will after.'

'I could look in the index cards for you,' said the librarian's assistant.

She made it sound as if that would be a favour or clandestine.

'That would be grand of you,' Will said.

The librarian's assistant had dark hair, smoothed then waved in those false curls Will disliked so much, but she had kind eyes above her pout of scarlet lipstick. She looked remarkably like he had imagined the mysterious and missing Felicity Bell might look.

The girl walked off slowly, swaying her ample behind at Will. Half a dozen newspapers sank below eye-level as the pseudo-readers watched her go.

Will hurried his step to walk beside her and she took him into the centre of a maze of stacks and towards several large, mahogany cabinets. Each monolith of wood had dozens of tiny, square drawers running along its façade.

'Every item in the library is listed,' said the librarian's assistant. 'Not just books but magazines and newspapers, journals, periodicals, posters, reference sheets, government forms and so forth.' She spoke in the slow, articulate manner of a kindergarten teacher.

'So, I can look up "G" for your Golden Door but unless that's the actual title of a work, I can't see that we're going to have much luck. I'd give the Department of Commerce a ring if I were you. Oh, have you tried the telephone directory?'

That seemed too obvious and Will didn't like to admit that he hadn't thought of it.

'The city operator might even be able to tell you if there's an out-of-state listing. Is it a Manhattan enterprise?' she asked.

'I don't know much about it,' said Will. 'That's why I'm here.'

The girl opened one of the drawers. It pulled out quite a way and in it, stacked one behind the other, were thousands and thousands of index cards – one card for each item housed in this library which might be one of the biggest in the world, for all Will knew.

He thought how remarkably similar these cards looked to the little notes he had printed up for Isobel. They were the same size and shape as the cards he had seen on notice boards all across the city, taped in shop windows and tacked onto lampposts. Will thought that if each card represented a missing person, then all the missing people in the world could be catalogued into mahogany drawers like these. Their names would be endless. Will felt his hope thump to the floor and lie ragged there, like a drunk finally passing out.

'Here we go,' said the librarian's assistant.

She began to flip through half a dozen cards.

'*Golden Age, Golden Band Melodies, Golden Children* . . . No, sorry that's a poster on the third floor, not a book . . . *Golden Dawn, Golden Fleece* . . . Golden . . . Golden . . . Golden. It's a popular colour,' she said with a little snort of laughter. '*Golden West, Golden Winter* and *Golden Vistas*. That's the last one. Plenty of golden somethings but no golden doors, I'm afraid, businesses or otherwise.'

'Thanks for helping,' said Will.

He was disappointed.

'Hold on,' said the girl.

She removed one of the index cards and marked its place in the drawer with her finger.

'That "*Golden West*" one has a subheading "*Doorway to Opportunity*". Not what you're after, I suppose?'

'I might take a look at it,' said Will.

The librarian's assistant gave him directions and Will used the marble stairs to reach the second floor. The railings of the staircase were tinged in gold leaf that had started to peel away years ago. Will thought of the gold braid on the shoulders of Commissioner S. W. Oak's jacket, the way it had started to jade.

Though Will didn't know it, replacing the gold leaf on the staircase railings had been a priority for the last library director. The funds had been authorized and earmarked for the project to beautify the staircase but then the Crash had swept that notion away. All grand plans had been diminished, until benches had become the director's legacy and not gold.

Will found the volume he was seeking after almost an hour of searching the stacks. The books were classified in a system even more complicated than the alphabetical order of a dictionary. Will asked another man for help and the Dewey Decimal System was explained to him: it went by numbers. The book was in the 900s. Will pulled it off the shelf. It was enormous with many pictures and sketches in it. It showed canyons and prairies. There were mountains with holes blown right through them by a thousand years of burning wind. Will had never seen a desert except in cowboy movies where the cacti looked like carved foam rubber. He thought the vast landscapes were beautiful.

The book was about the promise of the West – from the orange groves of California to the cattle ranches in Montana. The rails could take you out there in a matter of days. The rails had made the West great and Will wondered if Isobel might have seen a book like this and been taken in by it, the way he was taken in by it. Maybe the Golden Door list was simply a record of people who had purchased rail tickets to go out to California. Isobel might still call him one day, her voice crackling over the long-distance wires, saying how sorry she was but that she was finally free in a place where there was space enough for her. Will smiled at the thought. Isobel's story needn't only be a tragedy. It might be a new start.

Will was about to close the book when a page slipped free under his thumb. The glue in the spine binding was old and the page came out clean and straight. Will knew he ought to leave the leaf in its place and close the book on it but he didn't.

The page consisted of a single, large photograph taken from the engine of a train. In the shot, none of the carriages was visible – only the track, stretching ahead, and an expanse of land with gentle hills and a river lying low in their cradle. Ahead of where the picture was taking him, Will saw that there were mountains and beyond that, the Pacific – a flat, young ocean Will had never seen – soft and blue as a baby's eyes, and as indolent. Will suddenly wanted to see the place for real. The picture promised him he could, if only he kept following those tracks. Will folded the picture in half and slid it into the inside pocket of his jacket.

On his way down the stairs, Will encountered 'golden' again. The word sprang from the poster the librarian's assistant had mentioned earlier: its letters glowed from a wall on the third-floor landing. There was a boy and a girl who looked like brother and sister and behind them the red, white and blue of the flag. 'Golden children: Keep America's future safe!' was its sentiment. It was yet another exhortation from The American Eugenics Society. 'In every state, we're growing stronger!' ran along the bottom of the picture. Will couldn't help thinking he was being asked to be a part of something but that the implications of joining the association wouldn't be fully explained to him until he was signed up.

Will went down the stairs and back into the impressive, marble foyer. The tops of the newspapers slid down to reveal sets of hard, curious eyes as Will passed. A man would be forgiven for feeling paranoid. Those on the benches had nothing to do but watch and pretend to read. Those who were coming and going on business unnerved the readers who had forgotten what it was like to have someplace to be.

Will went out into the traffic horns and squealing brakes

of Fifth Avenue. He had discovered two bits of gold in the library but neither of them had much to do with Isobel or the fact of her name on Jonas Trichardt's list.

In his study in Number Seventeen, Jonas Trichardt sipped a whiskey as he ran his eyes over another set of returned plans. He wished the Board wouldn't insist on tenders for the final finishes; a project like this couldn't be allowed to go to the lowest bidder. It was too vital to the future of the country. His teams had completed the construction work perfectly but now the old blowers wanted a legitimate name on the final seal, as if that would give the whole enterprise an elevated stamp of approval. It was true the procedure had glitches but those could be handled in-house; there was no need for outsiders at this point.

Starret Brothers & Eken were the most keen to win the work. They had submitted their plans and suggestions regularly over the past few weeks and they had been professionally incurious about the need for discretion and secrecy; they had been willing to forgo explanations in return for money. Their new building was doing well and would come in under budget, it seemed. They needed more work to add to their prestige and they were savvy enough to know that bills on government contracts usually got paid, even during these difficult times.

Jonas still thought that bringing in legitimate firms at this late stage was a mistake. The pedantry of some of the members of the Board was a colossal waste of resources but Jonas understood their need for appearances. He was pre-occupied with dragging their great country out of this mudslide Depression while they wondered what people might think. When Jonas had achieved their end for them, he knew his name would be revisited in the light of history – that soft, forgiving glow in which old men with rosy memories sit down to write the nation's textbooks.

Jonas heard Lily's feet approaching before he saw her and then her body was half in and half out of the room. She loved to hang in doorways. It was one of her foibles that fascinated and simultaneously maddened him. Perhaps Lily's behaviour was indicative of her underlying refusal to commit but Jonas wasn't sure of that. It might be more of an underlying refusal to accept the truth.

'You look beautiful,' Jonas told Lily.

It was something he said to her, in different ways, almost every time he saw her. She never responded to it. Never said, 'Do I?' or, 'No, I don't!' the way other women would have, depending on their mood. It was more like a form of greeting they had unconsciously developed and a reminder that beauty was what had cemented them together years ago when Jonas had been as powerfully attractive as Lily was now. Aesthetic appreciation was what Jonas felt most when he was near her.

Tonight, Lily was wearing one of his shirts – the one from Moss Bros in London with stripes in a dozen different blues. The longer tails at the back covered the tops of her thighs, half-concealing the creamy lace of her French knickers.

'Are you working very hard?' Lily asked.

'I'm quite busy,' Jonas answered, leaving room in which she could cajole.

Lily went behind Jonas's chair and leaned over his shoulder. She unpinned her hair and it came down the side of his neck in a wave that was a spill of scent rather than hair itself.

Jonas started to breathe heavily. Always, there came this catching of the breath when Lily decided to close in. Jonas's need for air was heightened by her proximity and Lily said, 'Just relax, Jo,' as she ran her hands under his coat and along

Kerry Jamieson

the tops of his shoulders, gently massaging his wasted muscles.

Jonas turned his head sideways and inhaled from his mask. There was a demand valve built into the equipment, so Jonas got little air without the mask being firmly affixed to his face but it was a comfort still.

Lily sat down very gently across his lap and Jonas let his papers fall to the carpet. She snuggled her cheek against his chest. It was a familiar act of contrition, her coming to him like this, and Jonas forgave her by putting his arm around her shoulder and feeling her skin through the expensive linen of his shirt. Jonas felt the heat of Lily's silent tears slip down his chest and he loved her more intensely in that second than ever before.

Who had it been? That Will Carthy fellow? Of course, he was the culprit. Will who had walked into Jonas's study only a month or so before with the sweat of the building site still on him. Jonas envied the man's physicality, the self-possession of his taut frame. At times, Jonas imagined he could smell Will around his house. He knew the smell was more likely to be that of the grainy paste Mrs Harrigan used to clean the silver but that was just what Will Carthy would smell like. Jonas was surprised Lily had taken to it but, then again, she had been surrounded by farm boys and boatmen when he had met her in New Orleans.

Lily's upbringing had been uncouth and yet she had come to Jonas with refined taste. She chose clothes with fastidious class; her garments were stylish and risqué, so that seldom a month passed without Lily's picture making the society pages. She decorated their home in enviable fashion and designed menus that were the toast of New York's dinner-party set and she did it all without the benefit of good breeding. The ability was in her cells, her make-up. She was a Lafayette – practically French royalty – and even if Jonas removed her length of bone, her perfect teeth, her grace, there would remain the beautiful, red cells of her white blood.

Jonas kissed the top of Lily's head and her face lifted. She kissed him back. Normally this apology of hers would become instantaneously passionate. Lily would delve her rich, dark tongue into his mouth and press her hipbone against him in invitation. Jonas would let her move South on his body, to the places she knew best, and he would let her relieve him in the only way he allowed these days.

Only twice before he had left for the War had there been a full consummation. Jonas's mind returned to these occasions at the moment of climax. There were never images of another woman's face; it was only ever Lily, and the way she had looked during those two perfect moments of pleasure when he had enjoyed her fully. The first time had been in the garage of a country club and the second had been in the passageway of a night train to New York. He had entered her with her skirt bunched up between them and Jonas recalled how it had stayed creased for the rest of the journey – an illicit, tactile touchstone to remind him of their sex.

Jonas began to respond to the penance of Lily's lips. He kissed her roughly and waited for her contrition – that slow sinking to her knees before him – but it didn't happen this time. Her lips remained cool and soft beneath his. This apology was not filled with shame or guilt or remorse. It said merely that a slip had occurred but not that the indiscretion was over.

Lily pulled away from him and stood up.

'You're almost out of air,' Lily said.

She leaned over to see the oxygen bottle and noted the level of the needle on its gauge.

'And you've used up your spare, Jonas,' she said, chidingly. 'I'll get you another.'

Lily's words were short; frustration cut through them.

She went into the kitchen pantry and dragged one of the chrome cylinders from where they lay stacked on the floor. She balanced it between her legs as she caught her breath.

On the top shelf, Lily noticed the gift she had assembled for Will's sister. He had asked her to keep it for him until Isobel arrived. The girl had not turned up yet and Lily wasn't sure what to do with the offering. She would keep the gift forever if necessary, she decided. Nobody but Will's Isobel would have it.

In the dark pantry, Lily saw the shape of peaches in their preserve jars – thick and swollen with orange syrup – and thought of Will. She touched the sharp edge of the shelf with her fingertips and remembered the vein that ran like a ridge along the length of Will's inner arm. Lily rested the side of her face against the shelf and felt its cusp at the edge of her mouth. She opened her lips, so that the very tip of her tongue could run along it. Lily moved back and forward along the smooth surface of the cylinder – just half an inch, an inch, two inches – and longed for Will's fingers where she burned.

'Are there spares?' Jonas shouted from the study.

It wasn't a question but a bellow; he sounded as enraged as she was.

'Yes,' Lily called out. 'Yes, I have one. I'm coming.'

16

The sign was painted in yellow on the glass of a shop window
– an amateur hand (but one with some skill) had created the
letters. At first, it was difficult for Will to decipher if he had
read the words correctly because the sweeps of the brush were
unusual; the signwriter must have been more familiar with
another alphabet. Will was in the East Village and he had been
passing the strip of kosher stores which had held firm against
the invasions of the German and the Italian shopkeepers.

Rows of strangled ducks hung bald and pale from their
knotted throats; cherry wheels of cheese and piles of blinis
and bagels were neatly arranged in the gleaming windows.
Most of the shopfront glass had Yiddish writing but the
window that had brought Will to a standstill had the words
GOLDEN DOOR GROCERY painted on it in English.

Will had seen it because of Isobel. He had been searching
for her name on his walk home from the library as he had
subconsciously searched for it since the day she had failed to
meet him. Will had started looking for 'Isobel' in places where
her name couldn't possibly be: on the plastic pricetags the
butchers looped around their ham hocks, in the small print of
newspapers, on the travel posters in the subway, on the stubs
of tickets in the gutters at his feet. He looked for her name
among the manufacturer's marks on his daily rivet hammer
and on the paper napkins that came with his sandwich at
lunch. He looked for her in shop windows and on the labels
of broken bottles in trashcans and on the flapping banners the

municipality hung from the street lamps in the park to tell everyone it was summer.

Will had taken to reading every sign he had seen since July 10th. His eyes never rested for too long on any place he had already examined; they kept moving, seeking out the next possibility. It was because of this eye-hunger that Will had seen the reference to the golden door. He knew this window of clean glass – wedged between two other shopfronts on an obscure street – could have nothing to do with Jonas Trichardt; still, he decided to go in.

Will entered the shop surreptitiously but a bell above the doorway tinkled its wake-up call and gave his presence away. Will could discern the outline of a man sitting in a back room behind a gossamer curtain.

'Who is that?' said a voice with a thick accent. Polish, maybe.

Will wasn't sure how to reply. The man slid back the curtain; it was fashioned from makeshift rings made out of clothes pegs which ran along a stretch of wire. The man stood up from his stool and shuffled out onto the polished floor of his store. He was in his shirtsleeves and he had bedroom slippers on his feet. Will saw that both the man's eyes were milky spheres held in place by a ruching of wrinkles. There were no retinas – just two, pure, pearly windows onto blindness.

'That a customer or what?' the man demanded, his voice like wind through a drift of fallen leaves.

'I like the name of your store,' said Will.

'Irish fellow,' said the old man, matter-of-factly. 'I like the way you say your words. Singing-like.'

So Will's own tongue had betrayed him as readily as the old man's did.

'You doing some shopping here?' the old man asked, as if the idea was surpassingly strange.

'You're the only one open today,' said Will. 'It's your holy day, isn't it?'

The old man nodded.

'Up to sundown only. But I'm always open for business 'cause I'm a rebel. Irishmen know something of the rebel,' he said and he made a fist so softened by arthritis that Will could have crushed it in his own.

'I just saw the name on the window and liked it,' said Will. 'I wondered if there was a story to it.'

'Irish fellows like their stories and their fair Colleens,' the old man said and he chuckled again.

'I'll make tea. It's *Shabbat* for a bit longer but God is in favour of tea. I know that like I know my own mind.'

The old man motioned for Will to follow him into the back room and Will saw that the small space was papered in sepia. There were a hundred photographs pinned to the walls, depicting men and women and families clustered together in the tight, formal style favoured by traditional photographers. Not at all like Will's snaps of Isobel; those had captured the girl's spirit, having been taken at unexpected moments when she was most herself. This man's photographic collection seemed strange in light of his failed eyesight.

'You like my family?' the old man asked Will and his arthritic fingers ran lovingly across the smooth surfaces of the pictures, pretending the countenances were in Braille.

'They're very grand,' said Will.

The old Jew filled his kettle from a tap and lit a gas ring with a match. Each job required his hands to make a hundred delicate probings and explorations like a beetle negotiating a rose bush. The old Jew's fingers flitted and fiddled and Will wondered where the man would be when the arthritis froze his hands completely. When the kettle was stabilized on the gas ring, the man ran his hand up one corner of the wall and touched a photograph which held pride of place at eye level.

'That's me there,' he said to Will. 'With Miriam and the boys in Krakow. That's in Poland. When she died, they brought me over here and said what a great place it is to live in and grow old – lots of heat in the winter. That's true but now I find I miss the bones of my wife to visit and the boys are out working all the hours God sends.'

'Is it your shop?' Will asked.

He was surprisingly unwilling to hurry the old man.

'It's my boys' shop and their wives work in it but I sit here for luncheon hour, so they can do their laundry and what not. But you asked me about the name,' the old man said, 'I named this place after a great lady . . .'

Will wondered if the old Jew was making sense. How could the Golden Door Grocery have anything to do with a lady?

'Golden Door?' asked Will. 'How does that fit?'

'It fits quite beautifully,' the old man said and his voice seemed to warn Will that a story, like a mouse from a skirting board, would come out in its own time. 'We came across a wide sea to get here and there were storms. It was a few years ago and my eyes could still see back then. They were worried, my boys, because the medical men would look to see for the eye sickness I got.'

'On Ellis?' asked Will, suddenly sensing connections like webs.

'You got it!' said the man. 'Trachoma they call it. I got it but I didn't have it so bad back then in them days . . . You know the trachoma?' he asked Will.

'No,' said Will. 'Is it bad?'

'They don't like it here. No, sir! If they only catch you with it, you get sent away again. You go blind after a while. Red eyes and pain but you get used to it.'

Will thought of the old man's arthritis and the pain of a blinding disease; he admired his spirit.

'Anyway, we came into New York City harbour with the lights. I never seen such lights.'

Will remembered the glinting lights so well, too – that delectable invitation in the showers of bulbs.

'They anchored us down for the night but next morning I'm up early 'cause I can't sleep for the nerves and I see her: the Statue of Liberty. You know her real name? The name the Frenchmen gave to her before they presented her to America?'

Will shook his head.

'You shaking your head?' asked the man and Will smiled.

'Yes,' said Will. 'I mean no, I don't know her real name. I'm sorry.'

'Not all that many who come here do,' said the man. 'She's called "Liberty Enlightening the World" – just like the lights of the city in the water. Like that, but for the whole world.'

The old man ran his fingertips across the side of the kettle to ascertain whether or not it was heating up and Will wondered if his story was over and where the words 'golden door' found their place in it.

'Then somebody told me that inside that lady's belly, on the stairs where you can walk up to her crown, is written a poem. In that poem, they say that the lady is standing watch over a golden door. You can go see that poem for yourself. I can't see it no more but I got it up here,' the old man said and he tapped his forehead with his right hand and winced as his swollen fingers jarred against the bone of his skull.

'It was golden for me 'cause I passed right through it. No eye exam to find out my trachoma. No nothing. They missed me out by accident, you see, and when I got through and we got off the boat at Battery Park, I looked back and that great lady out in the harbour water winked at me as if to say, "I let you through. Now you make good."'

The old Jew chuckled at his story and Will decided he would take one of the Circle Line boats out to visit the poem for himself. He wanted to read it aloud and see if he could make any sense of it.

The kettle's whistle started to shriek and the old man began his painstaking scrabbling to take it off the heat without getting burned. Will let him potter about and do the job without any help. The old man was not so useless that he should be prevented from enjoying the few, small chores he could yet manage.

When the pouring and spooning was done and the old man had handed Will a mug of creamy, sweet tea, he waved his hand to indicate the whole room and said, 'My family for many generations. We sure did have a love affair with the photographing camera.'

Then he leaned forward and whispered, as if it was a secret he kept from his sons and daughters-in-law who were beginning to imagine he was senile, 'I could tell you every single one of their names.'

A few minutes later, one of the daughters-in-law came in and was flustered to find a bulky Irishman crammed into the back room with her father.

'Could I help you perhaps?' she said with her polite, refined Polish accent.

'Your father has helped me plenty, thank you Ma'am,' Will said.

He tipped his cap and she blushed where her dress rested against her neck.

'My name's Will Carthy,' said Will.

He took the old Jew's hand ever so gently in his own. He didn't shake it. He held it tenderly in almost the same way he had held Lily's hand in her kitchen – a similar connection but without the passion this time. It was a mark of respect between two men who had lost their homes and their ancestral bones.

'I'm Abraham Weissman,' the old man said.

It was a name Will would not forget. For some reason, he knew that it was one he would carry with him for no particular reason, the way he sometimes carried things about for days in his pockets. This name – like Felicity Bell's – had become a part of the story, of Isobel's story.

Abraham Weissman – a man who had seen the Statue of Liberty wink at him before he went blind.

Rose Marie did her laundry in a concrete sink out in the razor-weed yard behind Tully's. Normally, she stood with her back stalwartly towards the privy and she ignored the whistles of the unemployed men from the back tenement who stumbled down to use the facilities during the day. But because of the memory of Aidan's body, Rose Marie had taken to standing on the far side of the sink where it met the wall of the house. She would bump her hip against the wall as she washed but at least the privy door was in clear view to her right.

Aidan's body had crushed the weeds flat but now, only two days since his body had been removed, they had bloomed back – seeming greener and sharper than ever before, as if they had fed off his dead weight.

By chance, the first shirt Rose Marie chose from the basket was one of Aidan's. She knew all the boys' shirts by sight and size. Aidan had discovered some source of money over the past few weeks, that was certain – a secret source about which he had been tightlipped. He had bought Rose Marie a few drinks when he came across her in the Fields. Aidan had even gone to the garment district – to a factory shop that sold seconds on to the public from a vast bargain basement – and purchased this new shirt. It was very modern with a gauche burgundy stripe running through a lilac background. When Will had first seen it, he had called it a flashman's shirt – no good for an honest working man – and so Rose Marie had felt disdain for it when Aidan had twirled around in the kitchen like a Paris fashion model, showing it off. She would sell the shirt, maybe to Quinn or Calum who were sharing the bunks in the cellar. It was too small for Will or he would have had first option on it.

Rose Marie slapped the cotton of the shirt against her washboard and added a slip of soap to work into the grubby patches. Not the fine face-soap Will had stolen for her – a deed of cunning but also of love, Rose Marie knew – that would be saved for finer days and finer things than sweaty shirts. No matter how thin the green, carbolic bar grew before her father gave her a few cents to purchase another one, she wouldn't use Will's gift.

As Rose Marie took items from the basket, she caught her breath whenever she came across a thing of Will's. A shirt or a pair of the heavy canvas trousers he worked in. Those were hard to clean because they were always crusted with concrete dust and smudged with rivet ash but she took special care with them. Sometimes, Rose Marie would lift the cuff of one of Will's shirts to her nose and, when she took in his scent, she would close her eyes tight, as if stung by some sharp insect. Rose Marie always placed Will's clothes to one side – a ritual this – so that she could attend to them last as something to look forward to. Between her father's garments and those of their male lodgers, there was over an hour's worth of wet socks and stink to get through before she could care for the only items with which she had any patience.

Rose Marie went through Will's trouser pockets – her fingers stealing in daringly, as if his thighs were inside them –

only a thin lining away from the ridges of her fingerprints. If she felt something, she was delighted and wondered what it might be. Lately, there had been so many of those cards about Isobel which Will had painstakingly printed out by candle-light at the kitchen table. Will had allowed her to help him with the wording and she had done her best. He had seemed pleased and Rose Marie was glad of that. Will was so difficult to please these days.

Before, a specially thought-out meal – something Irish that Will had mentioned his mother making – would have brought a grin to his face. Rose Marie had used to show off her new shoes by pretending to do some Irish dancing in the hall until her father yelled at her to shut up; that had made Will smile, too.

Something had changed and Rose Marie felt it had to do with another woman. Isobel? That had been an awkward thing. Rose Marie had tried to be supportive but was truth-fully delighted the girl had not moved in with them. Rose Marie had seen Isobel's picture; she had wanted to take it and use it to light the stove because the girl was so lovely. But Will kept his sister's pictures near his bed and never put them in his pockets where Rose Marie could find them and claim she hadn't.

Today there were two items in the pocket of Will's trousers. One was an 'Isobel missing' card but the other – which wasn't in Will's handwriting but rather in the elegant penmanship of a woman – said 'Felicity Bell'. It was just a torn strip of paper with nothing else on it but that grand-sounding woman's name. Tully would have scoffed and said, 'It sounds like a bloody, high-falutin English girl's name.'

Was this Will's new girl? Had she given him her name printed on a torn card?

Yes, that was it. So there was a rival and Felicity Bell was her name. Rose Marie had suspected as much. It was alright; Rose Marie was alright. Now that she knew what she was up against, she felt better. Rose Marie had the girl's name and that made her easier to identify and easier to hate. Rose Marie dragged Will's trousers back and forward across the washboard while she thought about Felicity Bell. She worried about them until her wrinkled fingers started to crack open and bleed.

Will's shirt pocket also held a shred of paper. It was a piece of newsprint this time. Rose Marie looked at both sides – one mentioned a winning horse at Yonkers and the other side had something to do with a fire in a meatpacking warehouse. Rose Marie didn't think Will bet on the horses and the fire was obviously nothing to do with him, so she presumed Will had torn the strip to use as cigarette paper, now that buying the real thing was so dear.

Why did Will carry these scraps around with him: strange, random bits of tit-tat garbage? Only someone not right in the head would collect such oddments but Rose Marie loved Will for these eccentricities. She often felt he was giving her clues about himself, knowing she went through every one of his pockets and accumulated all the items he left there for her, trying to piece him together.

That meant Will had wanted her to find out about Felicity Bell. Rose Marie suddenly felt more settled; it was a test for her. A plan was formulating in her head. Will needed her to prove her love for him. She could do it, too.

At that moment, a man came crashing down the back tenement's fire escape and Rose Marie stopped daydreaming and pulled the plug out from the bottom of the sink, letting the drain suck the dirty water away. There were only five pieces of clothing left to wash but Rose Marie would do them in good, clean water; they were Will's things.

*　　*　　*

The two words were there beside each other as Will hadn't really expected them to be: *GOLDEN DOOR* – looking just as they had done beside each other on the pages of the file in Jonas Trichardt's office. Will had left Abraham Weissman's shop at two o'clock and had made his way straight to the Circle Line ferry which carried tourists out to Liberty Island. It was scorching hot and even the wind off the Hudson was thick and clinging. The ferries were new, they had been built only the year before to transport visitors to the great monument, but they weren't being maintained and they were almost barren of passengers.

Will thought of the trip he had taken out to Ellis Island a month ago and of the listening man who would have gone under if Will hadn't saved him. There seemed to be nobody nearby to save Will on his journey, even though he felt certain that he was close to drowning.

One of the guides on Liberty Island had answered Will's questions in a bored tone and directed him over to the base of the green lady. Liberty looked out – not down at the masses swarming at her feet. Perhaps from her great height, she had a better view of things to come and so could maintain her stoicism.

The poem was engraved on a brass plaque inside the base of the statue where a few families were lining up to attempt the three hundred and fifty-four steps to the statue's crown. Will would have liked to have seen the view the way the statue saw it but he was here to read the poem and find the two words that might offer a solution to Isobel's disappearance.

> *Give me your tired, your poor,*
> *Your huddled masses yearning to breathe free,*
> *The wretched refuse of your teeming shore,*

Send these, the homeless, tempest-tossed to me:
I lift my lamp beside the golden door.

A woman named Emma Lazarus had written it. Will had brought a sheet of paper with him and he quickly placed the sheet on top of the two words he had come to see and ran the lead of his pencil nib across them, so that he ended up with a tracing of the carving.

'Golden door': it was about immigrants, that was for sure. It promised a warm welcome and opportunities which glinted. Will went out of the statue's base and looked across the water to where the buildings of Manhattan twinkled in the afternoon sun. What could be the meaning of a list which used the golden door as its metaphor? And why had they chosen a door that wasn't open far enough for anyone to see inside?

Will waited for the ferry back to Battery Park. It churned through the river water towards him; its white paint appeared ever so slightly tawdry.

Will boarded the vessel and stood as far to the stern as possible. On their journey back to Manhattan, the boat passed between Liberty and Ellis islands. Ashore, Will could see a few claimants, leaping from the Department of Commerce and Labour ferry and hurrying up the stairs towards the enormous doors of the Great Hall. If he had been on this Circle Line boat a month ago, he might have seen himself and the listener walking up the landing plank.

Will's gaze returned to the Statue of Liberty. He saw that he was lost from her view. From this position on the river, beside the great, red structures of the Immigration Department buildings on Ellis Island, it was as if she had turned her back on him.

17

The Trichardts' guests were the kind of people who didn't drive their own cars. They had chauffeurs who wore uniforms which always looked new; their gloves were soft and their boots were made from leather that was darker and slicker than that used for ordinary shoes. Their starched jackets kept the drivers' postures upright as they stood beside their cars which were parked outside the Trichardts' house like a row of shining, black pearls beneath the twilight trees.

The trouble with the Trichardts' street was its lack of commerce. There was no way for a man loitering in it to look inconspicuous. There were only houses here and, though he might pass for a gardener, Will had no spade or wheelbarrow with him which could act as a prop. So he just leaned his back against the wall of the house directly opposite Number Seventeen and watched. The large front windows of the Trichardts' house – which seemed to suggest a frank openness with the street – were actually designed to reflect the late, evening sun which made them completely opaque.

Will noted another car pull up at the end of the row and a man and a woman stepped from it in a proliferation of glitter. The last of the evening sun sparked off the man's gold tiepin and off the gold bows on the lady's shoes. It was not exactly ostentatious but gold did seem to settle everywhere about their persons in tiny, dripping tears.

Will thought he recognized some of the faces of the people who arrived in the cars. They were the men who posed on the front pages and magazine covers he passed each day on the newsstands but couldn't afford to buy. They weren't actors or Broadway stars, not the faces that glowed from the stage at Radio City – nothing so frivolous. These were the serious, grim faces of men who had been senior liaison officers during the War, or the sons of the men who had run it. And their wives all had that indefinable, American polish that was emulated by the women who came in on the ships but somehow seldom equalled. Will hoped that Isobel, if she had arrived safely, would not have been one of those girls who pored through the ladies' journals and practised for hours with hot tongs to wave their hair in that manner Hollywood approved.

By seven o'clock, there were eight dark cars parked along the sidewalk. Will lit a cigarette and sat down on the neighbour's wall where the shade was darkest. Seven of the chauffeurs were intending to start a dice game down behind the area gate – the eighth driver was a Negro, and so not included. He stood apart from the rest and shone the front wheel of his owner's vehicle with a white rag. Just then, Mrs Harrigan, the Trichardts' cook with the enormous bosom, came out and approached the men. They all snapped to attention.

'This won't do,' she said. 'You're cluttering the street.'

She waved a dismissive hand at the cars.

'We're lawfully parked,' said one of them, confused.

'Yes, but it's common,' said Mrs Harrigan.

'None of these cars is common, Ma'am,' said another driver. 'They're all worth more than twenty years of my wages.'

'Mr Trichardt doesn't like it,' Mrs Harrigan said.

At that, several of the chauffeurs began to delve in their pockets for keys.

'It looks as if he's trying to be conspicuous. Mr Trichardt

doesn't like to be obvious. It doesn't look well for the house,' she said.

The drivers murmured between themselves and a few moments later three of the cars pulled away with low purrs and moved around to the next block, leaving the façade of Number Seventeen clear and discreet.

Mrs Harrigan caught sight of Will then; she peered at him, trying to make out his countenance among the shadows. His cigarette was glowing garishly in the dusk and his slouch was an eyesore, but she couldn't distinguish his face.

'And you're some sleazy pressman, I suppose?' Mrs Harrigan called across the street to Will. She sounded disdainful and she stood with her hands on her ample hips.

'No, Ma'am, I am not,' said Will.

'Then what are you standing there for?' she demanded.

'It's a free country,' said Will.

A few of the remaining chauffeurs snickered.

'Not that free,' said Mrs Harrigan.

Will stepped forward into the pale glow of the streetlight and Mrs Harrigan saw his face.

'Oh, it's you,' she said. 'What do you want?'

'I'll know it when I see it coming,' said Will, cryptically, and Mrs Harrigan backed away from him a little nervously and huffed back into the house.

Will wasn't sure what he had hoped for. When it happened, it surprised him and unnerved him, too. Mrs Harrigan came out of the house again with her lips set in a firm line. This time, she crossed the street to speak to Will.

'Mr Trichardt requests the pleasure of your company,' she said.

Will crushed the butt of his cigarette under his boot and strolled behind her with his hands in his pockets. He had the sudden, irrational sense that he ought to have somebody watching his back or at least aware of where he was going – as if he might never come out of the house again. It was the way Aidan must have felt when he had asked Will to come with him on his night errand for Foxy Nolan. But Will was going to a swell's dinner party, not a rough warehouse in the meatpacking district. The gentlemen going in to dine at the Trichardts' house had been dressed in tuxedos with white silk scarves thrown around their necks even though the evening was balmy. They were not roughnecks or gangsters.

Inside, Will was not greeted. Mrs Harrigan shut the front door behind him and looked him up and down.

'Normally, I'd offer you one of Mr Trichardt's evening jackets as a courtesy. It might make you feel more comfortable in the assembled company but his garments would never fit you.'

'I'm comfortable as I am,' said Will. 'This is my best suit.'

Will had dressed knowing he was going to the public library that morning and such was his respect for books that he had dressed well.

'I just don't know . . .' Mrs Harrigan tut-tutted to herself. 'What do you call yourself then?'

'Will Carthy,' Will said.

Mrs Harrigan pulled open a set of double doors and said, quite properly, 'Mr William Carthy, Sir,' before departing.

Jonas walked smartly over to Will, dragging his oxygen cart behind him, and patted him on the shoulder.

'Good of you to come, Will,' said Jonas.

They were in the red room which was decorated in a Chinese style – overly plush with a bizarre mixture of art deco angles and twisting scarlet dragons. Cigar smoke was already accumulating in a purple haze close to the high ceiling and the women were draped like slim bolts of glowing cloth across the furniture, their lithe bodies tantalizing and their eyes devouring Will beneath thick lines of black kohl.

'Will's in construction,' said Jonas. 'And a particular favourite of my wife.'

All the eyes in the room flashed to Lily. Will expected her to make one of her clever remarks about him being a whiz with chandelier maintenance or something like that, but she didn't.

'He's become a friend,' Lily said.

Everybody felt very awkward at that and began to count the ice cubes in their glasses. None of the guests seemed eager to introduce themselves and Will got the impression that – now that an interloper had been included – they were reluctant to be remembered as having been in attendance.

Lily came over to Will, making a straight line for him across the room. She was in silver – a dress that slipped across her thighs and breasts as she walked.

'What will you drink?' asked Lily, then she lowered her voice to a whisper and added, 'And why were you outside the window so we couldn't help but see you?'

Around them, conversations started up like reluctant motors. Will waited until there was a significant buzz of speech in the air before answering her.

'Do you imagine I'm here in a mad bid to confront your husband?' he asked her in a low tone.

Lily seemed hurt by that but then she rallied lightly, 'A girl can hope, can't she?'

'I saw something in Mr Trichardt's study and I'd like an explanation.'

Lily turned her back on the room, so that only Will could see how round her eyes had become.

'Jesus, Will! Have you been going through his things?'

'No, I haven't. It was lying there in plain sight.'

Will kept a smile fixed to his face as he spoke but his eyes glared into hers.

Lily seemed genuinely afraid.

'His work is top-secret. Half the men here are in government. The man behind you is Mr Darwin Brenner, a top advisor to the governor. He's only here because the venerable Governor Chase himself can't make it tonight. That gentleman over there is all the way from Washington just for this evening, an advisor to President Wallace. The other, with the impressive gut, is the Honourable Horace Metcalfe, our fair mayor.'

'They look fatter than their pictures,' said Will and Lily's champagne almost bubbled up into her nose.

No matter how solemn his intention, making Lily laugh had become a highlight in Will's life these days. He loved the way her eyes screwed up and her lips split in a long, happy line across her face.

'To these men, I'm just a trained monkey like the drivers out there. I'm here for my sport value only. Don't worry, I'm ready for it.'

'I'm afraid for you now,' Lily said. 'Jonas asking you in like this. It's strange.'

She couldn't say more. Jonas was making his way over to them; his trolley wheels squeaked across the carpet. Several of the woman looked over at Jonas as he passed their chairs, smiling to themselves about the eccentricity of keeping the cart in such a noisy state but Will remembered what Lily had said, 'It warns me when he's coming' and he understood that she was wise.

Jonas placed his hand on Will's shoulder in a proprietorial fashion and faced the assembly.

'Will is the immigrant success story,' Jonas announced.

When he raised his voice like this, it was clear that the

speech was intended for the whole room. Amid the small solar systems of glimmering guests, silence descended.

'How much cash did you have with you when you came to America?' asked Jonas.

Will felt he had been dragged into the light like an audience member pulled on stage by one of those dreadful conjurors. Will ignored the crowd and turned to speak only to Jonas, subtly twisting his body so that Jonas's hand was forced to fall away. Will glanced into Jonas's yellow eyes which had retinas of a peculiar shape – elongated and feral like a cat's, equipped for sight in the dark.

'You needed twenty-five dollars,' said Will. 'I came in 1924 and that was what you needed to get in. It's likely a little more now.'

'Twenty-five dollars,' said Jonas to his guests but he kept his eyes on Will.

There was a significant difference in their height, but standing next to the slight, slim man Will felt at a disadvantage because of his weight. He felt cumbersome and as uncouth as the rough cloth from which his cheap suit had been cut. Jonas had refinement: a length to his fingers and his throat that spoke of generations of breeding for sleek effect.

'Will came here with twenty-five dollars and he has a job building our city. He's working on the greatest project man has ever conspired to erect and he lives and supports himself and a wife?'

'No wife yet,' said Will.

He wanted to add that he had been offering support to Jonas's own wife but that would be petty and foolish.

'He's young, strong, single, successful. He is, most importantly, healthy and disease-free. He's able to speak our language. This is the kind of man we desperately need,' said Jonas.

Will's prediction that he had been hauled in to this party as an exhibit was proving founded. His presence was intended to strengthen an argument. What that argument was, Will wasn't yet sure but he intended to find out.

'I live in a tenement building on the Lower East Side,' Will told the room. 'For those of you so eager to know me better: I have my own room and count myself lucky. They're living eight to a hovel down there in the coldwater flats. I share a privy, winter and summer, with fifty other people. I may speak the same language as you but I doubt we understand each other.'

'And he has spirit,' said Jonas. 'The kind of spirit that makes America great. He's the true believer in the American dream. This is the man we aim to protect.'

'I can protect myself, Jonas,' said Will. 'It's you that ought to be worrying,' and he made a fist and gently pressed it against Jonas's cheek.

The man didn't flinch. Somewhere in the room, one of the women uttered a high, hysterical giggle and a few of the men joined in. Will gave a small chuckle, too, to indicate that he was joking but Jonas only smiled his weird, false smile that looked as if two fishhooks had been slipped through the skin at the edge of his lips and yanked up.

'I'm afraid you're not convincing them I'm worthy,' said Will.

'They're already convinced,' said Jonas. 'Any doubt they're entertaining now is just a case of cold feet,' he added.

One of the men walked over to where Jonas and Will were still locked together, neither man willing to walk away and break the tension.

'This is Titian Decatur,' said Jonas, introducing the man. 'He's in shipping.'

Will shook Titian's hand and the man looked knowingly at

Jonas and said, 'I'm with you in principle, Trichardt. We all are . . .'

'That's all we need,' said Jonas. 'Men of principle who stick by their principles. I'm more than happy for you to leave the actual practice to men with stronger stomachs.'

Jonas lifted his glass until it chinked against Titian's and announced that they should all go through to dinner.

Lily looped her arm around Will's elbow and led him through the house. Will smelled her skin; it was warm with the purple smell of evening lilac. There was a flower the size of a moon behind her ear and Will let her pull him along like a man floating in a strong current.

Mrs Harrigan made a show of adding the extra place setting at the last minute and Will saw that he was seated opposite Lily. Jonas was at the head of the table and Titian Decatur was at the far end. The various women, who were outnumbered two to one by the men, were dotted about, shining like jet in their jewelled dresses.

There were more forks and knives than Will had ever seen. From across the table, he saw Lily take the outermost set and eye him knowingly, showing him which ones to use. Will had had enough of it. He collected the pieces of extraneous cutlery into a bunch in his fist – keeping one knife, one fork and one spoon – and handed them to Mrs Harrigan like a posy of steel flowers as she passed. One of the men coughed uncomfortably. Will was beginning to enjoy himself.

The conversation started out politely and kept going in the same innocuous vein. Will wondered how someone like Lily could stand it night after night. The men talked about stocks that had failed and why, about racehorses, which tennis clubs were worth belonging to, the worthlessness of niggers and the Central Park beautification project.

Will looked across at Lily and saw that she was holding her

fork with such pressure that her knuckles were turning as blue as the veins in her wrists. He thought how he had first seen Lily from the bottom up – the soles of her feet leading finally to her lovely hair – when he had walked in on her in the kitchen that day. It seemed a long time ago, as if Lily was a childhood friend or, like Isobel, a sister he had always known. He thought how Lily would rather be sitting in the kitchen with him now, trying to mend that broken jug, not knowing that Will had the last laugh – that he held the final piece without which she would never complete the task.

'What we know to be the expedient solution,' said the man who was obviously a politician judging by his obsequious manner and his careful choice of words, 'is sometimes a hard sell to the public.'

'Democracy is the greatest good for the greatest number of people,' said Jonas. 'Not equal rights for all. That's not possible.'

Every head around the table nodded except for Lily's. Will had no idea what he might be assenting to, so he remained still, too.

Jonas continued, 'A policy of equal rights just isn't rational and it's not as if we're talking about Americans here . . . They're foreigners; their allegiance isn't to us.'

'Then again,' said Titian, 'our allegiance clearly isn't to them, is it?'

'A disease-free America,' said Jonas. 'That's all I ask. That's noble, surely.'

'Yes,' said Lily. 'You're terribly noble, Jonas. Not to mention cultured and polite and polished and hospitable. I think we've all witnessed that tonight.'

She pushed her chin out in defiance and Will thought how he wanted a picture of her at that moment. An image to keep which showed her like this: brave and foolhardy.

'It's been a mistake to include the women in all this,' said Jonas. 'I appreciate their sensibilities find the necessary hard line a little harsh. I apologize, my dear.'

There was a lull in the conversation.

'Is this about Golden Door?' Will asked.

There was a profound and heavy silence. Titian Decatur wiped his lips and placed his napkin to the side of his plate.

'What exactly is Golden Door?' Will persisted.

Jonas wouldn't bow down, though.

'It's an unlegislated immigration policy,' he said. 'Commissioned by the highest levels of government.'

'Jonas,' said Titian.

It was a warning.

Will looked at Lily. She seemed genuinely thrown by his question and nobody seemed to have anything to add. Will decided to find out more about the men with whom he was breaking bread.

'What type of shipping is it you're into, Mr Decatur?'

'Let's not talk business,' said the man and he laughed to show he wasn't nervous.

'Trawling, is it?' Will kept on.

'Liners!' said his wife, outraged by the suggestion that her husband made his living by scraping the bottom. 'One of the greatest shipping lines in the world,' she added.

'Elizabeth!' her husband warned. 'Mr Carthy doesn't tour much on liners, I don't imagine.'

'Gateway,' said Mrs Decatur. 'The Gateway Shipping Line. We own the whole company.'

'And you, Mr Brenner?' asked Will.

'I'm a civil servant,' said Mr Brenner.

'What kind of civil servant is that?'

'One you wouldn't have heard of,' said Brenner.

'Enough interrogation,' said Jonas.

'Jesus, Trichardt!' said Titian. It sounded as if he was pulling the power of his voice in, lest he unleash it at full volume. 'What the hell are you thinking bringing this man in on it?'

'I am not ashamed,' said Jonas.

'Then at least be discreet,' said Titian.

Will saw that Titian Decatur was powerful, too. Jonas and he were on an equal rung on society's ladder but Will sensed in Decatur something of the street whereas Jonas was all college libraries and debating clubs.

'Cigars and cognac for the gentlemen?' said Jonas and he rose to his feet, indicating that the men should follow him back into the study. Nobody mentioned that they hadn't had dessert or coffee yet. The men stood up quickly; the women remained seated.

'I don't believe I qualify,' said Will and he got to his feet, too.

He would find out about the men he had met tonight and their companies. Perhaps he would discover something that would further his investigation. Lily didn't try to stop him. He left the dining room and went along the passage to the kitchen. The room was dense with steam and the round aromas of plummy duck. Three cooks had been employed for the occasion. They all watched Will pass them. He picked up an apple from the fruit bowl under the disdainful eye of Mrs Harrigan and went out the back door.

It was as hot as a mohair blanket outside, the evening air wrapped in around Will's shoulders and clung to him. He hadn't heard anything that helped him much and he had succeeded in making a few more powerful men edgy. Will made his way along the side of the house, down the path where the magnolia trees trembled, burdened by their sagging blooms.

The chauffeurs were playing cards now, crouched down low to the ground, so that the new leather of their boots creaked as they shifted their weight. Will navigated carefully between them. They didn't greet him. He went up the stairs to the side gate and into the street. The lamps here were bowed arcs of ornate steel, each painted green, and the light they threw was designed to enhance the façades of the grand houses without glaring in through their windows.

Beneath the dripping trees, Will saw the form of a man and presumed it was the Negro chauffeur, smoking in solitary stillness. The man was the only human form in the street. The tortoiseshell cat, which imagined itself to be the dominant tiger of this stretch of the city, looked down at Will from the wall and licked his forepaw to show he meant to offer no assistance.

The man stepped out from the shadows and raised his hand. Will had the impression the man was about to swat a fly, he raised his hand just so, but there was a dark club in it and it crashed down on Will's head with a crack he heard distinctly before the blackness gulped him down.

18

There was the smell of engine oil and unwashed dogs. Smell was the sense that came back to Will first and it came back powerfully, flooding his nose with those two, distinct aromas. Something was pressing into his back – a bar of some sort; Will could feel its pressure against his spine. He tried to open his eyelids and even that small movement shot pain like tatters of orange lightning through his head.

Will realized he had been knocked out and moved somewhere, probably in the trunk of a car. His coat was splotched with oil or gasoline and its greasy smell made the juices swim sickeningly up the sides of his stomach. Will tried to touch his forehead. He felt the need to confirm it was still whole – it felt like a broken egg – but his hands were tied behind him. He was seated on a chair, roped to it, and he attempted to look around the place where he was being held but his eyes wouldn't focus and then, snapping back to use, they suddenly did.

Will found himself in a low-ceilinged room with brick walls that had once been painted an institutional shade of green but now looked like aging vomit. There were dozens of cages lined up along the wall, small rectangles of wire. Will tried to turn his head to see what was being kept in them and the side of his face pressed up against the front of one of the enclosures for a second.

The snarling maw of a dog came for his eyes. Will threw his weight in the opposite direction and his chair toppled over and crashed to the floor. Will wrenched his neck, trying to prevent his skull from cracking on the concrete floor; mercifully, he was spared that.

The dog that had snapped at him was restrained by a leather strap lashed to its collar and it was securely held behind the mesh of its cage – that was clear to Will now – but it strained so frantically that Will felt sure it would break its own neck to get at him. Its gums were bleeding and its ears were torn into ragged strips, so that they looked like war banners. 'Rabies!' Will thought at once. Dr Challis's story of the man slowly dying on Island Three came back to him in vivid detail but there was no foam at this mongrel's mouth – just dead, black eyes in a scarred face that seemed horribly intent.

There were other dogs, too, all penned in, all snapping and snarling madly – feeding off each other's rage. One bull terrier attacked the wiring of his cage and, with a twang, Will heard one of the dog's teeth snap free and fall to the ground not far from his face. Will tried to work his arms free but they had no strength; no nerves or blood flowed through them. It meant he must have been tied this way for a while; it must be the earliest hours of Sunday morning.

The sound of Will's chair falling over had brought a man to the doorway. He looked enormously tall from where Will was lying and the muzzle of his shotgun seemed improbably long. They were in a basement. Fragmentary facts zinged in and out of Will's brain as his full consciousness returned. There were tiny windows high on the walls. Their panes had been painted black but Will could hear taxi horns from somewhere up there; there was a street not too far away. The dogs went on and on until Will wanted the cracked eggshell of his head to break open and allow the yolk of his brain to dribble out onto the floor.

'God, the Father!' came a smooth, Irish voice. 'Did I say to put the man in with the dogs?'

The voice was a cool pool in Will's burning head. Its timbre was lilting but not strongly so. The smooth-voiced man slapped the man with the gun across the back of the head.

'Are we gangsters here or something?' said the man.

He came over and, with difficulty, he lifted Will's chair, so that it stood upright again.

Jonas Trichardt was quick, Will thought. Will had barely left the party when these men had nabbed him. They were going to beat him until he gave up how much he knew about the Golden Door. The terrible truth was that Will didn't know enough to satisfy them. He had been bluffing and that was a bad situation to be in when these men were going to pummel him until he told them everything.

The smooth-voiced man sliced through Will's bonds with a switchblade; Will finally had a free hand to touch the welt across the back of his skull and feel that it wasn't bleeding. Even with both hands loose, Will didn't try to get up or move. Nausea lolled around inside him and he felt a bone-deep exhaustion. He wanted to lie down on the floor and sleep – even the infernal dogs wouldn't keep him awake.

'To your feet, Mr Carthy,' said the smooth voice. 'Head up those stairs, if you please.'

Will did as he was told. Behind him, the two men spent a few seconds kicking at the dogs' faces through their cages until the animals were demented with fear and their jowls heaved with bloody saliva. Then they followed Will up.

The narrow staircase dead-ended in a space that looked like the box room where a janitor or an elevator operator might spend the slow hours of the night. A cheap wireless set sat on a three-legged table that looked as if it had been whipped off a bonfire pile and there was a military cot wedged into the corner with rough blankets on it. A gas primer stove stood in a central position supporting a kettle. A ledge above a sink held a shaving mirror and a grungy face towel. Deeper into the room, where the light didn't reach brightly, were dozens of towers constructed from chairs.

Will felt disorientated; the chairs were small and low, lower even than the sump of the bed. They were children's chairs, Will realized after a few seconds, stacked in piles. It must be a school, or a church room where Bible lessons were taught.

'I'd offer you tea but it's not actually my place,' said the smooth-voiced man.

They were alone in the room; the man with the shotgun held the shadowy perimeter of the doorframe. It was deep night outside, Will figured, making it gloomy in here where only an oil lantern was burning. Will watched the man. In contrast to his controlled speech, the man's fidgety energy made him childlike. The man moved a lot, gesturing constantly with his hands and bouncing on the unsprung mattress.

After a few seconds of this agitation, the man leaned over to light a cigarette beneath the hurricane glass of the lamp and Will saw him clearly for the first time. The man held his face beside the lamp for a few seconds to be sure that Will got a good look at it. This wasn't one of Jonas Trichardt's men, Will realized with a lurch. He was the unwilling half of a personal dialogue with Foxy Nolan.

Everybody said that Foxy Nolan was the best-looking man in America and now Will saw what they meant. Foxy was from Kildare, fair-skinned and blond with a perfect, full mouth and a tall, lean body. When he smiled, Foxy grew even more beautiful. Will remembered hearing that they had used his face in a toothpaste commercial for *Gleam* out in

California and sales had rocketed. His eyes were green and his hands had nails that were as round and smooth as starfish arms.

Will saw the ring around Foxy's thumb as the man lifted his cigarette to his lips. The ring was a regular band of gold but attached to it – so that it curved out from the side of his hand like an extra claw – was a steel spike sharpened into a point at the end. This was a cock spur, the vicious tool cock-fighters attached to their birds' own talons to increase the lethality of their strikes. Will felt a momentary jolt as he realized that if this myth was true, how many others might be halfway accurate as well? The spur Foxy Nolan wore was legendary but it was the only lethal-looking thing about him.

Other than the vicious spike, Foxy was impossibly clean and crisp.

'So, Aidan Moran's slit his throat,' said Foxy.

'Actually, someone did it for him,' said Will.

Foxy tut-tutted and handed Will a starched handkerchief.

'You bit your tongue,' he said and Will realized that, while the flow of blood had stopped, his lips were still crusty with the stuff. The cut was sending a coppery, red taste into his mouth every time he spoke. Will dabbed at it.

'Aidan was working for me,' said Foxy. 'I sent him out to play a little night baseball on my behalf a week or so ago.'

'I went with him,' said Will. 'You know that already.'

'I surely do, Mr Carthy,' said Foxy. 'And I'm grateful to you for your candour on the matter. God rest Aidan's soul but he wasn't half a useless little bogtrotter. My mother taught me not to speak ill of the dead, though. My mother taught me not to speak ill of a man who had a shilling to spend on a whore as well, but that's another story entirely . . .'

'I wasn't there when he caught it,' said Will, not sure if this tack would save his skin but not sure if anything else would either.

'I know. Nobody was there. I've asked about it and asked about it but nobody knows of any thieving-turned-to-murder that night. I've asked quite hard and the local petty criminals assure me a ghost did it,' said Foxy. 'So now I have to assume he died because of his business with me.'

'I thought you did it,' said Will.

Foxy laughed; he had a superior laugh, almost musical. Will even smiled a little in spite of himself.

'No,' said Foxy. 'Not my style at all. A fool like Aidan Moran is just useless enough to be useful sometimes.'

Will tried to see the face of the man at the door; there was no way he was the man Aidan had described as girlish.

'Aidan never could keep his mouth shut,' said Will. 'That was his problem.'

'So true,' said Foxy. 'I only wanted him to skulk about and pick up any word that was dropped. I'm after jobs for a few specific friends of mine. We'd heard they were bringing in scabs and I asked Aidan to find them for me.'

'He got under someone's skin,' said Will. 'With his skulking.'

'You see,' said Foxy, jumping on the mutual ground they had established. 'You understand me, Mr Carthy.'

'You sent a man round the next day, to ask what he'd found out? Aidan described him as quite feminine-looking.'

'Not me,' said Foxy. 'I had my dog pack on you that night – they saw the unexpected fireworks from a short distance away. I heard all about it before you knew what had happened.'

'And the newspaper gag-job?'

'Interested me enormously,' said Foxy. 'That must have thrown you all right. It threw me. Now, why don't you tell me what you saw that night and I'll determine if we have accord?'

Will decided to tell the truth and started in on everything he remembered.

'There were about twenty-five or thirty men, French-speaking, housed above the meat plant in truckle beds. Sleeping rough and being changed, according to Aidan, for new blokes every week.'

'They look like plasterers to you? Masons? What?' said Foxy.

'They looked a bit like steelmen to me. Their clothes had those ash marks like riveters get. They were furnacemakers or boilermakers maybe. Or heating men, I don't know. That's me guessing.'

'It sounds like a good guess,' said Foxy. 'Keep going.'

'Aidan and me were spotted and in the skirmish to get away, I ended up throwing a stick of dynamite we had found and blew half the place to the ground.'

Foxy let out a whoop of delight and bounced up and down on the bed in the exact way he had bounced on the two dozen institutional beds he had been assigned in orphanages and almshouses and insane asylums across Ireland during the first half of his life.

How had Foxy Nolan been allowed into this country? Will wondered. Had he snuck in through Canada? No, he had come through Ellis Island with all the others. He had walked the line, tall and blond, and he had smiled his movie-star smile and shown his MGM papers and they had welcomed him.

'So some bastard is trucking in Frenchies to do New York Irishmen's jobs. And I think we both know who that bastard is . . .'

Foxy let it hang.

'I went as a favour to Aidan,' said Will, genuinely nonplussed. 'I don't know who the builders are or where the site is or what the hell this secrecy's all about.'

'Ahhh,' said Foxy. 'That line of ignorance might have worked if my man hadn't just picked you up right outside the bastard in question's house.'

'Jonas Trichardt?'

'Him and a few of his worthy friends, no doubt.'

'He's not a builder,' said Will. 'He's a designer like. He plans the way crowds are going to move through big buildings like museums, so that they don't get bottle-necked and such.'

'He's only a part of it. He's got friends who own construction companies and friends in government and friends in planning offices all over the state.'

'He's got something to do with my building, though,' said Will. 'The grand one on Thirtieth Street. That's how I met him, ferrying papers from the site.'

Foxy shook his head.

'They've put some finishes up for tender is all and your contractors are bidding for them but I don't know where the site is. The plans don't give so much as a clue and they haven't been lodged with the City. Now that's strange, don't you think?'

'I've seen the plans – I can't figure them out either,' said Will.

It's to do with the Golden Door, thought Will but he didn't want Foxy Nolan to get wind of that name; he didn't want him involved with the list and Isobel.

'Maybe it's not a skyscraper, but the plans are for something pretty big,' continued Foxy.

'Well, he's not building a city project with twenty men,' said Will.

'That's just the little nest of vipers you found,' said Foxy.

'My other men have located dozens of their dens but they keep moving the workers on before we can get anything out of them. They keep them locked up tight as virgins in Marseilles. Add up all those bunkhouses across the city and you have a major project that could be employing plenty of my friends.'

'But we'd see the site,' said Will.

'That's the puzzler,' said Foxy. 'Where the hell is the place?'

'Underground?' suggested Will.

'Quite right,' said Foxy and he clicked his fingers rapidly five times. 'The exact conclusion we came to. They're extending the subway somewhere and they're keeping the work wrapped up tight. That's corruption.'

'Over in Queens?' asked Will.

'Not sure,' said Foxy. 'We're still searching.'

Foxy took a hipflask from his pocket and poured the contents into a teacup he took from a hook beside the stove. He swigged the liquor then jumped up exuberantly and shook Will by the hand.

'Good to have you onboard, Will. You never know when I might need a man like you,' Foxy said.

'I have a job,' said Will, flatly.

'No reason you can't be on a second payroll!' exclaimed Foxy. 'That's the beauty of working for me. Now for your standard-issue equipment.'

Foxy reached under the pillow of the bed and pulled out an oiled rag. He unfolded it carefully. Will already knew what the rag contained. The gun revealed itself, slick and nestled in the rag like a small, armour-plated animal you might catch in the desert. It was a nickel-plated Colt government automatic; the grip swirled with deeply embossed ivory, as if Foxy still imagined he was one of the cowboys MGM had been so keen to have him play. The eye of the gun's five-inch barrel stared Will down as Foxy swayed the weapon hypnotically from side to side. Will saw, as the piece passed his nose, that the safety was flipped down and breathed again.

'Welcome to Nolan Enterprises,' said Foxy.

Will took the gun quickly, wrapped it up again and put it in the waistband at the back of his trousers.

'You know how to shoot?' asked Foxy.

'I know how,' said Will.

'Thought you would,' said Foxy. 'I've heard about you,' he added in a whisper.

'I'm no secret,' said Will.

'Not here,' said Foxy, 'back in the old country.'

The Republicans thought of Will as an ally back home on account of his leaving the boy to rot beneath the seaweed. They didn't know it had only been cowardice.

'I've heard all sorts of impressive stories,' said Foxy.

'Have you now?' said Will, refusing to be baited into reminiscing about those days. 'I heard about you back home, too. All sorts of stories . . .'

Foxy's face went twisted in the lamp shadows and for a moment he looked less than beautiful.

Will decided he would keep the gun and, if Foxy ever came near him again, he would shoot him in the head. It would be like putting down a pup that had been born wrong – a mercy killing. Because he was thinking about dogs, Will heard again the yelps and whines coming up from the basement.

'We'll have to have them out next week,' said Foxy, indicating the dogs below them by pointing at the floorboards. He said it with some concern. 'School's back then, and little kids and those type of dogs don't mix too good.' Foxy slapped Will on the back, 'I learned that fact the hard way!' he said and his laughter was manic.

*   *   *

What Will didn't need was Rose Marie's frantic welcome when he came up the stairs of Tully's. She was sitting in the front room in her dressing-gown, waiting for him. It was almost six o'clock in the morning by the time Will got home and his head was still pounding. Rose Marie shrieked when she saw him and threw her arms around his neck, compounding the ache in his brain. Will had to splash some water on his face before he could begin to calm her down. He had the rest of the day to recover but by Monday he had to be back at the site or Frenchie and Frank and Lem would have no wages. He couldn't let them down.

'Where have you been?' Rose Marie demanded. 'You left the house at seven yesterday morning, heading for the library, and you've not been back since!'

Even Will's own mother – sometime after his fifteenth birthday – had ceased asking questions like that.

'I got into a sticky situation,' said Will. 'I'm alright now.'

He touched the bump at the back of his head. Rose Marie swivelled him around and, standing on tiptoes, inspected the gash.

'Oh Mary, Mother of God!' she said with a little cry.

'I'm alright, Rose Marie. Be quiet, will you? Can I have a cup of tea?'

Rose Marie clucked about, boiling the kettle and taking the bottle of milk from the icebox. Once she had poured some into their mugs, she wrapped the bottle in a tea towel and made Will hold it against the swelling.

'The bang's hours old now,' said Will. 'It's too late for this.'

Will didn't like how cultivated Rose Marie's hysteria had become. Had she lost all normal responses? Natural compassion. Proportional grief.

'I'm still going in to work tomorrow,' Will said.

'You can't,' she said. 'Get a doctor's note to excuse you.'

'It makes no difference,' said Will. 'They'll dock the others' wages.'

'Then let them,' said Rose Marie. 'You're not to blame for the whole world.'

She sounded so bitter that Will could hardly believe it. He stood up and put his arm around Rose Marie's shoulder. He felt her tangibly soften back to her old self.

'I've been so frightened since Aidan died,' said Rose Marie.

If that was the truth, Will was relieved. Rose Marie's nervous energy was the result of fear and probably lack of sleep. She likely lay in her bed all night and listened for the creak of the privy gate or the wet, fleshy crunch of weeds beneath a boot.

'When you're not here,' Rose Marie said, 'I'm almost always afraid.'

'There's nothing for you to worry about,' said Will.

'Are you sure?' she said.

She held onto him. The way she kept clasping at him, Will began to worry that she might feel the gun in his waistband.

'I'm sure,' he said, gently pushing her away. 'Are there eggs at all?' he asked.

Rose Marie nodded.

'Any chance of a scramble? I'm dying of the hunger.'

Rose Marie looked delighted.

'I'll make you something nice. There's even some bacon drippings.'

'That'll be grand. I'm going to wash up. I'll be down before you're done.'

Rose Marie went about making the perfect omelette. As long as she was occupied, Will could buy some time. He went up the stairs as quickly as he could without sounding suspicious. At first, he thought of hiding the gun in his own room but he had so little furniture that there was nowhere to conceal it safely. He heard a frying pan clank on the stove and knew he had to hurry. Will ran his finger around the ring of six .45 bullets as he thought. The safest place would probably be Rose Marie's room. None of the lads would dare snoop around in there.

He crept up the last flight of stairs to the attic and, for once, didn't give a second's thought to respecting Tully's views on callers in his daughter's bedroom.

He entered quietly and went over to Rose Marie's dressing-table. He opened the top drawer. It contained a disturbing collection. Will recognized some of the items instantly; others were only vaguely familiar.

There were dozens of his 'Isobel missing' cards, as if Rose Marie had sought them out across the city and taken them down as quickly as Will had pinned them up.

There was the broken piece of china Will had intended to give back to Lily as a joke one day: the piece without which the puzzle of her broken jug would never be deciphered.

There was the dead, brown remnant of a single flower – a lily – pressed between two clear sheets of plastic.

A few dozen objects Will had misplaced over the preceding months were also there; he hadn't bothered too much about them because they held meagre intrinsic value. There were matchbooks from places Will had been and – most unsettling of all because of its sheer uselessness – there was the fishbone he had pulled from the cafeteria table while speaking to Sam Fisk. The bone lay in Will's hands like a tool for which he could not imagine a use.

Will opened the second drawer and pulled it fully off its runner, placing it on the cover of her bed. There was ladies' underwear in the drawer and the slivers of soap Rose Marie hoarded but the backboard was loose and could be eased in a few inches, so that the container of the drawer was a fraction narrower than it ought to be. Rose Marie wouldn't notice that, surely? The drawer opened normally and, provided it wasn't opened too far, there was now a secret space where a hidden treasure could be stashed.

Will took the Colt from his waistband and rolled it tightly in its cloth, so it was snug and compact. He wedged it into the hidey-hole and replaced the drawer.

'It's almost ready,' sang Rose Marie's voice from the kitchen.

The thought of runny eggs made Will sick but he went quietly down the stairs and faced Rose Marie. Her eyes practically glittered with excitement.

Rose Marie looked at Will and felt the full measure of his attention on her. He seemed as nervous as she felt. There was no thought of Felicity Bell in his mind now, Rose Marie knew.

'Those look good,' said Will, sitting down in front of the plate of eggs. 'Thank you, Rose Marie.'

She loved it when he used her name. He even smiled at her. Will's whole heart was hers alone.

19

Will was so late for work on Monday morning that Lem had doused the coals in his stove and come down from the fifty-seventh floor to see what was holding the team up. Will saw that Feeney was back in the site office. He was swollen in the face and his arms looked like plump salamis; a hundred tiny sticking plasters covered the red lumps where the bees had stung him. Feeney's skin had taken on a yellow pallor but he was determined to show the men on the site that he wasn't afraid of a few trouble-stirrers or their nasty practical jokes.

Feeney was on the telephone as Will passed the door of his site hut. The man leaned out and wagged a finger at Will – indicating that he had noted Will's tardiness – but he didn't pause the conversation he was having.

'You've kept us waiting!' said Frank when he saw Will.

'So what?' said Will. He was too tired for Frank's whining this morning. 'You getting paid for piecework or something?'

Frank went silent at that.

'We still got the record, don't we?' asked Will, softening his tone but his query didn't elicit a positive response.

'No, we don't,' said Lem, shaking his head. 'Petrovski and his crew overtook us on Friday. They're up on fifty-eight already. Feeney made them the senior crew for the week.'

'Well, let them have it,' said Will. 'There's no bonus for killing yourself with the work.'

They all agreed with that in principle but some source of

pride had gone from Will, along with the quiet sense of dignity he had always displayed without ever having to try.

'We're just builders,' said Will, driving their spirits lower. 'When we're done here, they won't remember our names.'

'That ain't true,' said Frenchie. 'They're making a wall with all our names on it for the lobby.'

'Only some of our names,' corrected Lem. 'The master builders will get a mention, not us.'

Names had taken on a new meaning for Will in the past month. He had seen thousands of them: names on lists, names on cards, names in library catalogues, names on ships' manifests. But if they didn't attach themselves to a person you knew then what point did they serve?

The four men in the team walked despondently towards the elevator cage and waited for it to come down to street level. Will looked over at the workers' notice board – it had become an inexorable habit with him – and he saw what they all saw: Isobel's card was barely visible beneath the signs advertising rooms to rent and bicycles for sale and iceboxes going cheap. Even a lost cat had taken priority over Isobel. Just three letters '—bel' at the end of her first name – peeped out from behind the other postings.

Lem walked over to the board and started tearing the rogue cards down.

'Don't worry about it, Lem,' said Will.

The desolation in his voice made Frank and Frenchie stop smoking. They both looked at their boots. As one, they dropped their cigarettes into the dust and stomped them out as a sign of solidarity.

Will knew he had to find out what had happened to Isobel, even though he was entertaining the crushing thought that he would never find the girl herself. He had Lily to worry about now, too; she was vulnerable. There was also Jonas who made

Will indescribably nervous and, worst of all, Foxy Nolan was on the scene. Aidan's funeral was scheduled for the following afternoon; Will would have to attend that, and he was growing increasingly concerned about Rose Marie's detachment from the world and strengthening attachment to him.

A gun was nestling in her upstairs drawer.

Foxy imagined Will was his newest ally.

A building had been blown up by dynamite.

It had all happened since Isobel had failed to arrive only four weeks before.

Lem had almost cleared the notice board of the bits of card.

'They ought to know better, those bastards,' said Lem.

He held up a card that said TYPEWRITER FOR SAIL. RUNS GOOD.

'They gotta show a little respect,' he added.

'It's OK,' said Will.

'No, it ain't!' said Lem.

He was mad now. He ripped the notices into small pieces, leaving a wasteland of cardboard snow around his boots. Lem wiped Isobel's card across the front of his shirt and succeeded in removing some of the concrete dust it had gathered then he took four pins and placed it back in the centre of the board.

'Till you find her, ain't nobody using this board for nothing else,' said Lem. 'I'll let it be known round the site today.'

With that emphatic statement they got into the elevator and started their ascent. Will looked over at Lem as they were going up. Lem looked at him and they stood like that, not speaking, comforting each other, until they reached the top.

The sun was a blowtorch by noon. The sweat streamed off Will and the whole team worked with their shirts tied around their waists. The small sparks, like daytime fireflies, died in tiny cremations against their skin; they smudged into black commas when Will flicked at them with his fingers. For Will, the work was a numbing automation. The physical pain of pushing his body to its limits felt right, punitive. This job would last a few more months. After that, he wasn't sure what he would do. A man of his size, with his skills, needn't worry too much about finding new work. There was always the numbers rackets or the protection schemes – Will only had to make advances to the right people – but he had developed something of a conscience since coming to America, demanding from himself a new start and honest work.

Curtis brought round the water bucket and a few ladles an hour before lunch and the four of them stopped for ten minutes to sit in the bars of shade thrown down by Petrovski's team a storey above them. Will angled his body so that the slim, cool line of shadow lay across his eyes and he didn't have to squint.

'How much did you say?' said Curtis, quietly.

He had crouched down next to Will like a trench rat delivering a message along the line.

'Huh?' asked Will.

'You asked a few days back about missing girls,' said Curtis. 'How much did you say for news?'

'It was about his sister, you dolt,' said Frank.

'How would I know?' said Curtis. 'He never said nothing about a sister to me, you dolt!'

Will stood up casually and put his arm around Curtis's shoulder in a way that was anything but avuncular; the boy's tone was getting above his station. Will walked the boy away from his crew and sat him down on a girder that swung above the street. Curtis was unwilling to show his fear but the water-boys usually stuck to the sturdy walkways which had been assembled for the wheelbarrows. They were constantly nagged to stay away from the edge.

'So you've heard something about missing girls?' asked Will.

'I've just been asking around like,' said Curtis, sullenly.

'You hear anything?'

Curtis nodded his head then went rigid with fear at the sight of the taxis beetling along Fifth Avenue.

'You wasting my time?' asked Will, very softly.

There was no need to speak louder. Curtis shook his head, carefully.

'It wasn't girls, though. It was a boy and a woman,' said Curtis. 'I'm not sure if that counts.'

'Spill it,' said Will.

'How much?' asked Curtis.

Will applied pressure to the small of the boy's back, nudging him gently off-balance but not enough to push him fully.

'You won't fall,' said Will. 'That's how much.'

'OK,' said Curtis, as if he had negotiated and won, 'I've been asking around but I only heard about it now because the guy's new. He only came on site last week and it took a few days for the story to get through to me.'

'Who is he?' said Will.

'I don't really know his name on account of them speaking another language down there but he's working with the Jewboys, finishing up in the lobby. He's from Greek,' said Curtis.

'Greece,' said Will.

'Greeks then,' said Curtis and he shrugged to show he didn't care. He had to grip the girder beneath his thighs because the nonchalant gesture made his body wobble.

'He's working as a carpenter down there?'

Will had seen the superior wood coming in on trucks and he knew they were already painting and doing fine finishes in some of the lower levels. That's why the Jewish artisans had been brought in like magnanimous latecomers to do the work that got the praise.

'He's more like a carver. There's these blocks of wood for the walls and the biggest has a picture of the building going to be carved in it. I seen the drawings he's got planned and now he's making the drawing onto the wood. Etching it in like,' said Curtis.

'He's carving the lobby panels,' said Will.

'That'll be it!' said Curtis. His own vocabulary was primitive and he was always pleased when somebody deciphered his sentences. 'He's carved on some churches back home and you can tell the others think he's really something, even though they mostly speak another language.'

'How did you hear anything then?' asked Will.

'He's got a boy who sharpens his tools and hands them to him when he's up the ladder and stuff. He's also from Greeks but he's American.'

Will wondered how Curtis had come to that distinction. Was it the generosity of the young towards someone of their own generation that had allowed Curtis to bestow on this foreign boy the title of 'American'?

'He's been telling me how the old boy's sad over something. I asked him over what and he says the old boy's wife and his little son – he's got a really little son who's too young for a man so old – they were expected in last month only they didn't come. He thinks they got sent back to Greeks.'

'Why would they get sent back when he's their support?' asked Will.

Curtis shrugged a more controlled shrug this time and managed to keep himself steady on the girder.

'That's all I heard.'

Will had his doubts about the hodgepodge story. The circumstances were similar to Isobel's on the surface but this new case concerned two family members travelling together, not a girl on her own. Not an Isobel Phelan or a Felicity Bell.

'That's all I got out of him,' said Curtis.

'I'll go see him later. Does he speak no English at all?'

Curtis was disinterested now that there was no money in his errand and he was beginning to control his fear of falling.

'He can speak a little, I guess. He speaks it to the boy sometimes.'

When Will saw the panel, he appreciated how great the building was going to be. He comprehended its magnificence fully for the first time. The carving was still in a raw state – just outlines and grooves that gave impressions of its height and scale.

It was late afternoon. The site was quiet at last. The riveters had packed up for the day and the buzz-saws had been silenced. Will could hear the old man's feet as they shuffled along the rung of his ladder and he could hear him whistling to himself as he measured with a tape and made notes in pencil on his panels as to depths of carving and length of planes.

On a workbench, a sheet of paper fluttered beneath a chisel paperweight. Will looked down at it and saw a sketch the old man had made of what he was trying to create. It was his idea of what the building was going to be – a soaring, steel structure with a spire at the top and the sun behind it. Rays poured down in tangible streaks, as the beams of the angel must have rained down upon Saul's shoulders on the road to Damascus. It looked like the Tower of Babel and perhaps it was – a number of languages had built it – but it seemed to Will that this building was the opposite of that divisive enterprise. This building had brought them all together with a common aim: to construct a monument that would shine down on the city like a second luminary.

The panel was hardwood. The intention was that it should

be varnished and lacquered until it gleamed and, if the termites didn't get to it, people might look at it in the lobby as they waited for the elevators for a hundred years, maybe two hundred. This man's work was going to be the biggest panel: the one that people would see as they came deep into the heart of the building. They would walk towards it as they approached the bank of elevators to go up and the sun would be the eye of God on them from the moment they entered. The work had a power and a consoling kind of permanence.

'Yes, please?' said the old man.

He had caught Will fingering his plan but he smiled graciously down through his chest-length beard.

'It's good,' said Will.

The words didn't express his reaction to seeing the building depicted in its completion like that but Will wanted to use a phrase the old man would know. The man nodded happily.

'I work with the steel upstairs.' Will pointed up, as if to God.

The old man nodded and smiled again. Will decided to jump straight in.

'Your wife is lost?'

The man came slowly down the ladder and walked over to his workbench.

'Also my boy,' said the man.

'Where?' asked Will. 'How did it happen?'

The man didn't inquire as to why Will was asking. He was just pleased to have somebody who cared enough to ask him about it at all.

'They come on a boat from Piraeus,' said the man.

His accent was very thick and, except in the Greek part of the city, he was liable to get a kicking for that one of these days.

'They must go through the tests, you know. I wait for them

but they don't come through. I don't ever see them,' the man continued.

Will's blood thumped through his ears.

'On Ellis Island?' he said.

'Yes,' said the old man. 'But they don't come through.'

'Have you checked the hospital?' asked Will and the old man nodded.

'I got my brother who speak good English to make questions with the telephone but no, they not in any hospital.'

'My sister, too,' said Will, touching his own chest.

The old man reached out his hand and patted Will consolingly on the shoulder. His hands seemed to be made out of the papery shavings that covered the floor; they were so brittle and so rough.

'I'm sorry for you,' the man said. 'They send her back?' he asked.

'No,' said Will and then, because he didn't know what was certain anymore, 'I don't know.'

'They must have sent Thula back,' he said. 'I will hear she is well when she is home to Piraeus.'

'Her ship hasn't got back to your home yet?'

The old man shook his head.

'Tomorrow,' he said and he smiled.

Will wondered if the man would be lucky. He might still get news that his family was safe.

'Then we make new plans,' the man said and he sighed deeply. 'I hoped for America but it was all very unsure because of the boy . . .'

'Why's that?' asked Will.

'I am almost sixty years now,' said the old Greek. 'My wife is now forty-five years. She had our boy only five years ago; he is the son of old parents. He has the face of the Mongol, you know?'

Will had seen a child like this once in Gort and suspected Foxy Nolan had seen many more of them in the institutions he had called home for the youngest years of his life.

'He's a good boy,' said the man. 'A loving boy with a heart like the sea,' he spread his arms to indicate a vast expanse.

'They'll be fine,' Will said to the man.

'I know,' said the old man. 'God is good. We make new plans to be together. God is good,' he said again. 'My wife would have been fine but if they test the boy they would have said no and then she would go back with him. No choice. He is our son.'

Will was no closer to Isobel but he was developing a dread that he wasn't the only man in the city who was going through this hell. Were others following the process he had pursued over the previous weeks? Had men all over Manhattan been tacking up cards and writing letters to police stations and telephoning various bureaucratic offices, insisting on assistance and being denied? Were the authorities finding the volume too large to handle and so ignoring the complaints? These thoughts made Will go cold, as if an outdoor tap – not quite frozen – had begun to drip into the drain of his stomach.

Suddenly, Will thought of an idea he had been meaning to pursue. When he had trespassed on Ellis Island Three that night, he had made a mental note of the scratching on the odd, round window. He had tried to memorize the shapes, carving them into the surface of his own mind. He had lost the cigarette box on which he had scrawled the lettering . . . Could he recall it?

'Sir,' he said. 'Could you help me? I want to ask about some writing; I think it may be foreign.'

The old man – with his patience and his old man's grace – made an encouraging gesture with his hand for Will to continue. Will took a screwdriver and an off-cut of wood that was lying on the floor and tried to recreate the shapes. He remembered the first few letters clearly and he etched them shallowly into the soft wood with the tip of the tool. Then his memory failed and he improvised a little, knowing how difficult English would be to read if written by somebody who was forming the letters incorrectly.

After a few minutes, Will turned the small carving around and showed it to the man.

The man looked at it for a few seconds and said, 'This is not Greek letters.'

Will deflated. It probably meant nothing but he wanted to see what the rambling mind had felt was so important that it had tried, in its puny way, to reveal it to the world. What solitary word summed up what that mind had felt impelled to convey?

'It is maybe Russian,' said the old man. 'You wait just one minute, please.'

He went through the wall of hanging plastic that was preventing his shavings from drifting throughout the lobby.

A few minutes later, he came back with a boy and another man. This was probably the boy who had gossiped with Curtis; he seemed reluctant.

'This is Kolya. He speaks Greek and he speaks also English and maybe a little Russian, I think. And this is Olek. He speaks only in Russian.'

The old man handed Olek the carving and his brow furrowed at once into deep, brown ridges like a ploughed field.

After a few seconds, the Russian nodded to confirm that the language was familiar.

'He says it is in a type of Russian,' Kolya translated as the Russian spoke.

So, it had not been written by either of the two men who were there when Will had visited. They had been from Tunisia, hadn't they? Dr Challis had told him a few facts about them when he had told Will how they had tried to corner the dog on their ship. '*A ship from Tunis . . .*' Challis had said.

'Can he make out what it says?' asked Will.

Kolya passed the query on and the Russian shook his head. He babbled for a few minutes in his native tongue and Will wondered how he had managed to secure a job on the site. The Russian took the screwdriver from Will's hand and made a few alterations in the carving. Will saw at once where he had gone wrong. Now the letters looked exactly as they had done on the glass – just so.

'He says if it looked like this, it would be a word,' explained Kolya.

'So what does it say now?' said Will, wondering if it would be a girl's name, the way he had written Isobel's name all over the city.

Kolya passed the message on to the Russian and Olek gave a convoluted answer that Kolya seemed to have trouble with.

'It's like when there's a killing,' Kolya translated.

The Russian took hold of the boy's arm fiercely and spoke some more – clarifying, it seemed.

'Not just only a killing,' said Kolya. 'It says in Russian: MURDER.'

20

Contrary to Rose Marie's dogmatic assurances to the police, the Hibernian Society had been unwilling to fork out funds to bury the likes of Aidan Moran. Rose Marie had moved on to Plan B and had used a stash of cash she had found in the ticking of Aidan's mattress to purchase the cheapest plot of land she could find. It was situated in a corner of one of the dreariest cemeteries in Brooklyn. The patch was owned by the Irish Unity Society which had its headquarters on the fifth storey of a dilapidated walk-up. The Society had allocated Aidan a burial site for a fee and had given Rose Marie a map to give to the gravediggers.

Tully had called in a favour from the man who owned the ice-truck and the vehicle was dispatched to collect Aidan's body from the city morgue and drive it out to Cobble Hill. Space in the front of the truck was limited – what with the driver's Great Dane and Rose Marie in her most precarious heels – so Will had taken the subway. He had left work two hours early, sneaking out and begging the team to try and cover for him. By the time he had found his way to the cemetery, it was late afternoon but still ninety degrees.

Will made his way through pewter-coloured graveyard gates and saw that he had entered a valley of ashes. There was a construction site right beside the cemetery wall where the builders were pile driving through the old concrete of a gas station forecourt. The resulting fine, grey dust had coated the neighbourhood, so that the grass was the same colour as the pallid headstones. The flowers were dipped in chromium and the only thing that wasn't black or grey was the stripe of red lipstick that formed a thin, solemn line on Rose Marie's face. The sun made the conditions even worse. It beat on them and there were no hosemen to dampen down its heat.

Back home in Ireland, the weather conspired with funerals. The rain grizzled down on the widows; it bent the heads of the grieving willows and bowed the aspens. It rained so hard on funeral days that the churchyard paths were trodden to slurry, as if to boast of how many mourners had passed that way. In New York, the passing of humbled feet left no marks; the ground was stony. It was a city built on a foundation of granite.

Will breathed lightly but still the dust got into the gaps between his teeth, so that his mouth tasted of grainy toothpaste. Rose Marie tried to wave the powder from her face but only succeeded in creating a small, ashen whirlpool of dust like a cloud of gnats before her face.

A local priest had been persuaded, for a contribution, to say a few words but the drills hammered into the mourners' heatstroked brains and the cursing and hollering of the men on the site filtered over the wall. The priest decided to make do with a hurried prayer. The bearers dumped the coffin into the shallow hole which the gravediggers had excavated and began to cover it over. The priest tried to pat down his robes and dust flew from them in white wafts like talcum powder. The powder settled in the wrinkles around Will's eyes and mixed in with his sweat until he resembled an old man who had received the shock of bad news. Will imagined he looked like Lem with the black soot from the rivet fire in his eyes.

Rose Marie's black suit grew greyer and limper by the minute and her patent heels were turned to pumice stone as she shuffled them in the silver grass. The whole event took less than ten minutes and, under the circumstances, that was quite long enough. Aidan had always been unlucky.

Will led Rose Marie through the stone cemetery and back out onto the street. The construction noise was still bad here and Will wondered if the workers realized they were encroaching on part of the cemetery. Had they taken the bodies away and deconsecrated the ground? Will could see where they had broken through the wall of the old gas station; the new foundations they were digging were well within the boundary of the cemetery's far corner. It shivered him a little.

'They're not taking over the whole place with that site are they?' Will asked Rose Marie.

She looked behind her, puzzled.

'They can't be, can they?' she said. 'How could they sell me the plot otherwise?'

'Did it come with any papers at all?' Will asked her.

'Just this,' said Rose Marie. 'I showed it to the diggers when we arrived and they've put him where it said to put him.'

The map Rose Marie handed to Will had hundreds of numbered plots demarcated on it and the one Aidan was to have had been outlined in red pen. Will orientated the map, using the unique shape of the far wall as a frame of reference. The diggers had been way off. The site Rose Marie had circled in red was a few hundred meters to the right of where they had laid Aidan to rest. Will said nothing. The diggers knew what they had done as well as they knew that Aidan's body was going to be dug up and disposed of, as soon as that building site needed to expand. What would they do with the body? Will didn't like to think but it made him aware of the fact that bodies, though decomposing, took up space.

'Potter's Field would have been a lot worse,' said Rose Marie, self-righteously.

'When it quietens down, it'll be a grand spot. Will you ever visit?' Will asked her.

'I didn't have much heart for Aidan,' she confessed. 'He was just a boy.'

'It was good of you to see him buried then,' said Will.

He was thinking that the people who ended up in this ugly stretch of land were all alike – all like Aidan. The folks who buried them did so out of duty. The plots were the cheapest pieces of ground besides a pauper's grave and the grievers – the few there were – would probably never visit again and would likely not recognize the exact spot if they did. They would think themselves mistaken when there was a shop over where they thought their kin's grave had been. They wouldn't care too much either way. There were no expensive head-stones or melancholy, marble angels to be accounted for. Not like the grand crypts at the heart of Woodlawn in the Bronx – nothing so permanent as those memorials.

Will took off his hat and banged it against his trouser leg. A grey cloud puffed from it and he felt unbearably hot and harassed and sad. Always, there was the possibility that Isobel had ended up in a place like this. The voices of the dead whis-pered across the ashen grass and a seagull – incongruous and white as a soul – soared like a ghost . . . invisible . . . a ghost . . . invisible . . . between the tangled, wooden crosses.

Rose Marie bent down and tried to wipe the ash from her shoes. She was brightly determined to reveal their sparkling faces again and, as she leaned over, Will could see past her to a café across the street where Foxy Nolan was drinking a glass of Coca-Cola. He looked as cool as an ice-cream sundae in a pinstriped, navy suit and a natty, pink shirt.

Rose Marie looked over to where Will was gazing and abandoned the task of shining her shoes in favour of snooping. She linked her arm through Will's – the way she always did when she thought anybody might be watching them.

'That's a friend of Aidan's,' said Will, dubiously.

'He wasn't at the service,' said Rose Marie.

Will could already tell that the hurried prayer would be 'the service' when Rose Marie spoke of it from now on. There would be flowers at the service, in her mind. There would be sun and trees with shade and it would all be clean and American whenever she related it. That was what was happening to Rose Marie: a glossy American coating was being applied to every unsavoury event.

Foxy tipped his hat at them and Rose Marie impelled Will across the road towards the café.

'We should be gracious,' she said.

'It's a funeral,' said Will.

'Hello, lovely couple!' announced Foxy as they approached.

Foxy twinkled and his grooming glistened. Rose Marie actually giggled when she saw him up close and put a dusty, black glove to her red lips.

'I think a toast to Aidan is in order,' Foxy suggested and Rose Marie hurriedly took a seat before Will could spoil her fun.

'A cherry Coke for me,' said Rose Marie.

'Cherry Coke for the lady,' said Foxy to nobody in particular but then, miraculously, a waiter in a white apron appeared – as if an extra from a movie set had been shoved into the shot just in time.

'And for you, Will?'

'Water,' said Will.

Foxy didn't register the slightest disdain at Will's insult; asking for water from a man who was offering you a proper drink was less than polite.

'And an ice cold water for my friend, Mr Carthy.'

The waiter practically curtsied and scurried away.

'You missed the interment,' said Rose Marie but not in a critical tone. 'It was lovely.'

'I watched respectfully from the gate,' said Foxy. 'So dusty in there,' he added earnestly, convinced that such a trite explanation would suffice.

'Oh, that it was,' said Rose Marie. 'But such a moving service. So much to arrange.'

'And you managed it all yourself?' said Foxy, acting the awestruck innocent.

'I did!' said Rose Marie, sincerely. 'On top of everything else these men get me to do,' she sighed.

Rose Marie touched Will lightly on the jacket sleeve and he realized how tremendously she had come to irritate him.

'A woman's work,' said Foxy, 'is never fun.'

Rose Marie practically roared at that and Will was glad when his water arrived and he could gulp down some of his anger as he swallowed it.

'You came to see the site really,' said Will.

'As a fortunate by-product of the funeral only,' said Foxy. 'It's not the place we're searching for, Will. More than half those boys are good and Irish.'

'You might have asked them to stop for a few minutes then,' said Rose Marie. 'Out of respect.'

'Progress stops for nothing and nobody, Ma'am,' said Foxy.

Rose Marie concurred with a 'So true!' and an accepting nod.

At that, Foxy looked across the street and made a sharp, nodding gesture of annoyance. Will followed the direction of Foxy's eyes and saw a man standing about fifty yards away. Will hadn't noticed him before – he was discreetly tucked into the shade of a shop window – but Foxy's signal sent the man off at a jog. Half a minute later, the jackhammers went silent. Quiet flooded the street and the whistle of busy birds came back into earshot. Rose Marie clapped her hands, as if a show had just ended; Foxy made a mock bow and grinned.

'You're still keeping your eye out?' Foxy asked Will. 'And keeping your eye in?' he said pointedly. He made his hands into two guns, like a kid playing cowboys and Indians. 'You gotta practise or you'll get rusty,' he added with a mock, western drawl.

'What do you mean?' said Rose Marie.

Her eyes had become small and sharp with focus; she had caught wind of something that was none of her business and she wanted to root it out.

Foxy made the twin-shooters gesture again at Will but said, 'It's nothing to trouble your sweet head with, Ma'am.'

Rose Marie's face pinched up and her jaw stiffened with resolve.

Will had no intention of touching the gun. He remembered his determination to shoot Foxy in the head the next time he happened to run into him and thought now that he must have been very afraid when he had indulged in those thoughts. Foxy Nolan was an easy man to have a drink with and his reputation was constructed from fictions not facts, wasn't it?

Why did Foxy seem to feel he had a hold over Will and why did Will feel oddly the same way? Because they both wanted to know the truth about who had killed Aidan? Will didn't care that much about Aidan but if Jonas Trichardt was involved, as Foxy suspected, then Lily would be involved and Isobel might be, too. The police weren't going to do anything; they had probably put Aidan's file at the bottom of some dusty box and shoved it to the back of a deep shelf.

'Have you found your sister yet, Will?' said Foxy.

He said it in a way that implied he knew everything about it.

Rose Marie's fingers went still on her straw and she eyed the men from side to side like a woman at a tennis match.

'Don't pretend you know something,' said Will.

'But perhaps I do,' said Foxy and he laughed.

For no reason at all, Rose Marie laughed too. It was out of discomfort, Will imagined.

Foxy took a card out of his pocket. It was one of Will's hand-lettered cards that gave the details of Isobel's disappearance. Foxy placed it on the table.

'It's true I don't know where she is at this moment. I do hear things, though,' explained Foxy. 'I have this pack of dogs, you see. I tell them to fetch and they go out and dig things up for me. One of them came back with this the other day.'

'Isobel's gone,' said Will.

'You don't mean that,' said Foxy, in a gentle voice. 'You don't believe that, Will. People don't just disappear clean off the face of the earth. Now, I know people and I know people who know people. Together, as a team, we can find your Isobel for you. I have no doubt about that.'

'Could you?' asked Rose Marie with enthusiasm and Will thought how matter-of-factly she had told him to give up on Isobel during their one drink together in the Four Green Fields.

'I could, Ma'am. Will only has to ask me.'

Foxy eyed Will with his gorgeous, sea-pool eyes and waited. Will wanted to punch the man in his perfect teeth but he couldn't give up a chance to find Isobel because of male pride.

'If you hear anything, I'd be grateful to know about it,' Will said.

'There!' said Foxy, jubilantly. He leaned over boisterously and clanked his glass against Rose Marie's in celebration. 'That wasn't so hard, was it?'

'No,' said Rose Marie who hadn't had to eat so much as a crumb of the humble pie.

'Tell me what happened and I'll spend a little time on it for you,' said Foxy.

Will told him about Isobel leaving from Cork, about Mr Kelly's nephew seeing her off and the girl who had befriended her before they boarded. He explained how Sam Fisk had taken her name on the deck of the *Aurora* and had said she looked fine and of her last night in New York harbour before going ashore. Will related that a crewman had seen Isobel in one of the tender boats heading towards the immigrations blocks but her name had not appeared on the Ellis Island register. Will told Foxy of his attempts to get the authorities to look into the matter and Foxy made a dismissive, belittling gesture. Will mentioned his investigations but not his night trip out to Island Three.

Foxy listened intently throughout the long tale.

'I have plenty to start with,' Foxy said when Will had finished.

Will was amazed; he thought every avenue had been fully explored. He felt an odd sort of relief to have somebody as competent, if dangerous, as Foxy Nolan on Isobel's side and he wondered what the bill would be.

Foxy laid a dollar note down on the table and waved at the waiter.

'You'll see me soon, Will,' said Foxy and he tipped his hat.

In a cool, uncreased movement, he said farewell to Rose Marie and started down the street. As Foxy turned the corner and disappeared from sight, the jackhammers started up again – conjuring their clouds of dust from the concrete – as if they had been afraid to ruffle Foxy Nolan before then, as if it was a mistake to inconvenience him in any way.

Will drank the rest of his water. Some ice went down with it, tearing at the soft skin of his throat like glass, but he swallowed without flinching.

21

It unsettled Will that Foxy Nolan was as good as his word; he hadn't expected an old-fashioned courtesy like honesty from the man. Will had just come through the front door of Tully's after work on Thursday – just two days after Aidan's funeral – when the telephone rang in the front room.

Tully creaked out of his chair and answered it in a bewildered fashion. People seldom rang Tully's and the sound of the telephone bell had startled the old man.

'Hello?' Tully said.

Will listened to the conversation from his chair at the kitchen table. Rose Marie was cleaning her room – he could hear furniture being bumped around up there – so for once Will had been able to come into the house and sit downstairs in peace. The kitchen was the only room, besides the entrance hall, which had a door opening onto fresh air. There was a small, hot breeze puffing its way through the fly-screen. It was welcome, if ineffectual.

'You certainly may not!' Will heard Tully shout down the receiver.

The apparent dispute made Will listen more intently. He got up from his chair and went across the hall to stand in the parlour doorway. When Tully saw him there, he didn't hang up the telephone. He held the handset away from his body like a man holding a squalling infant and said to Will, 'Have you been giving this number out to strangers?'

Could it be Isobel on the other end of the line?

Will tore the receiver from the old man's hand.

'Hello?' he said. 'It's me. It's Will.'

It seemed as though minutes passed before the person on the other end responded. It was a man's voice when it came and the pathetic desire to weep overwhelmed Will again.

'Aren't you even allowed the use of the telephone?' said Foxy Nolan.

'What do you want?' said Will. 'I just got home.'

'I know that,' said Foxy in an irritated voice, as if he expected Will to understand that he was being followed all the time. 'There's somebody I want you to meet.'

'Who is it?'

'It's a pretty, young Irish girl, Will,' said Foxy.

His voice susurrated with secrets.

'Not Isobel, though?' said Will; he could feel his pulse thumping in his lips as he spoke.

Beside him, Tully was trying to grab the phone like a petulant toddler.

'I'll not say any more.'

'Foxy!' shouted Will and beside him Tully Tulliver froze in mid fuss.

'I didn't know!' whispered Tully to Will, clasping at him with hands like claws. 'Tell him I didn't know it was him!'

'He doesn't care, Tully,' said Will and he gently turned his back on the fretting, old fool.

'Can you get away at lunch tomorrow?' Foxy asked.

'I can find an hour maybe.'

'Good. You won't believe this . . . but she's about three blocks from your site – we'll walk to meet her together.'

'Don't meet me at the site!' said Will. 'Meet me on the corner, outside the tobacconist's.'

'Right,' said Foxy. 'Just after noon then.'

'Who is the girl?' demanded Will.

Foxy held the line open for a few more seconds, so that Will could hear that he was there but choosing not to respond. Then the exchange clicked off and the dead signal droned into Will's ear.

Will ran out onto the street and tried to see if he could spot one of Foxy's men, hanging about, watching Tully's. He knew at least one man would be somewhere nearby but Will couldn't see anyone suspicious. A firm of second-hand furniture salesmen were carrying a rolled-up rug from the tenement opposite. A barrow woman was wheeling a load of winter coats along the sidewalk. There were no layabouts, smoking suspiciously in low-brimmed hats. Will looked for the girly looking man, too – just in case – but the men all looked hard, baked to rock by the sun.

Will needed to find one of the dog pack and insist that he be taken to where Foxy was staying. He couldn't wait until tomorrow to hear if Foxy had found Isobel. At the same time, there was no way he would be told where Foxy lived unless Foxy himself wanted him to know. Foxy kept rooms in half a dozen choice hotels across the city. He had private suites in clubs and the kind of brothels that looked so upmarket they might be mistaken for Catholic Girls' Schools.

After ten minutes of fruitless inspection, Will went back into his tenement. As he passed Tully, he patted the old man on the shoulder. He felt the brittle skin quivering tenuously against his fingertips.

'You're alright,' said Will, reassuringly.

'I didn't know you were one of his, Will,' said Tully in a plaintive voice.

'I'm not,' said Will.

'What are you then?'

'I don't know, Tully,' said Will. 'I suppose I'm a new acquaintance of his.'

'A friend of Foxy Nolan's . . .' said Tully with awe and Will didn't correct him.

Foxy was waiting outside the Smoke Screen, beneath a sign that read PURVEYORS OF FINE TOBACCO PRODUCTS SINCE 1880. He had taken the opportunity to buy cigars while he waited and one of them hung unlit from the side of his mouth. Will crossed the street and approached him. He saw Foxy draw a silver cigar tube from his pocket and slide a Cuban down into it. He tossed the tube over to Will.

'Save it for a celebration,' he said.

Will put it into his pocket. It was the second time in a matter of days that a man he didn't care for had offered him an expensive smoke.

'Where are we going?' Will asked.

'You can practically see it from here,' said Foxy, as he started off down the street.

Will followed. Foxy was wearing a burgundy suit with a chocolate stripe and he looked like a Hershey wrapper or a dirty barber's pole but somehow nothing he wore detracted from his blond perfection. His hat sat jauntily on his head; the angle allowed the sun to catch one of his green-blue eyes and turn it into a panther's.

'If you happened to be looking at the right moment, I expect you'd have seen her leaving work,' said Foxy and he pointed up to where the steel frame of Will's building towered above them.

'You'd have seen her hair at least. Apparently her hair makes her easy to spot – so my boys tell me.'

Will's heart fluttered strongly. He would not let hope overwhelm him. This might be just the kind of prank Foxy would enjoy.

'We're getting closer to your sister, Will,' said Foxy. 'I can feel it.'

They had stopped outside an opulent shop on West Twenty-Seventh Street.

'Normally, I'd go in this way,' said Foxy, indicating the chrome and glass doors that opened onto the sidewalk. 'But today, alas, we're taking the side way in.'

Will followed Foxy down a dreary alley. There were trash-cans stacked along its sides; they made the going narrow. Somehow, though it seemed unlikely, there was the smell of decomposing animals. Not fish – Will was familiar with the reek of sea creatures rotting in the kelp they had dragged ashore – this was an earthier stench.

Where the bins were overflowing, thick brown sacks tied with wire had been piled on top of their lids. These wept a foul, purple-red fluid. Foxy skipped from side to side, avoiding the toxic puddles, and eventually stopped outside a door with a shiny brass bell beside it. It was the kind of bell that they sold off steamers that were scheduled to be scuttled and it looked out of place here among the rancid alley juice.

'I have arrived, Harvey!' announced Foxy to the man who responded to his convivial ringing. 'Will, this is Harvey Blix, Harvey, this is Will Nobody-You-Need-To-Know.'

'Pleased to meet you,' said Harvey.

He didn't seem pleased but he held out the white lump of flesh that was his hand. Will shook it; it felt damp and sticky like raw dough.

At first, Will thought Harvey Blix was a butcher. He had his sleeves rolled up to the elbows and he wore a rigid, leather apron around his waist. The handles of several instruments protruded from its pocket.

'Come in, I guess,' said Harvey, reluctantly.

He was fat and pasty. Sweat sparkled along the grooves of his jowls and he had a tape measure draped around his neck and loosely tied, so that it resembled a noose.

Will followed Harvey and Foxy up several flights of stairs. There were vats boiling in the downstairs rooms and Will's impression of the place swayed. At times he was sure it was a laundry and then it began to seem more like the cookhouse in a cheap hotel.

On the fourth storey, they came to a padlocked door off the landing. Harvey took a key from his apron pocket and unlocked the enormous chain that held the handles closed.

'For security only,' said Harvey – though nobody had asked him anything.

He pushed the door open and let Foxy and Will enter first.

'Don't keep her,' said Harvey. 'My girls have to work for a living.'

Harvey glared at the women who had looked up to watch them enter.

'What are you looking at?' he yelled. 'You all know your union representative here,' he said. All thirty heads in the room went down over their tables immediately; sixty hands went busily back to work.

The women were working at trestle tables. There were no chairs. They stood as they sorted a mountain of silver and black fur.

Harvey closed the door behind them, leaving Will and Foxy alone with the women, but Will didn't hear his footsteps going down the stairs. Will got the impression Harvey was waiting to escort them out, so he could lock up again.

The heat in the room was unbearable. Will tried to take in a deep breath, he was almost desperate for oxygen, and inhaled instead a mouthful of fine, wispy hair from the pelts.

It was a furrier's workshop and the ladies were marking out

the coats with chalk and matching the silk linings to the available fur.

From a neighbouring room, Will could make out the beehive drone of a dozen sewing machines. The noise never ceased, drilling on and on into his head, so that it was almost worse than the buzz-saws on the building site.

Foxy started down one of the rows. Will paused to look around the place. The windows were covered in the beige rice paper they sold for lantern-making in Chinatown. The light that came through these screens was diffused and no air seeped in. One of the windows must lead to a fire escape, surely – especially if the door was kept locked – but which one? Did the women know?

The petrified wallpaper was as brittle as ash. It spiked in patchy rosettes along the watercourse of a toilet that was leaking down the wall from somewhere above. There was a single porcelain basin in one corner and, as Will passed it and looked in, he saw a cockroach scuttling round and round in a kind of hypnotic dementia, following the lip of the plughole.

Will looked back at the door through which they had entered. He saw an enormous, steel contraption suspended on the wall above the frame. It was so rusty and savage in its structure that Will stared at it for a few minutes before he realized what it was: a bear trap – one of those antique, Black Forest bear traps with teeth the size of tiger claws running along its jawbone. The choice of this article as a form of decoration chilled Will.

He caught one of the women looking up at it and knew it meant more to them than it did to him. He saw, too, that the trap was primed to snap shut – not so much a display as a piece of working equipment.

'Harvey's quaint with the things he collects,' said Foxy over his shoulder.

He had stopped at the furthest row. This was the hottest corner and the newest girls probably had to endure it for months until they were promoted to the front of the room, nearer to the crack under the door where a sliver of a breeze drifted through.

Will didn't want to look at any of the women; he didn't want to see how young or old they were or what their eyes had to tell him. He watched the back of Foxy's head determinedly and then, as he realized that Foxy was waiting for his reaction, he turned a little and saw Isobel's face looking up at him.

Will slapped the palm of his hand down onto her table for balance. After a second, his mind told him that something was wrong. Isobel's eyes were wrong. They were a different colour and the left one didn't have its appealing, characteristic wink.

'Meet Carmel McDonald,' said Foxy.

It wasn't Isobel. This was a redheaded girl of Isobel's age and so similar to her in appearance that Will wished he could simply substitute her – go over and hold her and take her away from this awful room and care for her in Isobel's stead.

'Hello,' said Carmel. She seemed very afraid. 'I have my documents,' she said.

'None of that nonsense! We're going to luncheon, my dear,' said Foxy and he held out a manicured hand to her.

Carmel McDonald took it like an exhausted woman reaching for a rope.

Foxy escorted the emaciated girl down the stairs. As he passed Harvey Blix, he tipped his hat and said, flippantly, 'We'll have her back before dark, Harv.'

Carmel blinked like a frightened animal at the sunlight. Foxy dragged her by the hand and they crossed over Thirtieth Street and went into the Empire Diner.

'I have to go back,' said Carmel. 'I'll lose the work.'

'You will not,' said Foxy and he snapped his fingers at the soda jerk. 'Didn't you know I was your union man?' he asked.

'I didn't know we had a union,' she said.

Carmel held the menu nervously and when she looked up, Will smiled to reassure her.

Will ordered a pastrami sandwich and Carmel copied him exactly. Foxy ordered all three of them malteds, as if Carmel was ten years old instead of almost twenty. Will had to admit that she gave an impression of immaturity. There was something of the disappointed child in her. She had once expected more from life and was now too afraid to complain about it. She would never write home and tell them she needed help; she would never admit she worked in a stinking furrier's workshop.

Her letters would gild the story. And a furrier . . . that could be made to sound rather fantastic, as if little Carmel McDonald was modelling the coats on some stage-lit catwalk on Fashion Avenue.

In truth, she was a tall, narrow beam of a girl with lustrous red hair pinned back in a hairnet. She seemed awkward about eating in a restaurant, even one as brash and bawdy as the Empire.

'What's all this about?' Will asked Foxy.

Carmel grasped on that, thankful that someone else had given voice to the question that was racing about in her own head.

'Tell Will about your journey over . . . where you came from,' said Foxy.

He nudged Carmel quite hard with his arm.

'I come from Offaly originally . . .'

'And the name of the ship you came in on.'

'The *Aurora*. We docked on July 10th.'

'Bingo!' yelled Foxy and a few fellow patrons looked over at him. Foxy ignored them completely. The Empire Diner was his stage for the next thirty minutes.

Will made the connection. This was the girl Mr Kelly's nephew had seen boarding the ship with Isobel in Cork. This was the girl who had shared a cabin with his sister less than two months ago.

'You knew my sister?' he begged. 'You met Isobel? Isobel Phelan?'

Carmel looked up at him and her tentative smile became a genuine grin.

'Will!' she said and she reached her hands over the table and clasped his fingers in a tight grip. 'You're Isobel's brother Will. I should have known you from the picture she showed me.'

'Yes,' said Will. 'Do you know where she is? Have you seen her since the ship? Anything at all, Carmel.'

Carmel dropped Will's hands from her own.

'She's with you, isn't she?' asked Carmel. 'She said you would meet her at Ellis Island and take her home.'

Will imagined Isobel sharing her excitement with this girl who was so like herself – a sister, at last, to gossip and plan with.

'I think you'd better start at the beginning,' said Foxy. 'You left from Cork together . . .'

'We met on the quayside amid all the baggage and those bold boys who think they're coming over to make their American millions. We laughed a little at how similar we looked – cursed with the red hair and all that. We had such a good start with that laugh together and I knew I had a friend for the journey. We asked to share a bunk in the same cabin and they put us in together. Me on top, Isobel underneath. When the others went drinking or dancing we would lie and talk and give each other the terrors about the ship going under like the *Titanic*.'

'Was she well? Did she seem well to you?' begged Will.

'She was grand, Mr Carthy. She kept me going when the nerves took over. She told me all you'd relayed to her about the immigration process and I started to feel as if things were going to be all right.'

'And are they?' asked Will.

'I have my job,' said Carmel and that was it. That was the full extent of what America was going to give her. 'I'm lucky to be in the city. Some of the girls who took the work with Blix got sent out to a farm upstate where they breed the animals and they say there's a terrible disease you can get from the leather, if it's not treated right. They're burying the girls up there by the dozen – dying from the anthrax, they are – and their families will likely never know where they ended up.'

Carmel coughed a little and picked up her napkin. She put it quietly to her lips and Will saw her trying to wipe something discreetly from her mouth and roll it into the fabric. When she put the napkin down, tucked under the side of her plate, Will saw that it was a small, wet ball of fur like what a cat might choke up after cleaning itself.

Carmel looked embarrassed and Will pretended he hadn't noticed.

'I've never eaten here,' said Carmel. 'It's ever so grand with all the silver.'

'It's chrome,' said Foxy and he looked disdainful at this little mouse of a creature. 'Will needs to know about his sister, Carmel. He hasn't seen her since she was off the ship.'

'That's a mistake,' said Carmel. 'Maybe she'll be in the hospital, though . . .'

'She's not,' said Will, growing frustrated.

He refused to acknowledge that this lucky break might be a dead end, too.

'It was awful luck,' said Carmel. 'We were so well the whole trip and then . . .'

'What?' said Will, brusquely.

'Isobel goes and gets sick on the very last night.'

'With what?'

'They said the pink eye was going around. Consumptivitis or something like that.'

'Conjunctivitis,' said Foxy.

'That's the one,' said Carmel. 'It came up sudden. The afternoon we sailed in she seemed fine but that night she started rubbing her eyes and I said, "You must be tired out from all the excitement. After tomorrow there's no more worries, Is. Just Will waiting for you and America." And she said, "My eyes are burning so much I doubt I'll get to see it properly." When she woke up the next morning, they were all gummy and swollen. She looked dreadful and I gave her my spectacles for the inspection, hoping they wouldn't look too close and they didn't. The young man just filled her name in and we thought it was all going to be well.'

'When did you see her last?'

'We got up the stairs and into the hall and they started to separate us and Isobel got taken to one side and me to another. I didn't see what happened to her. I waited for her with my aunt and uncle for an hour at the greeting gate until we had to go. When I asked, they said she might have been taken to the hospital and that I shouldn't stay any longer. Isobel had my address and she promised to write but she never did. I thought it was one of those friendships that flourish in the sea air but don't stand up to the excitement of new things. I thought she'd been distracted and . . . well, I was just grateful we'd been kind to each other on the voyage and that she didn't have to find out where I'd ended up.'

'It's honest work,' said Foxy.

He tried not to sound too condescending, though Will could tell he thought Carmel's work was the lowest of the low.

'Yes,' Carmel said, 'I'm ever so lucky to have it.'

'How did you find her?' asked Will when they were about to separate outside the tobacconist's. It was time for Will to go back onto the site.

'Friends at the shipping office, friends everywhere,' said Foxy.

'It's not exactly like you found Isobel,' said Will, trying not to let Foxy get too self-satisfied at his own prowess.

'We're getting closer, though, Will,' said Foxy. 'Closer and closer.'

That unnerved Will. He thought about the rusted bear trap hanging above the women's heads in Blix Furs.

'If you wanted to, you could help her,' said Will.

'Is that my job?' asked Foxy. 'Saving my kinsfolk from their own stupidity. Am I my sister's keeper?'

That was a jab at Will. He felt its sharp point enter his chest.

'I think you are,' said Will. 'I think we all have to be.'

Foxy tried to brush Will's conscience away with the brim of his hat.

'You wouldn't keep your dogs in a place like that,' persisted Will.

'My dogs make me money,' said Foxy.

'If it was in my power to help her, I'd do it,' said Will.

'I'll tell you what . . . I could do it on your behalf and then you'd owe me another favour. You're getting quite a tally going with me, Will.'

'Do it,' said Will. 'I'll pay what's owed.'

Then Foxy – seeming to think better of the deal – said in a flat voice that suggested he was annoyed at his compulsion to be decent in this matter, 'Never mind. It's already done. She starts as a maid in my hotel next Monday.'

He crossed the street before turning back and shouting at Will, 'And there's nothing in it for me. No offence to your sister, Will, but I've got no use for redheads myself.'

Will couldn't stop his mouth from smiling. Foxy's stride resumed its bounce as he hailed a taxi and his hideous suit disappeared inside.

On the subway home, Will started to feel angry. Angry that Carmel hadn't been Isobel. Frustrated that he seemed no closer now than he had been at the beginning. Why couldn't Foxy be finding Isobel a decent job in a fine hotel instead of helping Carmel? Then Will thought about the bear trap and something inside him was relieved that Isobel had avoided Carmel's fate. Whatever had happened to Isobel, she had evaded that: whoring and sewing for the rich, and the anthrax disease and an unmarked grave in an upstate farm.

Will suddenly wanted Lily; he wanted her body to take it out on. Her hot, gasping breath and her sweat against him. He needed her intensely. He would go to Lily tomorrow. After work, he would simply get up from his seat in the train and exit the carriage. He would leave at the first convenient, connecting station. The decision, now that it was made, was a relief beyond measure.

22

Will had to convince Mrs Harrigan to take a message in to
Lily. She was home; Will had seen her shape coast past the
series of windows in the exact same way the spectre of
the seagull had floated between the cemetery crosses at
Aidan's funeral. Lily hadn't seen him standing on the street,
though, and he had decided to go round the side of the house
and knock on the kitchen door. Will felt naked without the
cardboard tube of site plans and tender documents which had
always offered him a legitimate excuse for visiting. Mrs
Harrigan's bulk blocked the kitchen door and Will asked if
Mr Trichardt was at home.

'He's out,' said Mrs Harrigan.

She tried to shut the door but Lily must have heard Will's
voice by then because she hurried into the kitchen.

'Mr Carthy!' Lily said and she feigned surprised.

'Mrs Trichardt,' said Will. 'Your husband asked me to
come about the garden.'

'He did,' said Lily. 'I was expecting you tomorrow, only I've
gone and got the days mixed up again, haven't I?'

She shrugged and gave Mrs Harrigan her sweet, incapable
smile. Mrs Harrigan let out a sigh of recognition at Lily's carelessness.

'The spot I'm concerned about is just over here,' Lily said.
'And I'm sure you're the man to do the job.'

Lily came down the back kitchen steps at a skip. She seemed
so incredibly at ease. Will realized that she was an accom-

plished liar and felt uncertain of her. Mrs Harrigan stood at the top of the steps, rubbing her dry hands on a dishtowel, over and over again.

Lily was in pink – a floating, gauzy dress that smelled of rosewater and pearls. She was barefoot again and her hair was pinned up with half a dozen pink barrettes; it was still a little damp from a wash. She looked like a pale waterlily – half air, half the iris-coloured smoke that rises from low streams in autumn.

She walked Will over to the creeping lilac and touched it with her fingers, making gestures, as if to indicate that she wanted it cut and trimmed.

'I have to talk with you,' Will said.

'That wretched woman is always here,' Lily said. 'Mrs Harrigan was Jonas's nanny. She's the wall that has ears in this house. I have missed you, though. You left in such a hurry after the party.'

Standing beside her – so close, but unable to feel any stretch of her skin with his fingers or his mouth – was cruel.

'Can you meet me in the park?' Will asked her.

'I can take a walk a little later.'

Mrs Harrigan's shadow had moved away from the door-frame but still Will didn't risk a kiss. A dozen windows looked out over this garden and all of them were masked in the sunlit reflection of the birches, so that a face watching from behind them would be invisible.

Lily smiled at Will lightly and he did something he never imagined he would ever do to her: he spoke harshly.

'Don't smile at me! My sister may be dead and your husband's likely in on it. Just meet me at the old boathouse near Belvedere Castle and bloody hurry up about it.'

Will pulled out of her orbit and stalked across the grass, leaving Lily clutching a fistful of lavender – which was turning from sweet to pungent this late in the season – and with her mouth a little way open.

Mrs Harrigan came down the steps as Will passed the house; she was holding a letter. So, she had been watching all along.

'Mr Trichardt asked me to give you this when next you showed up,' Mrs Harrigan said. She handed Will the envelope. 'Like the proverbial bad penny,' she added.

Will snatched the letter from her and tore it open as he went down the secret slip of pathway at the side of the house. There was a typewritten sheet inside, perfectly centred by an efficient secretary. It read TERMINATION OF ERRAND SERVICE. ENCLOSED PLEASE FIND A FINAL PAYMENT IN LIEU OF NOTICE.

Will didn't like the use of the word 'termination'. It seemed heavy-handed, considering how light his workload had been. At the bottom of the sheet, slanting crookedly across the page, was a note in a gentleman's hand; the lettering was so convoluted and fine it was difficult to read. Its sentiment – when Will deciphered it – was simple, though: Thank you, Mr Carthy, your services are no longer required.

Lined up beside the note was five hundred dollars in new twenty-dollar bills.

Some romantic fool had designed the swan boats. In the late 1920s, they had been all the rage – cumbersome two-seater pedaloes with their bodywork fashioned from white plastic, so that they resembled enormous swans. The fool had imported the idea from the lake on Boston Common and, for almost a decade now, every wealthy, just-married couple had insisted on having their photograph taken beside them. The way the newlyweds in the Lower East Side had posed in front of Tully's door for their cheap, solitary snapshot – which usually showed a groom with a tight collar and a bride looking plump and regretful – so the Park Avenue wedding parties had seen it as quaint and rustic to sit side by side in one of the swan boats before moving stoically forward into their fiduciary partnerships.

The two boats were easily damaged by vandalism and rot and there was no City money with which to maintain them. They had been relegated to an old boathouse on the shore of Belvedere Lake and they bobbed on the building's strange, enclosed tide and disintegrated slowly, their skeletons showing through their peeling paint. The lock had been smashed off the boathouse doors months before but the building was so ruined that there would have been any number of other ways to access it.

It was dark and cool inside. Through the stolen planks of the boathouse door, Will could see the sunlit water of the lake beyond. The two boats creaked eerily and bumped into each other, the antithesis of grace.

Lily kept Will waiting less than ten minutes. She called his name twice from the boathouse door and he dropped the cigarette he was smoking into the scummy water and let her know where he was. She climbed in through a hole in the siding. She was wearing flat shoes, at least, but still she skidded in the mud.

'Is this where they went?' she asked nobody in particular.

She ran her hand along one of the swan's white sides but it came away black; secret soot had stained it.

'I have a wedding picture taken in one of these,' she said. 'It looks ridiculous. I'm embarrassed about it now.'

Will respected the fact that Lily could recognize what a cliché she had become. He caught a glimpse of the girl she must have been before – fierce and poor and perhaps more than a little brave.

'I'm sorry for my mouth earlier,' Will said.

'I'm not shallow really,' said Lily. 'I only pretend to be.'

'Well, don't pretend to be on my account,' Will told her.

'You reminded me of my father back there in the garden and I admired him a great deal,' she said. 'He earned whatever he had and he worked every day of his life for it.'

'A descendant of Lafayette,' said Will, remembering what Jonas had told him.

'Hardly,' said Lily. 'Jonas claims to have traced my family tree and come up with proof of my regal ancestry. Nonsense of that sort means something to him.'

Lily put one of her feet onto the baseboard of the boat.

'Will it float with me in it, do you think?' she asked Will.

'I believe it will,' he said.

At his word, Lily put all her weight into the boat and plopped down onto the seat. She reached forward and caressed the swan's neck. Its face was a tortured twist of metal; the plastic prettiness had worn away. Lily herself looked as lovely as ever but Will felt an odd discomfort – seeing her so close to such an ugly thing.

'This is a secret place,' she said. 'Like there's no world outside and, if we opened those boathouse doors, we'd drift out into nothing but ocean in all directions.'

'If you have a secret,' said Will, trying to help her still, 'you could tell me now and it could stay here.'

'With the swans,' she said.

'Let it rot away with them.'

Lily liked the idea of that but she still wasn't ready to talk.

'My sister's name is in your husband's study,' he said.

Lily's eyes came up wide and dark blue into his.

'Your husband had a folder on his desk and I glanced through it that day he nearly caught us together. I saw her name written down there: Isobel Fay Phelan. That's what I was trying to tell you at the party the other night.'

Lily shook her head.

'The folder is probably still there,' said Will. 'You could look it up, see it for yourself.'

'What kind of folder was it?' she asked.

'A blue one with the sign of a golden door on the front,' he said.

Lily shook her head even more fiercely.

'It can't be your sister then,' said Lily. 'I know what those folders are about,' she added and she clasped her hands in her lap and prepared to tell him. 'There are several of them.'

Will felt the air push out of him; his lungs scrabbled for it.

'They're usually in his safe, though. One for each month of the year since it began. So, there must be four of them – May, June, July and now, a new one for August. I don't know how you saw one left lying out.'

'How do you know about them?'

'I asked Jonas what they were,' she said, 'and he told me straight out.'

'What is it about?'

'Jonas has always taken me to their meetings, ever since he brought me to New York: the American Eugenics Society. There are some nice people involved, all very intellectual and fine. Not everyone is rich either,' Lily said it as if she was trying to excuse them. 'They spoke about the future and it was awfully bleak. This was way before the Crash, too – maybe as far back as the mid-twenties. Jonas has always had money, of course, and he had his various building projects but this idea of heredity and human make-up seemed to fascinate him: why some men succeed and some don't.

'The War had got him started on it, you see. He had been asked by military intelligence to attempt to justify the use of Negro troops and he had concluded that they did have their uses, as infantry and in the front lines. Jonas had made a study of their central nervous systems and he had learned about their brain capacity and apparently, scientifically, their brains are different. I don't understand it. I don't know if I quite believe it even . . .' Her voice held a begging note.

'Go on,' said Will.

'They can't take care of themselves,' she said. 'Have you seen them? They're wretched. They're squalid and stupid.'

'Negroes?'

'No,' she said. 'All the inferior nations and races.'

'We were both squalid once,' said Will. 'By Jonas's standards.'

'But we weren't stupid,' said Lily and the edge in her voice sounded like a razor cusp. 'Their diseases spread. Their epidemics rage through the poor first but they ultimately engulf the rich and educated, too, just like the Great Influenza after the War.'

'Influenza killed my mother,' said Will. 'And my stepfather.'

'You see!' said Lily, desperately. 'Jonas sympathized with the most radical members of the group. The bravest of them began to hold small meetings in our home and the homes of other men – at Titian Decatur's and the Metcalfes' – and discreetly, they began to approach the government.

'Some of the men were policy-makers and they drafted the National Origins Act. Jonas was one of the behind-the-scenes designers of that. It was supposed to put the onus for medical screening on foreign ports. We wouldn't let anyone into America until their own country had passed them as fit; that helped a lot – immigration levels dropped – but other countries don't care the way we do, you see. They keep sending the infirm and the unbalanced to us; they aren't strict enough. And then Margaret Sanger began to campaign about family planning and that seemed the solution . . .'

'Margaret Sanger's organization is involved?' asked Will,

trying to postpone where this was heading, trying desperately to stop it reaching its terrible conclusion.

'No,' said Lily. 'Not at all, but her ideas, taken further, made sense. She has a very levelheaded solution for preventing disease and the proliferation of the feeble-minded. It's only about people like them, Will, not like us – nobody healthy. That's why I know you're wrong about your sister being one of them.'

'What are they doing to them, Lily? Tell me. I have to hear it now.'

'They're sterilizing them,' she said.

In Will's mind, there was suddenly an image – as if in a movie – of Isobel strapped down on a table. An ether mask came down to cover her screaming mouth, her long, flailing legs went slowly slack and then the surgeon loomed in over her like a great, white gull.

'No,' Will said.

'It's for the best,' Lily whispered. 'It's the most humane thing.'

'No,' said Will again.

'It makes sense, Will. They will never bear damaged children. Plenty of States have laws authorizing the same kind of thing but here we do it quickly and quietly and they usually know no better. They go on to lead happy, normal lives afterwards.'

'How is that possible?' asked Will.

'They get sent back on the ships once it's been done. That way, they don't spread their diseases globally. They won't perpetuate their destructive traits here in America or back where they come from. It's an unofficial policy that's cleansing the world.'

'Unofficial?' said Will.

'Most people wouldn't accept it even though it's for the

country's good. It's obviously kept very quiet. It's not govern-ment-sanctioned really but, if they don't approve, where is all the funding coming from?'

Will needed time to deal with the shock. Somewhere he had known the truth would be as awful as this.

'You sterilize them against their will?' he asked.

'I don't think so. The doctors do try to get their patients to sign a paper of consent but most of them don't have the intellect to understand . . .'

'Who gets chosen?'

Will thought of all the people in the lines on Ellis Island, all the chalk marks on the backs of their coats.

'Only the feeble-minded and those with genetically-linked diseases.'

'And the people with physical deformities? The cripples? The hunchbacks? The deaf?' he asked.

Lily seemed shocked.

'No, Will! Those things aren't generally passed from mother to child. We're only worried about the children. We want America's babies to be healthy. If their babies are going to be OK, we leave them. Those conditions you mentioned are only unfortunate, not inherited.'

'Who decides what's inherited and what's not?'

'The doctors,' said Lily. 'The surgeons and the professors. They're working so hard to find cures but . . .'

'My sister!' said Will; it was a howl of grief.

'She's fine,' said Lily through her tears. She was desperate for him to understand. 'We'll find her. I'll ask Jonas which ship she got sent home on and why. If there was nothing wrong with her then she's fine.'

'It could have been a mistake,' said Will. 'She had a lazy eye and she caught conjunctivitis while she was on the ship. That might look like this eye disease they check for – this trachoma thing. The examinations are so quick!'

'Either way, Isobel's fine. She's not a candidate for sterilization because trachoma isn't passed on genetically, neither is conjunctivitis. She would have been in the hospital and then sent home. I'll find out for you.'

Will needed time to think.

'She didn't go home,' insisted Will. 'Not on the same ship she came in on.'

'They use all the Gateway liners,' said Lily. 'Titian Decatur was one of the first to allow his ships' passengers to go through the special screening for selection. Isobel could have been given a berth on any one of his ships.'

'They do the surgery in the hospital on Ellis Island?'

Lily nodded.

Will was remembering how uncooperative Dr Challis had been. Where had all the patients been housed when he had visited, though? There had only been those few beds with people in them . . .

'Only the best surgeons are employed. The patients are up and well again in a day or two: men and women. It's because of the babies, Will!' Lily said and she pulled a small booklet out of her handbag.

Will glanced down at it, not sure he could take any more in. At the same time, he was almost relieved. What he had stumbled on shouldn't have resulted in Isobel's death. If she had been sterilized through some tragic error, they would deal with that together. He didn't know how but they would. Isobel would not be allowed to suffer any shame because of it. She might still be alive; that was a distinct possibility now. Will only had to find her and explain that he knew what had been done to her and that none of it was her fault.

The pamphlet Lily had given him was from the Margaret Sanger Society. It was called *How to Plan Your Family*.

'It's how not to have a baby,' said Lily. 'It's how I learned to prevent pregnancy. I go along with everything it says because I know what it's like . . .'

Will looked at her earnest, stricken face and understood it all.

'There was a baby,' he said.

'He had no arms,' said Lily. 'Only little stumps like stunted wings. He died.'

A tear slid down her cheek. Only one. The grief was deeper than salt water, deeper than the sea.

'We think,' Lily explained, trying to keep it very detached and empirical, 'that it was because of Jonas and the gas they used on him during the War. We never risked another baby. I called him William. That was why I asked your name when I first met you – I'm so fond of the name William. You're only Will but that's close enough for me. Jonas held him, right after he was born, and he just slipped off to sleep and never woke up again.

'I didn't care that his arms were missing. I suppose he would have minded, as he got older. I would have loved him just the same but Jonas always says it was for the best and that no other mother in America is going to have to bear a baby like William. Because of me, they will be spared it.'

Will reached out to touch Lily but she gently shrugged him off. He remembered the soft, plump perfection of Isobel as a baby in his boyish arms. She was the only infant Will had known, the only one he had held and made safe, and she had been perfect. Her baby's face had been wise-eyed but bewildered like an old man in a busy room.

Lily pushed aside her own sadness and focused on Will's instead.

'I will find out about Isobel,' she said. 'Even if you never want to see me again.'

'Look for another girl, too,' said Will.

Lily nodded and wiped her nose on a tissue, calming down.

'The girl's name is Felicity Bell. I just want to know if she was one of them. She was supposed to arrive here in early July.'

Will didn't know why he asked Lily to do this. Only that Isobel and Felicity might be together somewhere and he wanted that to be true. Will had so much to think about now. He looked over at Lily and tried to generate some other emotion to the one he always felt when he was near her – an intense and painful tenderness – but there was nothing else. He thought about Jonas and the baby and he thought about their veranda near the sea.

Will thought of Foxy Nolan and he knew what he was going to do.

'Are there any new maps in the house? In among your husband's papers?'

'The ones you bring?' she said.

'I won't be bringing them anymore,' Will said. 'I mean other maps I haven't seen. Check his safe when you look for the folders and bring them to me.'

Will relayed his address and Lily nodded.

'I want to know by the weekend,' Will told her. 'I want this to be over. And when you've decided what you plan to do about me – if you want to be with me – I want to hear about that, too.'

Behind Lily one of the swans from the lake sailed in through the boathouse doors, seeking solitude and shade. Lily did not see it. It paddled silently beside the old swan boat, as if a swan spirit had come back to visit its corporeal remains. It drifted there, sleek and silent as snow, and then it skimmed out again – a brief visitor, a sudden soul, there and then gone.

'I could give you a baby,' Will said.

It came out without premeditation or intended malice. It might have been the cruellest machination a man could devise for Lily at that moment but it wasn't intended that way. She took it well. She knew Will had seen, as she had, a cradle between them and railway tracks that led to two chairs on a balcony overlooking the sea somewhere. A place that was golden and far West of where they now were.

23

Will didn't sleep much that night and, for some reason, neither did Rose Marie. Will heard her footsteps creaking back and forward above his head until they became the metronome for his own insomnia; he heard her move furniture and open cupboards in her constant restlessness.

He played back Lily's words in his head, her justifications. How big was this seeming conspiracy, and was it a conspiracy if the men in power had given it their sly nods? How high did it really go? It was surely too big to have been hushed up but, then again, rumours could be silenced – the way news of the warehouse fire had been. If Will went back to the police with this new information and asked them to investigate, would they take him seriously or would their seniors tell them to leave it well alone?

Will imagined Jonas's explanations: 'The man's obsessed with my wife, Officer. Just ask her. Ask our cook, Mrs Harrigan. He's lost his sister recently and made a nuisance of himself all over town. Ask Dr Challis out on Ellis Island; ask Commissioner Oak. They'll all tell you Mr Carthy's unbalanced. He's Irish, too, so it's likely he drinks. Ask the men in the Four Green Fields about that. He's also probably involved in the murder of a young man he disliked who lived in his building. Ask yourself, Officer, if Mr Carthy's not a prime suspect in that business. As for me, I live off the Park. I'm designing a new system for the whole world.'

It all looked very bad for Will and the more he thought

about it – though the thinking sickened him – the more Foxy Nolan seemed to be the only man Will could turn to. It had come to this: Will needed protection from a man who had a distortion of the heart. Will knew Foxy's dog pack was watching him. He felt their eyes on the back of his shoulders, sensed their cool shadows sliding around corners and into doorways as he approached – slick as eels and just as quick among the reefs of the sordid streets. And still, at the end of it all, there might be someone who knew where Isobel had ended up. An insane asylum? A women's hospital? Or had the anaesthetic used during the procedure accidentally killed her? Will's knowledge of medicine was poor but he had heard of mistakes like that. Had Isobel made her way home to Ireland but been unwilling to seek out familiar places in case they reminded her of her soiled dreams of a small home and a string of children?

Theories and explanations ran through Will's head for hours until he glanced over at his clock and saw that it was almost six o'clock. A few minutes later, Will heard the sound of the ice-truck coming down the street. There came the familiar sharp shrieks of the iceman's steel hook as it was thrust into the ice-brick, so that it could be dragged from the flatbed and dumped onto the doorstep.

The new baby in the back tenement started to cry and, for such a small creature, the sound it made was powerful. Its scream drifted; it hung in the air the way sharp, sunlit dust does. The sound didn't settle even when it stopped.

The light beyond Will's square of window was turning sour. For a few minutes, it was hard to tell if it was dawn or if night was coming – those twilight moments when a new beginning or an end are equally possible. Will made his choice.

*   *   *

Foxy accompanied Will to the site that Tuesday morning. He was dressed like a Spanish pimp in a purple suit with matching dress shirt and tie. Will didn't know where a man might buy such a suit but Foxy wore it happily. Foxy lacked the cane that would complete his ensemble but his gold fob chain was as thick as his baby finger and it gleamed almost as vividly as the gold spike that curved from his thumb ring.

Will was dressed in a suit, too. As soon as Frenchie and Frank saw him approaching, they started to shake their heads in disbelief. Frenchie took off his cap and hurled it down onto the floor in frustration.

'What the hell is this?' said Frank.

'Go up and get Lem,' said Will.

'You're not dressed for work!' observed Frenchie. 'Damn it, Will, we've been carrying you for weeks, months even. Ever since . . .'

He gestured towards the notice board where, true to Lem's word, Isobel's card was the sole message to the site. The shape of her name resolved Will.

'Go up and get Lem,' Will said again and Frank, cursing, went into the elevator and slammed the door shut, so that the cage shook.

'If Feeney sees him we're all for it!' said Frenchie, jerking a thumb at Foxy Nolan.

'We're all for it anyway,' said Will. 'Don't you get it? We build fast to keep our jobs and the faster we build the faster the place is finished and we're out of work then anyway. How much of your wages have you saved, Frenchie? There's a depression on. How long do you think you can keep body and soul together when this job's done?'

'You're starting to sound like a Bolshevik, Will. A man's gotta work. I can't lose this job. Not for you or your poor sister or whatever it's about. I have a kid!'

Frenchie was pleading – an enormous man in ridiculous, short pants. He looked pathetic. Will felt embarrassed for him.

'This is about kids,' said Will. 'I promise you, it's not about me.'

'Go!' shouted Frenchie. 'And get that waster out of here before Feeney sees him with us. Jesus, I'm begging you, Will.'

It was too late. Feeney came out of his site office with a baseball bat and strode towards them. His face and arms were still covered in allergic welts and scraps of sticking plaster.

'How are you feeling, Feeney?' Foxy goaded the man. 'I hear you tasted a little of my sting.'

At first, Will thought Feeney was going to swing at Foxy's head without saying a word; it would have been better for Feeney if he had done just that. Instead, the foreman paused and gave Foxy the second he needed to pre-empt Feeney's strike. Foxy swung his hand up and sliced through Feeney's cheek with his spur, leaving a thin line of red that looked like no more than a graze for a few seconds until it opened up and split apart like a ripe cherry, pouring blood. Feeney went down on his knees and Foxy took the bat right out of his hands.

If there had been a few more men around, they might have taken their foreman's side (or they might not) but Will had planned his arrival for a few minutes after eight fifteen, and most of the builders had already gone up in the Otis and were noisily working above their heads. Feeney was rolling on the ground, groaning and clutching his face when Lem and Frank arrived back on the scene.

'Jesus, Will!' said Lem. 'Who are you mixed up with?'

'You know who I am,' said Foxy, straightening his silk tie. There was not a bead of sweat on his face and he flipped the bat lightly from hand to hand, as if checking the grip for balance before swinging it again.

'I know of you,' said Lem with his mature, calm voice.

It was the voice which, Will realized, had been one of the few reasonable ones in his life for the past weeks.

'Will's out,' said Foxy. 'Your team is through here.'

'You didn't have to come all this way to tell us that,' said Lem. 'And shame on you, Will. You ought to have told us yourself.'

'I didn't bring him for moral support,' said Will. 'I've made a deal with him.'

'Then God help you,' said Lem and he stood upright. "Cause it's a deal with the devil.'

Foxy increased the speed with which he was tossing the bat.

'There's jobs for all of you,' said Foxy. 'Secure work.'

'Cat houses or breweries?' said Frenchie, sullenly.

'Building work in Brooklyn,' said Foxy. 'Secure for a year and that's a few months longer than you'll get out of this place.'

'Hey, I live out in Brooklyn,' said Frenchie. 'It'll be a short commute.'

His alliance shifted that easily.

'They're building over a cemetery,' said Foxy.

'Sounds like charming work,' said Lem. 'Who's the foreman?' and he looked at Will like a father bitterly disappointed.

'Not me,' said Foxy.

'Well, that's something at least,' said Lem.

'Is Will coming, too?' asked Frank but he asked Foxy, not Will himself.

Foxy looked questioningly at Will but found his answer on Will's tired face.

'Will's got a few things to tie up then he's off to pastures new.'

'So you came back just to sort us out with the jobs, Will?' asked Frenchie.

'Something like that,' said Will.

'It pays seventeen dollars a day,' said Foxy. 'And it's union rules all the way.'

'That's a rise!' squealed Frank.

'Show up on Monday,' said Foxy. 'And here's a goodwill payment to prove it's on the up and up. Just in case this job doesn't come through for you with wages for this past week.'

He pulled out a roll of fifties, thick as a fist, and peeled off two notes for each of the three men.

'I was hoping I'd see this job through,' said Lem and he looked up at the way the building's skeleton was crawling into the sky above them.

'I thought I'd be able to take in the view from up there when it was finished,' said Will.

'You can,' said Frank, buoyantly. 'When it's done, it'll all be open to the public and we can go up and view the whole world from a safe balcony.'

Somehow that wouldn't be the same. Will felt as if he had neglected to see something very important through. The rivets at the top wouldn't be his. It seemed like a failure that he would never walk out again at that height with nothing around him but the wind and nothing below but a slim strip of steel and the black ribbon of street.

Feeney gasped at their feet, 'You're all done anyway,' he flustered. 'All of you. Get off the site.'

'I left my fire stoked,' said Lem, wistfully.

'Someone else will put it out for you,' said Frank.

'Get out!' said Feeney from his hands and knees.

Foxy, as if irritated more than irate, cracked the bat down

on Feeney's back. It splintered near the handle and he threw the split remains down on Feeney's unconscious body.

'They probably buy those bats from China,' said Foxy.

'That's the truth!' said Frank, delighted to have someone else asserting his own bigotry.

Foxy led the four of them off the site.

From Fifth Avenue, Feeney's body wasn't visible. As he passed the foreman's hut, Foxy leaned in the door and spoke to Feeney's secretary.

'Your boss wants you, honey-pie,' he said and he flashed his brilliant smile.

Frenchie and Frank patted Will heartily on the back and wished him good luck. They were swimming with wealth and prospects. Lem walked off in the opposite direction. Will called out a 'Take care, Lem!' after him but the older man didn't turn around.

Lily was standing on Orchard Street when Will turned the corner. She was as out of place as if a peach tree were still growing there – in the middle of the concrete against the back-drop of black fire escapes. Will wasn't sure how long she had been standing about but her hat and her gloves made her wealth as obvious to spot as if they were sewn from twenty-dollar bills. Will saw that there was a roll of papers under Lily's arm and she held her purse casually, unaware that the tenement windows hid the eyes of desperate men.

Will took Lily by the arm and pulled her up the front stairs to Tully's doorway.

'Come inside quickly before they beat me and rob you,' he said.

Will looked into the front room. Tully wasn't in but Will could hear water running in the courtyard basin, so Rose Marie was probably out there doing the washing.

'Go up to the fourth floor and into my room,' Will said.

Lily obeyed him and took the stairs without a word. She didn't touch the wall or the handrail, Will noticed, but neither did she seem as shocked by the place's modesty as she might have been. Tully's was probably closer to home for her than where she currently lived. It was hard to remember that she had been born on a dirt road when all her slips were cream silk trimmed with black lace and all her dresses were finished by hand.

As if he had rung one of the bells that protected the laundry lines from thieves, Rose Marie was instantly aware that Will was in the house.

'You're home,' she said, coming into the kitchen and wiping her hands on her apron. It was the way a new wife might greet her husband.

'We're out of soap and so is the corner shop. I've sent my father further afield to look for some,' Rose Marie said.

'Use the bar I gave you,' Will told her.

Rose Marie's face fell. He had disappointed her once again and she was tired with the constant ups and downs of his moods.

'That was a gift,' Rose Marie said and she touched her heart in a gesture straight from the movies, one that said his words had actually hurt her there. 'It was a token of affection.'

'It was not, Rose Marie,' Will said, angrily. 'I stole it because it was there for the taking and I didn't have anybody else to give it to. Use the bloody thing and stop saving it up for a day that isn't coming!'

Rose Marie's face went still; her composure had returned. Her eyes gave no expression away – they registered neither shock nor loss.

'It's because of her,' said Rose Marie.

For a second, Will imagined Rose Marie had caught a

glimpse of Lily sneaking up the stairs and that peek was what had prompted her words but then he saw that she was speaking in vague terms.

'You would never have dared to talk to me like that a few weeks ago, Will Carthy. This new girl's changed you.'

'No woman's ever changed me except maybe Isobel,' Will said. 'She changed me back when I was a boy and the loss of her has changed me now.'

Rose Marie didn't want to show Will her ace. Didn't want him to know that she knew the strumpet's name – Felicity Bell. She would shock him with that later, when he least expected it.

'You talk of that sister of yours as though she was your secret love,' said Rose Marie. 'I'm starting to think there's something disgusting about it!'

Will turned on his heels and went up the stairs. Rose Marie clambered after him. As he passed his own door, Will noted, thankfully, that it was closed. He marched right passed it and up into Rose Marie's room. The bar of soap sat on her bedside table on its doily shrine. Will picked it up and slapped it into Rose Marie's hand.

'Use it!' he demanded. 'It means nothing.'

Rose Marie spun out of the room, her dark hair coming loose from its pins and giving her the look of a harpy. Her shoes banged on the stairs and, after a few seconds, Will heard the back door slam behind her.

'Is everything OK?' asked Lily when he got back down to his room.

She had the sense to speak in a whisper. She was sitting on the end of Will's bed; there was no other convenient place, not even a chair. She looked forlornly down at the gold buckles on her peach-coloured shoes.

'It's fine,' said Will. 'She had the wrong idea, is all.'

Lily pulled off her gloves and threw them down on the bedspread with a sigh.

'She was your girlfriend in the park that day.'

'No, she was never that,' said Will. 'I never let her think it either.'

'I feel you've let her down for me. I'm sorry for her,' said Lily.

'Don't be. I'm not to blame if she got it wrong.'

'We do get it wrong sometimes,' said Lily. 'Men never understand that. We want to believe that what you say, even casually, might be a promise.'

'I never said anything casually to you,' said Will.

He was thinking about his promise of a baby and so was Lily.

'You brought something?' he said, to move the conversation away from the impossibility of them and towards the possibility of Isobel.

'It's a map but not like the ones you bring. It shows more geography. There are a few actual place names.'

'What's it about then?'

'It's the new project. A hospital, I think, where they can do the procedures.'

Will frowned.

'They have one of the biggest hospitals in the country out there,' said Will. 'They don't need more space. It's half empty now. I've seen it.'

Lily held up a folder then. It was a Golden Door folder.

'Is that the one with Isobel in it?' Will asked.

He was afraid that Lily would say that she had looked but that Isobel's name wasn't there. She would accuse Will of imagining the whole thing.

Lily nodded her head. She didn't turn to Isobel's name,

though. She opened the folder and said, 'This is the other name you asked about. Here, for July . . .'

Lily handed Will the page and he saw at once what she had found. Printed third from the top was a now familiar name. BELL, FELICITY JANE, it read. The compilers had included the girl's middle name; Will hadn't known it was 'Jane'. He wondered if the person who had made her 'missing card' had even known it.

Lily looked ashen.

'So this Felicity Bell's name is there and so is Isobel's. What do you think that means?' asked Lily.

'It means they take the girls somewhere,' said Will. 'The young and pretty ones, it seems, after they're sterilized. Maybe they send the men back home, and the children and the older women, but they keep the girls for some reason.'

'Not as prostitutes,' said Lily, quietly.

It wasn't really a statement; more a question of whether Will thought it was a possibility.

'I don't know but I'm going to find out.'

They pored over the map again.

'Do you recognize the place?' Lily asked.

Will looked carefully at the map. The edge of Governor's Island was shown and so was Liberty Island. The place where construction was underway was Ellis Island Three. There was no doubting that, even though there was no name indicated on the map. The shape was so unique – there were the three bars of the 'E' and the spinal causeway that linked them.

'It's Ellis Island for sure. They're building out there even though there's no space for new buildings.'

'Could they be building inside an existing structure?' Lily asked.

It was the possibility Will and Foxy had considered. Foxy

Nolan's dogs – Aidan among them – had been trying to sniff out the location for months but they hadn't found it. Now it turned out that the secret building site Foxy suspected and Isobel's disappearance were both linked. They were two halves of the same puzzle like the two halves of Lily's jug but the missing piece was still missing. What was the function of the new building?

'Will Carthy!' Rose Marie's voice tore up the stairs in a shriek.

Will left Lily frozen over the map and opened his door just wide enough to make sure Rose Marie had remained at the bottom of the stairs. She was standing on the flight below him with her hands on her hips.

Rose Marie, in an act of spite, had gone out to the stone basin, pushing another woman out of her way, and had searched her laundry basket for the filthiest pair of her father's drawers she could find. She intended to use Will's soap on them. It seemed apt. Spite roared delightedly through her as she began the familiar process of rubbing the grey drawers along the washboard but then . . .

'You can keep it!' yelled Rose Marie and she hurled the soap up the stairs where it hit Will full in the chest.

Will fumbled for the bar and managed to get hold of it. It didn't feel slimy enough to be real soap. The water was making it slick but the bar itself was completely intact, strangely dry and firm.

'It's not even real soap, you liar!' Rose Marie screamed. 'It's only wax. A useless bar of wax and nothing more.'

24

The night was a perfect co-conspirator. It settled like black lacquer in the recesses of the tenement walls and kept the rings of the streetlights small and tight. Will and Lily walked the few miles across the Lower East Side to the quays near Battery Park. They avoided the park itself which had grown dense with human forms, made animal and unafraid by the setting of the sun. Will was keeping Lily close tonight – she could help him search the vast buildings on Island Three. If there were any girls hidden out there, Will would need Lily's help to calm them down and formulate their escape.

All Will wanted was to find Isobel and possibly Felicity. He would move out of Tully's the very next day and take his girls West. He didn't want to confront Jonas Trichardt or Titian Decatur; he didn't want to have to convince the police of wrongdoing or face a wall of governmental silence. He wanted his sister; the authorities could go to hell. The Golden Door committee could do what they liked with the rest of their diseased immigrants. Will was no crusader for the innocent, only those innocent who were his. Innocence was a vague notion anyway. Those other victims had unfamiliar names.

When they reached the Hudson, Will forced Lily into a narrow doorway and went off to scout for a boat. She was pliant and eager to follow his direction but she was strong, too. Will saw that now. Lily didn't shriek at shadows and she walked with purpose and without cowering.

Earlier that evening, after Rose Marie's screaming had stopped and she had abandoned Tully's for the solace of the Four Green Fields to sulk, Will had gone back up to her room and selected a few dark garments for Lily to wear. He had found her a pair of Rose Marie's walking shoes, too. The morose ensemble dulled Lily down; even her yellow hair was pushed up under a black cap. She looked like a guttersnipe or a cutpurse, hiding there in the doorway, and Will hoped the harbour police didn't find her with their searchlights.

Will slid along the walls of Castle Clinton and hurried along the concrete river wall. The small boat he had taken the last time – God, that seemed like years ago – was no longer tied to its cleat and Will had to settle for a larger, noisier option. Its outboard was more powerful and riskier but it was the only choice – the boat tethered alongside it was a coast-guard cutter.

With his target vessel secured, Will turned back towards the spot where he had left Lily waiting. While he was still a few hundred yards away from her hiding place, he saw an apparition hanging over her, a pale ghost glowing in the thick shadows. As he got closer to the doorway, Will saw that the tall, white shape which hovered behind Lily's shoulder was Foxy Nolan in a floor-length cream cashmere coat – just the thing for dockside enterprises. Foxy was puffing on a cigar and the red harbour buoys illuminated the cloud of smoke that swirled from its tip, so that the haze around him seemed to burn with an unearthly fire.

'Terrific kit for secrecy, Foxy,' said Will in a harsh whisper.

Lily melted with relief when she understood that Will knew the man who had approached her.

'I don't have to skulk about, Mr Carthy,' said Foxy with a chuckle. 'I rent a mooring not far from here where I keep my boat. Would you care to join me?'

'We're going out alone,' said Will.

'You and this charming creature?' Foxy asked, waving his cigar at Lily. He didn't wait for Will's response to his question. 'That's an impressive force. INS security will quaver at your arrival, no doubt.'

'I don't want trouble with you, Foxy. I think my sister's out there.'

'And I think my building's out there and I want to see what's so special about it that honest Irish New Yorkers couldn't have been entrusted to build it.'

Will didn't want Foxy to know about the sterilization solution. It seemed to allow him a glimpse of some part of Isobel's body that was intensely private.

'We're just scouting tonight,' said Will.

'Me, too,' said Foxy. 'So, please, make use of my boat.'

Will nodded curtly and Lily followed the two men down to a pier where the wealthy kept their sailboats. The vessels' wooden hulls shone beneath their silky tallow; they went out in small, moonlit flotillas for champagne cruises in the summer and were chained together in long sad lines for the rest of the year.

Foxy was alone but never unaided. Shadows conspired obsequiously at the edges of Will's vision. When Foxy was around, there were always subtle movements on the periphery and Will guessed there were four or five men hovering nearby in case Foxy was ever under threat.

'Just the three of us are going,' said Will. 'Any more and it'll be too obvious we're there.'

'There are only three of us, Will,' said Foxy and he smiled. 'Do you see anyone else?'

Will shook his head and Foxy rubbed his hands, obviously delighted that his troops had maintained their invisibility.

Foxy was as adept on boats as Will himself. Together,

the two men handled the pleasure craft like a practised crew.

'We might start a boat business in St Augustine's when all this is over,' said Foxy, noting the ease with which they worked together.

Will ignored the comment but considered the sentiment. Foxy Nolan made him anxious yet the man was likeable, too. He had a composed capability and a casual fearlessness that spoke of power. Will had a sudden desire to feel powerful; over the past few weeks he had suffered under a sense of utter helplessness.

St Augustine: they could rent boats to the tourists, take them on marlin fishing trips out into the blue-black Atlantic off a sugar-white beach. Lily would be waiting when they returned. She would hand Will a whiskey, her tanned belly beautifully swollen. Those dreams would have to wait for whatever would be discovered tonight but as the bow waves frothed under Foxy's acceleration, Will felt a buoyancy he had thought was lost forever.

Instead of making for the nearer side of the island, the side visible from Manhattan, Foxy nosed his boat in between two others on the staff quay of Island Three; it looked as if it belonged there. The best place to hide was in plain sight, Will thought.

Foxy stepped boldly up onto the pier – no wading through water to arrive in secret for him. He took an empty soda bottle from a stowage box on the deck of his boat and lobbed it up at the single lamp that lit the docking area. It smashed against the lamp's metal hood and the light bulb popped and fizzled. No dogs barked; no heavy boots came running.

The three of them hurried in a tight knot towards the buildings. They had disembarked on the far side of the island, the New Jersey corner, the side Will hadn't reached during his first escapade, and just ahead of them were the two large buildings. The furthermost structure – the one Will had identified as the heating plant for the facility – had no windows. Its smoke stacks were still against the dark sky.

They searched around this mammoth block and came to a concrete bunker attached to its exterior wall. There were no windows in this structure either.

Foxy fiddled for a few minutes with the lock on the solid doors; he had a contraption made of slender wires that he flicked continuously in the tumblers – a skeleton key, something Will had heard of but never seen. After nearly fifteen minutes, during which time Lily had sagged down to sit on the wet grass, the lock made an audible click and Foxy opened the door. There had been no point to the exercise: the room led nowhere. It was filled with huge tanks marked with hazard symbols. The pipes from their nozzles ran along the interior walls of the bunker and into the building but there were no gaps surrounding them through which a human body might squeeze its way in.

'It's only some chemicals for the hospital,' said Foxy. 'Damn it!'

The tanks looked like massive boilers. They were silver and cylindrical and reminded Will and Lily simultaneously of Jonas's oxygen supply.

They moved on to the second massive structure. This one had windows and Foxy and Will peered through them in the same furtive manner Will had employed weeks before. Lily was between the two men. Although she was too short to see through some of the casements, Lily's height gave her a unique view of the building's structure: she saw the subterranean level first. She grabbed Will's arm when they were halfway along and pulled him down beside her. Foxy crouched, too.

'Basement,' said Lily and she pointed out the row of six,

slim windows that ran along the wall at grass level. Foxy pulled at each of the catches but they all had large padlocks – still brassy and new from the store – clasped round them.

'Could you fit through?' Will asked Lily. 'If we broke one?'

Lily shook her head. The windows were only about six inches high.

'If there's a basement, there's probably a coal chute some-where near here.'

Will was beginning to feel that it was hopeless and he could see temper rising in visible, red streaks up Foxy's throat, even in the dark.

'Here,' whispered Lily, harshly.

She had heard the sound of her footsteps grow suddenly hollow beneath her and she looked down to see that she was crossing two wooden doors that lay flush with the lawn.

'The old coal-cellar doors,' she said.

Foxy went to work on the padlock. It was easier to trick than the one on the bunker room and its clasp snapped open in a few seconds.

One by one, the three of them dropped down into the cellar. Will risked the spin of his lighter wheel when their entry was greeted with silence. In the small light of the flame, the three intruders could see that the room they had entered offered good cover. It was the Immigration Department's storage facility for lost property: thousands of suitcases left by travellers or unclaimed on the landing station once immigrants had cleared through the inspection process. There were duffels which had probably been left on the ferries, and battered trunks and cardboard boxes, and blankets tied around bundles of possessions. It was rudimentary baggage and it stretched for miles. It looked as if this cellar ran the entire length of the two biggest buildings on Island Three and from floor to ceiling it was packed with this worthless debris of human diaspora. The room stank worse than any inspection line. Will couldn't imagine why the New York Immigration Service was keeping this garbage.

Foxy had ignored the storeroom in favour of the far stairs and he had already pushed the door into the main building open a crack to see if anyone was about.

He waved at Will and Lily to catch up.

'This place runs on a skeleton crew at night,' said Will. 'Last time there was just one nurse, I think. No guards, nothing.'

'You've been here before?' asked Foxy, impressed.

'I never got this far. I just scouted around from the outside.'

'Looking for your sister?' asked Foxy.

Will nodded.

'Not for my building?' Foxy pressed.

'We weren't in partnership back then,' snarled Will and Foxy smiled his toothpaste-selling smile.

'Is this the place you searched?' asked Lily.

Will nodded. 'Island Three,' he said. 'Where they keep the contagious arrivals.'

'What?' yelped Foxy and he wiped his hands along his cashmere coat.

'They're in the hospital building down the other end,' said Will. 'The East end.'

'So this must be where they do it,' said Lily. 'The procedures.' Her voice sounded contrite in the darkness.

'What procedures?' asked Foxy.

'Nothing that affects fair hiring practices in New York City,' said Will.

Foxy, completely unexpectedly, stepped out into the corridor. Light spilled through the open door into the storeroom and Will and Lily shrank away from it.

'There's nobody out here,' said Foxy in his normal voice.

'Jesus Christ!' whispered Will. 'Keep your voice down.'

'Seriously, there's no need,' said Foxy.

He leaned back into the cellar landing and pulled Lily out into the garish light.

'It's totally empty,' she confirmed back to Will.

The corridor smelled like a hospital. It was painted a soothing shade of blue and every thirty feet along its length, a chair had been placed with a stand beside it that housed a fern and a few old movie magazines. Once, Will might have stolen one of the magazines and rolled it into his jacket; usually, he would have ended up giving it to Rose Marie when he had read it.

Foxy began to check a few of the doors that were closed on the corridor. Will and Lily did the same.

'Don't let a pox victim jump out at you,' said Foxy as Lily's fingers began to turn a knob. She stopped at once, suddenly considering what Foxy had said.

'Wouldn't they be locked in?' she asked.

'This is all wrong,' said Will.

He flung a door open and saw the same set-up he had seen on the wards of Island Two. There were rows of neat beds with unrumpled pillows. Beside each bed was a table with a washcloth and a bar of soap, prominently displayed.

Foxy's voice cut in. 'This is no goddamn hospital.'

'It is,' said Lily. 'It's a sad one.'

'Then where are the patients?' asked Foxy.

Lily frowned. 'Maybe there were none today. I told you the policy was working, Will . . .' she said hopefully but her voice had no spirit.

'Hospitals have valuable equipment stored in them,' said Foxy. 'Men like me are always on the lookout for valuable equipment so, believe me, if this place was a hospital, it would be better secured than this. Have you seen any operating theatres, any of those machines they use, any drip stands and the like?'

Lily looked up and down the bright, blank corridor.

'But Will said he saw patients here,' said Lily.

'I only actually saw one,' Will said. 'A rabies patient or just a plain lunatic. Maybe he was here for show, too.'

Will thought of the man chained to the wall. His snarling had been enough to terrify anyone. There had been no guard dogs on Island Three the night he had visited. Except that maybe the authorities here kept their guard dog inside. He might not be a real dog but the service he performed offered an equal deterrent to snoopers.

'There was definitely a nurse about when last I came, though. I saw her dinner set out, so keep your voices down,' said Will.

'There's nothing to steal here,' said Foxy. 'I want to find my goddamn building!' he yelled and his face contorted unexpectedly into a mask of such vitriolic rage that Lily stepped back, having seen the true nature of the man for the first time.

'Then why all the locks?' she asked.

'Because they're hiding something here,' said Foxy. 'Something they don't want to get out.'

'Then surely there would be guards,' said Lily.

'You're right. There must be guards,' said Foxy.

Paranoia leapt into his green eyes and he looked all around him, as if expecting to see something that he had missed before, but there was nothing new in the shining corridor. Foxy reached into his pockets and pulled out two of his favourite Colts with their trademark ivory handles. The weapons were so ludicrous that Will almost found himself believing they were harmless movie props.

'They're watching us,' said Foxy. 'They're waiting for us to make our move.'

Will knew better than to tell Foxy to settle down. The man waved his six-shooters in the air and Will could hear that Lily's breathing had taken on the rhythms of conscious control. She was making the air go in and out of her lungs by sheer will of mind.

'We're in the second biggest building now, right?' asked Foxy.

'Yes,' said Will. 'There was that one without windows we couldn't get into. That's closest to the boat, then there's this one.'

'So that windowless building is back this way?'

Will nodded. Foxy spun around and looked down the half-mile of corridor to the far end. He started backtracking towards their boat.

There were two huge doors at the end of the corridor.

'No windows,' said Foxy. 'That must be our building. That's the ruse building they're working in.'

Lily and Will hurried after him; Will put his hand on Lily's arm, requesting with the pressure of his fingers that she avoid getting too close to Foxy. Their feet were as loud as bells tolling on the chessboard tiles. The din didn't stop echoing around them until a few seconds after they reached the doors and paused.

Outside the steel doors at the end of the corridor there was a basket – an old-fashioned, homely, handcrafted basket made of butter-coloured weave. It was enormous, as large as a stew pot, and piled into it – nestling like eggs on a snowy towel – were dozens of bars of the soap Will had stolen for Rose Marie.

Rose Marie's words came back to Will. '*It's only wax. A useless bar of wax and nothing more.*'

Will picked up a bar and felt it. It had a logo stamped into it. A small image depicting a pair of open hands – the kind of appealing branding a toiletries company would place on its products. Just like Foxy's face had been used to sell *Gleam*, so might a manufacturer choose a pair of outstretched hands as a symbol of cleanliness and beckoning on a bar of soap. Even to someone unfamiliar with the English language, the logo said, 'Join us. You are welcome.'

Will felt a trickle of sweat run down his forehead. The image was similar in style to the golden door on Jonas Trichardt's folders of names and Will knew that particular image was only a lure. The invitation was treacherous; Jonas's quarter-open door led somewhere terrible. The doors ahead of them now led to the same place.

'Why would they give them wax soap?' asked Will of nobody in particular.

'This whole place reeks of a set,' said Foxy. 'That soap there doesn't have to be real, it only has to look real. That way they can use it again and again. Like in the movies; it's only a prop.'

'But why soap?' asked Lily.

Foxy knew about enticement but he wasn't in on this diabolical deceit. He shrugged casually and stuffed his two firearms into the waistband of his trousers. Foxy rested his free hands on the steel handles of the doors in front of him, preparing to swing them open and discover the secrets of the room for himself . . .

But it was Will who suddenly knew the answer.

'You give them soap to make them go in,' he said.

25

The windowless building was a shell. Its exterior walls concealed another building – a box inside a box – just as Foxy had suspected when he had heard rumours of a secret construction site. Foxy entered the outer box first, followed by Lily. Will came in last – he had the most to lose to whatever they might discover within.

They found themselves wedged in a narrow vestibule. It looked innocuous enough. There were two sets of doors almost immediately inside the ones through which they had entered. A sign hung above each of the doorframes, lettered in exactly the same way all the hospital signs in the Ellis Island compound were lettered. Simple black words on a white background read *LADIES' WASHROOM* and *GENTLEMEN'S WASH-ROOM*.

Below these words were pictures, rudimentary black silhouettes, of a woman and a man for those immigrants who didn't read or whose first language wasn't English.

Will leaned forward and quietly opened the door demarcated for women. He wasn't sure if he expected bodies to tumble down on him or a concealed cache of bones to spill out and clatter like dry stones to the floor but when the doors swung back, Will felt almost disappointed.

'Like it says on the door,' said Lily. 'It's a washroom.'

The room was enormous. There was a low, tiled wall running down its centre, bisecting the space into two halves. Along both sides of this wall and along all the perimeter walls ran rows of white porcelain basins – there were about sixty in all.

'Bloody enormous washroom,' said Foxy.

'I guess they're processing hundreds a day,' said Lily.

'Thousands,' said Will.

'It's all way off,' said Foxy.

His fox's nose was sniffing out inconsistencies. He walked along the echoing rows and fingered the faucets on the basins. They were stainless steel.

'I washed in a dozen rooms like this as a kid,' said Foxy.

Will imagined the grim institutions and the cold, stone floors under Foxy's little feet. At the hands of priests and policemen and welfare officials, what might a beautiful boy like Foxy have been subjected to?

'There's something wrong here,' continued Foxy. 'There's one thing I always remember about communal washrooms and this isn't right . . .'

'What's that?' asked Lily.

Her voice was hushed with something like awe. Foxy held the stage and Will could see his power as an actor. What a career he might have enjoyed. Foxy held his hand up for silence and there was silence – absolute stillness in the cloying night.

'No dripping,' Foxy said. 'Not so much as one worn washer and no rust on the porcelain. You always get that sort of orange corrosion in institution basins, believe me. The tap heads get stained.'

'But you said it looks really new,' said Lily. 'No time for rust yet.'

They looked down at the flooring of steel mesh that acted as a drainage mat a few inches above the real concrete screed.

It was Foxy who spoke the second inconsistency. 'Haven't you looked at the basins?'

Will and Lily both stepped over to them and looked down.

'No plug holes,' said Will. 'No drains.'

'Try the faucets,' suggested Foxy.

Lily tried to turn one of the taps. It didn't budge.

'Soldered shut,' said Foxy. 'But they're connected up.'

Will knelt down behind the basin and saw the copper piping running from the faucet through the walls.

'Not to water but to something else.'

'It looks like a washroom,' said Lily, refusing to allow her mind to speculate.

'And this looks like soap,' said Will, and he dropped the bar of wax with a clatter onto the grid.

Up ahead, Will suddenly saw the small, round window – like a porthole – he had discovered on his last expedition. The window looked out from this room at the wall across the alley. Will touched the glass with his fingers; the pane had been replaced. The lettering was gone. There was no catch on the window, Will noted. It wasn't for ventilation; it was more like a viewing window. If he stood outside in the alley, a man could stare in but nobody, except the women in this room, would be able to see him looking.

Will, Lily and Foxy walked together towards the back of the immense compartment. The ceilings were low and the room felt cramped. Why had they done that when they had space enough within the enormous exterior structure to do what they wished? Huge cavities in the ceiling, covered by bolted grids, concealed the entrances to ventilation shafts.

The two sliding panels at the back of the room had a thick, rubber seal where they met and Foxy and Will, pulling with all their might in opposite directions, just managed to break the vacuum which held them together. With a hiss, the doors pulled apart and rolled into cavities in the walls to reveal the entrance to yet another chamber.

Will already had a suspicion of what they would find in there; he had seen the chimneys pumping out their black smoke that first night he had snuck ashore. There was a wide conveyor belt almost immediately inside the sliding doors. It ran along at a height of two feet above the ground for twenty yards and it led up to the steel maw of a giant incinerator.

'What does a hospital need a burner like that for?' said Foxy, distractedly, before his excitement took hold of him and he went off into a fit of finger-snapping. 'We've found it, Will! This is what your lads from Canada have been building – all these secret rooms. I reckon with this amount of steel and plumbing there's four months of riveting work here easy and they've built this engine from scratch. It's a one-off.'

Foxy ran his hands along the sides of the immense incinerator.

'I said I thought they were steelmen when I saw their clothes,' said Will.

To his own ears, his voice sounded dead now – dead because of a dreadful realization – but he kept talking, amazed that the inanities of speech would still come. 'They had all those little burns in their trousers just like Lem does.'

'You did say that!' said Foxy. He snapped his fingers again, delightedly. 'I remember you saying it. You're a regular mastermind, Will.'

'But Foxy,' said Will, 'this place is finished. It's operational and my guess is it's been working for months, so . . .'

'So why are they still bringing men in?' said Foxy. 'You're right.'

'Because there's another one,' said Will, in shock. 'Somewhere else. This place isn't big enough on its own. They must be building another incinerator somewhere close by . . .'

Will thought about the dozens of smaller river islands, unused stretches of the Jersey shore, miles and miles of vacant warehouses along the riverfront – they could be building a second incinerator anywhere. Will knew what the Golden Door was all about now. Even in his worst nightmares, when the lowest evil he could imagine came clawing at his eyes in the dark, he had not guessed this.

'Could it be anaesthetic they're pumping through?' Lily asked; her voice was ineffably soft, articulating this last, paltry hope.

'Don't you understand? They don't sterilize them, Lily,' Will said, turning to her. 'That seems almost merciful now. I can't believe I imagined that was the worst thing they could do.'

Lily looked at him blankly. She was still wandering aimlessly around the empty room. Suddenly, the incinerator belched and blared into life. Lily jumped at the unexpected sound but nothing could startle Will. The temperature in the room, though the mouth of the incinerator itself was closed, changed palpably. Heat was almost instantaneous.

'Hospitals have waste they need to dispose of, especially in a contagious ward,' said Lily. 'And after operations there are . . . Well, sometimes there are parts that need to be burned. It's better than burying them; it's more hygienic. It must be for the waste, Will,' said Lily.

'Yes,' said Will. 'It's for the waste.'

The poem came back to him, '*The wretched refuse of your teeming shore . . .*'

There were no definitive clues that people had passed this way. There was no smell that could rise above the whiff of strident antiseptic which drenched the chamber – that indomitable formula favoured by boarding school matrons and the sanitation workers who swab out station lavatories.

Will looked down at the conveyor belt again. It was so new that its black leather band still had sheen; its cog heads hadn't yet been dulled by grease. Will might have been able to convince himself that what Lily said was plausible. She believed that what she was saying was true, that was certain, but even as she was saying it, Will spotted something that confirmed his basest speculations.

It was an innocuous item in the right context but here, in this sterile room, it was as damning as blood on a thug's blade.

Clipped to the conveyor belt, at a diagonal angle, was a ladies' hairpin – a thin, brown twist of tin designed to keep a curl in place. Drugstores and milliners and haberdashers all over the world must sell pins like it by the million. It had snagged, as pins like that are apt to do, on the free side of the belt. The machine had rolled on perfectly well with it attached there. Unless a worker saw it and removed it, it might have rolled harmlessly through the cogs a hundred thousand more times.

Will pulled the pin off the edge of the belt and held it in his hand. Did Isobel wear pins like that to keep strands of her red hair out of her one ever-so-slightly-lazy eye? She might. Will held it up to Lily and Foxy and they both stared at him, as if he had gone quite mad. Then, as was his quirk and habit, Will placed the hairpin in the pocket of his coat and it settled there – the tangible proof of an inconceivable truth.

Isobel was dead.

It was unlikely that the pin had belonged to Will's sister or to Felicity Bell but it had belonged to one of the hundreds – Jesus, the thousands? – of women who had passed this way, their gassed bodies dragged along into the all-consuming fire.

The Golden Door committee did not ship the sick back to their countries of origin – of course they didn't. Who would foot the bill? Not the likes of Titian Decatur whose shipping line would have been bankrupted by such an altruistic enterprise. Nor did they attempt to cure those with serious ailments. Dr Challis didn't waste his scientific brilliance on treating contagion; he only sorted through it and catalogued those worthy of a chance. Then, he disposed of the rest. It was expedient and, humanity aside, it made sense.

Most of the arrivals they pulled from the immigration lines could be nursed back to health on Island Two in a matter of days. Those who remained – the unfortunate ones with incurable conditions – were marched over to Island Three where they were asked to leave their belongings at the foot of a beautifully made bed. How enticing those beds must have looked to travellers who had slept in steerage bunks for weeks. The founders of the Golden Door policy wouldn't need many staff sympathetic to their cause to handle the disoriented subjugates.

Will could almost hear the nurse's voice, '*Just place your luggage at the foot of a bed to reserve it. We know you're unwell and you can rest just as soon as you've washed. Take the soap . . . That's right. Each one of you has your own bar. Take the soap and go in to wash. Cleanliness is next to godliness – have you heard that saying? Just beyond those doors. Do you see them up ahead of you? Yes. That's good. Go in . . .*'

Will put his face in his hands and started to cry with great, heaving sobs of grief.

'Christ Almighty!' said Foxy and he looked helplessly over at Lily.

Foxy didn't see it yet.

'Don't you understand?' said Will. 'They gas them here. Those canisters outside – the ones being stored in the bunker – their pipes run in through the basin faucets. The gas is poison. They execute people and, after they've vented the washrooms, they come in and load the bodies onto this belt and make a production line into the fire.'

Lily stood stunned. She looked behind her to the women's washroom and back at the incinerator, as if she was trying to come up with another theory that might explain the bizarre configuration of apparatus.

'No,' she said. 'It's only so they can't have babies. It's only operations, Will. The people are fine after.'

Will attacked Lily then.

'Your husband annihilates them!' he roared into Lily's face. 'It's a massacre!'

Will shook her so violently that Foxy had to drag him off.

'You're telling me they're killing people in masses here?' Foxy asked Will.

It seemed bizarre that this genocide would offend a killer who preferred to pick his victims off one-by-one, but Will's words blanched Foxy's tanned face to a paler shade.

'The ones who are really ill. The ones they take out of the lines on Ellis Island . . .'

Foxy was quick on the uptake, '. . . Because it's getting too expensive to keep them. And it's too expensive to treat them, especially since the Crash. The shipping lines don't want to take them back. We don't want to support the useless ones here. It stops diseases being spread across the world . . .'

'Maybe they try to cure some of them,' said Will, 'but the hopeless, the most wretched, end up here. And the mistakes end up here, too. Like my sister,' he said. 'They made a mistake with Isobel. She had a lazy eye and then conjunctivitis, too. You know how fast the medical exams are. They must have thought she had trachoma. Either that or the judging's becoming indiscriminate and they're just filling number quotas.'

'It's not perfect yet,' said Jonas Trichardt. 'We're experiencing start-up problems.'

His voice came to them from the washroom but soon the

squealing of his wheeled cart and his physical presence caught up with his words.

Foxy's hands went straight to his sides; he pulled his coat closed around him to cover the guns.

'There are some glitches in the concept. Basins aren't ideal, you see. When they figure out what's happening, they try to block the faucets and then the whole process takes longer. They stumble around for a good few minutes before they succumb.'

'And they have time to scratch messages on the windows,' said Will.

'Quite,' said Jonas.

'Jonas,' said Lily. 'Tell them. Tell them it's only for the babies.'

In her desperation, Lily didn't try to explain away her presence there. Her obvious infidelity with Will had become so appallingly trivial in the past few minutes.

'This is Lily's husband,' Will said to Foxy. 'This is Jonas Trichardt. You've been watching his house. He's the man who designed all this.'

'I'm only one of a like-minded team,' said Jonas, modestly. 'I was only called in because of my skills in moving people. The policy itself originates a lot higher up than me.'

'You followed me?' asked Lily.

'I always do, my love,' said Jonas, gently. 'Though usually I have someone do it for me.'

'You're the one who's been building without my say-so and without my men,' said Foxy. As always, he was fixated on his own agenda.

'And you're the gutter-bred union agitator my men keep telling me about,' said Jonas. 'Doggy something.'

'Foxy,' said Foxy. 'Foxy Nolan.'

'Ahhh,' said Jonas. 'Foxy. That's it. I knew it was some kind of animal anyway.'

Jonas's approach was painfully slow and his squeaking wheels sounded like howling wolves in the barren space.

'Lilian,' said Jonas. 'It's about time you understood it fully because it's all for you really.'

Lily's head moved like a metronome. She backed away from her husband, as if she could back away from the reality of what she was hearing but, after a few steps, she hit a wall and couldn't avoid it any longer.

'You kill people?' she asked.

'It's a war,' Jonas shouted to her; he enunciated each word slowly and carefully as if intimidating a child.

'You killed Will's sister,' said Lily. 'I bought her opera glasses, so she could see her future.'

'Oh,' said Jonas and he rolled his eyes sarcastically. 'Well if I had known it was Will's sister, I would have called the whole undertaking to a halt.' Jonas swaggered around in a small circle, carrying the irony to humiliating lengths. 'I mean, what is the salvation of a nation when Will's sister is at stake? I mean, have we dared to misdiagnose some little, Irish slattern who will fill this world with a slew of retarded, illegitimate, broken babies . . .'

'Don't talk about my baby!' shrieked Lily and she went for Jonas's face with her nails.

The weight of Lily's body hitting him unexpectedly knocked Jonas off-balance. If she'd had the strength, Lily might have tried to tear his throat out but she was exhausted by the size of his iniquity. She scratched at him and his lip tore open, bleeding down his chin. She kept punching at his chest until he slapped her hard and threw her aside. Will went towards him but Jonas manoeuvred his oxygen cart between them and began to move in sly circles like a man charming a snake from a basket.

'We do have security here,' said Jonas. 'The guards on Island Two have been informed of your intrusion but I've told them I'll take care of it. They probably think it's just kids who've come out here looking for an adventure. We don't allow many staff on Island Three; there's nothing much to guard but, on some nights, there is a lot to see.'

'So you're taking me and Will on?' said Foxy with a chuckle.

'My man is outside,' said Jonas.

'The man who murdered Aidan?' asked Will.

'That boy was a menace,' said Jonas. 'He was constantly sneaking around the dormitories asking questions about my business. The little bastard spoke with some of the workers we were using out here. They were Canadians and we used different teams every week. They came in on rotation, so nobody ever saw too much of what was being constructed. They never got the whole picture, and what would they care if they did put two and two together? It isn't their country that's going to the dogs . . .'

Jonas looked right at Foxy when he said it and Will thought to himself, 'Doesn't he know not to look a dog in the eye like that?'

'We're going to the papers with it,' said Will.

'No way!' said Foxy. 'We'll settle it here.'

'We own the papers,' said Jonas.

His lip was still bleeding and his breath was rasping. His damaged lungs heaved inside him and it looked to Will as if the demon in possession of him was trying to blast its way out of his chest.

'We'll tell the world about you and about this,' said Lily.

'Why do people always threaten that? As if the public will

be outraged?' Jonas pointed a finger at Foxy and Will. 'America hates you!' he screamed.

'America just hates in general,' said Foxy.

At that, Will took Foxy by the top of his arm and started to encourage him and Lily back towards the exit. Jonas shook his head in amazement at their retreat.

'I am not ashamed,' Jonas shouted after them.

Foxy stopped walking at those four words. Will sensed a change in him and stopped, too. The dandy was quite gone; the Irish immigrant was back. Everything went very quiet in the chamber. The only sound was Lily's low and constant grizzling.

'What did you say?' asked Foxy.

'I am not ashamed!' roared Jonas, defiantly.

His voice echoed and the echo echoed.

'I've killed people, too, Mr Trichardt,' said Foxy, quietly, 'but I will share with you one secret thing about me . . .' He said it quietly but they all heard him, 'I am always ashamed.'

Jonas leapt forward at Foxy but Foxy saw him coming; he flung the sides of his coat open and took hold of one of the Colts. He didn't play at cowboys, using them both. They had become utilitarian to him for the first time. Foxy Nolan – once-upon-a-time darling of the MGM Studios and beloved toothpaste salesman – fired two bullets at the bloody man. The first hit Jonas in the chest and the second snapped his head back as it took him in the side of the throat.

Jonas went limp and fell down on both knees. His body slumped forward but he did not look penitent.

'Her name was Isobel,' said Will.

It was important that Jonas should know that before he died . . . that the shape of Isobel's name should suffuse his brain as he went down into the fire.

At the gunshot, feet came running through the washroom.

Foxy didn't hesitate; he was on a roll. He fired into the men's bodies as they came through the doorway with their own weapons drawn. One of the men made it through the gauntlet and Will was astonished to recognize him. It was Sam Fisk, the clerk from the Immigration Service inspection boat, who had helped Will with information about Isobel. As Will saw Sam's face, he knew immediately that this was the man Aidan had described as girly-looking – Will himself had thought the very same thing when he had first met him. Sam streaked past Will and ducked down behind the shelter of the incinerator. Bullets were ricocheting off the steel walls as Will tried to pull Lily to safety.

One of the stray shots hit Jonas's oxygen cylinder where it lay beside his gurgling body. The canister exploded and shot through the wall of the incinerator, disgorging flames.

As the bottle took flight, the tubes attached to it jerked Jonas's body up, as if he was a puppet, before they tore free from his mask. Will saw that the man wasn't yet dead. Sparks from the explosion of the tank had set Jonas's shirt alight; he was burning. His expensive suit was ablaze and the flesh of his face was melting; it was blackening and crusting as they watched and Lily was screaming a scream that never seemed to run out of air.

'Those gas bottles are going to go,' shouted Foxy.

Will understood that in a couple of seconds the heat would reach the bunker outside and the toxic gas, if it was flammable, would ignite.

Shots were still coming at them from somewhere in the smoke-filled room but they were infrequent now. Sam was alone behind the incinerator. Will, Foxy and Lily ran for the washroom; the plumbing contained no water with which the fire could be doused. The shining pipes that might have been

Jonas's salvation stood dumbly and dryly by and watched him burn.

Will pulled the screaming Lily by the arm and Foxy stopped to slam the doors closed on the ball of fire that had once been Jonas Trichardt's dream of utopia.

Beside the steel doors, the basket of wax soap showed its true face. It had melted into a sticky pool of yellow pus.

Will looked back to make sure that Foxy was still following them. The man looked like an angel. One of the angels of death the God of the Old Testament sends out to move across the surface of the earth and wreak His vengeance – a white and beautiful figure against the steel doors. Then, behind them, the incinerator exploded. The doors blew off the washroom with tremendous, buckling force. The white sides of Foxy's coat flew out like spreading wings and he seemed to soar for a second against the strange and terrible conflagration before he, too, was consumed.

Will didn't try and make Lily run for the boat. Pursued by fire, they tore along the corridor. Will threw the entire bulk of his weight against a door to the outside world and crashed through it; Lily followed a second later. There was fresh air and a narrow stretch of lawn. Will dragged Lily across it and turned her towards the water. They leapt together into the greasy, green Hudson. The heat engulfed the bunker and Ellis Island Three went up in an explosion that was unsurpassed by the hundred fireworks displays that had rocketed to heaven from barges set up near this very spot every Fourth of July.

Ten minutes later, while the sky was still lit by red-tongued flames, a bevy of inebriated Upper East Siders out on a cruise dragged Will and Lily onto the deck of their pleasure boat.

Loudhailer voices from the coastguard frigates and the fire tugs had ordered them to make their way to shore but the partiers were reluctant to leave the spectacular blaze behind.

'It's those bloody munitions gone up in smoke,' slurred one of the men.

'What do you mean by that?' said a lady in tipsy query.

'The military have used that island as a dump for arms during every conceivable war and now one of their secret stashes has gone off and incinerated the whole damned place. You'll see it in the papers tomorrow. I've always said it would happen one day.'

Against Will's chest, Lily's shocked breathing was ragged. Will held her body tightly. He remembered baby Isobel in his arms all those years ago – asleep and at peace – with only the tiny candle flame of her breath against his heart to tell him she was still alive.

Will kept Lily close to him as they docked and went ashore. The booze-soaked party guests let them go without much concern. Drunk as they were, they seemed reluctant to draw attention to themselves. Informing the authorities that they had fished two people from the river near the scene of the night's inferno hardly seemed worth the scrutiny their soirée might receive as a result. They had a secret whiskey source to protect.

Will and Lily made their way towards Tully's and, when Lily grew too exhausted to walk, Will gathered her strongly up in his arms and carried her.

26

The sound of the ice-truck woke Will on Friday morning. It was very early; the sky beyond the purple, velvet curtain was as pink as a baby's blanket; the tops of the buildings were keeping it afloat. After the flames of the night before, the stillness of the row of tenements at dawn was startling. Will lay beside Lily on the narrow bed. He left his arm curled beneath her, even though the weight of her body had deadened any sensation from it.

The sounds from the street were familiar. Will could hear the ice-man whistling to his dog; he wanted it to jump down from the back of the truck and relieve itself on the sidewalk. Will heard the swish of the canvas cover being pulled up to reveal the ice inside the bin. He heard the squeal of the ice-hook entering its chosen brick and the dull clunk as that brick was tossed to land on their threshold. The ice-man delivered his goods to several more doors across the street before he got back into his truck, called for his dog, and turned the engine over.

The noise of the departing truck woke the baby in the back tenement and it squalled loudly. The alarming sound set several noises going in the other apartments: a man shouted, a tap was opened in a kitchen, Will could hear a drain guzzling in the darkness.

He pulled gently away from Lily and looked down at her. The woman with the baby came out onto the fire escape that led down from the back tenements into the concrete yard. She

329

started to sing. It was a love song, not a lullaby, and Will knew the words. The song was from home. He didn't sing it, though, because Lily wasn't yet fully awake; he whispered the tune quietly to himself, '*She's so fair, she's so pretty. She's the belle of Belfast City . . .*'

He didn't want Lily to come to; he wanted to preserve her for as long as possible in that state of perfect peace because it would be shattered to splinters as soon as she was conscious.

When they had arrived back at Tully's the night before, Lily had taken off the sodden garments Will had pilfered for her from Rose Marie and thrown them down onto the floor. The night had been hot but Lily could not stop shivering or halt the fearful, vacant staring of her eyes. At last, Will had convinced her to lie down on his bed and she had fallen asleep almost at once.

Will had noted that her under-things were as fine as his best Sunday clothes, though a little skimpy. She had on a pastel slip with a cream lace trim – Orchard Street had its peaches again. The slip had dried in a few minutes as Lily slept; Will had leaned over to smell it. It was imbued with Lily's scent – the warm syrup of her skin – and he had thought how she would probably want to wash it as soon as she woke and how regretful that was.

Once Lily was deeply asleep, Will had paced for almost ten minutes trying to get a plan in order, then he went to work, moving quietly around the room, organizing their retreat.

Maybe he should escape the city first but he didn't want to leave Lily here alone if Foxy Nolan's men were going to come looking for their boss. When Foxy's disappearance became clear to them, they would make their way to Tully's. They knew that Aidan had lived there and that Will and Foxy had been consorting together over the past few weeks. They would want to know what had happened and it wasn't likely that Foxy's dogs were an amenable pack.

Will had gathered up his duffel bag. It was the one that had been his stepfather's – the one in which Will's meagre possessions had first journeyed through Ellis Island. He had used it to drag his worldly goods up to this cell of a room five years ago. The thought of moving away from Orchard Street filled Will with a type of awe. Now that the decision had been forced, Will couldn't believe that he had stagnated for so long in one place, that he had allowed himself to be lulled, like a hypnotized boy, by the bright lights of this terrible city.

He was a man who needed fishing and horses and places that had stood still for so long that the wind had made holes in their mountains, as if it intended to use those monolith stones as beads on a necklace.

Will had looked over at the picture he had pinned to the wall above his bed. It was the one he had taken from the book in the City library – the page that showed the tracks heading West into a world unpopulated by prejudice. That was where they would go.

Will had packed his money into rolls of socks for safe-keeping. He hadn't been sure what he would do with the five hundred dollars from Jonas Trichardt. Now, it was as if the money was Lily's – Lily the widow – and he would keep it for her. They needed every dime they could get for their new start. Will placed Isobel's photographs at the bottom of the duffel bag, too. He didn't look at his sister's image as he stashed them away. The time would come when he would feel strong enough to manage it but that time was distant.

Every now and then in the night, Will had stopped and listened as a noise came to his ears. Usually, it was somebody using the outhouse in the yard. He listened for the cottony creaking of Rose Marie's socks on the floorboards above his head but no sound came from that direction. Either Rose Marie had gone to bed before they had arrived back in the small hours or she was still out in the dark city. Maybe some man had taken pity on her in the Four Green Fields; maybe she had met somebody to care for her at last.

Will knew he would visit her as soon as he heard any sounds of life from her part of the house and broach the question of whether anybody had been snooping about in her room. He had to find the gun Foxy had given him and dispose of it before it fell into the wrong hands. Perhaps he should hold onto the weapon until he was free and clear of New York – maybe even longer than that.

He didn't imagine that members of the Golden Door committee would pursue him, especially if they decided to call the explosion on Ellis Island an accident. They might acknowledge that they had lost one of their key consultants – a Mr Jonas Trichardt – in the blast. They might choose to inform the press that Mr Trichardt had been at their facility on Island Three, examining some recent improvements the Immigration Service had authorized, and that he had been the unfortunate victim of a terrible tragedy.

There would be recriminations aimed at the Department of Defence for neglecting to clear the site of outdated munitions. The newspapers would give front-page space to grainy snap-shots of the dead being fished from the river. A solemn man with a gaffe hook would lean over the rails of a coastguard cutter and coax a body in a white coat towards its bow. As the body turned over, it would reveal the pale, ethereal face of Foxy Nolan – or had his perfection been charred beyond all recognition? Will shuddered at the image.

Had Sam Fisk escaped with his life? Will doubted it. Everyone on Island Three would have been lost. Shrapnel and burning missiles had rained from the sky for several minutes after the initial immolation and it was only by grace that burning debris had not hailed down on Will and Lily as they floated in the water.

By three o'clock in the morning, Will had packed everything that meant something to him. There was not much – photographs, that was all. He thought of Abraham Weissman in his back room at the Golden Door Grocery and of his family snaps – each one a person with value. Abraham Weissman's name would be a part of his life no matter where he went from now on. Felicity Bell would be remembered, too – a girl about whom he knew nothing, really – and Isobel Phelan, of course, his little sister about whom he would know nothing more. These people's names endured, though their histories and their futures had both been burned away.

Finally, Will had lain down beside Lily on the cot to sleep. She hadn't stirred or grumbled; she was in a distant, healing place. Will had wrapped his arm around her and pulled the sheet up to cover their near-naked bodies. As he slipped from consciousness, Will had known that, if he could fall asleep like this for the rest of his life, he would be able to endure.

Nothing disturbed Will's dreams until the ice-truck rattled into Orchard Street at five o'clock. He listened to it pull away from the curb to move into neighbouring streets. Suddenly, Will heard the driver thump his horn. He heard Rose Marie's high, shrill voice yelling profanities. She had probably stumbled into the ice-truck's path and the driver had just managed to stand on his brakes and avoid knocking her down.

Will heard a bottle smashing to the sidewalk. He could make out the sound Rose Marie's key made as it scratched across the lock of the front door. She banged her fists against the frame in frustration. Eventually, the tumblers turned and

Rose Marie came in. Will heard her trudging up to her room. Her feet slouched on the treads and her shoulders bumped against the walls on both sides of the staircase with alternating thumps.

When her footsteps paused outside his room, Will held his breath. Lily hadn't stirred beside him and he had the fleeting, irrational terror that she had died in the night. Suddenly, Rose Marie kicked at Will's door with her shoe and it swung open.

The crash woke Lily at last. Her right hand moved to shield her eyes and she propped herself up on her left shoulder, half-sleepy and beautiful – her yellow hair caught in the dawn light that streaked through the glass and illuminated their sheet.

Rose Marie's addled brain took a while to realize that Will wasn't alone in his bed. The girl was a wreck. Her jacket was inside out and the petticoat that lolled from beneath the hem of her skirt was torn; the lace trailed, like a dog's panting tongue, against her shin. Rose Marie's mascara had run in Japanese lettering across her cheeks and she had licked any cosmetic colour from her blue-bruised lips. Her hair was matted and there was, bizarrely, a leaf tangled in it.

Rose Marie stood so still that Will struggled to ascertain if time was actually passing. He saw her eyes blink wildly at Lily. She took in Lily's perfect skin, her neat, peach-painted nails, her satin slip.

'Lah-di-dah,' said Rose Marie. 'Lah-di-dah.'

And she closed the door again.

'Is she going to be OK?' asked Lily.

Will touched Lily's lips. He hadn't wanted her first vision upon waking to be the sight of a dishevelled Rose Marie. He had wanted Lily to look up at him, so that he could transfuse into her mind his own resolute certainty that things were going to be fine.

'Maybe you should go and see if she needs to talk it out,' said Lily.

Her face showed genuine concern. Will wondered if she had yet recalled anything of the night before, if the profound reality of events had started to come to the forefront of her mind.

Will leaned over and kissed Lily. He wanted to touch her before the memories shrouded her in. Lily responded to him, pressing against him and softly opening her mouth. Will was filled with temporal joy until he heard Rose Marie stomping about upstairs.

'Maybe she'll fall asleep. She's hopelessly drunk,' said Will.

'She's been disappointed, Will,' said Lily. 'I'm sad for her.'

'Should I go up and try and talk to her then?' he asked. 'After that, we need to decide about a few things, too.'

'Yes,' said Lily. 'Do it for me.'

Will was Irish and he knew the futility of trying to speak sense to a drunk but if the gesture would make Lily happy, he would attempt it. Also, he needed the gun. Will heard Rose Marie's door slam; she was coming back down the stairs again.

'There she is now,' said Lily. 'Go to her.'

Will began to rise but Lily stopped him for a second. There was a weird tone of desperation in her voice. 'No, wait,' she said and she pressed her lips to Will's again. She kissed him fiercely and long, as if she thought they might never touch again.

Will smiled.

Lily smiled, too.

'It's OK,' she said. 'Things always work out for the best, you'll see.'

That was when Rose Marie came through the door again.

If Will had stood up when he had first intended to, if he had gone upstairs when he had planned to, if Lily had not pulled him back for that final kiss, he would have encountered Rose Marie before she made it to the doorframe. He would have met her on the stairs and maybe the bullet would have caught him in the stomach.

Instead, the way it actually happened, Rose Marie had a clear view of Lily. She raised Foxy Nolan's Colt like an expert. There was no trembling in her. Lily's face didn't register surprise or shock. Later, Will was glad of that. He believed Lily had not even recognized that the object in Rose Marie's hand was a weapon. Lily was still smiling, her mind inflated with the afterjoy of that perfect kiss, when the bullet caught her in the left eye – her extraordinary, violet eye – and blew through her head.

For a second, the shape Lily's blood left on the wall was striking – a red flower of such intensity it might have been a piece of art but a second later the drops began to slide down in small dribbles and the flower was gone.

Rose Marie lowered her arm and dropped the gun to the floor. She stood still like a machine once its work is done. Will had never seen Rose Marie totally at rest like that; she looked content.

'Goodbye, Felicity Bell,' said Rose Marie.

Will was still, too. He didn't comprehend the reference to Felicity Bell; he didn't digest the actuality of the event. He didn't go over and touch Lily's body. Later, he wished he had, but Lily wasn't even there anymore. Her face was a shattered mess of veins and grey matter. Lily herself – the girl with hair in three distinct shades of yellow – was quite gone. Will didn't want to touch her corpse. He knew – illogically and irrefutably – that her skin would already be as cold as pewter.

Will tried to think, tried to take it in. Nothing happened. Then he did have one thought: it came into his mind like a newspaper headline in dark, black ink and it announced itself to him with a scathing voice that sounded a lot like Jonas Trichardt's, '*Did you imagine institutionalized hatred was the worst kind of malice?*'

'No,' said Will's own voice inside his head. It sounded resigned and somehow empty. 'Governments don't bring a man down. It's those he loves who kill him every time.'

Afterword

It was a landscape remembered from a dream: desolate and swept smooth by orange siroccos. Will watched the scenery pass by the windows of his carriage; he felt it mirrored a deeper, less tangible emptiness. The train ratcheted along between the cliffs and the stark mountains – blunt and bleached like cow skulls then baked red by the sun. The rails were taking Will West and several times – though he had left the image stuck to the wall of his room in Tully's and so had no real reference – he was sure they passed the exact spot from which the picture in that book, 'Golden West', had been taken. The sky was a high, cathedral blue and the earth was the burnt sienna of lava stones broken open a day after the eruption.

Will had left Lily in her peach slip and her burgundy blood and gone down the stairs of Tully's for the last time. He had summoned the presence of mind to pick up his duffel bag and he had shoved past Rose Marie in a kind of stumbling somnambulism.

Will had thought at once of the rails and he had made his way to their headquarters: the fortress of Grand Central Station. There, he had purchased a ticket. Despite the heat, Will made sure he kept his coat dragged closed to cover the tiny flecks of Lily's blood on his shirt.

The hallways of the station boomed with the sounds of people on the move – a dissonance of shouting and feet and luggage. It was cooler on the platform; Will stopped sweating under his coat and felt unnervingly calm. He chose a seat in a third-class carriage. When his train departed, it started his eyes swaying in time to its rocking motion and that was what he did for a good few hours – he swayed compulsively, consoling himself with repetition.

It was several hours before a railway steward offered Will some refreshment and asked cheerfully how far he was going.

'All the way to the end,' Will told the man.

'All the way to California then,' the steward said because he thought Will was talking about the train journey.

Will wondered what was happening back at Tully's. In a few days, the newspapers would tell him the truth – if they could be trusted. Had Rose Marie gathered the presence of mind to blame him for the killing? The police were bound to bother with fingerprints when they realized the victim was a society lady, so had Rose Marie wiped the handle of the gun and claimed that she had heard the shot and run downstairs to find Will standing over Lily's body?

'It was a lovers' spat, Officer,' she would say. 'Isn't it appalling how fond emotions can end in tragedy like this?'

Or was Rose Marie still standing there, dumbstruck, waiting to be found out?

Will decided he would find work on a ranch, if there was any going. He remembered, with slight bewilderment, that the countryside was what he had always loved most; he wanted to care for horses again. Will had not seen a horse – aside from carnival ponies and the carriage nags that trundled the tourists around the park – for years now.

Or he might find work in the movie studios. Hadn't the traveller's assistant on Ellis Island suggested Will might have a future in the pictures? Will thought of Foxy Nolan then, and about where the promise of a life of fame had led that boy. Will thought about Isobel dead and Lily dead and he wondered what made him bother to run and plan at all.

Only when he thought about Island Three did Will experience the smallest glimmer of pride. He had tried to stop what they had started to do. Perhaps his self-congratulations were naïve: maybe he had only managed to postpone the process for a while. Although, elections were due and there was a chance the new government might not approve expenditure on the programme or agree with its sentiment, presuming they had ever really known about it to begin with. Then he remembered the dormitory of sleeping steelmen and Foxy's suspicion that they were building a second site, too.

Will couldn't help that. He only knew that he had not been the good man who had said nothing. His motives had never been altruistic, it was true, but because of him the next man would go out to the immigration station and see his sister or his wife or his daughter waiting for him – that one, particular face he had anticipated for months or years would be there to greet him. The next man would have his lover's body in his arms, her warmth beneath his sheets.

On the second day of his train journey, Will found the strength to get up and make his way to the ablutions car. He stripped and washed as best he could in the tiny, steel basin. He wet his hair and combed it back with his fingers; he determined to shave as soon as he could find a drugstore close enough to a station where the train was scheduled to stop for a few minutes. Will would buy a new shirt. He had over eight hundred dollars tucked into the socks at the bottom of his bag. That represented a start.

Will looked at himself in the mirror above the basin and realized that he had more than he had brought with him to America five years ago. Much more than the twenty-five dollars he had started out with: he had construction skills and a more mature outlook. He had, too, a cauterized spirit that made him tougher.

For some reason, the dirty water swimming in the basin made Will think of the boy buried beneath the weed in that field near the sea in Kinvara. Once the boy's flesh had rotted away, the rebels would have taken his bones out to sea in one of their fishing boats and tossed them overboard. That boy was a wraith now. Will had been frozen on that long-ago day when he had seen the boy's body. He had erred with silence then. This time, he had chosen to do what was right rather than what was expedient. He had not given up. Isobel had paid the price for him to learn that lesson; Lily had paid. He was redeemed. Agreed, God? The debt is square?

Will walked back to his seat. As he passed between two carriages, he felt the swirling dust of a Great Plains State; the wind outside was sweeping clean the world. Will thought of the ashes that had pumped from the incinerator chimneys on Island Three. The ash had spread across the surface of the river and landed on his shirt as he had waited for the ferry. Those same ashes had dulled the face of the city, greying it down, but soon there would be the spire of his tower – the Empire State Building – a tremendous, silver spike into heaven that would never be buried.

The man seated across from Will was reading a German newspaper and Will saw a face he recognized from somewhere in the front-page photograph. The paper was probably about a week old, and Will couldn't understand a word of it, but the picture showed a prominent German politician with several of his cronies in a formal pose at a country home. There was a small lake in the background and mountains covered in trees.

Will leaned over and tapped the man's knee, hoping he would speak some English.

'What's happened here?' he asked, pointing at the relevant story.

The man seemed pleased to be invited to converse. His English was good, though formal, but he was unsure of his pronunciation and so glad of the opportunity to practise.

'There was almost a drowning incident near our party leader's home in the Obersalzburg but our Führer is a very strong swimmer and he has managed to save the man who is one of his assistants.'

'Which man did he save?' asked Will.

The man read the caption beneath the photograph. He pointed out a face with his finger; it was the man Will had recognized.

'It was this man,' said the German. 'He does not swim apparently and he was having difficulties after slipping off a dock by accident. Our party chairman swims out to him and rescues him just as a hero does.'

The German looked delighted at the chance to praise a leader he so obviously admired.

'What does this rescued man do?' asked Will. 'Does the story say?'

The German shrugged. He wanted to get back to his reading now.

'He is an advisor only. On matters of health and hygiene and so forth, he informs our leader.'

Will might not have made the connection if the situation of a near drowning hadn't jogged his memory. He knew now that the man in the picture who had been saved was the very man he had prevented from falling off the Ellis Island ferry on the day he had first gone out to claim Isobel. There was no doubt. The man being embraced by the leader of the National Socialists was the same man who had cocked his head, trying to hear the sounds of events that were still coming. It was the man Will had nicknamed 'the listener' and he spoke, it seemed, as well as listened.

Will didn't want to think what the picture or the association between these two men might mean. Ashes spread, that was all. It was inevitable.

Will went back to staring out the carriage window. He wondered how far he would try to go. There was this desert to cross but beyond it there were orange groves and fresh dreams to dream. How far West could he push in search of them? He would try California; when that disappointed him, he would move on. There were smaller landmasses West of America, Will knew. There was a swanky, offshore retreat called Catalina and after that the tropical islands of Hawaii but beyond those? As far as Will knew, there was only sea: the Pacific – pale and wide and shallow, with no Atlantis at the bottom of it.

THE END